I0549673

THE SPIRITS OF SIX MINSTREL RUN

MATTHEW S. COX

DIVISION ZERO PRESS

The Spirits of Six Minstrel Run

© 2019 – Matthew S. Cox
All Rights Reserved

ISBN (eBook): 978-1-949174-94-6

ISBN (Print): 978-1-949174-95-3

CONTENTS

1

PERFECT

FRIDAY, AUGUST 24, 2012

Sensitive to an unusual mood in the air, Mia couldn't shake the suspicion something more than a new house waited for them in Spring Falls, New York.

She resisted the temptation to stare at Adam until he confessed, and kept her eyes on the road. Not only did being so high up in their new Chevy Tahoe feel weird, she had also never before driven anything with a trailer attached. Her husband appeared far too enthusiastic for someone who'd resigned from a job he'd held for three years—and could've kept forever—to move two hours west. Despite having already secured a position teaching at Syracuse, he should have been at least *somewhat* nervous about such a big change in their lives, especially considering they'd committed to a new mortgage when they'd only bought the Tahoe a few months ago. Fortunately, the place Adam found sold *well* under market for the area. What they'd be paying each month for the house came in significantly lower than their rent in the suburbs of Albany. Perhaps the oddly low price had been what put her on edge. *Something* had to be wrong with the place. The eerie-as-hell feeling she'd gotten from it the first time they went to tour it didn't help either.

Mia eyed the rearview mirror, again struck by the amount of space between her and the back window… quite a change from the Chevy Malibu she'd been driving since college. It had been older than Adam's Nissan Sentra, which presently sat on the trailer behind them, so they decided to trade it in.

"Something bothering you, hon?" asked Adam. "It's not the trailer, is it?"

"No. Well, maybe I am a little on edge from it. Not used to handling something this big."

He kept quiet for a few seconds before he cracked up.

"Now I know why you wrote your master's thesis on Freud. Everything's a dick joke. You're hung up on the phallic phase."

He wiped laugh tears from his eyes. "Sometimes an innuendo has nothing to do with deep meaning. But you know what they say about Freud. If it's not one thing, it's your mother."

Mia snickered.

They drove in silence for a few minutes amid relatively light traffic. Pastoral trees rushed by on both sides, gaps offering the occasional glimpse of open grass or tiny lakes on the rolling fields beyond.

"Okay. I have to ask. Why are you so excited?"

"We're moving into our new house." He grinned at her. "What's not to be excited about?"

She snuck a sideways glance at him. "That's true, but you seem *too* excited. Aren't you the least bit worried about anything?"

"Oh, of course. Just not enough to diminish how thrilled I am."

She kneaded her hands on the wheel, wondering if she'd ever get used to driving the Tahoe. *How did we wind up getting talked into buying this enormous thing?* A sudden, sharp twinge of pain stabbed her in the left foot.

"Gah!" Mia jerked her leg back. Her foot appeared to be fine. The pain stopped as abruptly as it had started.

Adam jumped at her yell and looked wide-eyed out at the road for a few seconds before glancing over at her. "What happened? You okay?"

"Yeah. Guess I've just been sitting too long in the same position. Random muscle cramp or something in my foot."

He patted her knee. "You really need to stretch to reach the pedals in this thing. It's nice having so much room, though."

"Tell me about it. Remind me why we got this monster?"

"We're going to be out in the country more or less. The roads out there aren't nice to small cars in bad weather. Four-wheel drive is almost required."

"Do you believe everything a car salesman tells you?" She let out a weak laugh.

"Something is really bothering you and it isn't the truck." Adam's smile faded. "What's wrong?"

"I don't know. Maybe I'm only worried about all the what-ifs."

Adam stretched, smiling out at the passing greenery. "The only thing we need to worry about is Syracuse University not working out for me, since that's an unknown. There's nothing to make me think it won't. And even if things don't pan out there, I can easily get back in the door at U-Albany. Only real difference then is it will be me with the long ride each way to work."

Mia laughed, picturing two years' worth of that commute beating the crap out of her Malibu. Not that she went out of her way to find a position so far from where they used to live, but fine art restoration jobs didn't exactly pop up all that often, especially a full-time position at a museum. "We can't afford to go through a car every three years, so you better do everything you can to make the new job work here."

"You'd think they would've just shipped you the paintings to restore at home. It's not like you're working on priceless masterpieces."

"I wouldn't have even asked them to. The last thing we need is to be considered responsible if something happened. While they're not *masterpieces,* some of them are still worth more than the house we bought."

He raised his hands in mock surrender. "Okay, okay. So, really. What's bothering you?"

"Why are you pressing?"

"Because, hon, I know something's bothering you, and for some reason, you're dodging the question."

"You're going to take it the wrong way."

"Hmm. That means you expect me to attribute it to your very real talent."

Mia sighed. "I'm about as psychic as the air freshener the dealership forgot to give us."

He smiled in silence at her.

After two minutes, she gave in with a shake of the head. "Fine. Ever since we left this morning, I've had this strange feeling of dread. Remember when you were a kid how it felt getting sent to the principal's office… that mood that hit you on the long walk down the hall?"

"Can't say I do. They never sent me to the principal's office, my dear, delinquent wife."

She smirked. "You expect me to believe you were a perfect angel?"

"Hah. No. I was merely careful enough to avoid detection when committing my nefarious deeds. Do tell. I never pictured you as much of a troublemaker."

Upon noticing their exit coming up, Mia triple checked the mirrors and guided the ponderous vehicle over one lane to take the off ramp. She'd driven this route every day for years to get to the Everson Museum of Art in Syracuse, but today, she'd be skipping the exit for the city and going farther north. Having only a twelve-ish mile ride to work would make her days so much longer. Life during the week could be more than work, driving, or sleep.

Memories of grade school brought a frown. "I wasn't a troublemaker. The most unforgivable thing I did as a kid was think critically. Let's just say I didn't get along with the nuns. They really hate the term 'Catholic mythology.' I'm honestly surprised I didn't get expelled."

Adam laughed.

"I also have the weirdest feeling there's something you're not telling me."

"Assuming there is, in fact, some piece of information I haven't shared with you, the reason would be due to objectivity in observation."

Mia shook her head. "Did you marry me because you loved me or because you think I'm psychic and wanted a ready test subject?"

"Definitely because I love you. That you are gifted didn't even occur to me until long after."

"Okay. I'll forgive you." She smiled, slowing for a traffic light. "We're almost at the point where I don't recognize the area."

Adam turned the GPS on, keyed in the address to their new house, and set the device on the dash. "There you go."

"So it's something about the house you're not telling me?"

He twiddled his thumbs, grinning like a boy at Christmas.

"You're not at all worried about me having an ominous feeling that something isn't right?"

"Perhaps I should be, but I'm not. More excited." He pulled out a notebook and jotted a few lines. "Can you describe the feeling?"

"I already did. Dread mostly. Like I'm about to get into a whole bunch of trouble… but it's strange."

"Stranger than a random bit of intuition?"

She chuckled. "No, I mean it's dread, yeah, but… it also feels right somehow. Like I have to do something really unpleasant that I'm afraid of doing, but the end result is going to be worth it."

"You've just described higher education."

"Right…" Mia laughed. "It's eerie, like I've wanted to move out here for a long time."

"Well, you *have* been dealing with a horrible commute." He nodded, humming as he wrote a few things down. "What about the unexplained pain in your foot?"

"Adam, honey, sometimes a muscle cramp is just a muscle cramp."

"You've been taking this ride twice a day for two years— thereabout. Have you ever had a similar muscle cramp?"

"You're impossible." She sigh-laughed. "Look, if one of us drops something on our foot in the first couple days, maybe I'll believe you."

"What were you thinking about when you got the twinge?"

"Uhh, I dunno. Mostly about the truck being so big and unfamiliar."

He continued writing without a word.

"What do you think it means?" she asked.

"Not sure yet. I'm merely taking notes in case it does wind up meaning something."

AFTER NEARLY THREE HOURS DRIVING, MIA TURNED ONTO Minstrel Run, the street upon which their new house waited.

A few minutes of winding tree-lined road later, she pulled into their driveway, a long sloped stretch of asphalt up to a two-car garage, and parked beside a silver Mercedes. Their realtor, Joe Dello, hopped out of the car and flashed a huge grin. He had a vaguely Italian look to him with short spiky brown hair and a goatee that hadn't quite fully grown in yet. Short, he only came up to Adam's shoulder. His shirt and pants seemed somewhat big for him, so she figured he'd recently lost a good deal of weight. The man's contagious smile and warm demeanor had won them over while they'd been checking out various realtors, but something about him felt off.

They're supposed to be happy when they sell a place, but this guy looks like he just earned a commission on Buckingham Palace. The instant Mia looked at the house, at the large 6 on the wall by the door, an unexplained sense of gloom came over her. She tightened her jaw, glancing around at the woods. *This place was a lot cheaper than anything else in the area. There has got to be something wrong with it.*

Adam had been equally distrustful of the price at first, and paid for three separate inspections. None of them found any problems. It didn't seem likely that an owner with something to hide could've bribed all of the inspectors… so they proceeded to make an offer.

Except for having forest on all sides and a small creek running behind it, the two-story home resembled most suburban houses she'd seen, albeit noticeably larger. Its front porch spanned the full width, shaded under a roof extension held up by plain white columns. A prior resident had left a pair of giant wicker chairs there, but they were in dire need of cleaning. The beige siding looked immaculate, perhaps even new or at least no more than two years old. New-ish rain gutters trimmed the sides and roof. None of the windows had curtains, drawing the emptiness of the interior out into stark obviousness.

Mia froze with her foot on the brake, not even shifting into park. The instant she took in the entirety of the house, an ill malaise swirled around the bottom of her gut. It had to be all of Adam's talk of psychic stuff and not wanting to tell her anything about the property that could 'taint' her impression of it. She mentally rolled her eyes. He probably didn't even *have* information he'd withheld. Merely saying he did would have primed her into expecting there to be strangeness here. Of course, she couldn't deny the pronounced sense of foreboding in the air around the apparently innocuous home.

It reminded her of the same dread she felt back home as a child living with her parents every time she went into the basement. The laundry machines had been down there, and whenever she went to them, she kept her head down, too terrified to look off to her right into the darkness. It always felt like a person she couldn't see glared at her in anger. Even at nineteen, being in that basement alone got her hands shaking. She hadn't been anywhere near that house for eight years, though the creepiness of the basement had nothing to do with it.

Her gaze fell from the house to her hands on the wheel, knuckles white. Adam had already hopped out of the Tahoe to talk to the realtor, not having noticed her frozen there. She glanced over at them. Joe shook hands enthusiastically with her husband, grinning as wide as if he'd won a massive lotto jackpot.

That man is far too happy.

Fragments of conversation about 'how much they'd love the place', 'how perfect it was for them', and 'no problems at all with the inspections' pierced the fog in Mia's thoughts. She shifted her gaze back to the house, still gripped by the sense that someone—or something—malign stared at her.

Joe handed the keys to Adam and gestured at the front door. "C'mon, let's do a quick walkthrough. Just got a few things for you to sign and we'll be all set."

Mia eased the Tahoe into park and put the emergency brake on due to the inclined driveway. The instant her foot touched the e-brake pedal, the same sharp pain stabbed into it. Mia gasped in shock, gritting her teeth for the few seconds it took the cramp to go away. *I need to walk around a bit.* She killed the engine, unable to peel her eyes off the house.

"Great." Adam turned toward the truck. He finally appeared to notice the look on her face—and grinned from ear to ear. "Yeah, Joe. I think we're going to love it here."

She gingerly opened the door and climbed down. A soft breeze laced with the fragrance of forest and wood smoke teased at her hair, long, straight, and brown as it had been her whole life. Joe and Adam hurried inside, her husband emitting a delighted squeal at the keys working. It took her a moment to break the mesmerizing spell that staring at the house put on her. She looked down while following a footpath made of irregular flat stones in various colors from the driveway to the front porch. Three steps led up to a painted hardwood deck, the house's front door a short distance directly in front of her.

Air in her lungs thickened to a dense mass, heavier and heavier with each step she took forward. By the time she crossed the threshold, she couldn't breathe in or out. Mia pressed a hand to her chest, wheezing under a burden like she had a man sitting on her shoulders.

Seconds before she collapsed, the feeling abated. She coughed and took a few huge gulps of air before lifting her head to gaze around at the stark, empty room. Plain white walls and new beige carpet the only remnants from the former tenants. An archway connected the living room to the dining room and the same carpet continued out the other side down a short hallway leading to the kitchen. Standing inside the front door, she could see straight through the house to the back door and a hint of the countertop. To the right, stairs against the wall led up to the second story. Left, another small arch led to a room with hardwood floors and a huge bay window.

"This is awesome," echoed Adam's voice from the kitchen. After the squeak of a door hinge, he walked into view, Joe the realtor behind him. He grinned at her while entering the little hallway between kitchen and dining room, stopping to poke his nose into a side passage.

"Wow, that's kind of a small bathroom. I could wash my hands while sitting on the darn toilet."

"Technically, it's a toilet closet," said Joe. "No tub or shower. There's a full bath bathroom upstairs."

"Right." Adam backed out of the doorway. "I forgot about this little one down here."

Joe shook hands with Adam. "Everything looked good to me. What do you think?"

"Perfect." Adam grinned. "Absolutely perfect. Mia?"

She scratched at her chest, still a touch dizzy from whatever spell came over her. "Uhh, yeah. Perfect."

2

MOVING IN

SATURDAY, AUGUST 25, 2012

Sleeping bags on carpet made for a restless night.

Mia spent most of it holding on to Adam like a little girl clinging to a huge teddy bear. The weird unease she couldn't quite shake had been bad enough, but the *emptiness* of the house worsened her fears, especially in the dark.

They'd spent the remainder of the daylight hours unpacking the few things they'd loaded into the Tahoe and crammed into every inch of usable space in the Nissan. Not knowing what—if any—delivery food existed in this area, Mia had made sure to bring a box of canned goods and pasta. She prepared a basic dinner of spaghetti and they had an inglorious feast sitting on the living room floor watching a movie on Adam's laptop.

Once it ended, he'd asked her about her feelings toward the house.

Despite not wanting to feed his almost boyish preoccupation with parapsychology, she'd been honest with him. He already knew about her childhood home, specifically that Robert Williams, her paternal grandfather, had died in the house in his later sixties from a heart attack. Mia had only been a year old at the time and never really knew the man. All during her childhood, she'd hear footsteps on her ceiling at night, like someone walking around the attic. There, she refused to go alone. For no reason she could put her finger on, the attic terrified her more than the basement. She'd gone up there once when she'd been around six to ask her mother for something—she'd been puttering around, getting rid of old stuff they didn't need. Mia didn't remember much of the day, only that she'd been in such a hurry to get out of the attic she'd fallen down the stairs and spent about an hour afterward scream-crying. Mia had refused to go near the attic ever again. She didn't even like being near the door at the bottom of the stairs.

Not until her father's younger brother, Uncle John, visited for Christmas the year she'd been twelve, did she hear the stories her parents wouldn't discuss. The house had been built in 1902, and back in those days, most people held funeral visitations right in their homes. In addition to her father's father, Great Grandpa Williams had also died in the house, as did his parents, all of them lying in state right in the living room. To Mia, that had explained why the living room became scary at night, though it didn't bother her in the day—probably because all the ghosts went up to the attic to hide until the sun went down... or something.

None of the old relatives had suffered particularly bad deaths, but she felt they all disliked her or at least didn't want a child anywhere near them. They probably felt the same way toward her little brother Timothy—perhaps even more so—but he didn't react to them to the same degree Mia did. He, too, refused to set foot in the attic and hated being sent to the basement for errands.

Hearing that this house gave her the same feeling her 'haunted' childhood home did had made Adam's day. Probably made his month. At that point, he confessed to having heard some rumors that this place might have a restless spirit in it, but hadn't looked into any of the details of who they'd been or how they died. Truth be told, this house had been listed for a seriously low price for the area—not that real estate in the area had been bad to begin with. But, their new house's price was so low it did seem suspicious. Worse, it sat on the market for almost three years without being snapped up at that price as though everyone else in this area knew better than to go near the place.

On the upside, they both now had a roughly half-hour commute to

Syracuse, hardly *that* bad. Joe the realtor said the little town of Spring Falls had one police officer, and any internet connection they wanted would have to be either dish or radio based. None of that really explained why no one else had jumped on such a deal, if only to flip the house and make a quick profit. Though, the listing sat on the market for a long damn time at a ridiculously low price. That had to have scared away anyone who might've tried to flip it. If it wouldn't sell low, it definitely wouldn't sell 'normal.'

After they'd set up sleeping bags in the master bedroom, she'd spent much of the night staring at the ceiling waiting to hear footsteps go overhead... or watching the door, expecting it to swing open all by itself. Adam had no trouble falling asleep and passed out within five minutes. Eventually, dark became light in an instant, and she remained there in a groggy half-awake state, only partially aware of voices downstairs.

Ugh. I must've fallen asleep, but only a few hours ago.

Heavy tromping snapped her out of a brief catnap. She groaned and sat up, rubbing her face. The alarm clock on the rug beside her showed the time at 10:04 a.m. A spaghetti-flavored burp slipped out as she stood and headed into the upstairs hallway. Four feet to her left, a door led to the upstairs bathroom, more than double the size of the one in their last apartment. It had an enormous closet on the left wall with three pairs of louvered doors. Walking from the door to the toilet practically counted as 'hiking.' She took a seat on the bowl with her face in her hands. Once finished, she returned to the master bedroom. It occupied the front left corner of the upstairs, the only bedroom with windows on two walls. The house theoretically had five bedrooms upstairs plus an atrium at the rear right corner with more windows than wall. Of course, having no furniture anywhere yet to turn any of them into actual *bed*rooms, four of them would remain purposeless for some time. Part of her felt a little weird that they might have 'stolen' a house like this from a couple who wanted—or already had—a big family. Mia didn't *not* want kids, but she'd never felt in any great rush. Also, if it happened, she'd be content with one or two... nothing she needed a five-bedroom house for.

After getting dressed in the same T-shirt and jeans she'd worn the day before, she jogged down the hall to the stairs all the way at the end. A washer-dryer nook stood to her left at the top of the stairs in an alcove recessed back from the hallway that intruded on the atrium room, giving it an L-shape. At least whoever built the place had been nice enough to take the need to go up and down stairs out of laundry day. Even better, doing laundry wouldn't require her going anywhere near a basement. Mia paused to smile at the machines... which also looked suspiciously new.

"Laundromats are something I will *not* miss."

Much of the house's creepy vibe vanished in the daytime. The place *did* have an attic—the door roughly at the midpoint of the upstairs hall—as well as a basement. Her old childhood home had done the same mood thing: fine during the day, creepy at night. She eyed the attic door and decided against checking it, mostly out of old fears and not real time feelings.

Downstairs, the movers went about doing their thing, lugging heavy objects and boxes back and forth. Adam, coffee in hand, watched them and pointed out where to put things. Upon noticing Mia awake and at the bottom of the stairs, he walked over for a kiss.

"Morning, babe."

"It is." She yawned. "Sorry for oversleeping."

"It's fine. I know how you are with new surroundings. Couple days, you'll be fine. Oh, and our bed is here."

Mia eyed the movers. "I noticed."

She kissed him again, then followed her nose to the coffee machine, already unboxed and with half a pot left. Adam had also opened one of the kitchen boxes with mugs and glasses. Several dirty mugs sat in the sink suggested he'd given the movers coffee already. For the next few hours, she did her best to stay out of their way. The curtains in their old place had belonged to the apartment management, which meant they would need to buy all new ones for the house.

Ugh. That's another few weekends shot.

Between sips of coffee, Mia repositioned boxes the movers had left stacked against the wall in the living room. Anything marked with a K went to the kitchen, D to the dining room, and so on.

"Hello?" called an older male voice from the front door.

Since Adam had gone upstairs to assist the movers with the bed, Mia put down the box she'd been about to carry to the kitchen and stepped out onto the front porch.

A sixtyish man with neat grey hair stood at the base of the porch stairs in a powder blue button-down shirt and khaki pants. His somewhat large nose bore two red marks from eyeglasses nowhere in sight. He leaned toward the house, wearing a hopeful smile somewhere between friendly neighbor and insurance salesman.

"Can I help you?" asked Mia, approaching the top of the steps.

"Hello, are you the lady of the house?" He offered a hand. "Welcome to Spring Falls. I'm Weston Parker."

"Yep." She smiled and accepted the handshake. "Mia Gartner. We just got here yesterday, my husband Adam and I that is. Do you live nearby?"

"Oh, not quite so close. Not too far either." He emitted a wheezy chuckle, then gestured at a forest green Jeep Cherokee parked out on the street at the end of the driveway. "Were I your age, I might've walked."

"Well, still neighbors then even if we don't live next door."

"That we are. I'd like to do everything possible to help you folks settle in here." Weston eyed the house, his smile weakening. "You and your husband ought to join us tomorrow for services. My church is just a ways from here down Brownbriar Road. I'm the pastor."

"Ahh." Mia leaned back, folding her arms. "That's nice of you to invite us, but we're not religious."

Weston shifted his gaze from the house to her, his expression as incredulous as though she'd told him they didn't eat food and derived all their nutrition from the air. "It would do you well to seek His protection. Dark things have happened in these woods, Mrs. Gartner. I'd hate to think you and your husband might fall prey to the same."

"Really, we're fine. I don't think there's any sky wizard up there watching me. And, even if there is one, you people always ramble on and on about how he's got this great plan for us. If that's true, then whatever is going to happen is going to happen regardless of what I do —unless you think your god is so weak that humans can overpower him and change that plan."

Weston stared at her, shocked mute.

Footsteps crossed the porch behind her.

"Oh, we have a visitor?" asked Adam, sidling up to stand next to her.

"Pastor Weston Parker." He offered a hand. "I was just telling Mia here that you should really join us tomorrow for worship service."

Mia shot Adam a flat look.

"Yeah, umm..." Adam emitted a humorless chuckle. "She hasn't exactly had the best experience with religion. It's a bit of a sore point for her. Please don't take it personally, but you'd have an easier time selling SCUBA classes in the middle of the Sahara desert than talking her into attending church."

Mia stifled a chuckle.

"I'm not interested in selling you anything, Mr. Gartner. It's your souls I'm concerned about protecting. You don't need to give me anything but your time. I beg you to consider it. Just go left on Minstrel Run to Deer Path, two miles down, hang another left onto Brownbriar. The church is on the right 'bout four more miles. Can't miss it."

"Let me guess, you've got a twenty-foot-tall cross on the front lawn? How many poor people could you have fed for what that cost?" asked Mia.

Weston chuckled. "No, ma'am. Ours is a simple building, none of that ostentatious display stuff. It's ungodly."

Mia locked stares with him. *This guy is too insistent, but aren't they all.* "Thanks for stopping by, but I really need to get back to unpacking. If God wants me to visit your church, he can ask in person."

She waved and ducked back inside. Shuffling on the porch suggested Weston tried to follow her but Adam got in the way. The two men resumed talking, though she tuned them out and resumed carrying boxes around. Four movers thundered down the stairs, all nodding in greeting on their way out the door to the truck.

They re-entered in a few minutes, two carrying Adam's dresser, two lugging hers.

She ferried boxes around the various rooms, saving the ones destined for the second floor until later—both out of laziness and not wanting to get in the way as the movers would be monopolizing the stairs for a little while more. If they'd hit the bedroom stuff, the truck had to be nearly empty.

Adam walked in, shaking his head.

"I know, I know," she muttered. "I shouldn't have bit his head off like that, but he tweaked a nerve."

"This is about your brother, isn't it?"

"Of course it is, but can we not rehash that now? This is supposed to be a pleasant, exciting day of moving into our new home." She draped her arms around his neck. "The last thing I want to do is think about my parents."

"All right." Adam started to come in for a kiss, but froze at a long, slow *creeeak* from the back of the house.

Mia leaned to the side, peering around him down the hall at the kitchen. "What was that?"

"One of the movers using the toilet closet?"

"They're all upstairs wrestling with the box spring and mattress." Mia pointed. "I'd swear the bathroom door had been open, sticking into the hall, but it's closed out of sight now. The spot of sunlight on the rug is gone."

"Wind?"

"Aren't you the paranormal nerd?" Mia poked him in the side.

"I am." He grinned. "But, I am a scientist first. All reasonable explanations must be exhausted before considering the unreasonable."

"Right... But you want there to be ghosts."

"I do." He kissed her. "And I know you believe in them. The stories you told me about the house you grew up in..."

"Yeah. I'm far more inclined to believe ghosts are real than I'm psychic. As far as that goes, I think you're only seeing what you want to see."

Adam shrugged. "You're not a very good atheist, you know. They don't believe in ghosts."

"I never claimed to be an atheist. It's the cults I don't like. Whether or not there's anything up there, out there, under there, or whatever, I have no idea. If there's a god, he, she, or it can recruit me personally. Anything that comes out of a human being's mouth about what 'god' wants is a hundred percent bullshit. Isn't it funny how what 'god' wants always seems to be the same thing the person saying so also wants?"

"Right. Hey, you don't need to soapbox me." Adam pulled her into a hug. "You're still riled up about that pastor?"

"Ugh." She rested her head against his shoulder. "Yeah. I really can't stand the pushy ones like that."

"Well, I didn't get the sense he wanted money."

"Some people don't. They just have this creepy need to rope everyone into their little cult." Mia scooped up another box and tromped to the kitchen with it.

Adam trailed after her. "This guy didn't give off that vibe. He seemed genuinely worried 'for our souls.'"

Mia laughed and set the box on the counter. "Right. They always say that."

"Do you believe in souls?"

"Not really."

"But you believe in ghosts. Aren't they the same thing?"

Mia paused. "Okay. Maybe there *are* souls."

Four sets of boots came down the stairs.

"Mr. Gartner?" asked a deep voice from the living room. "That's the last of it. Wanna give a quick look around and let us know if you'd like a hand rearranging anything?"

"Sure." He patted Mia on the butt. "Be right back."

She shook her head, smiling at nothing in particular while opening the first box of plates, which she proceeded to unwrap and set in the cabinets. A few minutes later, a soft skitter slid across the kitchen behind her. She turned, noticing one bit of wadded up packing paper by the dining room entrance, well away from the pile she'd made.

Draft or something.

Adam and the movers' boss came downstairs. They sat at the dining room table—which looked comically small in this house—and proceeded to go over the paperwork for the moving contract. Both men seemed happy, so Mia disregarded them and resumed packing away kitchen stuff in the cabinets.

She attacked the open box of mugs next, muttering to herself about why a family of two owned over a hundred coffee mugs. Both she and Adam worked in places where every secret Santa turned into a coffee mug, all the relatives they still talked to sent them gag coffee mugs for Christmas or birthdays, and Adam couldn't resist buying funny mugs if he saw one.

Something bumped into Mia's leg.

She jumped with a yelp and stared at the lower cabinet door. It had swung open.

"Hon?" asked Adam.

"I'm fine. Might need to check the magnets on these cabinet doors. One just drifted open and I wasn't expecting it."

"Cool," said Adam.

"What happened to 'scientist,' huh?" She grinned. "Reasonable explanation first?"

"Of course. I'll check the doors out."

"Thanks a lot, Mr. Gartner. Congrats on the new place," said the mover. "Appreciate your business."

"I appreciate you guys' saving my back. Drive safe." Adam added a cash tip to his handshake.

"Thank you again! Take care."

"Bye!" Mia waved at him.

Adam walked the mover out and closed the door. "Well, we're officially home."

"Yeah. Home." Mia glanced over her shoulder to her right at the thin white door covering the basement stairs at the corner of the kitchen. *Childhood trauma. I'm going to be afraid of basements for the rest of my life.*

"The living room and dining room can wait for now. I'll get started in the bedroom."

"Okay," called Mia. "Save your back? You're what, twenty-nine going on fifty?"

"Ha. I am a psychology professor, not an athlete."

"Hey, what are we going to do for food? It's almost four and we haven't eaten a damn thing."

"We went past a diner on the way here. Pine something..."

Mia shrugged. "We just got here and you want to go out?"

"We don't exactly have a choice." He walked in, pulled the empty fridge open, and gestured at it like a game show hostess. "There has to be at least one pizza place. We're not *that* far out in the sticks they won't deliver."

"This is pretty far out in the sticks. Only way we'd be even more remote is if we'd bought a log cabin."

"Hah. We still have cellular signal, so we haven't left civilization." Adam's face flickered different shades as he browsed his smartphone. "Yep. There is one pizza place."

"Do your magic." She winked.

Adam paced around with the phone to his ear. "Hi, yeah. Do you guys deliver? Six Minstrel Run. Uh huh. Yeah, we just moved in, why? Heh. I'll take you up on that. Okay, can we get a large with pepperoni and an order of garlic bread? Mm-hmm. Yeah, cash. Thanks." He hung up.

"What was that about?" Mia glanced at him.

"Oh, nothing. The owner just said he'd send us a free pie if we last six months in here."

She stared at him. "What?"

"I don't want to needlessly alarm you..." Adam flashed a sly smile. "But apparently, people who move into this house usually leave fairly soon, according to local folklore."

"If you are going to keep priming me with stuff like this, I'm going to start jumping at shadows. Do you want to have to peel me off the ceiling every time a cloud goes by overhead?"

"Aww, babe." He walked over and hugged her. "It's nothing Joe didn't already mention. Past few people to own this house have all been fast turnover."

"Yeah, yeah…" Mia shook her head.

While Adam ran upstairs to start unpacking their clothes, she continued stacking mugs in the cabinet, then moved on among the various boxes of kitchenware. The stove seemed brand new, barely used, an electric range with a ceramic cooktop. She remembered reading somewhere the house had been built in the early 1960s. No way was it the original range. Whoever installed it couldn't have gotten much use out of it before they sold the place.

"Hmm. Odd." Mia crouched in front of it and pulled the oven open. "Still smells like 'new appliance.'"

When she closed the door, a dark spot in the reflection on the window made it look like someone stood behind her. She whirled, clinging to the oven door handle… and stared at an empty kitchen. Her heart resumed beating in a few breaths. Gradually, she turned back to look at the glass, dreading what she'd see.

The reflection appeared normal, no trace of anything standing behind her.

"Ugh." She covered her face with a hand. "Dammit, Adam. You've put ghosts and spookies in my head, so I'm going to be imagining crap for weeks now."

A soft *thud* shook the ceiling along with a short grunt of exertion from Adam.

Mia gathered loose packing paper back into the boxes. "These are so much easier to carry without all the dishes."

Click.

She spun, staring at the basement door. It remained closed, but she couldn't help but get the feeling someone had recently been standing in the corner and slipped out of sight with no sound other than the snap of the latch.

"Hey, look…" Mia bit her lip. "If there are any ghosts here, we don't want to get in your way, okay? The last time I lived in a house instead of an apartment, it had a bunch of ghosts and we got along pretty well. So, play nice with me and we won't have any issues."

Nothing moved, made noise, or answered.

Another *thud* from overhead almost made her jump onto the counter.

"Dammit, Adam." She glared up. "Do you have to throw stuff around like that?"

The kitchen no longer felt like someone stood there with her. Though, she expected that would change as soon as the sun went down.

3

SAFE PLACE

SATURDAY, AUGUST 25, 2012

Mia crawled into bed feeling like a pizza-stuffed whale settling onto the sea floor.

After an entire day spent running around the house unpacking, she barely managed the strength necessary to roll on her back. Adam climbed in the other side and let out a hard breath.

"You sound exactly how I feel," said Mia.

He squeezed her hand. "It's good to be home."

"It's good to be in a real bed."

"We only had to put up with one night of sleeping bags."

"One night too many." She closed her eyes and smiled.

"Any creepiness?"

"Not at the moment. But I did feel watched all night."

"So did I. It's starting sooner than I expected."

She looked over at him. "What's starting?"

"Activity. I should probably try capturing EVPs or something tomorrow night."

Mia poked him in the side. "You kept saying stuff to make me think about ghosts. It could all be in my head."

"Yeah, that's another possibility. If the recordings come back without any unexplained voices on them, that will tend to agree with the 'all in your head' idea."

"But you'll be disappointed." Mia's voice slowed with oncoming sleep.

"True enough. So, do you want there to be ghosts, or not?"

She swished her feet side to side. Her need for normality conflicted with an inexplicable sense of hope. For a moment, she shared Adam's enthusiasm like a kid about to get something they'd desperately wanted for a long time—but that sense of anticipation faded under the memory of how intimidating the house had seemed when she looked at it the other day.

"I dunno. Guess I'll just try to keep an open mind and not jump to any conclusions."

MIA FOUND HERSELF AWAKE WITHOUT EXPLANATION.

She glanced left at the clock. 11:58 p.m. To her right, Adam lay asleep. They'd put the headboard against the front wall between the two windows on that side. Mia lifted her head off the pillow enough to peer past her feet at the bedroom door. Nothing appeared unusual, or even felt strange, so she started to settle back down—but a sudden smear of darkness zipped out the door into the hallway.

"Hello?" whispered Mia.

She waited four breaths before sitting up. The door hung open only a few inches, not enough for a person to have fit past it. Worse, she couldn't remember if they had closed it or left it ajar. Adam typically preferred to have the bedroom door closed since he said it would be safer in the event of a fire. It had taken her years to get used to that. Her parents hadn't allowed either her or Timothy to close their bedroom doors at night, and became irate if they even asked about it.

Desperately terrified we might touch ourselves and go straight to hell.

Grumbling mentally about her parents, she let her head sink back down and closed her eyes. Her brain focused on the sensation of fullness in her bladder, distracting her enough from sleep that she relented after only a minute or two.

Mia slipped out of bed and padded over to the door. She hesitated, nervous about what might be waiting for her in the hallway. *Still seeing stuff. Just Adam and his fascination with ghosts.* She pulled the door open and stepped out.

The door across the hall from their room remained closed, though the next one to the right on that side was open. *Okay... I know we closed the other ones. At least... I think we did.* Moonlight from the window at the head of the stairs illuminated the whole stretch of hall. Other than the one door open that shouldn't be, nothing appeared out of place. She shook her head and walked four steps left to the bathroom.

When she'd gotten halfway to the toilet, a tingle ran down her back as if someone else had walked into the room with her. She paused, certain someone stared at her from behind. Most of the left wall consisted of a storage closet with a recess on both sides. The alcove in front of the door had a window, the other one in the far corner held the toilet. The tub/shower took up the middle of the right wall, open and empty. A faint hint of bubblegum scent crossed her nose.

Mia turned to look at the open door behind her. Despite there being only Adam in the house, the urge to close—and lock—the door hit her. Too tired to ask questions of herself, she did so, then hurried to the toilet.

She struggled to stay awake while peeing, her head constantly lolling forward and bouncing back up.

A whisper floated out of the bathtub. "Shh..."

Mia jumped and stared at the shower curtain. *I'm only half awake and dreamed that. Holy crap. Good thing I'm already on the toilet.*

She kept watching the bathtub for as long as it took to finish. The floor in the hallway creaked like a man walking up to the bathroom door.

"Adam?" asked Mia.

"Shh..."

Mia froze at the second whisper from the tub, too frightened to even stand off the toilet. Her brain raced for any explanation of what could possibly have made that sound. The shower curtain moving an inch might've sounded like a harshly whispered 'shh'—but the curtain hadn't moved, and she couldn't even reach it from the toilet. If it *did* move, that would mean someone else hid in the bathtub. Someone neither her nor Adam.

Maybe it's a branch at the window?

Sitting on the bowl didn't offer a great view of the small window on the wall to the left, but it didn't look like any trees came close enough for a branch to make contact. Again, the floor creaked in the hall. Mia opened her mouth to call for Adam, but the sudden fear that something bad would happen if she made a sound kept her mute.

An increasing sense of anger wafted from the opposite end of the bathroom, seemingly coming from behind the closed door.

Mia stared at the knob, paralyzed with dread at the thought—no *expectation*—that she would see it start to turn on its own. The unmistakable feeling that an enraged man loomed right outside kept her pinned to the seat.

A rustle came from the bathtub.

She snapped her gaze from door to shower curtain.

It twitched as though someone behind it fidgeted.

Mia gasped.

Another creak came from the hall.

"Who's there?" whispered Mia. "Is someone here?"

"Shh," whispered no one.

Mia sat there for a few minutes, unsure what to do, mentally kicking herself for not turning the light on. As long as she kept hidden in the bathroom, she'd be safe. The instant that thought crossed her mind, she sat up straight and blinked. *Where the hell did that come from?* She eased herself to her feet and approached the sink in front of the toilet. Nothing reacted or made a sound while she washed her hands and dried them on a towel hanging from a ring between sink and bathtub.

She padded past the tub, her bare feet squishing into the plush bathmat. Three steps later, a sharp tug on the left side of her nightgown made her jump away with a startled yelp. She stumbled against the closet doors, gawking at the still-closed shower curtain.

"Adam?" she called in a not-quite yell. "Adam!"

Silence hung over the bathroom for another minute. No response came from her husband, but the not-voice also hadn't shushed her again. Mia swallowed a bit of saliva, steeled herself, and approached the door. The anger she sensed in the area had faded away along with the sensation of not being alone.

"I'm not fully awake and highly suggestible. Maybe I was sleepwalking."

She opened the door to an empty hallway... and the faint smell of beer. Eyes narrowed, she backed up to the tub and pushed the shower curtain aside to look in—at nothing.

"Yeah. I definitely need sleep."

4

PANCAKES

MONDAY, AUGUST 27, 2012

Sunday went by in a blur of grocery shopping, curtain shopping, curtain hanging, more unpacking, and Adam exploring the house with a digital sound recorder while talking to the walls. Mia couldn't tell if all the activity and running around simply kept her too busy to notice anything weird or whatever might be here disliked the commotion and avoided them. Of course, she also considered the possibility that having real, physical things to focus on prevented her brain from teasing her with imaginary spooky stuff.

ON MONDAY MORNING, THE HORRIBLE SCREECH OF THE ALARM clock dragged Mia out of a bizarre dream. It hadn't lasted long, and all she remembered of it upon opening her eyes had been walking along an official-looking corridor, surrounded by people in suits or professional attire. She'd been looking down at her arms, covered in a plain brown coat. A pastel blue purse dangled from her hands. She went past several doors and a stairwell before a man in a police uniform stepped in front of her. She stopped.

"Are you sure?" asked the man.

"Yes," replied Mia.

"You understand what will happen."

"I do," said Mia.

The officer nodded and reached for something under his jacket. Before his hand came out, the alarm had gone off. She groaned and sat up, whining at herself for putting the alarm clock all the way across the room on the chest of drawers. Every day she got up for work, she hated that she'd done that... but by the time she ambled over to make it stop blaring, she gained enough consciousness to realize she needed to stay up. Putting the alarm within reach of the bed would get her fired.

Mia grumbled at forgetting to change her alarm after moving. She didn't need to get up that early anymore. No point going back to sleep for an hour and a half, so she took a nice, relaxing shower, then returned to the bedroom while Adam ran in to clean up. She sat by her little cosmetics desk, ran the blow-dryer, then... proceeded to hunt around for the hairbrush. Grumbling, she gave up on it and borrowed Adam's, then got dressed. He breezed into the room right as she stood to go downstairs.

"Have you seen my hairbrush?"

"All the time." He flung off his towel and opened his underwear drawer.

"Smartass."

Adam wagged his butt at her.

"I mean today."

"Can't say I looked for it. Why? It's not on the thing?" He stepped into a pair of boxer briefs, then turned to face her.

"For a psychology professor, you're astoundingly obtuse. If it *was* 'on my thing,' why would I be asking you where it was?"

"When a guy asks 'it's not where you think it is?' that basically means we have no idea where the missing object is." He pulled on a T-shirt, then moved to the closet. "Probably lost in the move."

"Ugh."

"Your hair looks fine."

"I used your brush."

"So, what's the emergency then?"

She pointed it at him. "Your brush isn't my brush."

He stepped into his slacks and shot her a smirk.

"And on that note... what do you want in your oatmeal?"

"Raisins are fine... or raspberry jam, or plain."

Mia headed down the hall to the stairs, but froze at the top. She glanced back at what she thought she'd seen... and blinked. The middle door on the right had once again opened. *Adam's been in and out of that room all yesterday. It's become a giant closet.* Despite the house having far more space than their apartment, a handful of boxes and other stuff (like lamps) wound up in there for the time being until they'd settled in enough to look at unpacking all the stuff that formerly sat forgotten in closets.

"Adam probably left it open."

Shaking her head, Mia went downstairs to the kitchen and set about preparing two bowls of oatmeal. She set them in the huge microwave and stood there watching the tray spin around. *Their* microwave— another object sitting in the storage room upstairs—was about half the size of the one the prior occupant of the house left behind.

A sudden craving for pancakes came out of nowhere. She eyed the box of mix on the counter, then the clock. Mia blinked at it, unable to remember buying pancake mix when they'd gone to the store, or even why she would have. Neither she nor Adam had pancakes at home once since they'd married. Yet, there it was, so clearly they'd bought it. Maybe seeing the pastor had caused her to think of her brother, which somehow triggered a subconscious memory. The last time she'd had pancakes had been when she'd made them for him, a couple months before they left home. *Damn. I haven't had pancakes in forever. Tempting... but there isn't enough time and I've already got the oatmeal cooking.*

The craving proved distracting enough that she picked up the box of mix and read over the directions, re-familiarizing herself with *how* to make pancakes. At a *ding* from the oven, she set the box down and took the bowls out—unprepared for how warm they were.

"Hot! Crap! Crap! Crap!"

In her haste to set the bowls on the counter before she involuntarily dropped them and spilled oatmeal everywhere, she accidentally elbowed the pancake mix off the counter. It hit the floor with a loud *whap*, popping open and spewing a light dusting of powder on the tile.

"Dammit." Mia sighed. At least she hadn't wasted much mix.

She crouched to retrieve a dustpan from under the sink and got the oddest feeling someone hurried past her despite not hearing anything. When she pivoted to her right to begin sweeping—she stopped short at the sight of footprints in the pancake mix. Five distinct spots in the shape of a small child's bare feet crossed from one side of the spill to the other.

"Oh, crap..." She stared for another moment before yelling, "Adam!"

Mia dropped the dustpan and brush, sprang upright, and grabbed her cell phone from her handbag on the table.

"Yeah?" called Adam from the stairway. "Did you yell?"

"Get in here!" She swiped open to the camera app and took several pictures of the footprints.

He sauntered down the hall in no great hurry, pausing at the doorjamb. "What are you doing?"

"Look!" Mia pointed. "I derped the pancake mix off the counter and spilled a little. There's *footprints!*"

Adam's lackadaisical attitude evaporated. He dashed over and squatted. "This is incredible."

"Incredibly sad. Those feet are so small."

"Hey..." He pointed. "Make a footprint next to them for scale."

She shifted her gaze to him. "Why do *I* have to do it? I've got stockings on."

"Okay, fine. Just hold your foot over the dust. Don't step down."

With a sigh, Mia slipped one shoe off and balanced on one foot while Adam took a few pictures.

"Yeah, that's a kid all right."

Mia stepped back into her shoe and grasped his left arm in both of hers, chin on his shoulder. "That's so damn sad."

Adam rummaged a tape measure out of a drawer, extended it a bit, and set it down beside the prints before snapping a few more images.

"I thought I felt someone walk past me." Mia circled around to the other side, close to the little hall that led to the dining room. "Looks like they were running to the back door, maybe to go outside."

"Felt someone?" asked Adam. "Did you hear anything?"

"No… You know how people just *know* when someone's around? That. A sense of not being alone."

He smiled. "Dare I say, because you *weren't* alone?"

"You're trying to make sure I never sleep again, aren't you?"

"Well, you grew up in a house full of ghosts." He picked up the oatmeal bowls and moved them to the table. "This shouldn't be that much different."

"It was way different back home. There, I only heard distant footsteps or got creepy feelings. I never heard ghosts speaking or saw footprints or even… okay, I *did* feel like I wasn't alone… all the time. But only at night." She took her seat and ate a spoonful of oatmeal. "Umm. I'm not sure if I should sweep that up or leave it."

"Good question. If you don't mind me asking, how did you manage to knock *just* the pancake mix over out of that whole row of boxes against the wall by the jars?"

She got up to grab raisins. "Got the weirdest craving out of nowhere for pancakes, so I picked the box up to read the instructions. Put it down too close to the edge when the micro dinged."

"Interesting… Wonder where that itch for pancakes came from."

"Don't say it." She sat again and dumped some raisins into both bowls.

"Thanks."

They stared at each other while eating for a minute or three.

"Kids like pancakes." Adam wagged his eyebrows.

"Knock it off. I'm too sad to smile at any jokes about that."

He suppressed his smile. "I'm not trying to make a joke. We've just witnessed legit evidence of the paranormal. I'm excited about that, not… well, yeah."

Mia sighed. "Great. I'm going to be in a bad mood all day."

"Over spilling a little pancake mix?"

"No, dammit. Over the thought that a kid might have died here."

She rested her elbow on the table, chin in her hand. "It's just not fair. Some people shouldn't be allowed to be parents."

Adam raised an eyebrow. "What makes you think the parents—or a parent—did it?"

"Umm. I don't know…" Mia paused, searching for an explanation as to why she felt so certain the ghost died at the hands of a parent. "I'm not sure. It just came out without any real thought involved. Felt right." She sighed. "I dunno. Maybe my parents make me expect the worst from everyone."

"Maybe." He gave her a look that said 'they weren't *that* bad,' but wisely didn't open his mouth.

5

FREAK EVENTS

MONDAY, AUGUST 27, 2012

Excited at the appearance of the footprints, Adam hummed to himself for most of the ride to Syracuse University.

He found it difficult to contain his restless enthusiasm; however, the dean, the HR department, and the bulk of the faculty/administration he dealt with upon arriving assumed his mood to be related to his new position teaching a freshman psychology class. His first session didn't start until 9 a.m., so he had a little less than an hour to situate himself in his new office.

A few minutes into arranging the small box of desk kitsch he'd brought, a light knock came from the door. Adam looked up at a young man with short platinum blonde hair and a plain tan sweater. By looks, he could've been anywhere between eighteen and twenty. The backpack over his shoulder and ID hanging around his neck on a lanyard gave him away as a student. Slight hesitation in his slate-blue eyes suggested he might be lost.

"Good morning." Adam smiled and set his Luke Skywalker pen holder next to the lamp. "Can I help you with something?"

"Professor Gartner?"

"Yep."

The young man stepped in and offered a hand. "Hi. Good to meet you. I'm Paul Reitman, your UTA. Shame about Professor MacLeod."

Adam rested his hands on his hips. "I'm sorry. I didn't know her. All they told me was that a position opened unexpectedly. I hope nothing too bad happened to her."

"Bone cancer. She's still in the hospital as far as I know, but at her age, it's…" Paul shook his head. "I heard she'd been feeling off for a while, but put off going to the doctor. Kept right on teaching until she collapsed. That finally made her go to a doctor, and they found out how sick she really was."

"I'm sorry. Now I almost feel guilty for being happy a position finally opened here."

Paul scratched at his arm. "It's all right. I only knew her from taking her class. She's amazingly insightful and connects with her students. It's because of her I'm considering an educational track instead of clinical. Most of the reason I volunteered as a UTA this year is to get a taste for being on the other side of the desk. Still not sure which way I'll wind up going, but I at least wanted to see it."

Adam chuckled. "Both are rewarding, though *teaching* psychology has the added benefit of preserving your sanity. As a clinician looking into other people's lives, especially the aberrant ones, a lot of that stuff comes home with you. Kinda like cops. Getting to see the worst in people haunts you."

"Are you saying clinicians all wind up divorced alcoholics before fifty?" Paul laughed. "So, you've been waiting a while to come here specifically?"

"Yeah. My wife's been working over at the Everson Museum for the past few years, commute was kicking her butt. I've been trying to get my foot in the door of anything close enough to this area that we could move."

"Oh, nice. Welcome to Syracuse."

"Thanks. We're not actually living *in* Syracuse. We got a place up in Spring Falls." Adam wagged his eyebrows. "It's supposedly haunted. Parapsychology is somewhat of a hobby of mine, though I'm primarily focused on spirits and the possibility of psychic phenomena." He raised a hand. "Strictly from a scientific point of view."

Paul's eyes widened. "Wait… did you get *that* house?"

"On Minstrel Run?"

"Yeah, that's the one. Minstrel. I remember reading about it."

"Oh?" Adam resumed transferring little figures from his box to the desk. "Nothing too bad, I hope."

"The place has been on the market for years. Anyone who buys it always leaves in months. Two women who lived there at different times both almost died in freak accidents. One even wound up paralyzed from the waist down."

Adam paused, holding his R2-D2 paperclip magnet, staring at Paul. The idea that Mia could in any way be put in danger by their new house had never occurred to him. Everything that had happened so far all seemed fairly tame, but they had only been in the house a few days. At the first sign of serious risk, he'd get her out of harm's way. No amount of research data would be worth her life, or even permanent injury. "Are you serious or are you messing with me?"

Paul wagged his eyebrows. "Check the *Spring Falls Gazette*. They have records. Might even be digital now."

"Hmm." Adam rubbed his chin, feeling remiss in not having researched the house's history more deeply than 'it's haunted and people keep leaving.' "The house was listed considerably lower than everything else in the area. Our mortgage is less than the rent on our old apartment."

"Yeah. I'm telling you, the place is totally haunted. Not so much down here in Syracuse, but up by where you live? All those small towns like to talk."

Adam leaned back, folding his arms. "If word hasn't reached Syracuse, how'd you hear about it?"

"You're not the only one in this room with an interest in the paranormal." Paul grinned. "A friend of mine thought it would be fun to go over there and look around. No one lived there at the time and we didn't break in. Spent two hours walking around the property. Got an EVP that sounds like a little kid crying. Kelly thought she heard a deep male voice growl at her in the backyard, and Cayden's box said 'lonely.'"

"Cayden's box?" asked Adam with a head tilt.

"It's this device that supposedly lets spirits manipulate electromagnetic energy to pick words out of a database. It's finicky and doesn't always work, but at your house, it repeated 'lonely' several times. Kelly thinks it's really a demon because of the deep growl and the little kid voice."

"Oh, one of those things. Yeah, I've seen them before. Most people who are considered any sort of legit authority on the paranormal state that child haunts are malicious spirits pretending... but check this out." Adam took his phone from its belt holder, opened to the photos app, and pulled up the pictures from earlier. "My wife bumped a box of pancake mix off the counter this morning. She turned her back on it for only a minute to grab a dustpan... and found this."

"Whoa." Paul gingerly took the phone and studied the photo, zooming it. "This happened in the daytime, with her right next to it?"

Adam nodded.

"Not that I'm any sort of expert on ghosts, but"—Paul handed the phone back—"being active in the day makes me think it's a pretty powerful manifestation. And being active in the room right next to your wife suggests it's territorial. If that *is* a demon, you should be careful, professor."

"Yeah. Mia hasn't mentioned picking up on any hostile feelings or negative energy yet."

"Your wife, is she sensitive?" asked Paul.

"I'm sure of it, though I haven't been able to prove it to any scientific standard. However, she *did* react right away to the house when she saw it, both the first time we checked it out months ago and Friday when we officially took ownership." Adam chuckled. "That kinda explains why Joe was so happy."

"Joe?"

"The realtor. You'd think he'd won the lottery or something."

Paul laughed. "He basically did. That house is like a cash vacuum for the agency. They sell it and make commission all over again every few years."

"Not this time." Adam shook his head. "I don't think we're going to be giving up on it that easily. I chose it specifically because it had a haunt."

"Good luck, but I bet most of the people who moved in there said the same thing, or didn't believe in ghosts. Pretty sure they believed in ghosts when they ran out the door screaming." Paul glanced at the clock. "Class starts in twelve minutes… takes about six to walk there from here. Got any notes or anything you need help with?"

Adam opened his case. "It's only the first day. Work hasn't quite piled up yet." He dropped a manila folder in front of Paul. "That's my lesson plan. Why don't we go over it so you know what you're getting into?"

"Sounds good." Paul flipped the pages, skimming. "Looks fairly close to what I remember from Professor MacLeod's class."

Adam gestured at the door. "Might as well talk on the hoof. No sense being late the first day."

"Sure thing." Paul closed the folder and carried it out into the hallway. "If you don't mind, keep me updated on what happens with the house?"

"Of course. If you can't tell, I love talking about this stuff… as much as I love talking about psychology. Only real difference is one pays the bills, one gets me laughed at."

Paul laughed.

Adam playfully narrowed his eyes.

6

SENSITIVE

MONDAY, AUGUST 27, 2012

A twenty-six minute ride to work blew Mia's mind almost as much as arriving before she finished her coffee.

Between having time to finish waking up, eating something, and allowing for traffic, it had been her reality for the past two years and some months to drag her ass out of bed at a little after five in the morning so she could make it to work by nine. More often than not, she arrived early. Leaving work at 5:30 p.m. usually let her get home by eight or a little later. That left only two hours for everything normal people did after a work day unless she cheated herself out of sleep.

Needless to say, walking out the door at 8:30 a.m. had been amazing. She equally looked forward to being home by six. For the commute alone, moving to Spring Falls had been worth it. Everyone she met on the way to her work area in the back of the museum picked up on her overabundance of energy. After six brief conversations explaining what a drain on her soul a two-hour-plus drive had been, she reached her studio.

The room reeked of various chemicals, paints, old glue, wood, and concrete dust. She hung her coat in the storage closet and resumed working on the painting she'd started Wednesday before leaving work. She'd taken Thursday and Friday off for the move.

Inch by inch, she dabbed a Q-tip soaked in cleaning solution around the old canvas, clearing away the effects of exposure to air for two centuries. The donor claimed it was the work of Henry Raeburn, from around 1802, done as a private commission for some long-dead relative of his. Based on the amount of grunge, Mia had little trouble believing it had been either displayed in someone's home or left in an attic for an extended period without proper care.

She hummed to herself while making her way across the canvas, noting places where small areas of damage would require patching and repainting. She found color-matching the most tedious part of the process, but also the most rewarding. Breathing life back into something thought dead fulfilled a deep, internal need. She often wondered if the original artists had been as happy to create the paintings as she was to restore them to the way they should appear.

While working her Q-tip along the jawline of the young woman depicted in the painting, she caught a spell of maudlin at the thought of the footprints in the pancake dust. Ever since she'd graduated college, she'd worked on countless paintings, many of which had been portraits of people who had long ago died.

It seems I'm fated to work with the dead... either the ones preserved in oils or roaming my kitchen.

With each successive cycle of dabbing and wiping, an increasing sense of love and sadness surrounded her. The young woman in the painting smiled in the way that newlyweds tended to smile, joy and nervousness and mischievousness and embarrassment all wrapped up in one subtle curve of the lip. She appeared to be staring at the artist as he worked, but a dark undertone of loss and sorrow gnawed at her as well. Mia pictured the woman being restless, fighting her urge to jump up and embrace the painter, wanting to be close to him. Her feelings didn't at all fit what the donor had told the museum about it being painted over in London as a simple commission.

That didn't sit right with her, so she spent almost two hours analyzing the style, color use, composition, brush technique, and the signature. It resembled Raeburn's work, but fell short of an exact match. The style approximated his, but after looking up a few of his other works, she felt certain the painting she'd been working on was *not* a Raeburn. After another half hour or so of research—and lunch— she determined what the acquisitions guy mistook for the big H R in the signature was, in fact, a stylistic M. She eventually tracked down that the artist most likely to have painted it had been named Mendelson. She took some notes, intending to finish the documentation process later, since the actual restoration work called to her more strongly.

She resumed cleaning the painting, hoping to finish at least the first pass today. Gradually, the dingy canvas brightened under the ministrations of her Q-tip. The monotony of dabbing, wiping, and dabbing took her out of reality into a haze of contentment.

"Hey," chirped a nearby woman.

Mia jumped, having been so absorbed in her work she hadn't noticed the woman walk up to her. She grasped the huge table to steady herself and glanced over at Julie Wolfe, one of her colleagues who restored primarily vases, pottery, and statues. "Sorry. You startled me."

"You don't need to make up for taking days off, yanno." Julie winked. "That's why they call them days off. Or did you intend to stay late? It's 5:36."

"Oh crap. I didn't notice." Mia checked her phone to confirm the time and grinned at the idea she'd be home in less than a half hour. "I got absorbed in this painting. There's so much love in it, but it's also somehow really sad."

"What do you mean?" Julie tilted her head.

"The way the woman's looking at the artist, you just know they were deeply in love. And I think one of them probably died too young. It's almost like, I dunno. Like someone poured a lot of emotional energy into this painting."

Julie scrunched her nose. "Isn't that the Raeburn?"

"That's what the guy said, but it isn't." She explained the signature and style not being a match. "It's close, but this is a Mendelson."

"Oh, isn't that the guy who painted almost exclusively women's portraits?" Julie scratched her head. "I remember reading somewhere about it. Sticks out because it was so sad. The last painting the guy ever did was of his wife. He had some disease or something and knew he would die, but didn't tell her."

"Did he die young?" asked Mia. "Or did he marry a much younger woman?"

"I have no idea. Why, you think this is that painting?"

"Could be."

Julie fiddled with her phone while Mia packed away her supplies for the day. "Okay, I was wrong. Says here that this Mendelson guy painted his wife's portrait only a few months before *she* died. The poor woman caught a stray bullet from two idiots dueling in a field near her house. According to this article, he fell into a deep depression and never did another painting. He kept the portrait of his wife, and supposedly talked to it all the time thinking she could hear him."

"Wow." Mia blinked.

"Holy crap, what are you psychic or something?"

"Hah. Probably just a good guess based on her expression, though Adam thinks I'm sensitive."

Julie made 'wee-ooo' creepy noises while waving her hands around. "You just totally freaked me out. Wait, you read that article already and you're playing with me."

"I didn't, but I'm also neither trying to freak you out nor prove I have ESP. So, take it as a coincidence."

"Right..." Julie walked backward a few steps, pointing at her. "One hell of a coincidence."

Mia faked a smile as her thoughts went back to that moment in her bathroom. Someone had been terrified, someone else, furious. After seeing those small footprints earlier, she couldn't help but think that the kid had been the one hiding in the bathtub. A sick sort of sorrow twisted around in her stomach, wondering how long some poor child had lived in fear of their father before the unthinkable happened.

With a sigh, she finished packing up and headed home.

MIA PARKED HER TAHOE IN THE DRIVEWAY AND STARTED TO GET out before remembering to put the parking brake on due to the incline. As soon as she pressed down on it, a mild twinge of pain washed over her left foot.

"Damn. Did I bruise the bone or something? Don't remember dropping anything on my foot. Must've stepped wrong." She rolled her ankle around a few times, stretched her toes, and gingerly put her weight down on that leg—no pain. "Huh. Weird."

She shut the door, then turned toward the house—and stopped short under a heavy wave of dread. The place didn't feel warm and welcoming like 'home' should. It also didn't exactly fill her with the urge to run away and never return. An inexplicable notion of 'not quite right,' as though she looked at a house seconds before a lava flow obliterated it, kept her standing there for a minute or two.

"Okay, this is…" She sighed. "That painting was pretty messed up. Maybe Adam's right and I *am* sensitive.

The instant she entertained the idea that her husband's insistence she had some degree of psychic talent could be true, something moved in the middle upstairs window. Mia gasped and grabbed her purse tight to her chest, staring at the curtain. Her imagination filled in a small person watching her from the window and randomly darting away.

Unsure how to feel about anything, Mia walked up the stone footpath to the porch and went inside. No particular mood hung in the living room. Her happiness at having a much shorter commute took over, and she managed to smile on the way upstairs to her room.

"Adam?"

No one answered.

She checked her phone, and sure enough, she had a text from him that he expected to be home soon. Telling him about the painting could wait until dinner conversation, so she replied to let him know she'd arrived home safe, then tossed the phone on the bed. After changing into a T-shirt and sweat pants, she grabbed the phone and headed downstairs.

The pancake mix remained on the floor as they'd left it. Now barefoot, Mia made a footprint beside the ones theoretically caused by a ghost. Hers, other than being larger, appeared cleaner with almost no mix wherever her skin touched the floor. The smaller footprints didn't completely clear the tiles.

"Of course. I have physical substance. My skin picks up the powder." Mia brushed her foot off, then took a few close-up photographs of where she made a sample print.

That done, she gathered the supplies to cook dinner, going for the salmon filets as they wouldn't last. She set them in a baking pan flanked by asparagus and drizzled olive oil on it before adding minced garlic and some parmesan.

While shaking the cheese onto the tray, a faint chill moved up behind her along with the sense of not being alone. Mia froze, holding the canister over the food. She found her nerve and twisted to look back. No one stood behind her.

She glanced around nervously. "Hello. I have no idea if you're here or not, or if I'm imagining it all. But, if you're real, my name is Mia." When her gaze settled on the pancake dust, she gasped.

Another small footprint had appeared beside the one she made, not 'walking,' but a deliberate placement beside hers.

Mia stared at the new footprint, the overt playfulness of it causing her to choke up. She took a few breaths to calm down. "It's okay. I'm not going to hurt you."

No response came.

I'm talking to thin air. Am I nuts? Adam does it all the time, but I don't have one of those little recorder things. She smirked at herself and slid the baking tray into the oven. A soft *thump* came from the living room. Curious, Mia padded out of the kitchen. Motion pulled her gaze to the rug.

Halfway across the dining room, small depressions in the carpet approximated footsteps, but they didn't compress much, not even enough to recognize the shape of a foot... merely that *something* moved.

Barely breathing, Mia crept after the trail, staring intently at the point where the rug pile dented. It continued into the living room, curving to the left toward the sofa. She started to smile at the innocence of it when a much darker energy gathered in the little hallway by the toilet closet. A distinct sense that something malevolent glared at her locked every muscle in her arms and legs rigid. The entity felt as though it gathered strength for an imminent attack.

Bing-Bong.

Mia screamed at the sudden, loud doorbell.

An oldish voice outside also cried out in surprise.

The negative presence vanished, and with it, the paralytic dread.

One hand over her chest, Mia headed to the door and pulled it open, revealing a rather surprised Pastor Weston Parker. He still wore a blue button down shirt and khaki's but had added a cloth boonie hat.

Mia's mood darkened, but she caught herself before making a comment. Though he probably shared the same ideology as her parents, this particular man hadn't yet done anything to her personally.

"Sorry for startling you, Mrs. Gartner." Weston offered an apologetic smile. "Didn't notice you at Sunday Service."

"Probably because I wasn't there." She smirked.

He drew a breath, shaking his head. "I understand you may have had some bad experiences in the past, but I think you really ought to consider getting right with Him before it's too late."

She tapped her foot. "Since I don't know you, I have no idea what your personal goals are here. However, regardless of the theoretical existence of any sort of god or gods, I don't trust any person telling me what they think said theoretical deity wants. If there is something up there, or multiple somethings out there, they're more than welcome to contact me in person. A true god wouldn't need a mortal to do his talking for him. Only cults need people to do their dirty work."

Weston shifted his jaw side to side. "I realize you've got your opinions on religious folk. And darn sure there's quite a few people out there who misuse the name of the Lord to deceive people. What matters here is your and your husband's souls."

She glanced back over her shoulder upon catching a noticeable waft of garlic from her dinner. "I still think that if a supposed loving god had any intention of 'saving our souls,' he'd do it whether or not we spent a couple hours on Sunday singing off key in a fancy little building. If his love-slash-protection is conditional, then it's not coming from a position of benevolence. Do *this thing* or the bad stuff that happens to you is your fault sounds like an abusive spouse—or the mafia—not a heavenly being."

"Mrs. Gartner, I don't think you're taking seriously the amount of danger you're in."

She smiled. "I take it about as seriously as the notion that there's a Jewish zombie up in the clouds who will protect me if I telepathically tell him how much I love him, but if I don't, he'll let all sorts of evil happen to me because he loves everyone. Or, can you explain to me why this god of yours cares so much about the souls of a young, suburban married couple in upstate New York but all those starving people in third world countries are on their own?"

Weston set his hands on his hips and stared down.

Mia bit her lip. "Sorry. That was a little harsh. I appreciate your concern, but I still think if any benevolent god was going to offer my soul his protection, he'd just do it without being asked. That's what parental figures do for their children… they protect them without being asked. If you had a three-year-old, and he was running around near traffic, you wouldn't just stand there watching him zoom in front of a UPS truck because he didn't *ask* you to save him from being run over. You'd keep a hold of him. All you religious types keep talking about 'love,' but the minute someone doesn't conform to some arbitrary set of rules, all that love goes straight out the window and supposed families rip themselves apart."

"I apologize for upsetting you." Weston lifted his gaze from the porch. "All I ask is that you don't judge everyone based on the actions of a few people. Please think about what I said. This house has a dark past. The Devil has his eye on it." He tipped his fishing cap. "Have a good rest of your week."

"Drive safe."

She hovered in the doorway, watching him amble off to the road and hop in his Jeep Cherokee. A smallish dog sprang to life in the back section, separated from the rear seat by a wall of cage-like mesh. The —possibly bichon—barked and yipped happily, tail wagging.

"That guy is too persistent."

Mia shut the front door and walked back to the kitchen. She eyed the little side hall to the toilet closet, still worried that something there might want to hurt her. Her train of thought regarding dinner had derailed, but salmon and asparagus really didn't need anything else as a side. It also had a bit more time before being done. She started to head for the living room to sit, but froze, staring at the countertop.

Her missing hairbrush sat beside the can of parmesan cheese.

7

BEDTIME

MONDAY, AUGUST 27, 2012

Thoughts of students flew around in Adam's head on the ride home.

He had three classes, each an hour and forty-five minutes, plus an official 'office time' of 4 p.m. to 5 p.m. to meet with any students that had additional questions or required help. Paul, his undergraduate teaching assistant, shared much of his interest in the paranormal. Considering it had been the first day of class, no one showed up with questions at office hour, so the two of them had swapped ghost stories—and run late.

As he usually did at the start of a school year, he mentally categorized the students who stood out: the ones he expected to excel, the ones he figured would struggle and need a lot of support, and one or two he expected to be problematic. Those usually fell into either overt troublemakers, or the sort of person who complained to the administration over every little thing.

Content with how his day had gone, he smiled the whole trip to the house—though he did need to use the Garmin to find his way at least to Minstrel Run.

Ehh, couple weeks and I'll be able to drive this in my sleep.

He narrowed his eyes at a distancing green Jeep with a fluffy white dog in the back window.

"Great. What the heck does *he* want now?" Adam rolled his eyes.

While he didn't share Mia's active contempt for religion, he considered himself a skeptic. The psychology of it sometimes bore alarming similarities to cults, especially wherever the people craved authoritarian leadership and became hostile in the face of dissent or any perceived lapse of complete belief. Also, there remained a rather astounding lack of proof. He prepared himself to fully accept any deity that showed itself or created phenomena science couldn't explain. Until someone presented peer-reviewed studies proving the existence of a god or gods, he regarded religious people as either victims of fraud or perpetrators thereof. He had to admit a little jealousy at how the vast majority of people in the country readily accepted the 'truth' of a deity without any proof more compelling than someone saying it existed, but start talking about ghosts or psychic powers and everyone demanded mountains of evidence. Sometimes, the same people who laughed at him over ghosts and called his proof fake also completely believed in 'god' without any corroborating evidence.

"Ugh. Okay, maybe I am as bad as Mia." He pulled the Sentra into their enormous driveway, parking to the right of the Tahoe.

Eager to spend a few hours running around the house with a digital recorder, he hopped out and jogged up the walkpath to the porch.

"Mia?"

"Hey," came a soft voice from the kitchen.

He sniffed at something fishy-veggie in the air with a load of garlic. "Ooh, that smells amazing. I've got a short day tomorrow, so I can cover dinner."

Mia didn't say anything.

Adam crossed the living room to the arch and hurried past the dining room to the kitchen, where Mia sat at the table, staring at a hairbrush she turned around and around in her hand. "Oh, hey, you found it."

"It was on the counter."

"Weird." Adam removed his light jacket and draped it over another chair, then put his briefcase down by the door.

"No, I mean one minute it wasn't… the next, it's there."

He rounded the corner of the table to stand in front of her. "What's wrong?"

"There's a ghost in this house. And it's probably a kid. That's depressing as hell."

"It is." Adam took a knee and embraced her. "And as sad as it is, there's nothing we can do about it but try to make contact. If we have an actual intelligent spirit, maybe we can work out a way to communicate."

"The spirit is smart. Look at the pancake dust."

Adam gave her another squeeze, then let go and stood. "That has to be your footprint."

"Look next to it. After I did that for a size comparison, the ghost stepped there, but only there. Like he or she was playing."

"That's amazing." Adam's grin widened with awe.

Beep.

Mia set the hairbrush on the table.

"I got it. You prepped it." Adam winked. He took the tray out of the oven and distributed the contents evenly over two plates. "This looks phenomenal."

She chuckled. "It's not exactly difficult to dribble stuff on a tray."

While they ate, Mia told him of her 'psychic impression' on the painting at work. It fascinated Adam, but he couldn't use it for any of the papers he wanted to write since none of the conditions had been controlled or even documented prior. That didn't stop him from trying to squeeze every last detail out of her and listening with the eagerness of a kid hearing a campfire story.

"They say it's possible for items to soak up emotional energy. Did you have any visions or anything when you touched it?"

"No. Nothing like that. Only a general feeling. It's not psychometry."

He grinned.

"Yes, dear, I do listen when you talk about the weird stuff."

Adam chuckled, then told her about meeting Paul and his mutual interest in all things paranormal. Other than that, his first day at the school had been pleasant if unremarkable. "I'm not the least bit psychic, but I have a good feeling about the place. I'd like to say I'm going to be there for a long time."

"Don't taunt fate like that."

"Fair point. Well…" He gestured at the footprints. "Being there for a long time doesn't necessarily require I remain alive."

Mia almost dropped her fork. "Please don't joke about that."

"Sorry." He cringed. "So what did that priest want?"

"He's a pastor, not a priest."

"There's a difference?" Adam scratched his head.

Mia smiled. "I'm going to resist the rather obvious temptation to make a disgusting joke, and say yes. And, what else do you think he wants? Trying to sell his cult door to door. Oh, I didn't see you there Sunday. You really should attend. Your souls are at risk, and so on."

"Ahh. No problem with him?"

"Other than being pushy, not really. Can't tell if he's a sinister cult leader or a kindly older guy who genuinely believes he has an imaginary friend in the sky."

Adam laughed. "We've got an imaginary friend in the kitchen."

"As soon as god leaves footprints in our pancake mix, I'll change my mind." She stabbed her last piece of asparagus.

"I'll get the dishes."

Mia leaned her weight on her elbows and flashed an alluring smile. "Why do men do that?"

Adam picked up the plates and carried them to the sink. "Do what?"

"Whenever they do some simple domestic chore—like washing dishes—that normal people just *do*, they announce it like they're about to singlehandedly charge a German machine gun nest."

"I'm a man. I deserve a back pat for performing any form of housework that doesn't involve lawn care, power tools, or breaking my neck on a ladder outside." He grinned at Mia via her reflection on the window over the sink.

"The obvious sarcasm in your voice has saved you from my vicious reprisal."

"Oh?" He ran hot water and added dish soap. "What sort of reprisal?"

"Something truly vicious… like leaving a candy bowl mixed with M&Ms, Skittles, and Reese's out for you to find."

"Vicious."

"I am." She examined her fingernails.

While he scrubbed the dishes, Mia finally decided to sweep up the pancake mix, then headed into the living room. Adam looked around for a drying rack… and stared at the dishwasher. "Dammit."

"You finally noticed we have a machine, now?" asked Mia from the living room.

Adam hung his head. "Yeah. That's going to take some getting used to." He looked up and finished scrubbing the baking pan. "Not like we generated many dishes tonight. No big deal."

Once he finished, he headed upstairs, changed into a T-shirt and shorts, and returned to the living room to recline on the couch next to Mia and enjoy the absence of shoes. She scrolled for a little while before putting on *Zootopia*.

"This is a kids' movie," said Adam.

"It's supposed to be funny."

"Random inclination to put it on?"

She glanced over at him. "I don't think so. Just seemed like a good idea. They don't have anything else on this thing that we haven't already watched, looks lame, or is not my cup of tea."

"Fine." He smiled. "It's okay if you put it on for the kid."

Mia playfully elbowed him in the side, then snuggled against him. "Oh, it was so wonderful to only have a half hour ride to work. Having free time at home is such a bizarre feeling."

"Anything I say to that will result in revenge of some form."

"While you have had a short commute for your entire life, you did offer to move up here for me before you found a job. I'm the one who insisted we wait. So I don't blame you."

He kissed her.

The movie, though meant for children, did have its funny moments. It ended around 8 p.m., at which point, Mia tossed the remote to Adam to pick the next show. He started scrolling between dramas and documentaries, but paused at the soft thudding of footsteps. Adam glanced at the stairs, the apparent source of the noise, and stared at the ceiling as they passed overhead.

"You heard that, right?" whispered Mia. "Sounds like someone's walking upstairs."

"Yeah."

She sat up and nudged him. "Go check."

He stood. "You should come with me."

"Are you crazy?" She stared at him.

"We have spent the past almost two hours sitting in full sight of the front door. Whatever is upstairs is most assuredly *not* any sort of living burglar. For interacting with spirits, you are far better equipped."

She whined out her nose.

"Stay behind me, but you should come with." He took her hand.

"Okay, fine."

Adam crept across the living room to the stairs and eased his weight onto the first step with a minimal of creaking. Mia followed close. He spent a few seconds listening, but the upstairs had fallen silent. In an effort to make as little noise as possible on the way up, he placed his feet close to the sides of each step.

"I hear something," whispered Mia.

Adam strained to listen, but the hallway above remained silent. He shrugged.

Mia slipped around him once they reached the top. She tilted her head a bit to the side to put an ear forward and padded all the way to the bathroom at the far end, hovering at the doorjamb. Adam moved up to stand behind her, staring expectantly at her. He tried to ask 'what do you hear?' with his eyes.

She glanced back over her shoulder and whispered, "Someone brushing their teeth."

He nodded.

"Just stopped," whispered Mia. She peeked in. "No one there... but okay, this is weird. I smell bubble gum."

Adam's heart sank a little. "Kid toothpaste."

Mia frowned. "Night, sweetie."

They stood there listening and looking around for a minute or so.

"I'm going to try to capture an EVP."

She patted his shoulder. "You do that. I'm going to watch something."

While Mia returned downstairs, Adam grabbed a digital voice recorder, turned it on, and hovered in the corner between the bedroom and that bathroom.

"If there are any spirits here, can you say something in this little box I'm holding?" He waited ten seconds. "What's your name?" He waited another ten seconds. "How many spirits are here?" He waited about fifteen seconds. "Did you die in this house?"

Mia screamed.

"Crap." He ran down the hall to the stairs. "Mia?"

"I'm okay. The TV turned itself off. Startled me."

"Oh." Adam laughed.

A few seconds of 'cop dialogue' came from downstairs, but cut off.

"Ack! It did it again."

The TV came on… and died.

Adam descended the stairs.

Mia shook the remote at the TV. *Law & Order* appeared on the screen, but the TV shut off four seconds later. "What the hell?"

Adam held the recorder up. "Are you doing something to the television?"

Mia turned the show on again, but the set crapped out in four seconds to a black screen. "Grr."

He stopped recording, rewound thirty seconds, and pressed play, listening to the device close to his ear.

"Are you doing something to the television?" asked Adam's voice from the recorder.

Two seconds later, a scratchy rasp answered.

"Ooh!" Adam gasped. "There's a response."

"What did it say?" Mia looked over at him.

"Not sure. Gotta replay it."

He rewound ten seconds and hit play. Mia turned the TV on again, but it died.

"Atime," rasped a toneless voice.

"Sec, hon. Let me hear."

Mia folded her arms, still holding the remote, waiting for him to listen before she resumed her war with the TV.

He rewound and replayed, straining to listen.

The phantom voice spoke fast, still a blip of a whisper that sounded like 'time.'

"Anything?" Mia cocked her head.

"One sec. Let me try replaying this at eighty percent speed. Spirits are on a higher frequency." He tinkered with the speed setting, backed up ten seconds, and hit play again.

"…omething to the television?" asked Adam from the recorder, his slowed-down voice low and nearly demonic in pitch.

Two seconds of silence passed.

"Bedtime," whispered a child.

Mia covered her mouth with a hand.

"Might as well go to bed then." Adam smiled.

"It's only 8:30." She tried to turn the TV on again, but it switched off. Mia leaned back, staring at an empty spot of floor. "Okay… okay…"

Adam took a step toward her. "What?"

"I… think the kid's getting angry with us for being up past our bedtime." She set the remote down on the coffee table. "Okay, okay. Bedtime."

"What?"

Mia stood and hurried over to him. "A feeling. Like they're standing there glaring at me. I felt a distinct sense of annoyance. Besides, I don't want to spend the next hour fighting the TV."

"I'm picking up a distinct sense of annoyance, too." He tapped her on the tip of the nose. "From you. That the TV won't stay on."

"Come on. Let's just go upstairs. You can still try to talk from bed."

Adam checked both front and back door locks, then followed Mia up to the bedroom. "How's that for backward? The kid's sending us to bed."

8

CONTACT

TUESDAY, AUGUST 28, 2012

Mia awoke to the sensation of the bed moving, as though a cat crept up from the foot end between her and Adam.

As she didn't have a cat, she froze still while her heart raced. Too terrified to open her eyes, she waited as the inexplicable motion passed her knees, coming closer. Bedding tugged at her from weight pressing down, the mattress compressing in the space between her arm and Adam's chest.

A semisolid mass pressed on her shoulder, another near her hip. Mia couldn't bring herself to move, her fear deepening at the realization it felt as though a small child had curled up beside her.

Why am I scared?

Mia swallowed the saliva that had built up in her mouth. *It's a kid. I shouldn't be afraid of a child... but what if it's a demon?* All the horror movies she'd ever watched with creepy killer children came back to torment her with what the entity beside her might want to do.

In the absolute stillness of her bedroom, Mia lay frozen in dread, as though she shared sleeping space with a lion that could snuggle as readily as decide it wanted to tear her apart. Gradually, she became aware that the small gathering of substance between her and Adam swelled and shrank... as if breathing.

Mia pictured a head resting on her shoulder and a knee on her leg. The footprints in the pancake mix didn't look *that* small, so this poor kid couldn't have been a toddler. She hadn't been around kids much since babysitting for the neighbors as a teen. Between the size of the footprints and the feeling of substance beside her, she guessed the spirit to be between five and eight years old—if in fact it had been a real child.

Bedding near her left collarbone squeezed inward with the distinct sensation of small fingers.

The sorrow of a child that young being a ghost chipped away at her fear, though if that pastor's persistence meant anything, there might be a darker entity in the house. Other than her body's primal reaction to being around a paranormal entity, she didn't pick up any sense of dread... not the way the house had hit her at first sight.

There has to be more than one spirit here. This kid isn't a threat.

Still too frightened to open her eyes, Mia slipped her left hand out from under the blanket and reached up as if to pat the head leaning against her shoulder. Only a cloud of cool air lingered between her and Adam, her fingers brushing at nothing.

Her fear lessened, blooming into an inexplicable sense of security.

Mia's eyes snapped open. *The fear wasn't mine... I'm somehow feeling this kid's emotion, like I did in the bathroom.* She gingerly turned her head to the right. A faint impression in the top of the comforter hinted at the form of a child, one leg curled up and resting on Mia, the other straight. Slight weight across her chest felt like an arm, the hand clutching the bedding by her neck.

"Hi there," whispered Mia.

The weight pressing into her vanished, and the comforter shifted as though the child had simply floated straight up off the bed.

"It's okay. You don't need to go." Mia waited a moment, and when nothing happened, she sat up to look around.

Her bedroom appeared normal, nothing out of place, no feelings of being watched.

She let out a long, sad sigh.

Years ago, Mia decided the whole heaven or hell thing had to be a myth, partially because her parents insisted on force-feeding her religion, partially because she kept finding contradictions everywhere. For example: who would ever wind up in hell if God forgave anyone who asked for it? Even if the greatest sin imaginable was for someone not to believe in him, how could a 'loving' god not forgive that when he'd allowed the person to live their entire life without ever showing proof of existence? Upon death, and seeing God in person, only a complete idiot would refuse to ask for forgiveness, and the 'loving god who always forgave everyone' would do so. Therefore, twelve-year-old Mia had concluded hell had to be a lie told by men to control the behavior of other men. A true, loving god would never send anyone to a place like that.

A child ghost lying beside her threw her mind spinning back into some of those same old quandaries. It seemed unlikely for a kid so young to not be innocent, so why wouldn't they have been welcomed into heaven *if* it existed. Adam had always been fascinated with the paranormal, ghosts primarily, and at least one out of every four haunts he talked about involved kids. Mia, naturally, took that as a strong sign that no benevolent deity watched over humanity. While there *might* be something 'out there' arguably considered a 'god,' it didn't bear any resemblance to anything described by most organized religions. Surely, such a being wouldn't permit children to be murdered at all, much less slam the 'pearly gates' in their faces and leave them out of paradise.

She drew her legs in and wrapped her arms around them, chin on her knees. Her father's shouting echoed in her memory, such cruel things he'd screamed at her brother. He'd only been fourteen then, Mia sixteen. That had been the final straw for her about religion... and all the proof she needed that her parents' talk of 'love' had been lies. Their beliefs had nothing whatsoever to do with love.

Mia hugged her legs the way she'd hugged Timothy later that night when she found him in his room trying to keep her from noticing the bottle of pills in his hand, and wept. She knew without a doubt, had she not been there for him, he'd have taken his own life.

"Hon?" whispered Adam. "What's wrong?"

She wiped her tears on her hand. "Just being maudlin for nothing.

Oh, we had a visitor."

"Visitor?" he asked, sounding slightly more awake.

"The ghost crawled into bed with us. I said hello, but they left." She patted the space between them. "Curled up right here."

Adam rolled onto his side, facing her, grinning. "That's awesome!"

"Not even a scrap of doubt?"

"Nope. I gravitated to this house originally because I found a post about it on the spirit forums. The low asking price only reinforced what I suspected. No one sells a house this size for so little without there being something genuine going on—or a serious physical problem. When the inspections came back clean, I felt pretty sure the place had to be a legit haunt. And the stuff we've been seeing these past few days confirms it."

Mia blinked. "You chose a haunted house on purpose. Who does that?"

"Me." He smiled weakly. "You should use your gift and try to make contact."

"I thought I did that by saying 'hello.' The kid took off." She ran her hands up over her head, combing her fingers through her hair. "Please tell me our new home isn't an experiment to you."

"No, it's not *only* an experiment. I have every intention of us staying here for the long term. If I thought of this place as purely a research project, I'd be looking to leave as soon as it's finished. But, that's not the case."

She groaned into her knees.

"Hey…" He sat up and put an arm around her. "I can't really explain it, but something told me we're needed here."

Mia chuckled. "Aren't I supposed to be the psychic here? And this house filled me with dread more than anything on first sight. But maybe you're right. The first time we came out here to look at this house, it scared me to death but it also felt *right* somehow."

"I'm sure you picked up on latent emotional energy. Places take on imprints if highly-charged events happen there. Hey… try this. Close your eyes and concentrate on clearing your head."

After sighing at him, she sat up straight, crossed her legs under the blankets, and rested her hands on her knees. "I've never been good at meditating. Clearing my head is hard. There's a lot of crap rattling around in there."

"Picture an open void of nothingness. Just black."

Mia closed her eyes and tried to tune out her thoughts of her brother, the ghost, the house, the alarm clock that would be going off in four hours...

Adam waited a moment, then spoke in the voice of a hypnotist. "There's nothing but void."

"Working on it... not quite there."

"Picture a distant spot of white in the black field."

Mia briefly thought of a train coming at her in a tunnel, but reframed it to a single star in an overcast night sky. Gradually, she imagined away the clouds until she had only a glowing dot. At that point, she nodded once.

"The speck of light is gliding closer to you, growing. Soon, you realize it's not a star, but a closed fist."

Mia focused on the image of a disembodied hand clenched into a fist and rotating clockwise, floating in a vast void of emptiness.

"The hand is your psychic potential. Your mind is relatively closed," said Adam in a soft, soothing tone. "As soon as you desire the hand to open, your mind will open. See the fingers relaxing, the fist softening. The thumb moves away, unfurling. Fingers stretching... an open palm."

In Mia's mind, the too-white hand bloomed like a flower, but flickered back and forth between gradually opening and a flat palm, fingers splayed. She forced herself to slow it down, stop it from jumping to fully open. Over the next fifteen seconds, she imagined the fist uncurling without the alternating snapping image. Finally, she stared at an open palm.

"It's open," whispered Mia.

"The hand is open to your eyes. Your mind is open to the world. As your ears bring sound, your eyes bring sight, your mind brings awareness beyond perception. Listen only to that sense for now. What do you feel?"

Mia sat in silence for a minute or two, waiting tentatively, reaching outward with a desire to read her surroundings. Amid the blankness, the faint notion of feeling ridiculous started to sneak in, but she brushed it aside. Adam had coached her with the 'hand opening' thing several times before, but it had always struck her as silly. She could never take it seriously. For whatever reason—perhaps truly believing she'd read emotions from the painting at work, or maybe that a ghost had touched her—she managed to convince herself it might actually be real.

A creeping sense of melancholy came out of nowhere, heavy loneliness threaded with sorrow. Strong anger crashed into it, falling rapidly to grief before she once again felt as lonely as if she were the last survivor of an apocalyptic event struggling to find a reason to keep on living.

Mia recoiled from the crippling sorrow. Her eyes snapped open. All the outside emotions raced away like a tangible mass fleeing into the house. With a gasp, she grabbed her head and shook it hard side to side to clear it.

"Hon?" Adam pulled her close. "Are you okay?"

"Yeah. Just... wow." She lowered her hands from her face and looked up to make eye contact. "It worked... it really worked."

"It?"

"The psychic thing. I felt such overwhelming loneliness and anger and grief, but I could tell it wasn't mine."

Excitement flashed in his eyes, but his expression remained one of concern. "You turned white as a ghost. If it's too much for you, we can stop."

She leaned against him. "First time's always a little painful and awkward, right?"

He chuckled and continued holding her. "The same thing I said then applies now. We go at your speed."

"You're so bad." She almost managed to laugh, but couldn't quite get out from under the heavy mood in the air.

"That's enough for tonight. We should both get some sleep."

Mia snuggled back under the covers with him. "Yeah."

9

PRINCESS RABBIT

TUESDAY, AUGUST 28, 2012

Mia fidgeted, unable to get comfortable enough to sleep again.

The clock on Adam's nightstand read 12:42 a.m. He'd managed to fall asleep in only a few minutes. Perhaps her brain retaliated for being forced 'empty' by flooding her with random worries and insecurities. The ghost hadn't returned to the room as far as she knew.

At 12:56 a.m., and being no closer to sleep, Mia let an exasperated sigh out her nose, got out of bed, and headed for the kitchen to make a cup of chamomile tea. The window at the end of the hall by the top of the stairs let in enough moonlight that she didn't bother turning on any lights. Her bare feet found the carpeted steps cooler than they ought to be, as though she'd walked into an inches-deep layer of dry ice fog, but nothing looked unusual.

The ghost was here. She padded down to the living room. *Or... it's a draft. When did I start reaching for the paranormal explanation first?* "Oh, I dunno," she whispered. "Probably right around the time I saw footprints appear in pancake mix."

As soon as she neared the couch, a spike of anger exploded inside her. Quiet, seething anger... fury like she wanted desperately to kill someone, but had to bide her time. Desperate, sorrowful anger, the sort of rage that robbed her of any care what happened to her in the aftermath.

Mia stopped short, staring into space.

The desire to kill seemed directed at a specific person yet simultaneously at no one in particular. She'd happily die if she could only take that bastard with her. *What bastard? Who?* Mia grasped the couch for support as her knees weakened. She pictured a cop reaching into his jacket.

Again, the external feelings dissipated as abruptly as they'd come on.

"Ugh. I'm probably sleepwalking. Or maybe I'm really asleep and only dreaming that I can't sleep."

Grumbling to herself, she trudged down the hall to the kitchen and put on the kettle.

"Little chamomile will relax me."

She prepared a small mug with half a spoon of loose tea. No sense staying up for an hour sipping or drinking enough that she slept through the alarm. Once the water boiled, she poured it into the mug, set the kettle back on a cold burner, and sat at the kitchen table.

Alas, staring into the steam didn't help her make sense of her feelings.

A bit of fanning and blowing on the tea cooled it enough for tentative sipping. She rested her elbow on the table, head in her hand, and half-closed her eyes. Plenty of people claimed to be psychic. Adam adored any sort of paranormal investigation show he could find, except the ones which reeked of obvious fakery. Almost all of them occasionally brought in supposedly psychic guests who threw the term around as though the world at large had accepted such things to be real and possible. Up until a year ago, she'd thought them silly. As of tonight, she didn't know what to think.

Mia swirled the tea around her half-full cup, staring into it. Between the overdose of strong, negative emotions, the shock that she really did have the 'gift' Adam had been telling her she had for the past two years, and a clingy sadness at the notion a dead child roamed her house, she wondered if she'd ever have a good night's sleep again.

Sudden pressure squeezed around her middle in the shape of a small person's arms.

She froze in shock at being touched, but only for a few seconds before staring at where she expected a child's head to be. Nothing appeared, though she suspected if there had been pancake mix on the floor, it would show footprints to the right of her chair.

"It's okay," whispered Mia. *I really hope this isn't a demon. I'm such a sucker... wait, no. I'd rather it's a demon than a real kid being dead.* "Are you a boy or a girl?"

"Shh," said a disembodied voice, too whispery to sound like anything other than 'child.'

Mia glanced down at her nightgown, visibly flattened where she felt the presence of a little arm. The spirit wanted her to be quiet... but why? She sat and listened to the faint whirr of the fridge, debating what a demon could be trying to accomplish by clinging to her. Emotional manipulation? Slow drive to insanity ultimately leading to her death? Could that desire to kill have been 'future Mia' and not 'past unknown woman'?

The silence seemed to swell down on her from the ceiling, the very air thick and suffocating.

Right as she started to ask what scared the child, the kitchen floor shook under a punishing of heavy footsteps. Mia jumped with a shriek, reflexively trying to grab the kid in a protective embrace, but hugged only herself. She cringed back, guarding her face with both arms at the sense of a huge man storming closer, every strike of his feet resonating in the chair. The entity thundered past her toward the back door. The footsteps ceased with a tremendous clattering crash as though a giant metal toolbox had been hurled to the floor in anger.

Abject panic seized Mia's mind. If she didn't run *right now*, she'd die. Screaming, she bolted from the chair, knocking it over, and raced out of the kitchen. The downstairs passed in a blur. She scrambled on all fours to get up the carpeted steps. At the top, she pushed off the floor like a sprinter and raced toward the bathroom, intending to hide in the tub. At the last second, that struck her as a stupid idea and she swerved into her bedroom.

Mia dove over the foot of the bed like Supergirl and scrambled under the covers, curling up in a shivering ball.

Someone grasped her arm.

Mia screamed again.

A man spoke indecipherable words in a soothing tone.

The fear she'd felt toward the touch shifted to a need for protection. She clung, shaking.

"Mia? What happened?" asked a man.

"Where's Princess Rabbit? She's missing," whined Mia. "I need her!"

The man kept silent for a moment. "Uhh… What?"

She sniffled.

"Mia, is that you in there?"

She looked up at the man holding her. It took her a second to process his face… Adam, her husband. Fear burst like a soap bubble. The need to flee for her life evaporated. Mia blinked at him, glanced at the door, and exhaled.

"Hon?"

"Damn…" She sat up and breathed into her cupped hands. "That was freaky. It felt like someone was about to kill me."

Adam squeezed her shoulder and rubbed her back. "Breathe… You're safe. For what it's worth, I didn't hear or see anything."

"Thanks for not being excited at paranormal stuff… at least obviously." Mia managed a weak smile.

"Are you okay?"

"Rattled, but I'll be fine. So much for that tea calming me down."

"What is Princess Rabbit?"

She glanced at him. "Huh? I have no idea. Where'd that come from?"

"You just said it."

"That's not funny." Mia stared at him. "That's really not funny."

"No, it isn't…" He smiled. "It's amazing."

"I'm completely lost now."

"Hon…" Adam took her hand. "I think you might have channeled the spirit. Either she jumped into you or you invited her in… that voice didn't exactly sound like you. You kinda whined like a child who'd been crying over a lost toy. Going to guess the ghost is a little girl."

"Because there's a doll or stuffed animal named Princess Rabbit?" Mia leaned against Adam. "That doesn't necessarily prove anything."

"Did Tim have dolls?"

Mia shook her head. "No way would my parents have let that happen. Not even sure he'd have wanted them. Maybe he played with mine when no one was around to see him, but if my parents ever caught him, they'd have had a stroke." She rubbed her face, then sighed. "I should at least try to get back to sleep."

"Okay."

Again, she lay down and cuddled up to him, deliberately refusing to look at the clock. If she saw a number too close to 7:30, that would add to her anxiety, and her need to get to sleep as fast as possible would have the paradoxical effect of keeping her up. She stared at the ceiling, bluish in the moonlight, and tried to let her mind clear of thoughts.

Mia did *not* attempt to picture an opening hand.

Minutes later, a random notion took root in her head without explanation or cause.

She's a girl.

10

ENTITIES

TUESDAY, AUGUST 28, 2012

Much to Mia's surprise, she had little trouble waking up the next morning.

She opened her eyes two minutes before her alarm would've gone off, lay there for a bit, and got out of bed in time to reach the clock within seconds of it blaring. Adam walked in from the hall, surrounded by a cloud of shower steam and wearing only a towel draped around his neck.

"Tub's all yours."

"Thanks."

After removing her nightgown, she hung it from a hook on the back of the closet door and headed to the bathroom. Thick, steamy air swirled around her, heavy with the fragrances of soap, antiperspirant, and cologne. Adam had left footprints in the condensation on the dark grey faux-stone tiles, going from the plush bathmat to the door. She stepped into the tub, smiling again at the larger accommodations compared to the dinky bathroom at their old apartment.

The shower proved almost too relaxing, making her want to go straight back to bed. She envied Adam his ability to shower at night and go right to bed if he wanted to. Not only did her long hair take forever to dry, the warm water usually energized her and made sleep impossible for at least a few hours.

Mia washed herself with neither urgency nor a lack thereof, having plenty of time to make it to work. Once finished, she stepped out onto the bathmat and grabbed a towel. A minute or two into drying, the almost inaudible pattering of small feet made her stop and hold perfectly still.

Small, bare footprints appeared one after the next in the condensation, darkening the tiles. The trail entered from the door, heading directly toward her. Mia could only stand there watching in sad awe as an invisible tiny person approached her.

"Hi there. Good morning, sweetie."

The footprints stopped at the edge of the fuzzy bathmat, and a cloud of chilly air coalesced next to her leg. Mia choked up, near to the point of crying, but couldn't tell if the sadness came from inside her or from the entity.

"I'm really sorry for what happened to you," said Mia in a soothing, soft voice. "I'm not sure if there's anything I can do to help, but if there is, I'll find it. You don't need to be afraid of me or Adam."

Nothing touched her, though the chill remained.

"I don't have the little recorder thing so I can't hear you if you're trying to talk to me. What's your name?"

She waited a moment.

"My parents were mean, too. I know what it's like to be scared of your own parents." Mia bit her lip. Never would she have imagined her parents killing her—or even Timothy—but she still sometimes had a flinch response whenever an angry man moved too rapidly toward her. Dad loved taking his belt to her bare backside, though he never walloped her anywhere near as hard as he did her brother... girls being 'delicate' and all.

"If you know what I can do to help, please tell me."

Still, nothing happened.

Mia resumed drying herself off, unsure if she should feel embarrassed at 'not being alone' while naked in the bathroom. Then again, if ghosts—as they appeared to be—were real, then most of the people in the world likely had unseen eyes watching them all the time. If indeed she stood beside an actual spirit and not some malign entity seeking to trick her, that poor girl had experienced far worse than watching her shower.

"I'm sorry… you didn't deserve whatever happened to you." When she tried to pat the invisible child on the head, her hand found no trace of the chilly cloud. "Are you still—?"

The bathmat jerked backward and to the left, ripping her feet out from under her. She went down in a twisting motion, but reflexively brought her arms up before her chin crashed into the edge of the tub as she fell flat to the floor like a bundle of broom handles, elbows and knees banging on hard tile.

"Ow…" She lay draped off the tub, in too much pain to move. "What was that for?"

A few minutes later, she shifted to sit and scowled at the fuzzy black bathmat squished into the wall by the door. No way could a small girl have had the strength to do that. She hated the idea that what she thought of as an innocent child might be a far more malignant entity.

No. That can't be true. There's more than one ghost here.

A FEW MINUTES LATER, MIA—DRIED, DRESSED, AND READY FOR work—walked into the kitchen, trying not to limp too obviously.

Adam smiled at her and gestured at the plate of pancakes he'd just set on the table.

"Seriously?" asked Mia. "We're getting too old to eat like that. We'll become enormous."

"Old? Neither one of us is thirty yet. The occasional sugar bomb breakfast is a guilty pleasure." He winked and poured more batter into the pan. "Never too old for pancakes. It's like anything else. Taken in moderation, everything is fine."

Mia sat. "Does that include crystal meth?"

"I stand corrected." He shook his head. "I was talking about normal guilty pleasures, not toxic crap."

"Had another visit. Oh, and the bathmat tried to break my neck."

Adam whirled, spatula involuntarily raised as if about to smack a fly with it. "Oh?"

"At first, little footprints in the condensation. Felt like the ghostly kid was standing next to me. Minute or so later, she's gone and I got a rather close look at the floor. You know, those tiles are really nice. Bet they were expensive. I doubt they're original to the house. Wonder who paid for them only to move out in a few months?"

"Whoa. Wait a minute. Go back to the almost breaking your neck thing." He wagged the spatula at her.

"I was trying to talk to the kid, but didn't get a response. Next thing I know, the bathmat goes flying out from under me like that stupid magician's trick with the tablecloth. Only, I didn't stay there undisturbed like the dishes. Went down pretty hard, but I'm okay."

Adam shot her a worried stare, then turned back to the stove and prodded his pancake. "You're sure?"

"Fine. I still feel bad for whoever spent all that money redoing the bathroom only to up and leave."

"Yeah. Which makes me wonder exactly what happened that drove them to that point. They had to lose a lot selling so soon after moving in."

Mia poured a conservative amount of syrup on her pancakes and cut them. "By the way, I think the ghost is a child."

"Didn't we establish that already?"

"No, I mean an actual child. A little girl. Not a demon or something pretending to be one. And I also don't think she made those thuds. There's something else here."

"Which thuds?" Adam twisted to look at her. "No butter?"

"Nope. For whatever reason, I never cared for it on pancakes." She impaled a few slices on her fork and told him about the heavy footsteps when she'd had tea.

Adam shoved his pancake out of the skillet onto the stack he'd started, then poured the last of the batter in to cook. "Either there are multiple entities here, or it's one pretending to be a kid part time."

"No, Adam. It's not. She's really a small girl. I'm sure of it. It has to be multiple entities."

"Okay. I'll trust your feelings then." He fussed at the cooking pancake. "Tonight when I get home, I'll set up some equipment in the kitchen. Maybe scatter some more pancake powder on the floor."

"Don't waste it. Use baking soda, or better yet, talc."

He grinned back at her. "That's not a 'don't mess up my floor, you idiot.'"

"I'm not quite the same skeptic I was a year ago."

"Oh, great. Maybe we'll invite Pastor Weston over."

She pointed her fork at him. "There are some things you shouldn't joke about with a woman holding sharp objects."

"Oh, he's harmless. Little off base, but harmless."

Mia ate two more forkfuls. "Mmm. I haven't had pancakes in years. Not since I lived with my parents."

"You poor deprived woman. My... sorry."

"No, it's okay. I know *your* parents are normal. Don't feel guilty."

"My mom still makes them at least twice a month, and my grandfather on my dad's side has them every Saturday morning without fail."

"Traditions are nice." She teased the fork around in the syrup. "Do you think I was too harsh with the pastor?"

"Something new happen or are you referring to the last time you ripped his head off?"

"He came back the other day. Maybe I let him have it a bit too hard. I just don't get why he'd insist we have to go to his church in order to be protected or saved. Wouldn't God—if it existed—just protect people because it's the right thing to do? It seems so contradictory and *convenient* that he only looks after the people who show up on Sunday."

Adam slid his final pancake onto the stack and shut off the stove. "I don't claim to know the mind of God... or the workings of the universe enough to say what's out there. I do, however, know the inner workings of Mrs. Butterworth."

Mia whistled. "That sounded *far* dirtier than you probably intended."

"Did it, now?" Adam wagged his eyebrows.

"It did. Besides, that mix is store brand."

"We're cheating on Mrs. Butterworth?" Adam fake gasped. "Grandpa would have the vapors."

Mia nearly choked on her next mouthful when she tried to laugh.

"See?" Adam leaned in and kissed her before sitting catty-corner at the table. "Pancakes make everyone feel better."

11

THE MAN

TUESDAY, AUGUST 28, 2012

Three cups of coffee got Mia through a fairly boring day at work.

She finished the cleaning and spent the remainder of the day patching small tears or holes in the canvas, remounting it on a new frame, and painting over faded or patched spots to look as close to original as possible. The whole time she touched up the oil paints, she spoke to the young woman in the portrait like a dental hygienist chatting with her patient. That the patient, in this case, *didn't* reply reassured her that some normality remained in the world.

At 5:30 p.m. on the dot, Mia left the museum. She arrived home roughly twenty minutes later with a big, stupid grin at her wonderful commute. *I hope this never feels old... having such a short ride.* She'd never gotten used to the dreadful two-hour-each-way slog. While she somewhat missed the familiar surroundings of Albany, having no time whatsoever to enjoy said familiar surroundings made it a moot point. A random craving to visit an old restaurant or something could always be satisfied on a weekend.

Adam sent her a text suggesting she just relax and he'll cook dinner since she did so last night. She smiled, replying 'don't worry about it,' and 'I'm already here. Besides, you wanna ghost hunt tonight.'

'You are the best wife.'

She grinned and headed upstairs to change. A moment or two later, she had one foot in her sweat pants when a heavy *thud* rocked the floor from somewhere down the hall.

"Gah!" she jumped, tripped over the sweat pants, and landed in an ungainly heap with her face on the rug and her rear end in the air. "Ouch." Not bothering to stand, she rolled over onto her back and pulled the sweat pants the rest of the way on, then sat up and wriggled into a T-shirt. "What the hell was that?"

She didn't expect an answer, and nothing surprised her with one.

Grumbling, Mia climbed back to her feet and crept out into the hallway. A lingering note of anger in the air raised the hairs on the backs of her arms. Other than that it happened upstairs, she couldn't tell exactly which room the bang came from. Whatever caused it had been heavy enough to feel as a tremor in the floor. Perhaps one of the boxes of books had fallen over? Neither she nor Adam had yet been inclined to deal with lugging those around and unpacking them. They still hadn't settled on *where* they'd put the bookshelves permanently. Maybe downstairs in the living room or maybe upstairs in one of the unused bedrooms, making a library out of it.

Door by door, Mia advanced down the hall toward the stairs, peeking in each one. The second room on the left—the same door that had opened itself the other day—held most of their still-packed stuff. Like the other bedrooms, it had been devoid of furniture, the walls painted a cream color. The rug in here seemed newer than everywhere else.

Mia tried not to think about the implications of that and contented herself at not seeing anything knocked over or broken. The remaining rooms plus the atrium at the left corner offered no clues as to what had hit the floor.

"I either imagined it, or something ghostly fell over."

She collected herself and went downstairs to start on spaghetti.

A LITTLE AFTER SEVEN THAT NIGHT, MIA PERCHED ON THE LIVING room sofa with a plate of spaghetti in her lap on a tray. Adam had arrived home before the noodles finished, accompanied by a young man with platinum blond hair he introduced as Paul, his teacher's assistant who he'd talked into helping out with the ghost hunt.

Fortunately, Mia had made plenty of spaghetti.

Adam and Paul and got straight to setting up a night vision video recorder, two digital audio recorders, three hockey-puck-sized devices they called EM detectors, and a box that supposedly allowed spirits to somehow pick words out of an electronic database. Mia couldn't even begin to guess how such a thing could possibly work, so she left him to it.

The men joined her with trays in the dark living room where they ate in near-total silence, listening for signs of activity. She couldn't take it after about ten minutes and proceeded to chat in whispers about her day—her rather boring day—at work. Adam didn't seem to mind and shared somewhat more interesting notes about some of his classes. Paul occasionally smiled, nodded, or *hmm*ed at the conversation, most of his attention on a laptop connected to the equipment.

When everyone finished eating, Mia collected the dishes.

"I'll get it. You cooked," whispered Adam.

"It's fine. You guys are busy and I'm bored. Tomorrow, you can cook *and* do dishes." She winked, then headed to the kitchen, careful not to step on any wires or bump anything.

For the duration of loading the dishwasher, she had a light on over the sink. It didn't take anywhere near as long as she'd hoped, and soon, she found herself back on the sofa beside a pair of guys acting like overgrown boys having a sleepover where they stayed up late looking for monsters—only with a few thousand dollars' worth of electronics involved.

She made a valiant effort to be interested, though watching her darkened house didn't rank anywhere in the top 1,000 ways to spend a fun night. Only the off chance that they might see, hear, or record something that could help the spirit of a child kept her from insisting they wasted time.

Adam and Paul took turns walking into the kitchen area and asking random questions of thin air. Whoever remained with the laptop monitored an audio level indicator that, theoretically, would graphically show EVP responses in real time.

A little after 10 p.m., Mia yawned. "Is looking for ghosts always this exciting?"

"This is fairly typical," said Paul. "Ghost hunting is usually dozens of hours of boredom for thirty seconds of OMG did you see that."

She offered a sleepy smile and closed her eyes. At least they had a comfy couch.

MIA AWOKE TO A LOUD CRASH AND A SERIES OF HEAVY THUDS, squinting at Adam kneeling on the floor by the couch, gawking at the laptop screen, his face lit bluish from the glare.

"Whoa," he whispered.

She looked around, noting Paul's absence. "Your friend leave?"

"I just heard that, without the mic. Like actually *heard* that." Adam grinned at her. "And yeah, Paul left over an hour ago."

"What time is it?"

"1:03 a.m."

"Ugh," moaned Mia. "I'm going up to bed."

"Hang on a sec, please? Something just tromped across the kitchen. Can you try taking a psychic look again?"

She stretched, sat up, and yawned. "Sure, but I'm giving this ten minutes tops before I go up to bed."

"Deal. Something is active right now... the EM detectors are wigging out."

Mia turned to face over the back of the couch and stared through the dining room at the doorway to the kitchen. Small lights flickered in the dark wherever one of Adam's various electronic gadgets had been placed. After a brief moment of trying to 'clear her mind,' she thought about wanting to pick up on whatever energy the little blinking dots reacted to.

A moment later, heavy footfalls—not quite the smashing thuds she'd heard in the kitchen—rushed closer, wobbling the moonlight glinting from the windows of the china cabinet doors. Mia gripped the back of the sofa, resisting the urge to hide. It sounded too much like the way her father would pound across the house on his way to her or Timothy's room whenever he thought they'd done something bad. Of course, Dad regarded all children as little sinners, so any denial of wrongdoing was a lie. All it took was the mere belief they'd done something wrong and their butts would face the belt.

The moment the footsteps reached the arch between the dining and living room, a large-framed man appeared for an instant as though he'd walked into a spotlight in an otherwise dark room. Disheveled black hair hung to the shoulders of a dark blue jumpsuit. He marched toward the stairs in a forward-leaning gait, dead brown eyes staring fixedly forward with not a trace of humanity left in them. His stare chilled her to the core. A glint of metal, something in his hand, flashed by too fast to recognize.

Mia turned her head to follow the source of the noise, which passed a few feet from her. The stairs creaked one after the next. When the disturbance reached the upstairs hallway, it ceased once again to silence.

A mixture of motor oil, grease, beer, and body odor settled in Mia's sinuses. She gagged on it, coughing, her eyes watering.

Adam put a hand on her back. "You saw something."

"That wasn't a question."

"It wasn't. You don't usually turn pale for nothing."

Mia let the air out of her lungs. "Yeah… I saw a man. Big… dirty. Black hair. Some kind of mechanic or janitor. He had on a jumpsuit with a name tag. I'm smelling grease or oil… body odor, beer. Guy seriously needs a shower."

"I think he's a little past that point."

She smirked.

"Where did you see him?" asked Adam.

"Right by the arch."

He got up and walked over to the point the living room became dining room. "How tall is he compared to me?"

"Umm… go to your left like two feet and come closer one step."

He did.

"The top of your head is about where his nose would be, and he's wider than you by at least the size of your arms on each side."

"Whoa."

Mia crawled over the sofa back and hurried into a hug. "He had such a horrible look in his eyes. I… don't want to think about what he did."

"Yeah, let's not." Adam cradled the back of her head and held her. "I'd rather not think about it either."

Mia absorbed the love and protectiveness radiating from him while catching her breath. "I'm okay. Just needed a moment. Did you hear him go up the stairs?"

"No. Only the heavy pounding in the kitchen and the crash."

"What about the stomping through the dining room *to* the stairs?"

"Nope. You heard that?"

She nodded. "Yeah."

"Congrats. You're a medium."

Mia twirled her finger in mock cheer and headed for the stairs. "Yay. This medium is well done. I'm going to bed."

"Wanna check the video?"

Mia didn't slow down. "I'll watch it tomorrow night when we try again."

"You're up for another go?"

"I'm too tired for *that*, but if you're talking about ghost hunting tomorrow, yeah I guess I can give it another shot."

ADAM SMILED, WATCHING MIA GO UPSTAIRS.

With the giddiness of a schoolboy, he attacked the laptop, stopping the recording from the night vision camera. He restarted it to a new video file, intending to let it go all night in case it caught something else. In another window, he pulled up the last file and dragged the slider near the end. He soon found the timestamp of 1:00 a.m., and let it play.

At 1:03 a.m. in the video, the heavy stomping echoed from the kitchen along with a giant metal crash like a dropped toolbox. At 1:04:21, a fist-sized ball of faint light floated out of the kitchen and glided toward the camera across the dining room before zipping off to the right in the direction of the stairs.

"Awesome." Adam backed up and re-watched it a dozen times.

Light anomalies, as people called such finds, happened all the time. Sadly, no one but the 'paranormal community' accepted them as *proof* of anything. However, if they could find something more substantial, a catch like this would only help back it up.

He yawned. "Might as well crash for the night."

Adam got up and went to the kitchen, taking a glass from the cabinet and running it full of water. Faint motion flickered in the corner of his eye. He froze, gradually turning his head.

A tall humanoid figure made entirely of wispy shadow hovered beside the door to the basement. Abnormally narrow, the body warped and bent in an inhuman posture, more like a great gnarled root of a tar-black tree. Two pale eye spots in the head locked on him. Its stare caused a sensation similar to icicles piercing his chest.

For two seconds, Adam stood there unable to move, the water overflowing the glass into the sink.

The shadow figure leaned as if to rush toward him.

Adam screamed; lost to blind panic, he ran. The next thing he knew, he lay flat on his back outside, gazing up at the night sky. The toes of his left foot throbbed in time with his racing heartbeat. He couldn't remember how he got from the kitchen to being on the grass in front of the house. The stone walkpath that connected the driveway to the porch lay a short distance behind him. Blood—and a cracked nail on his big toe—told him he'd tripped over the path.

He peered back at the still-open front door. No trace of the shadow figure remained.

"Holy, shit… there's something serious in there. Ow…" He cradled his foot, wincing at the sight of his big toenail separated from the bed, lifted up like a tiny car hood. "That's going to hurt as soon as the adrenaline wears off."

Adam got up and limped back into the house. The living room once again felt normal, no trace of paranormal strangeness. *Hmm. Damn thing is messing with me. Caught me off guard.* He brushed grass from his leg, then went up to the bathroom in search of a Band-Aid for his toe. Wincing, he raised his foot to rest on the closed toilet lid, blood bubbling out from under the nail. He held a wad of toilet paper down on it until the bleeding mostly stopped, then used the Band-Aid to essentially tape the nail back down.

It's going to take more than a little parlor fear trick to run me off.

12

STONE TAPE THEORY

WEDNESDAY, AUGUST 29, 2012

Impressionist meadow blurred into a disorienting smear of vibrant yellows, oranges, and greens.

Mia swayed on her feet, stooped over the giant worktable at the museum. Three cups of coffee offered little help, or maybe they did as she hadn't yet collapsed asleep. Usually, restoring an old painting—tedious as it could be—paradoxically excited her. Today, scrubbing at the canvas with a Q-tip felt like mowing a mansion's lawn with scissors.

Despite being the only person in the large studio room, she kept glancing around under the weight of eyes on her back. Almost a year ago, a high school class came by on a tour and watched her work for about ten minutes. The mood in the air reminded her of that, minus the constant chatter. Only a shelf of as-yet-to-be-restored paintings stood behind her. Her museum contracted out her services to other museums in the area as well as private collectors who had pieces in need of help. She didn't mind working on artwork that wouldn't be shown here as it offered job security.

Several days in a row of fitful sleep plus staying up too late last night made her susceptible to the mindlessness of her task. She moved the stark white Q-tip in little circles over and over again, etching a creeping line of clean across a canvas as big as two refrigerators. Every eight circles, she'd pause to dab the painting with a soft cloth... over and over again she repeated the cycle until the cotton tip blurred as much as an impressionist work up close.

"Ugh." She pushed up from the table, leaning over backward to stretch, then yawned. "I need air."

After walking around the parking lot twice, she swung by the cafeteria for an iced tea, then returned to her studio. Her boss, Janet Newman, popped in around four to ask how her move went, talk about the new house, and complain about the director of finance. Mia liked Janet, and got along with her more like another co-worker than her manager. Not wanting to be thought of as nuts, she omitted any mention of ghosts, though admitted to having some difficulty sleeping. That, she blamed on the major change of moving and expected to adjust soon.

The last hour in the day shot by fast enough that Mia briefly questioned if she'd fallen asleep standing up. She cleaned up her area, covered the canvas she'd been working on, and trudged out to the Tahoe. If she still lived outside Albany, she'd have been sorely tempted to spend the night in a motel close by rather than attempt such a long drive in her current state of fatigue. However, with a roughly twenty-minute trip between her and home, she figured she could make it.

Loud music and the air conditioning on high helped her stay awake. For the few minutes it took her to drive through downtown Spring Falls, the odd looks she caught from pedestrians or other drivers kept her on edge.

Upon arriving home, she found a paper stuck in the front door—a flyer inviting her to Sunday worship at Pastor Weston Parker's Christian Fellowship church. Mia shook her head, crumpled it up, and went inside. Everything appeared as it should, nothing out of place except for Adam's ghost sniffing stuff, which he'd left set up. She groaned in her head at her offer to stay up with him again tonight.

Mia trudged to the kitchen, tossed the church ad in the trash, then went up to her bedroom to change out of her work clothes. In a T-shirt and shorts, she wandered back downstairs while texting Adam that he would be cooking dinner tonight.

Without waiting for his reply, she fixed herself a mug of chamomile tea and curled up on the couch. A sense of not being alone made the hairs on the backs of her arms stand on end. Amid a sudden surge of wakefulness, Mia looked around for the source—and spotted her hairbrush on the cushion beside her.

That wasn't there when I walked in the door. She picked it up, not quite sure if it had been there when she'd carried the tea into the living room. As bleary as she'd been, maybe it *had* been there the whole time. However, even if she simply failed to notice it when she'd gotten home from work, she still hadn't put it on the sofa. Whether it happened minutes ago or hours ago, someone other than Mia moved it.

She leaned forward, resting her elbows on her knees, and turned the brush over, examining it. The idea that a ghostly little girl might be stuck in her house brought on a pang of sorrow. Having no true understanding of how the universe worked, she couldn't say for absolute certainty that the entity *was,* in fact, a child. Weston appeared to be of the mind that a demon lurked in the house. If such creatures as demons existed, one of those could be responsible for both the angry male presence as well as the innocent one.

"That doesn't feel right…" Mia turned the brush over and over. "You're real, aren't you?"

Her eyes tingled with imminent tears, but rather than cry, she let out a long, slow sigh at the depressing thought of a dead child.

A chill gathered in the air by her leg. Mia looked up in search of an air conditioning vent above her, but the ceiling had no openings. She sat up straight and reached around at the air in front of her, discovering a cold spot roughly four feet high hovering close by. Within a second or two of sticking her hand into the chilly air, a strong sense of loneliness came over her.

"Hi, sweetie," said Mia in an almost whisper.

The chilly spot moved a bit to the left, tucking between her knees. Mia bowed her head at the somberness of the moment, and noticed faint footprints in the carpet at the base of the sofa, toes pointing away from her.

This kid is standing right in front of me with her back turned... what...?

Mia glanced at the hairbrush she still held, and pictured a small girl standing patiently in front of her. *Oh, no way...* She felt around for the top of the cold spot, then went through the motions of brushing the girl's hair as best she could guess where it would be. Neither her fingers nor the brush made contact with anything more solid than chilly air.

"This would be so much easier if I could see you. What kind of hair do you have? Is it long like mine? I'm sure it's pretty."

The radiant loneliness abated over the course of a few minutes. Eventually, she noticed the cold spot had gone away. Mia leaned back on the couch, hands draped in her lap, and tried to understand why the ghost would show up only for a little while if she were that lonely.

MIA AWOKE TO A DARK ROOM AND ADAM GENTLY NUDGING HER shoulder.

"Hey, hon. Dinner's ready."

She closed her eyes again long enough to take a breath of garlicy air, then sat up. "What time is it?"

"A little after eight. Waited a while to start dinner since you looked exhausted." He took her hand and helped her up.

"Thanks." Mia yawned hard and followed him to the kitchen.

He'd cooked chicken cutlets with a side of butter-garlic pasta. While they ate, she mentioned the brush being on the sofa and the cold spot that had hovered nearby for a few minutes.

"I don't understand why she would go away so fast, if she's as lonely as she feels."

Adam nodded while chewing. "That is odd. I'm still not entirely convinced we're dealing with an actual kid. Careful and don't let your guard down just yet."

"She feels genuine to me."

"A radio plays whatever signal it picks up."

Mia rushed a mouthful of chicken and took a sip of wine. "What?"

"You're basically a radio picking up psychic broadcasts. Whatever is in the air, you receive. If some other entity with dark intentions is broadcasting 'hey, trust me, I'm a real little girl,' that's exactly what you will feel."

"I dunno..." She replayed her 'brushing' moment in her head while nibbling on pasta. It could've stood to be cooked a little longer, but he liked noodles on the firmer side. "What you're saying does make sense, but I don't see an entity like that standing there while I brushed its hair."

"It could be acting that way on purpose to get into your head, build you up to think of it as innocent."

She stabbed another piece of chicken. "But why?"

"Isn't it obvious?" asked Adam with a serious expression. "It wants your soul."

Mia blinked.

He cracked up.

"Ugh." Mia gazed at the ceiling. "Speaking of which... he was here again. Left a paper in the doorway."

Adam shook his head. "He'll eventually get the hint."

"Here's hoping." Mia sighed and ate another forkful of pasta.

They finished dinner amid a conversation about setting up an auto-payment for the mortgage and a notice from the town that had been in the mail claiming that their property value assessment 'had some irregularities' and they wanted to send an appraiser. Mia grumbled that some politician in the city wanted them to pay taxes based on an overinflated estimate rather than the sale price, which had been admittedly low. Adam felt that because they didn't know the seller or have any relation to them, the city would find no evidence of fraud and allow the value to stand for tax purposes.

After eating, Mia loaded the dishwasher. Adam went upstairs to run the laundry machines. She returned to the sofa intending to watch television, but didn't stay conscious long enough to reach for the remote.

MIA AWOKE TO ADAM'S LESS-THAN-GENTLE SHAKING OF HER LEG and the metallic crash of a toolbox in the kitchen. Thick emotional energy hung in the air, the room saturated with a pervasive sense of imminent doom. She sat upright with a poorly-stifled yelp of alarm. If not for her husband's grip on her ankle, she might've bolted for the door.

"1:03 a.m. again," whispered Adam.

Shivering from nerves, she twisted around to peer over the back of the sofa at the kitchen doorway far on the other side of the dining room. The same grungy male figure appeared a few paces short of the archway to the living room in full view, unlike the prior night where she'd only caught a flash of him as if he'd crossed a spotlight beam. She stared in awestruck horror at the man in dirty blue coveralls walking toward her, still with the exact same dead expression in his eyes.

A small white oval on his chest bore the name Vic in curvy red letters. What had been an unrecognizable metallic glint in his hand now looked like mini sledge hammer. She couldn't move, barely able to breathe, as he came within arm's reach of her. The stink of body odor, engine grease, and beer overwhelmed her senses. Mia leaned away, half expecting the man to take a swing at her with the hammer, but he turned toward the stairs. As soon as he stopped looking *through* her, Mia's fear lessened enough to let her breathe. Except for being faintly transparent, and not existing much below the knees, the apparition had a remarkable amount of definition.

She continued watching him until the wispy traces of his lower legs vanished into the upstairs hall. As soon as he moved out of sight, the freakiness in the air went away. She twisted to look at Adam, who gazed with intense focus at the laptop screen.

"Did you see that?"

"Are you referring to the light anomaly?"

Mia shook her head, but he didn't notice. "No. I saw him. All of him... well, above the knees. His name was Vic."

"What?" Adam looked up with wide eyes. "He spoke?"

"No... I think he was a mechanic or something. He had a jumpsuit on with a name tag. White oval, red letters. Smelled like he hadn't taken a shower in a week or two... probably drunk. He..." She shivered. "Oh, no..."

"Oh no?" Adam knee-walked closer to her and took her hand. "What did you see?"

Mia steeled herself before she burst into tears. "He carried a hammer. I think he killed her with it."

"Damn..." He climbed up to sit beside her on the couch and pulled her into an embrace. "I hope you didn't see that."

She leaned against him. "No. He had such an evil look in his eyes, and he went upstairs holding a hammer. There's a child ghost in the house... what do *you* think happened?"

He sighed out his nose, warm breath puffing over the top of her head.

"At least he died, too. The guy didn't look that old."

"Hmm." Adam made a series of contemplative noises, then scrunched his face. "I'm not sure he's an actual spirit."

"As opposed to what? A hologram? Did you see him?"

"Nope. Just a light ball on the video, gliding along the same route you most likely observed him walking."

"So... I'm hallucinating now. The demon you think is here is making me see stuff to, what, drive me insane?"

He kissed the top of her head. "While that's an outside chance, I don't think so. This guy appeared at the exact same time he did last night. Same series of noises. While you were mesmerized by something on the stairwell, I played the audio from last night and tonight simultaneously and compared the waveforms. After I eliminated any sounds you or I made, the rest matched exactly."

"Okay..."

"This isn't an intelligent haunt. It's a psychic impression. Whatever he did had such a strong emotional/psychic charge it imprinted itself in the house, maybe even on the land itself."

"Oh, that stone tape theory thing?" She sat up again and looked toward the kitchen. All the electromagnetic sensor devices had gone dark.

"Basically."

Mia glanced at him. "So every night for the rest of however long we live here, we get to hear that stupid crash at 1:03 a.m.?"

"Until we find a way to erase the tape, that's probably going to repeat every night, yeah. Good thing you sleep like a rock."

"*If* I can get to sleep in the first place. Haven't been sleeping too well lately."

"New place, ghost stuff, or are you worried about something?"

"A little of everything."

He leaned his head against hers. "What are you worrying about?"

"Not so much worry as I can't stop thinking about that poor child. How scared she had to have been living with that man... and then to have... okay. Sorry. Curiosity is getting the better of me."

Mia stood and approached the stairs, peering up at the hallway in front of the washer/dryer nook. A fleeting sense of warning came and went, similar to how she'd felt as a child looking at the attic stairs of her old home. No force on Earth short of a literal gun to her head could have made her go up into the attic of her parents' house alone, but this dread didn't hit her that hard. Fists clenched, she made her way up.

"Sec, hon."

She paused at the top of the stairs, gazing down the hallway to the left. All the doors were closed except for the middle one on the right. Adam came up the stairs behind her with the night vision video camera. Mia walked past the first door on the right, which led to the atrium.

Nothing appeared out of place, nor did anything break the silence from the middle room, but she *knew* Vic had gone there.

Her bare feet all but glowed in the moonlight as she padded up to the door and stopped with her toes an inch from an invisible line where hallway carpet became room carpet. The door hung open about a quarter of the way, the room beyond a morass of shadows. Mia stood there, listening both with her ears as well as her mind, but picked up nothing out of the ordinary.

Heart racing, Mia reached out and touched her fingertips to the door, finding it freezing. Against her better judgement, she pushed it inward. The room had three closets, each with louvered double doors, on the left, no furniture, and a henge of unopened cardboard boxes at the center.

"I know he went in here."

Adam nodded and leaned around her to point the camera into the room. "Just boxes. Closets are all empty."

"I know that."

"I'm narrating for the camera," whispered Adam.

"Yeah… but what's here now doesn't mean anything."

The instant Mia stepped past the door, she cringed at a crushing sense of aversion that hadn't been in the room before. Some part of her did *not* like being in the room and wanted to back away as fast as possible. She looked around at the boxes, her hands trembling. The day they'd carried them all in here, this room hadn't seemed any different from the rest of the house, merely another empty bedroom in a house with four extra bedrooms.

In that moment, Mia Gartner *knew* beyond a shadow of a doubt that something horrible had happened there. She wound up staring to the right, fixating on a spot near the wall in the far corner beside one of the two windows. The patch of floor gave off a strong sense of significance, though she couldn't bring herself to look at it for more than a few seconds.

Her resolve faltered, and she backed out of the room, desperate to get *away* from such a sense of evil. As soon as she entered the hallway, weight lifted from her, even her breathing grew easier. Light-headed, she swooned into the wall on the other side, cringing from the bad energy in the room.

Adam remained inside, aiming the camera around, oblivious. "You okay, hon?"

"I'm not sure."

He lowered the camera to look at her. "Not sure?"

Mia covered her mouth with one hand, shaking her head, unable to speak.

Adam emerged from the doorway and stood close. "Hon?"

She raised a shaking hand, pointing. "Something… something *bad* happened in there."

13

FAREWELL

WEDNESDAY, AUGUST 29, 2012

Minutes passed in silence, Mia unable to look away from the bedroom.

"What did you see?" asked Adam for the fifth or sixth time.

His voice broke the trance she hadn't realized she'd fallen into. "Umm. Nothing. Only a feeling."

"You look pale."

"I'm a little freaked out, Adam. I'm feeling stuff that I shouldn't feel. It's like I'm a kid again back home at night. I haven't been scared of the dark since I was little."

"Okay." He flicked the camera off. "Why don't we go to bed?"

She shifted her weight off the wall and took a step away, but stopped, gaze fixated on the door. "This is weird. I went from being afraid of that room to feeling like I really ought to look again."

"Only if you're sure." He touched foreheads with her. "I don't want anything to happen to you."

Mia hugged him, clinging for a minute or two. Her need to look again didn't weaken. His asking her what she'd seen made her feel like she'd gone back to high school chemistry class and missed a basic but important step. Whether it came from personal pride or a supernatural pull that wanted to share information, she couldn't tell.

"Okay. I'm going in." Mia released her hold on Adam and approached the door.

He turned the video camera back on.

Hands braced to either side on the doorjamb, she peered into the room, wanting to *see*. Amid the towers of cardboard boxes, she caught a fleeting glimpse of a white dresser directly opposite the door right in front of her. Left of it, a small desk. Empty rug and cardboard returned for several seconds, then gave way to a scattering of Barbie dolls, which promptly disappeared.

Mia's stomach twisted into a knot of anxiety.

She stepped into the room, arms slack at her sides, and made a deliberate effort to desire seeing the 'not here.' The room blurred. She simultaneously perceived empty rug as well as a large toy chest beside the door. As if reality in front of her had become a movie projected on a claw-shredded sheet, the room existed in two versions at once. Within the rips, the walls appeared covered in patterned wallpaper. Furniture that didn't exist anymore still stood around a child's room. She stifled a gasp at blood spatter on the white dresser.

Cringing, Mia kept looking around. Empty space at the inner corner on the right traded places back and forth with a small bed, sheets turned down as though the child who slept in it had gotten up in the middle of the night. Red past the foot end drew her attention toward the *bad* spot of floor.

Droplets of blood ran down the wall from a tall arc spray, flowing around letters smeared in the crude finger-penmanship of a drunken adult.

All the breath leaked out of Mia's lungs at the sight.

With one shaking hand over her mouth, tears streaming from her eyes, she started to lower her gaze down past the letters, but the instant she caught sight of a small, lifeless hand laying on the rug by a bloody mini sledge, she screamed and turned away—refusing to look at the body she knew would be there.

A woman's voice screamed in anguish, distant, yet loud. The cry continued despite the woman running out of air, too grief stricken to remember how to breathe in. That same grief—and the same scream of horrible heartache—erupted from Mia.

She clutched her chest and fell to her knees, her body wracked by great, heaving sobs. Nothing mattered anymore. The only thing in the world she cared about lay dead in what should have been the safest place in the world for her. Guilt crashed into grief, as biting and cold as though Mia had murdered the girl herself.

The rug came up to hit her in the face. She curled on her side, wailing in sorrow, unable to move. She could only lay there wanting to die while staring up at the three unspeakable words painted on the wall in a little girl's blood:

Bye bye Mommy.

14

WILHELMINA

THURSDAY, AUGUST 30, 2012

Mia walked along the fancy corridor of a large building, probably the courthouse. People in suits or dresses passed by, everyone offering sympathetic looks or sorrowful nods. Their hair appeared strange, the women's attire most noticeably older, out of style.

She peered down at herself, in a black dress, clutching a decidedly un-fancy pastel blue purse close to her gut. A plain brown coat covered her arms to the wrists. The words 'Room 4' repeated in her thoughts at a whisper while she made her way deeper into the stark corridor of black and white tiles, gazing at small signs on the wall by every door.

A young police officer, perhaps halfway into his twenties, stepped in front of her. "Mrs. Kurtis…"

"Yes," said a different woman's voice from Mia's mouth, heavy with sadness, mostly whisper.

"We're all so very sorry for your loss." He bowed his head, glint flashed from a small gold bar on his chest engraved with the word 'deputy.'

Mia nodded. Guilt kept her silent. She should have done more. Should have left sooner, skipped work that night, taken Robin with her…

"Are you sure?" asked the cop.

"Yes," replied Mia in a toneless voice.

"You understand what will happen?"

Mia didn't much care if they shot her, arrested her, executed her, or whatever. Robin was gone. Nothing mattered anymore. "I do."

The deputy nodded and reached under his jacket. He looked around, then pulled out a small revolver, which he dropped into her purse. "It's a snub. Not much for accuracy. You'll have to be close. If it was my kid, I'd do the same thing."

Mia nodded. "Thank you."

She tugged the zipper on the purse shut. The instant it closed, she lurched upright in bed, squinting at sunlight.

Her brain tripped over itself at the sudden transition, reducing her bedroom to an environment as alien as if she'd been abducted by creatures from a UFO. She couldn't fathom where she'd wound up or how she got there—until her alarm went off two minutes later.

Reality crashed into her. Home. Bedroom. House. Ghosts…

Dead child.

Ignoring the blaring clock, Mia buried her face in her hands and wept. The raw grief that had consumed her the previous night lessened by an order of magnitude. Rather than finding *her* daughter, it hit her only as hard as if it had happened to a friend's kid.

Get it together, Mia. That poor girl died years ago. Nothing I can do. She forced calm over herself, then crawled out of bed to kill the annoying alarm. Adam being out of bed already struck her as unusual since she hadn't yet adjusted to the new paradigm of living here. Back in their apartment, she woke up much earlier than him to mitigate the horrendous commute. His new job required him there a little sooner than she had to be at the museum, so he'd become the one who had to get up first, if only by twenty minutes.

The note on his pillow, however, *did* stand out as odd.

She snatched it up to read.

Hon, had to go in early today for a meeting. Call me if you need to talk. I need to know you're okay.

"I'm okay." Mia set the note down and sighed. "Except for not remembering how I wound up in bed."

After hurrying a shower and getting dressed, she sat on the edge of the bed to put her shoes on. While she fixed the straps around her ankles, the bed to her right shifted from weight settling down. She peered up at a small indentation... like a child sitting beside her.

"Robin?" asked Mia, thinking back to her dream. "Is your name Robin?"

A disembodied whisper replied, "Yes."

Mia attempted to hug the air beside her, and wrapped her arms around a cold spot. She tried to say 'I'm sorry,' but her voice hitched in her throat as grief resurfaced. Sudden crying came from the hallway, the distant voice indistinguishable between a woman or a child.

ADAM STOPPED AT THE COFFEE MACHINE IN THE STAFF ROOM AFTER the meeting ended, refilling for the second time. It annoyed him that he'd been dragged out of bed an hour and twenty minutes early to listen to the dean talk about the library and some improvements to the athletic field, then touch base with the various department heads. Nothing that came up in the meeting required him there, all of it every bit as easily conveyed by email.

He exited the room grumbling to himself, though he had no intention to complain about anything, especially not on his first week. In fact, he probably wouldn't rock the boat for at least another few years unless something serious happened.

"Professor Gartner?" asked Paul from behind.

Adam stopped and turned.

His TA walked up to him, along with a large-framed woman with long silvery-grey hair and a warm expression. Her blue eyes still held a spark of youth despite faint wrinkles around them suggesting she'd gone past fifty. She wore a number of necklaces made from wooden beads of various sizes, each bearing a small medallion or talisman with markings in an unfamiliar written script. The most prominent resembled an oak tree enclosed in a circle.

Adam nodded in greeting. "Hello, Paul, and…"

"This is Professor Wilhelmina Marx. She teaches history. She's also interested in the paranormal. I showed her the images you took of the footprints and the orb video. She said she knows about your house already and was surprised someone had moved into the place again, much less also worked here."

"Miss Marx?" asked Adam, offering a handshake.

She accepted. "That's right. Mr. Gartner."

"Paul tells me you've moved into number six a few days ago." She clasped her hands in front of herself. "I live just down the road in ten."

Adam's eyebrows perked up with interest. "Oh. That's a coincidence and a half to be working at the same school as one of my neighbors."

"Quite." Wilhelmina smiled. "Welcome to Syracuse University."

"Thanks. Still feeling my way around, but I like it so far. Hoping to be here for a good while."

She nodded once as if to say 'but of course.' "Psychology?"

"Yep."

"I mostly teach history of western civilization, though I also run a few electives on ancient European groups and traditions. Been teaching here going on twenty-two years now."

Adam blinked. "Wow. That's impressive. Hopefully, I can enjoy the same kind of stability."

"That's good. So, Paul tells me you chase ghosts as a hobby."

"My interest in paranormal research goes beyond hobbyist, though it's far from easy to get any administration to take parapsychology seriously. Even asking about it usually results in everyone calling me a nut."

Paul chuckled. "Showed her the footprint pic with the ruler, she thinks the ghost is around seven years old, uhh, if it's really a ghost."

"Tell me, professor," said Wilhelmina with a glint in her eye, "how do you feel about druidy, witchcraft, that sort of thing?"

"I don't really have much of an opinion, to be honest, but what little I've seen of it seemed fascinating."

Wilhelmina fidgeted with her tree amulet. "I dabble a bit at it."

"She's basically a paranormal Wikipedia," said Paul.

"Amazing." Adam grinned. "I'm guessing you probably don't get along too well with that Weston guy?"

Wilhelmina smirked. "We don't see eye to eye. I think he's a fool, he thinks I should be burned at the stake."

"Whoa." Adam whistled. "He's one of *those?* The man didn't strike me as that unhinged."

"Well, I doubt he'd be inclined to literally burn me at the stake, but somewhere inside, I'm sure he wants to. And, don't get me wrong. I don't think he's a fool for being a Christian. He's a fool for thinking his beliefs are the only ones that matter."

"So, you think the spirit is seven years old based on the size of the footprint?" Adam scratched his head. "Are you an expert tracker, too?"

"Probably looked at a shoe size chart," muttered Paul.

Wilhelmina laughed. "Neither of those. I knew the family."

"You…" Adam stared at her, frozen in a mixture of curiosity and guilt. If this woman knew the family, that made them less 'ghosts to experiment on' and more actual people. His eagerness to find answers crashed headlong into his aversion to being disrespectful. "Knew them?"

"I did… babysat for them a few times when I was thirteen."

"Oh, man." Adam rubbed the bridge of his nose. "I'm sorry."

Wilhelmina shook her head. "It's all right. Enough time has passed that I can talk about it. I hadn't been particularly close to them, just a teenage girl in the area when a babysitter was needed. Of course, you know in a small town like Spring Falls, everyone knows everyone. Not like the big cities where people can live there thirty years and not even know the name of the people next door."

"Vic," said Adam. "Was the man's name Vic?"

"Yes." Wilhelmina's white eyebrows rose a tick. "Before I get too impressed, did you find that on Google?"

"No. I actually haven't done all that much research yet. I didn't want any preconceptions to influence my experiments. And gee… it sounds so wrong to think of it as experiments if you knew the people."

"They're all dead, Mr. Gartner." Wilhelmina looked down. "As I said, in a small town, everyone sees everyone else's dirty laundry. Vic was a mean drunk. Worked most of the day at O'Riordan's Garage. Used to go home most nights and get a bit physical with his wife."

"And the daughter…" Adam sighed.

"Robin. No, not so much. With her, he mostly screamed. None of us are really sure what got into him that night, but violence wasn't exactly out of character for him. Best I can figure, Evelyn—that's Vic's wife—finally had enough of him knocking her around and planned to take off with the daughter. He got wind of her plans. She worked at a diner over in Fulton. Bit of a ride but paid better than the Pinecone, our local diner. Usually didn't get outta there 'til well after midnight."

Adam hooked his thumbs in his pants pockets and stared at the floor. "He wanted to hurt her in the worst way imaginable. Likely, he had no particular anger toward Robin, but she represented the best way to destroy her. Guessing he didn't put much effort into avoiding the law? Men in that situation are typically either suicidal themselves or indifferent to their own survival, or they feel they have every right to do what they did."

"Well, yeah. He ran, but didn't go far. That wretch killed that beautiful little girl before Evelyn came home. She found her."

Adam gasped. "Oh, no… That explains…"

"Hmm?" asked Wilhelmina.

"My wife. I'm convinced she's gifted"—he tapped the side of his head—"and she picked up a vision of… something in the girl's bedroom. It had to be. She let out this god-awful scream and collapsed in sobs, probably re-living the moment the mother, umm, Evelyn, found the girl's body. It hit her so hard she passed out."

"Wow," said Paul. "Is she all right?"

Adam looked at his phone. One text read 'I'm okay, about to leave for work. Thanks for putting me in bed.' "I think so."

"Intense." Paul fidgeted.

"What happened to Vic?" Adam looked back to Wilhelmina.

"The Coopers in number seven heard Evelyn screaming and called the cops. They figured Vic was letting her have it bad. Police showed up, found her upstairs holding Robin, rocking back and forth. Anyway, make a long story short, they picked him up a few miles outside town on the bridge near the falls, drunker'n hell. Heard he still had the bloody hammer with him."

"Might've been trying to drink up the courage to jump?" asked Adam.

"The falls aren't that big. Wouldn't have killed him, but drunk as he was, being in water might have. Evelyn shot him in the back of the head during the trial. She'd been seated right behind the, ehh, what is it... the defense table. The judge called a lunch recess or some such thing and"—Wilhelmina pointed a finger gun at the wall—"*pow!* She emptied all six rounds into him from as close as me to you. 'Course ya don't kill a man in the middle of a courthouse and get away. She just stood there and let the police arrest her. Everyone knew the cops turned a blind eye to her bringin' that weapon into the courthouse. 'Least everyone I talked to figured the cops agreed with her. Poor Evelyn died in a cell awaiting her trial for killing Vic. We all expected her to get off, or maybe wind up in psychiatric care. Officially, they called her death a 'suicide by undetermined means,' but, if you ask me, the poor woman died of a broken heart."

Adam brushed a tear from the corner of his eye, thinking about the way Mia had been wailing last night. "I can believe that."

"That's so, so, horrible." Paul exhaled. "We think they're haunting the place."

"Wouldn't doubt it." Wilhelmina swiped some of her pewter hair from her face, wooden bracelets clattering. "No one's stayed in that house for long. Took forever to sell the first time since everyone 'round here knew what happened in there. Some out of towner bought it in '76, best I can recall. I don't remember the guy much. He had a city mentality, never talked to any of his neighbors. That man kept the house the longest. Something chased him out around 1988 or so."

Adam took out a small notepad and began jotting.

"The house sat empty until 1991, I think it was this girl Ellen L-something... Long, if I remember, who bought it. Poor thing. Only a year or two into her thirties. Made decent money, can't recall what she did for a living, though. She had the place a year before she fell down the stairs and landed wrong. Lost the use of her legs. Went back to Utica to move in with her folks. Place sat empty for a long time after that. Then it was Mr. O'Ryan. George. I want to say he moved in sometime in '96. Something spooked that man terribly. He took off in the middle of the night after a month. Wouldn't even come back to collect his things. Hired movers to do it for him."

Adam looked up from his writing. "After a single month, something in there scared him so much that he wouldn't set foot in the place again?"

"Correct." Wilhelmina tapped her chin. "Around 1999, maybe early 2000, the Vaughans moved in, a somewhat older couple. After about two months, they started having Pastor Parker there three times a week. Middle of the night, early in the morning, weekends. Mr. Vaughan always had bruises like he'd gotten into a nasty scrap over at Johnny's." She raised a hand and whispered past it. "Spring Falls has three bars, and that's the one the down-and-outs frequent. People go there to erase time."

"Ahh." Adam jotted that down.

"The Vaughans lived in the house about two years, but finally gave up on it after Mrs. Vaughan nearly suffocated in her sleep. They said some kind of 'demon' sat on her chest, so heavy she couldn't get any air. Even claimed to have little handprint bruises on her neck."

Adam squirmed at the memory of Mia telling him the ghost girl had crawled into bed between them. Could she have tried to kill Mrs. Vaughan by kneeling on her chest and choking her, or might she have had some manner of coronary event and blamed the ghost for it?

"Did they take pictures?" asked Paul.

"Not as far as I know. Most recent people to live there were Phillip & Arlene Weir, about three years ago. Really sweet couple. I remember them gettin' on towards forty but they didn't have any kids. They were friendly with Pastor Parker, but not to the same degree as the Vaughans. Maybe he learned his lesson that going in there and screaming scripture at ghosts only makes them angry."

"The Weirs..." Adam wrote that down. "That name sounds familiar. I remember it from the sale, but we never met them."

"How long did they last in the place?" asked Paul.

"About six months. Left a couple weeks before Christmas." Wilhelmina tapped a finger to her chin. "Heard they started arguing a lot. She wanted to leave, he didn't want to sell—for financial reasons. Arlene took off early one morning, but only made it a little ways down Minstrel Run before she wrapped her car around a tree. Damn near broke her neck. Cops couldn't determine if she swerved to avoid something or tried to kill herself on purpose since she hadn't hit the brakes. Either way, as soon as she got out of the hospital, they left the area."

"Well, Professor." Paul grinned at Adam. "Two years is the record to beat, but it sounds like things will become interesting between one and six months from now."

He chuckled. "They're already 'interesting.' I'm just hoping they don't become dangerous. How long ago did Vic kill his daughter?"

"September, 1970. The murder happened on a Wednesday. I still remember my parents telling me about it the next day. Didn't feel real. Still doesn't. Robin was such a cute, happy child... except when her father was around. That man chased the joy right out of her, but she bounced back whenever he left."

Adam shook his head. "Such a damn senseless tragedy."

"Oh, crap." Paul hurried a few steps away. "We've got five minutes before class."

"Drat." Adam stuffed the notebook in his pocket. "It was wonderful to meet you, Professor Marx. I'd love to discuss as much about ghosts, druids, or that poor family as you're willing to put up with. Would you like to stop by sometime for dinner?"

"It's been forty-two years since I've been in that house. I wonder if she'll remember me." Wilhelmina thought for a moment. "Sure. Perhaps I can even help the three of you get along."

"Great." He backed up. "Need to run to class."

"Me too." She wagged her eyebrows. "Nice meeting you as well, Professor Gartner."

With a final wave, Adam jogged down the hall toward his classroom.

15

ALONE

THURSDAY, AUGUST 30, 2012

A cloud of grimness fell over Adam while he drove out of the Syracuse University parking lot.

The same melancholy had dogged him ever since his conversation with Wilhelmina earlier that morning. It stood beside him during his classes, worsened by gazing into the faces of eighteen- and nineteen-year-old students. Even though it happened longer ago than he'd been alive, he couldn't help but dwell on the idea that a little girl who once lived in his house would never make it to college.

She might have turned out to be attentive and smart like Lexi Haney in his second class, or maybe she'd have had the 'this is boring, I already know it' attitude of Benedict Fletcher from his morning period, or daydreamed the whole time like Alicia McLaughlin in his last session. It didn't matter what kind of person she *might* have been. The girl never had the chance.

Once he no longer had to focus on his job, he distracted himself with a mental debate regarding the odds of the entity being an actual child spirit or a demon pretending to be one. Mia had been quiet all day, not sending any texts. That happened sometimes, especially when a restoration project absorbed her attention entirely. However, after what happened last night, he worried about her.

Watching his wife have a complete breakdown had been perhaps the single most difficult experience of his marriage. Though, technically, it hadn't so much been watching her that bothered him as much as his being powerless to stop it. Adam squeezed and relaxed his grip on the steering wheel at a red light while the formless blurs of traffic passed in front of him. He couldn't ask Mia to do that to herself again. As soon as he got home, he'd suggest she avoid that room. The most upset he'd ever seen her prior to last night had been a little over four years ago when they'd first started dating. Her cat had died of old age, but even then, she hadn't been anywhere near as devastated.

Mia's grief took the form of quiet tears, lack of interest in doing anything but sitting in one place and staring into nowhere. The scream-crying hadn't been her. It couldn't have been. She either read the emotional imprint Evelyn Kurtis seared into that room or perhaps the woman's ghost also occupied the house and had chosen that moment to inhabit Mia's body.

The light changed.

Adam didn't notice until a soft beep came from behind. He raised a hand in an apologetic wave and resumed driving. His mind jogged down a different thought path, sorting the types of activity he'd seen. If the child ghost was genuine, it would be unlikely—at least he hoped—that she gave off the dread Mia reported feeling from the house. That darkness either came from Vic or the psychic scar such a brutal killing could leave on an area. The sorrow clearly came from Evelyn, though none of the overt manifestations connected to her. Perhaps, like Mia's stories of her childhood home, that ghost lurked in the attic or basement and avoided living people.

Mia had wondered why Robin kept running away after such short visits. Perhaps Vic remained in the house as well and she ran away from him. Though, if Evelyn haunted the place, why would the child ghost give off such feelings of loneliness? Perhaps they had somehow wound up isolated in different parts of the house and couldn't interact.

He turned onto Minstrel Run a short while later, still no closer to understanding anything more than not wanting his interest in the paranormal to hurt Mia. The tree-shrouded street curved gradually back and forth for the almost mile between the corner and his house. He slowed to a stop by his driveway, gazing down the road toward Wilhelmina's house, not that he could see it from there with all the trees in the way. Older people always filled him with a sense of nostalgic wonder at the idea the world they had once known had changed so much.

His hope buoyed by the prospect that the woman might be able to help somehow, he pulled into the driveway and parked beside the Tahoe. Eager to check on Mia, he hurriedly shut the engine off and ran inside. The downstairs appeared dim and empty except for various EM sensors, the camera tripod, and a few digital audio recorders. He walked far enough into the dining room to see the whole kitchen, and found no sign of her.

"Hon?" called Adam.

He looked around, listening to silence for a moment before checking the toilet closet in the small alcove off the dining room. Still, no Mia. Adam jogged back to the living room turned right, peering into the mostly-empty room they hadn't yet figured out what to do with. Despite the early evening dimness, the two large bay windows let in plenty of light.

"Mia?" called Adam, his voice echoing off bare walls.

Worry rising, he ran to the stairs and went up.

Upon seeing a light on in Robin's bedroom, he froze, a chill creeping down his back. Soft muttering in Mia's voice leaked out into the hall. Adam's briefcase slipped from his fingers, striking the floor with a *thud* that startled him. Ignoring it, he walked to the door and peered in.

None of the moving boxes remained.

A child's bed occupied the inner corner to his right, a cute white dresser against the wall straight in front of him. In the left corner by the window stood a mound of cardboard scraps, likely the packaging material for one of the two pieces of furniture that hadn't been there earlier.

Mia lay on the floor in the middle of the room, curled up in a ball on her side, her hair fanned out on the rug. She muttered random nonsense that didn't make sense as words, a repeating pattern of syllables.

"You bought a bed?" asked Adam, hoping 'normal' might help snap her out of it.

She didn't react.

"Mia..." He took a knee and grasped her shoulder. The instant he touched her, she jumped as if startled, stopped muttering, and looked up at him. "Hon. What's going on?"

Her eyes fluttered; she looked around with an expression as though she didn't remember how she wound up on the floor. "Umm..."

Only her absence of alarm kept him from freaking out. He sat on the floor, holding her hand. "You seemed to be in some kind of trance."

"Yeah... something like that. A woman sat here for hours like that... probably Robin's mother after finding her." Mia grasped the front of her throat, choked up. "She found her body... right over there on the floor past the foot of the bed."

Adam's guilt got into a war with his excitement over validation. "You know the girl's name?"

"Yeah..."

"It's right."

Mia glanced at him. "What do you mean, 'it's right?'"

"I met a woman at the university today who lives down the road a few houses. She knew the family, said she babysat a couple times when she'd only been a kid herself. The girl's name was Robin."

"Is," whispered Mia. "She's still here."

Adam bit his tongue before musing aloud about the potential of a demon impersonating a child. "I've been worried all damn day about you. What's with the furniture?"

"I..." She looked over at the dresser. "Don't know what came over me. Called out of work sick and just wound up getting them."

He rubbed her back. "It's okay. At least kid furniture isn't too expensive."

"You're not upset?"

"No. I was worried about you." He exhaled out his nose, relieved.

Aside from appearing faintly disoriented, she acted normal. "I'd never seen you *that* upset before."

Mia leaned against him. "I think that came from her mother... I saw such awful things. He killed her and wrote 'bye bye mommy' on the wall in blood. I felt everything that woman felt when she found her child dead."

Adam shuddered, on the verge of tears at the thought of it. "Damn... shit like this is why I didn't go into clinical practice."

"She killed him. I'm sure of it. I think right in the courtroom or something. A police officer even gave her the gun."

"What?" Adam blinked. "How'd you find that out? Wilhelmina told me about it, but she didn't know exactly how the woman got a weapon. Of course, everyone assumed the cops helped her. It's pretty damn hard to sneak a gun into a courthouse."

Mia explained her dream. "It felt like a long time ago. Everyone's clothes looked dated. Like something out of the sixties. I have no idea if she wanted me to see that or if I picked it up somehow."

"It happened in 1970." Adam rested a hand against her cheek. "Please be careful... two women who lived here both suffered serious injuries. A third almost died. I'm not sure what made the spirits turn hostile or if that's just what they do... act harmless for a while and then go off."

"I... don't think so." Mia picked at the rug by her knee. "I know you're going to say it could be exactly what the spirit wants me to feel, but I feel like she won't hurt us."

"Maybe it's not Robin we should be worrying about." Adam glanced at the little bed. "Perhaps Evelyn is still here and if we get too close to the child, she goes all possessive and wrathful."

Mia kept picking at the rug.

"You sure you're okay?"

"I feel fine now. Just needed a day to recover from last night. It took a while for me to separate myself from that woman's grief."

Adam hugged her. "Promise you'll tell me if you start feeling un-fine?"

She nodded.

"Hmm. The bed and dresser could make for good trigger objects."

Mia emitted a sad chuckle. "Babe, I don't think we need trigger objects to encourage activity. There's plenty of it already."

"Right…" He chuckled. "All that's missing is a stuffed bear."

She flashed a weak smile. "Ordered one already… the store didn't have the right kind."

Adam started to laugh, but gave her a quizzical look. "Right kind?"

"A plush rabbit, not a bear. Like the one she used to have." Mia bit her lip. "I think you're right. I'm probably psychic. I shouldn't know what her toy looked like or her dresser, or even what her name was until you told me."

"Hon, that's great, but I'd rather spend the rest of my working life as a psychology professor with a healthy, happy wife by my side than be a successful parapsychologist. Please be careful."

"I will."

Adam kissed her. "I'll go whip up something for dinner."

"Okay. I'll be down in a few minutes."

MIA SAT ON THE FLOOR AFTER ADAM WENT DOWNSTAIRS, HOPING to see some sign that Robin liked her gifts.

It caught her off guard that he hadn't been upset about the furniture. While they didn't exactly live paycheck-to-paycheck, spending a couple hundred bucks on kid furniture would throw off the budget a little. Until she paid off the Tahoe, it really didn't make sense to throw money at useless things.

But they didn't feel useless.

A child *did* exist inside the house. Even if she couldn't use either bed or dresser, their presence here would help. Mia didn't know why she knew that, but it felt right. She'd spent hours earlier in the afternoon trying to find the exact dresser she'd seen during that awful vision. The bed, too, came as close as she could manage to the one that used to be here. A spirit might have compelled her to buy them, or perhaps the urge had bubbled up from her deep-seated need to destroy the darkness she'd seen here, adding things to the room to brighten it, make it the little girl's bedroom it had once been.

Perhaps her idea had backfired. She sighed at the empty bed. It struck her every bit as depressing as an empty room had been, perhaps even more so. Mia bowed her head, brushing her hand across the beige carpet. Which prior owner had installed this? It looked new, but given how sparsely the house had been occupied in the years since the murder, the rug could've been thirty years old and remained in good shape.

Cold air brushed over Mia's shoulders and a sense of being watched fell on her.

She looked up from the floor—and clamped both hands over her mouth to stop from screaming.

A little girl in a plain white nightgown stood by the foot of the bed, arms at her sides, tiny hands balled into fists. She stared at Mia with an intense glower, her eyes brimming with darkness well beyond her tender age. Long, straight light brown hair framed a delicate face frozen in an expression of territorial challenge. Unlike Vic, she appeared whole from head to her bare feet, though her entire body had a mild transparency. A blast of fear radiated from the spirit along with a raspy hiss.

Mia twitched in response to the wave of paranormal fear, but didn't otherwise move. The anger in the child's glare stunned her, but she forced herself not to look away or run. A sense that this girl radiated anger at her circumstances, not Mia, teased at the back of her thoughts and gave her enough nerve to hold her ground.

Trails of blood started to leak from Robin's nose and lip, dripping down onto the chest of her nightie. After a moment of silent eye contact—and Mia not fleeing in terror—the blood receded.

Mia moved her hands from her mouth to her chest. "Hi, sweetie. You're Robin, right?"

The child nodded once, still glaring at her with a 'why are you in my room?' scowl.

"My name's Mia." She couldn't help but start crying all over again, though this sorrow came from inside and manifested in her usual manner: silent tears rolling down her face. "Is it okay that I got you some things?"

Robin turned her head to peer at the bed. For an instant, her face flashed to a blood-soaked horror. Mia flinched. Again, the girl nodded once. Some of the hardness in her glare lessened.

"I hate that you're sad and lonely," whispered Mia. "I hate even more what happened to you. How can I help?"

Robin took a few steps closer, her hands relaxing open, no longer fists. Bloody footprints on the rug lingered for seconds before fading, though her legs appeared clean.

"That other spirit hurt you, didn't he?"

The girl nodded. "I'm scared of him."

Mia choked up again at the sound of the child's voice. It had a far-off quality, sounding as though it came from somewhere down the hall, part whispery, part tonal. "I am, too."

"Mia," said the ghost, her glare fading to a plaintive expression. "I don't want you to go away. I'm lonely. I want you to stay here with me."

"I'm not gonna leave." Mia raised her arms, inviting the girl into a hug. "Oh, you're still only a baby... so young."

Robin took another step closer, pausing inches from reach. "Don't go away and leave me alone. Everyone always leaves me alone. I don't like it."

"C'mere, sweetie." Mia smiled, the urge to hug the sweet, innocent child growing. "I'm not gonna leave you."

The girl appeared about to move closer but whirled to the left and went wide-eyed in fear. Without another word, she bolted back to the spot where her body had been, and disappeared. The rumble of Adam walking up the stairs came from the hall. Mia let her arms fall into her lap.

"He's not like your bad daddy. He won't hurt you."

"Hon?" Adam poked his head in. "Dinner's almost ready. Oh, crap... what's wrong?"

"Nothing."

"You're crying."

Mia stood and wiped her face. "Yeah. I know. I just saw her."

"Her? Robin or the mother?"

"Robin. I think she's afraid of you."

Adam set his hands on his hips. "Understandable. Between what her father did, then Mr. Vaughan and that pastor, I'm not surprised she's afraid of men."

"What did the pastor do?" Mia blinked at him in shock.

"Not sure exactly, but probably nothing worse than shouting at her to go away, calling her an unclean spirit or some nonsense like that." He sighed out his nose. "Hey, you up for a little validation test?"

Mia folded her arms. "Now what?"

"Just thinking I might grab some random photos of kids, stick one of Robin in there and ask you to pick her out."

"I think it would be obvious for being a newspaper clipping from 1970. I have a better idea." Mia let her arms fall and walked out into the hall. "I'll sketch her. Maybe even paint a portrait if I can find where my stuff is."

"Speaking of stuff... what did you do with all the crap we had in here?"

"Moved it across the hall to the other empty bedroom. This one's in use."

Adam glanced at her, then the bed. "Yeah... I suppose it is."

16

CERTAIN SORTS OF PEOPLE

FRIDAY, AUGUST 31, 2012

The alarm clock erupted in a beeping fit.

Already near conscious, Mia awoke in seconds, and smiled. She'd skipped the late night ghost hunting and crashed early, around nine. Unusually happy, she bounced out of bed and shut the alarm off. The patter of water in the bathroom told her Adam was in the shower. With a mischievous grin, she pulled off her nightgown and decided to join him.

MIA ZOOMED INTO THE KITCHEN AND WENT STRAIGHT FOR THE cabinet where she kept the oatmeal, pausing to look at the box of pancake mix out on the counter already.

"I'm sorry, sweetie, but I don't have time to make pancakes today. I promise I'll make them tomorrow when I don't have to work."

The pancake mix teetered and fell off the counter, hitting the floor with a *thump*.

"Oh, please don't be like that..." Mia set the oatmeal aside and picked the pancake mix up. "I'd make them if I could today but"—she blushed, thinking of what had occurred in the shower moments ago

—"there isn't enough time left. If I lose my job, we could lose the house and have to leave."

She replaced the pancake mix in the row of boxes by the wall on the counter, beside the coffee machine, then microwaved a portion of oatmeal. Adam rushed in only long enough to give her a quick kiss before hurrying out the door. Mia ate as fast as the temperature allowed, rinsed the bowl, and jogged to the front door.

The instant her hand touched the knob, the deadbolt flipped itself on. She opened it, and a *click* came from the knob. When she twisted the little thing by the knob to unlock it, the deadbolt threw again.

"Robin, please… I have to go to work. I'm not *leaving*. If I could stay home, I would, but we need money to pay for this place and food and bills… I promise I'll be back."

The deadbolt gradually opened itself.

"Thank you."

Did she get this possessive with the other people who lived here? Mia exited the house, locked the door, and climbed into the Tahoe. *If she wants me to stay, why did she try to scare me off when she appeared by the bed?*

She shrugged, started the engine, and backed out of the driveway. As the back tires hit the street, she looked up at the house…

And locked eyes with Robin glaring at her from the living room window. Before Mia could open her mouth, the girl faded away.

Mia worried about the baleful expression on Robin's face all day at work.

Despite her anxiety about the ghost, the day went by fast. Cleaning a giant painting absorbed her attention to the point she missed lunch, not even realizing it until the 'work trance' faded twenty minutes past four. She decided to just wait for dinner and kept working until quitting time.

A few minutes after six, she drove up Minstrel Run toward home. A green Jeep Cherokee parked near her house threw her into a bad mood, bracing for an argument. She pulled into the driveway to find Weston trading words with a tall, unfamiliar woman holding a pie. They both stood halfway along the walkpath to the porch, voices raised, but not fully shouting at each other.

The woman looked older, her long white hair streaked with darker bands of pewter. Her baggy shirt and long multicolored skirt plus all the necklaces and bracelets she wore made her look somewhere between an aging hippie and a fortuneteller. Despite that, Mia's initial instinct inclined her to take the newcomer's side of whatever quarrel went on. The woman radiated a sense of genuineness that appealed to her.

Both stopped barking at each other, turning to watch the Tahoe roll to a stop.

Mia hopped out and approached them. "Is there a problem here?"

"I'm merely wondering what *she* is doing here," said Weston.

The woman frowned. "I could ask you the same thing. Have you been invited?"

Mia's confusion made Weston smile.

"Stop with the deceit, woman. Mrs. Gartner clearly has no idea who you even are."

"Oh, you must be Wilhelmina Marx." Mia walked up to her and offered a hand. "Adam did tell me about you. I'd forgotten you'd be joining us for dinner tonight."

The woman shot Weston a 'aha, take that!' look and accepted her handshake. "Pleasure to meet you, dear."

"You shouldn't be associating with that sort of person." Weston almost took Mia's arm to pull her away, but thought better of it. "This house is tainted enough without her influence."

"All the screaming you did here with the Vaughans didn't help, now did it?" asked Wilhelmina. "I could hear the lot of you from my place."

"All you did was traumatize a child all over again." Mia glowered at him. "There's no demon here. If your god actually cared about children, he would've stopped that man from hurting her in the first place."

"God works—"

"In mysterious ways, yeah I know." Mia folded her arms. "That's the same thing you people say whenever you have no good explanation for why a supposedly loving god allowed evil to happen to innocent people."

"Mia, you must understand what's going on here," said Weston.

"I understand that you have an extremely narrow view that offers no room for anything outside the little book you love so much. Can't explain something? *Must* be Satan. Don't like something, just call it Satan anyway so everyone else doesn't like what you don't like."

"Weston…" Wilhelmina raised a placating hand. "The greatest problem you have is believing that your way is the only way. I've never said your god doesn't exist, only that he isn't the be-all-end-all you think he is."

"Atheism and paganism are going to be the ruination of this country." Weston scowled at the house. "Mrs. Gartner, you must listen to reason before it's too late for you."

"One, I'm not an atheist." Mia pointed at him. "Atheists don't believe in ghosts either. My opinion on god is that I don't know. If he's out there, he can speak for himself. I have a problem with people who use some theoretical deity as a justification to mistreat others. If your god is real, and as powerful as you think he is, then everything that happens is either his doing or happening with his permission. Evil exists because God creates it, allows it, or he's not powerful enough to stop it. Now, please… if ever I feel the need to seek your help 'saving my soul,' I'll come to you. I'd appreciate it if you stopped pestering us and harassing our guest."

"But—"

She ignored Weston's rambling about dire consequences and walked with Wilhelmina up onto the porch. The front door clicked on its own before she could even stick her hand in her purse to hunt for the keys.

"Thank you, Robin." Mia pulled the door open, held it for Wilhelmina, then entered, closing it on Weston's continued shouting about trafficking with the minions of Satan. "Ugh, that man."

Wilhelmina looked around the living room. "The place has changed so much. I don't even recognize it anymore. Though, it *has* been quite a few years since I've been inside this house." She faced Mia. "There's definitely energy here."

"Yes. Robin is here, though I'm still not sure if her parents are, too, or if I've only been catching glimpses of emotional imprints. Would you care for some tea or coffee?"

"Tea would be lovely, thank you. And, here." She offered the pie. "Blueberry."

"Thank you! It smells wonderful." Mia headed to the kitchen, set the pie on the counter, then put on a kettle of water. Wilhelmina trailed after her in no great hurry, gazing around at the walls. She reached the kitchen as Mia set two mugs on the countertop.

"Plain tea? Or we have a few different herbal ones."

"Plain is fine, dear." Wilhelmina took a seat at the table. "So, you're certain the girl is here?"

"Yes." Mia explained seeing her in the bedroom for a few brief minutes before Adam spooked her.

Wilhelmina's eyebrows notched upward. "That's most curious. I find it intriguing that rather than being chased off by such an apparition, you're inclined to help her. And I do think you're right about her being frightened of men."

The kettle whistled. Mia got up to pour the water, then returned to the table with both cups. "Cream? Sugar?"

"Just a little sugar, please."

Mia retrieved the sugar dispenser and sat again. "I kinda grew up around ghosts, though that didn't stop me from being afraid of them. After the experience I had the other night, seeing Robin appear didn't rattle me all that much. Poor kid looked furious though. Not sure if I annoyed her by putting some furniture in her room or why she'd throw off such rage if she's lonely. Adam's still not convinced we don't have a demon pretending to be a child."

"That's a valid worry. There is negative energy in here. It could be coming from Vic. As far as I am aware, nothing dark was ever summoned in this area, though who knows what any of the former residents might've done. Weston might have attracted something else with all his screaming about the Lord."

Mia rolled her eyes.

"You appear to have more of an issue with him than I do." Wilhelmina poured a teaspoon of sugar into her tea and stirred. "Mostly, I try to avoid him."

"It's not him personally. Pushy religious people all have that effect on me. It's because of my brother."

Wilhelmina sipped tea, nodding.

"My brother, Tim, is gay. Our parents are like Weston, maybe even worse. They used to say such awful things to their own son after he came out of the closet. I caught him once with a bottle of sleeping pills... he was only fourteen then."

Wilhelmina cringed.

"I had Timmy's back, though. No idea where I got the nerve to get in my dad's face, but I did. As a little girl, I'd been so afraid of him I could barely talk over a whisper around him. But, after finding Tim with those pills... I dunno, it just set off a fire inside me. We left home when my brother was seventeen. He lived in the dorm with me when I went to college, against regs. The whole floor basically adopted him. He's okay now, but I haven't spoken two words to my mother or father in about eight years."

"I'm sorry you had to deal with that."

"Nothing you need to apologize for. But, yeah... my issue isn't with that man, but his beliefs. Maybe I should see what he thinks of LGBT people before I lump him in with my parents, but the preachy stuff just gets me irritated so fast. Sounds exactly like my father."

"Oh, Weston's no shortage of preachy. He and his people used to pester me and mine, but they eventually gave up."

"Your people?" asked Mia.

"There are a few of us who follow the old ways. All that man needed to hear was the word 'coven,' and you'd think we sacrificed infants for Samhain. If I hadn't been thirteen—and quite secretive about my interest in witchcraft back then—I'm sure he would have blamed me for affecting Victor's mind. The five of us meet every so often. Weston used to show up with some people from his church and wave signs on my lawn. Lovely folks, mind you. They were all so happy to tell us how we'd burn in hell."

Mia sighed. "Sorry. Well, I suppose I should get started on dinner then."

"Want some help, dear?"

"You're a guest. It's okay."

Wilhelmina stood. "Nonsense. I don't mind, and cooking together is the best way to welcome a new friend into your home."

While they prepared a pot roast with onions and sliced carrots, Mia chatted about the paranormal events that had occurred thus far, and what she'd experienced. She'd only known the woman for an hour or so, but already, Wilhelmina felt like the friendly, supportive mother she'd always resented other people having. Discussing the moment she'd felt Evelyn Kurtis' grief proved difficult and emotional. Mia struggled to keep her voice from breaking up as she relayed the words she'd seen written on the wall.

Adam walked in. "Sorry I'm a bit late. Got ambushed by a student who needed help." He shook hands with Wilhelmina. "Thanks for coming. What did I miss?"

"I've been filling her in on everything that's happened... oh and Weston decided to warn us away from talking to her." Mia shook her head. "Please tell me he's not still out there."

"No, I didn't see him." Adam held up his briefcase. "Be right back, gonna drop this upstairs and change."

Mia resumed her explanation while cleaning green beans for a side.

Wilhelmina whipped up a batch of mashed potatoes. At the mention of Mia watching the cop give Evelyn the revolver, she gasped in shock. "Everyone suspected as much, but no one said anything. I heard the judge fainted at the gunshots in his courtroom. Guess he wasn't expecting it. Now, I'm no police officer, but I thought it unusual Evelyn had the time to fire all six shots before any of the cops managed to get to her. Way I heard it described, it sounded like a movie. She walked up behind him, emptied the gun, dropped it, and raised her hands. The police walked her out, didn't even cuff her." She grinned. "I also heard the defense attorney soiled himself."

Mia paused nipping the ends off the beans and stared at the knife in her hand. "I think I might be jealous a little. My mother wouldn't have avenged me—or Timothy—like that. Robin was Evelyn's whole world. That woman had a lot of guilt, too."

"I'd imagine. She'd been trying to leave Vic for a while, but kept losing her nerve. The man slapped her around all the time. Can't say if she blamed herself for not leaving sooner or because she thought trying to leave made him do it."

Mia set the knife down and scooped the beans into a steamer. "Maybe both. No matter what she chose to do, something bad would've come of it."

"Smells good," said Adam on the way back into the kitchen.

"We've called in professional help." Mia smiled.

"Hah," said Wilhelmina.

They sat around the table talking about ghosts for a while. When the pot roast neared done, Adam opened a tube of biscuit dough, arranged them on a tray, and threw them in the oven. Mia's dream experience and visions lined up with what Wilhelmina remembered, causing Adam to declare her a genuine psychic. He grabbed his laptop and showed Wilhelmina the light orbs he'd captured plus the EVPs he'd recorded. The woman fidgeted at her bracelets the entire time, occasionally gazing up at the ceiling. Once the food finished cooking and they proceeded to eat, their conversation shifted to how she might be able to help.

"My friends and I follow a belief system based on a combination of ancient Celtic druidy with aspects of witchcraft and a smattering of pagan lore. And before you ask," said Wilhelmina with a smile, "as far as I am concerned, the druids did *not* conduct human sacrifice. The Romans often accused them of it as a propaganda maneuver. They frequently ascribed barbaric traits to any outside groups or foreigners —including Christians—as a means by which to feel superior."

"So you can help?" asked Mia.

"Perhaps. It depends on what you're trying to accomplish. Are you attempting to exorcise the spirits and drive them away?"

An odd sense of apprehension filled the air.

Mia shook her head. "No. Not at all. Well, maybe Vic… He can go straight to hell."

The ambient worry faded.

"As far as Robin is concerned, I'm not really sure how to help her. What are spirits *supposed* to do in order to be happy? Is she trapped here and unable to move on? Or does she want to stay? I only want her not to suffer."

"We're still not entirely sure the entity *is* a real child," said Adam in a low voice. "Maybe it's a bit Judeo-Christian centric of me to think this, but why wouldn't an innocent be able to move on?"

"That is rather western of you." Wilhelmina chuckled. "However, I'm afraid I cannot offer much in terms of concrete answers for why she may still be here. Evelyn left here one morning to attend Vic's trial knowing she would never return to the house. She hadn't been eating much. They found the fridge full of spoiled food."

"She'd lost the will to live," said Adam.

Mia stared into her plate. "I'm sure she only lasted as long as she did because she hadn't killed Vic yet."

"Perhaps the girl is still here, somehow waiting for her mother to come home?" asked Wilhelmina.

Adam sighed. "Truly a wonderfully happy subject for dinner conversation."

"I guess I'll try talking to her and see if she knows what we should do." Mia had lost most of her appetite, but forced herself to eat. "Could there have been something else here before the murder that got into Vic and made him do that? The look in his eyes when he went upstairs didn't seem human at all."

"There is a definite darkness in this house, but I can't say for sure if it's the type of entity you are thinking of or merely an aftereffect of what happened." Wilhelmina grasped her tree amulet, rubbing her thumb back and forth over it.

"Of the prior residents," said Adam, "only the women had been seriously hurt. Do you think that's Vic's work?"

"It could be. That man definitely had issues with us." Wilhelmina rubbed her arm. "He pushed me into a wall once when I'd been here to watch Robin for them. Accused me of moving one of his tools in a shed that used to be out back. No idea why he'd have even thought I'd have gone out there, but he didn't believe me when I told him I hadn't touched it."

Adam scowled. "What kind of sad excuse for a man gets physical with a young girl over a missing tool? What were you, twelve or thirteen?"

"Around that age, yes. And he was a real piece of work. Not many people stood up to him due to his size. Thought he could do whatever he wanted." Wilhelmina frowned. "I probably should have stayed away, but I—and I know this sounds stupid considering how young I was at the time—but I didn't want to leave that little girl alone with him. As if my not babysitting for them anymore might've put her in danger."

"She likes pancakes," said Mia, trying to brighten the mood.

"Oh, that she did." Wilhelmina grinned. "Every time I watched her, she'd ask for them."

"Does. Not 'did.'" Mia stabbed a bit of pot roast. "I promised her I'd make some tomorrow morning."

Adam raised an eyebrow. "That should be interesting to watch a ghost consume pancakes."

"She'll probably inhabit one of you, likely Mia, while you eat."

"Should we be concerned?" asked Adam.

"That all depends on if the spirit is really who she appears to be." Wilhelmina winked.

From there, conversation took a turn toward the mundane, with Adam and Wilhelmina discussing the university while Mia played spectator. Though she felt like an outsider to the topic, her husband sounding so comfortable with his new job reassured her.

After dinner, they all had a piece of blueberry pie with coffee. That done, Mia brought Wilhelmina upstairs to Robin's bedroom. Adam followed with the video camera. The elder wrapped her arms around herself and shivered upon walking in. Her gaze went straight to the spot of floor where Mia suspected the body had been.

"You poor child," whispered Wilhelmina. "Yes, it happened in here. The energy of this room is scarred. Perhaps I can help change that."

"Would that have any effect on Robin?" asked Mia, a little defensiveness rising in her voice.

"If she is what she appears to be, it may do nothing or it may set her free. Assuming, of course, she is *trapped* here and not merely staying by choice. Now, if as Adam suspects, the entity is only pretending to be a child... it could have unforeseen results."

"I don't want anything to hurt her... more than she's already suffered." Mia folded her arms.

"It *can't* hurt her if she's really Robin." Adam pivoted around with the camera.

Wilhelmina fussed at the bracelets on her right wrist while gazing at the wall where the bloody writing had been. "She is quite territorial and protective."

"Sounds like Mia's taking on a bit of that protectiveness as well." Adam smiled. "Mama bear."

Mia smirked. "I'm no mama."

"Sure you are." He put an arm around her. "Timothy? You're more a mother to him than your mother was."

"I guess." She rested her head against his shoulder.

"Well." Wilhelmina clasped her hands. "Let me do a little preparation. I'll be ready in a few days, then we can try a cleansing."

"Sounds good." Adam nodded.

"We're not trying to get rid of her." Mia noticed the plush rabbit she'd left on the bed sat on the floor. She picked it up and replaced it on the pillow.

"Of course not. Merely whatever is giving off the dark energy." Wilhelmina glanced sideways at Adam and stepped backward out of the room.

He took Mia's hand and they followed her down to the living room.

"Thank you both very much for dinner. I shall have to return the favor soon." Wilhelmina made her way to the front door. "Alas, I'm afraid these old bones aren't terribly good for late nights anymore." She took her coat from the pegs on the wall, but paused with one arm in, glancing past them for a moment before she finished putting her coat on. "Mia, I do believe someone wishes to speak to you."

17

PSYCHIC

FRIDAY, AUGUST 31, 2012

Mia twisted to look back.

Robin stood near the top of the stairs, staring at her. Other than faintly transparent, she appeared reasonably normal: no blood or trace of injury, her legs didn't stop existing below the knees. The child's expression appeared mostly neutral, though had a hint of sternness.

"You see her?" whispered Mia.

"No," said Adam.

Wilhelmina shook her head. "I don't, but I can feel her. Thank you again for a lovely night. If you'll excuse me, I must be off."

"Of course," said Adam. "Can I offer you a ride?"

"It's not that far."

Mia couldn't bring herself to look away from Robin. "It was great to meet you, Wilhelmina. Thank you for the wonderful pie, too."

"You're too kind. It's only a blueberry pie."

"I don't mind." Adam grabbed his coat. "It's dark, little chilly…"

"And I'm old. You can say it." Wilhelmina chuckled. "All right. If you insist."

Mia turned back toward the door and smiled at her. "Thanks for coming."

"Oh, you're welcome dear." Wilhelmina hugged her. "And don't let that old pastor get on your nerves. He's like a rusty weather vane. Unsightly and makes a lot of noise, but won't cause any real damage."

Adam and Mia chuckled.

He left to drive her home.

Mia looked back at the stairway, but the girl had disappeared. "Robin?" She ran upstairs, finding the hallway empty. "Robin? Where'd you go?" She peeked into the child's room, also empty. Realizing she still wore her work clothes, she went to the bedroom, changed into her T-shirt and shorts, then returned to the girl's room. "I promise I won't let her do anything that will harm you. I know you're really an innocent little girl, and I'm *not* trying to make you leave. This is still your room, okay?"

She waited for a minute or two, but nothing happened by the time Adam came in downstairs. With a sad sigh, she headed downstairs to watch TV.

MIA SNAPPED AWAKE FROM A DREAMLESS SLEEP AND STARED AT the ceiling of her bedroom. Adam lay on his side next to her, one arm across her chest.

Distant thumps came from downstairs. The alarm clock read 1:04 a.m. *Ugh.* She reached out from under the blankets and rubbed her eyes. That stupid crash had likely been loud enough to knock her out of sleep. Mia figured Vic had learned of Evelyn's intention to leave him while at work, stopped by that dive bar on the way home to slurp down a few cans of artificial courage, and stumbled in the back door. Whether he dropped the toolbox or slammed it down in anger, she couldn't tell.

Evelyn had gone to work... was Robin home alone while that bastard drank himself into a stupor? Wow, she worked at one in the morning? Guess she had the late shift.

Mia slipped out of bed and trudged to the bathroom. Two glasses of wine and a large cup of iced tea had filled her bladder to the point she couldn't fall asleep again. On the way back to bed, she paused in the hall, staring at the door to Robin's bedroom. An ephemeral sense hung in the air, a noise she couldn't quite hear that sent tingles down her arms. The feeling reminded her of her grandmother's old-fashioned giant television set, the way she could just tell it was on even with a blank screen and no sound.

Someone's in there...

Worry that the girl might be hiding from Vic—or worse, re-living her death—urged Mia down the hall. The door hung a hair shy of halfway open, the room beyond dark. She hesitated and knocked twice on the doorjamb.

"Robin?"

The child appeared out of thin air in the doorway, staring up at her with a blank expression.

Mia jumped back, clutching her chest, and nearly landed on her ass. A hint of a smile played upon the girl's lips, as though startling her had been a fun game. Mia took a few breaths to calm down. *At least she's not stuck being killed over and over.*

"Hey. Are you ready for pancakes tomorrow?"

Robin smiled again, wider, her eyes sparkling with eerie intensity as though she could cheer about breakfast as easily as burn down a house. She stepped into the hall, her right shoulder and arm passing through the door. "Yes."

"I'm sorry if I made you worry when I was talking to Wilhelmina. I don't want you to go away. There's something else here that feels dark. It probably scares you, too."

Some of the eeriness in the girl's presence faded. She swished side to side making her nightgown flare.

Mia tried to take the girl's hand, but her fingers met only cold air. "Do you know if you're trapped here? Is something holding you?"

"I don't wanna go away." The girl's glower returned.

"Oh, sweetie…. I'm not saying that." Mia tried to ignore the part of her that wanted to react with fear to the unnerving presence in front of her. "What I mean is, if something is hurting you, I want to help stop it. My husband was confused why an innocent child would still be here."

"This is my room," said Robin in a matter-of-fact tone. "I like it."

"I like my room, too." *Even after what happened in there, it doesn't seem to bother her.*

"Mommy sometimes bought me dolls or friends for Princess Rabbit, but I had to hide them. Daddy would get mad."

"Aww."

"I know I'm a ghost. Don't be sad. It's fun to run through walls and make mean people scared. I'm not dead... I'm just"—she poked her fingers into her chest a few times—"squishy."

Mia almost laughed. Despite the girl giving off a bizarre mixture of sinister cuteness, like dealing with a seven-year-old holding a loaded gun, she found her adorable.

Robin resumed swishing side to side. "He yelled a lot 'bout money. That's why Mommy always had ta go to the work. Like you go to the work. Sometimes she'd stay all day, not come home 'til after I's in bed. Daddy was mean to both of us."

"I'm sorry he treated you like that." Mia brushed a hand over the girl's insubstantial hair. "My daddy yelled a lot, too. He hit me sometimes, too."

"Like in the face?"

"No... he'd hit me on the backside with his belt, yelling the whole time." Mia shivered at the echo of the voice telling her how disappointed God was with her for being such a disobedient daughter. Eight times out of ten, she hadn't even done anything wrong, merely her father assuming she had and not believing a word out of her mouth. Perhaps he'd merely enjoyed hitting her and Timothy, their screams begging him to stop giving him some kind of power rush.

Robin blinked. "Daddy yelled a lot, but he only hit me once. Mommy an' me was gonna leave. He got angry an' hit me with a hammer. My head went smush." A lone trickle of blood ran from the girl's left nostril.

Mia cringed. "I'm so, so sorry..."

"It didn't hurt, but I got all cold and stuff. Daddy went away. Mommy came home an' screamed a lot. I tried to talk ta her at night, but she didn't talk back... just cried. Every time I talked, she got upset.

Mommy made herself a ghost, too… but she went away." Robin narrowed her eyes. "Some people came to the house. They had a funny TV set like yours. Looks flat like a painting, but it's a TV. The other people who came to the house went away, too. I wanted them to stay, but they went away. I didn't like that."

An alarming amount of dread rolled off the tiny apparition, enough that even Mia leaned back against the wall. "It's okay, Hon. I'm not going to go away. Most people don't know how to be around ghosts. They were probably afraid."

The girl's scowl darkened further. "I didn't like the old people. They always said mean stuff an' called me bad names. I made them go away."

"What did you do?" whispered Mia.

Robin tilted her head forward, a dire stare shadowed under furrowed eyebrows. "I played bad games on them."

Mia blinked. *Adam said that woman almost suffocated in her sleep… is this girl capable of killing people?*

"Are you scared?" Robin relaxed, leaning back and once more looking at her with innocence. "I don't want to scare you. You're nice."

The kid's just acting creepy because it amuses her. She's old enough to be my grandmother. Is she still a child, mentally? Was this entity ever a child? Mia gazed into the girl's huge brown eyes. The spirit's current appearance seemed so far removed from any sense of malice, the thought of her hurting anyone was laughable.

"Is there anything we can do to help you?"

Robin nodded, smiling. "Don't go away."

Adam groaned.

The girl jumped, startled. At the soft thump of his feet on the floor, she ran into her room, disappearing into thin air after three steps. He emerged from the master bedroom, heading toward the bathroom, but stopped and peered back at Mia.

"What are you doing up?"

She bit her lip. "Had to pee."

"The bathroom's over here. You're halfway down the hall."

"I saw her."

Adam turned the rest of his body to face her. "Robin?"

"Yeah. We, talked."

His eyebrows shot up. All traces of sleepiness fled from his eyes. "Actual conversation?"

Mia nodded.

He rushed over and grabbed her hand. "Intelligent responses?"

"Adam, it wasn't like an EVP session. She was literally standing in front of me having a conversation like any normal kid."

"Whoa…"

"Yeah, whoa." She wrapped her arms around him and let her head fall against his shoulder. "Guess I'm psychic after all… or she manifested."

"Could be either. Won't know that until we're in a situation where you can see her and no one else can. If everyone sees her, she's manifesting."

"That happened a few hours ago when she was at the top of the stairs. I saw her; you and Wilhelmina didn't."

"Oh… right. Ignore me. I'm not fully awake."

Mia considered asking the girl to come back out, but didn't want to annoy her. Again, it felt as though she had to cope with a situation as dangerous as an armed child. Her gut said Robin was—or had at one point been—a real child, not a demon or some other malign spirit. But, what effect did spending forty-some-odd years as a ghost have on her? Could her and Adam's lives be in danger?

Nah. Can't be. She's just a child playing creepy. Those people probably only had accidents when she scared them.

"So what did you talk about? What did she say?" He held up a finger. "Hold on. Tell me after I deal with this…"

She headed back to bed while he hit the bathroom. Once he climbed in beside her, she explained what they'd talked about, though she omitted telling him about the subtle sinister air Robin had given off at times. If Adam became too worried, he might start thinking about giving up on the house and she didn't want to leave the girl alone.

"That bastard of a father of hers… It's tempting to start believing in

Heaven and Hell just so I can fantasize about him down there. Is it crazy that I hate someone who died before I was born?"

"Given the circumstances, it's understandable." He kissed her. "We should at least try to go back to sleep."

"Yeah…" She stared again at the ceiling. *Easier said than done.*

18

LATENT ENERGY

FRIDAY, AUGUST 31, 2012

Attempting to fall asleep lasted about ten minutes.

"Do you think Vic is here, too?" asked Mia.

"Mmm?"

"Sorry."

Adam yawned. "No, it's okay. What?"

"I asked if you thought Vic is haunting the house as well... or if he's just a, umm, 'ghost recording."

"An apparition doing the same exact thing in the same way over and over again is most likely a latent impression. But that doesn't mean the spirit isn't around, too."

"I haven't seen him."

"There's a good chance I did... shadow figure in the kitchen. However, it didn't look like anyone in particular, just a distorted human shape. Could have been Vic, a demon, a manifestation of pure evil... an IRS auditor..."

Mia chuckled.

"A few of the EVPs I caught sounded like a man, but I can't make out what's being said or even any tonality to the voice. Most of them aren't much more than demonic growls."

"She's not a demon."

"I didn't say she was."

"You implied it." Mia rolled her head to the right.

He rolled his head to the left, making eye contact. "You inferred the implication… though I admit I left it hanging there."

"I'm sure she's real. Everything you've ever told me about dark entities pretending to be child spirits is based on fleeting glimpses of apparitions or distant giggles, sometimes playful behavior moving objects. Do you think one of those 'pretenders' would stand there for ten minutes and have a complete conversation?"

Adam looked straight up. "That does seem unlikely."

"I hope she stops running away from you eventually."

"That would be nice."

Mia rolled her head straight again, staring up at the ceiling. "In your professional opinion, do you think she's afraid of men because of what happened to her?"

"Either that or… nah. You're probably right."

"What?"

"If you're certain she's a real child, it's just a wild outside thought that'll only freak you out." He squeezed her hand under the covers.

"Out with it." She returned the squeeze.

"Well… it occurred to me that another reason she might be avoiding me is that she's not really a child and is trying to work her way into your head, get you to trust her, feel bad for her, that sort of thing… then… I dunno. *Claim* you or something. Of the people who have lived here before us, only the women wound up being seriously injured."

Mia laughed. "You've been watching too many horror movies."

"Not feeling unusually drawn to her? I mean, you ran out and bought furniture for a ghost."

"No more than I'd be drawn to any other little kid in a horrible situation. Robin just happens to be in our house." She swished her feet back and forth. "Are you still ambivalent about kids?"

"What, like kids in general or are you going *there*?"

She grinned. "What if I was going *there*?"

"If I recall correctly—which I probably don't because this is a discussion about children and the mother is always right no matter what the dad remembers—the 'it can wait indefinitely' thing came from you."

"Yeah, well… remember I only had my parents to go by for what a 'family' would feel like."

"You are not your parents."

"So…"

Adam looked at her. "Are you asking if I want to have a kid?"

"Let's talk theoretically?"

"Hmm. Never really thought about it. It's neither something I looked forward to or particularly wanted to avoid."

Mia rolled onto her side and wrapped herself around his arm. "I'm still trying to cope with knowing a child died in this house. Maybe it's that."

"Could be. It's beyond thrilling my estimation of your gift turned out to be correct. So glad I heard those rumors and picked this house."

"Adam…" Mia pushed herself up to sit and glared at him. "Are you kidding? This is all just some kind of experiment to you? We're talking about a *real* child here. She's not some laboratory test for you to use so you can prove to the world that psychics and ghosts are real."

"Hon I—"

A book tumbled from the shelf over the bed and nailed Adam in the face with a dull *thump*.

"Oof."

Mia looked up at the empty space in the row of books. "I think you made her angry."

He pulled the book away from his face. "That's not what I meant. I'm excited you made contact. I'm glad I chose this house to suggest to you because it's resulted in us making that contact. Robin needed us. Now that we're here, we can help her. If we also wind up gathering enough evidence to change the world's perception of existence after death, great. If not, it doesn't matter." He sat up, rubbing his nose.

"Given a choice between earth-shattering evidence or helping that girl, we help the girl no questions asked."

"You mean that?"

"Absolutely… assuming she's actually a child spirit, I'm totally with you. We help her—but how?"

A hint of motion caught Mia's eye. She stared at a trail of footprint marks appearing and disappearing in the rug on the way out the door. "I'm not sure… other than being here for her. She didn't seem to know what we should do either. But, she's only seven."

"Hmm." Adam lay back down. "If after thinking about it, you still want to try for a baby, I'm open to the idea. Just hope Robin doesn't get jealous."

Mia bit her lip. The ghost had definitely given off a dark streak, though she still preferred to believe the former owners of this house had injured themselves while fleeing in panic from a spirit they didn't even try to—or couldn't—communicate with. The idea that she could potentially become jealous of an infant did worry her. It might be best to talk to the girl about it and gauge her reaction. But, that could wait for now. So far, only one set of owners had lasted more than a year here. If they could survive past the six month mark, Mia felt sure things would work out.

It's not like I'm in any great hurry to have a child.

MIA AWOKE TO A CRUSHING PRESSURE ON HER CHEST, AS HEAVY AS Adam sitting on her.

Coldness seeped into her mouth and nose, invading her throat. Tightness like a band of ice constricted around her neck. She couldn't breathe in or out. Her brain exploded with panic. Mia tried to scream, but couldn't even manage a wheeze. She raked her fingers at her neck while kicking at the sheets.

Spots danced across the darkness overhead. Pure malice saturated the air.

Something wanted to kill her.

She gave up grabbing at her neck and tried to push herself up, but the weight on her chest proved too heavy for her. Mia rammed her heel into Adam's leg hard, over and over, knowing she had mere seconds left before she passed out.

"Ow. Mia, what the hell?"

She slapped at him.

The lights came on.

"Holy shit!" yelled Adam.

Mia vaguely noticed his arms sliding under her back. He grunted, struggling to lift her. Mia grabbed the headboard and pulled, her vision shrinking down to a tunnel... then a pinpoint of light. Adam flopped over sideways, braced his feet against her side, and shoved. The instant she slipped off the bed, the crushing force dissipated. Air rushed into her chest.

She hit the floor flat on her front, dizzy, coughing, and babbling. Her breaths appeared as fog, as cold as a winter's day.

Adam jumped down beside her and cradled her face in one hand. As soon as he saw her breathing again, he pulled her into a shaking embrace. "I'm sorry..."

"Not... your fault," wheezed Mia.

"Coming to this house was."

She coughed, forcing herself to slow her breathing to normal. "It's fine."

"No, it's not fine. You almost died."

Mia leaned against him, rubbing her sore chest. She should've been frightened by such an attack, but it made her more angry than anything. Something didn't want her here, didn't want her reaching out to the child spirit. Whatever inexplicable *need* she had to help that little girl refused to back down. If anything, the dark spirit wanting her dead only made her more determined to do something for that poor kid.

"I'm not going to let it win."

"We have to accept the possibility that what you think is an innocent child, isn't. The same entity you've been seeing and talking to *could* be what just tried to kill you." Adam cradled her face in both hands, staring into her eyes. "I can't lose you. I *won't* lose you over a stupid house."

"It's not over a house. It's a child. She's real, Adam. I know it."

He squeezed her. "I'm worried."

"I know. I am too. But I am going to attempt the impossible."

"What's that?"

Mia sighed up at the bed. "Try and get some sleep."

19

WARNING

SATURDAY, SEPTEMBER 1, 2012

Crouched low, Mia found herself hiding in the washer-dryer nook at the top of the stairs.

The small hands braced on the carpet on either side of tiny bare feet didn't look like hers. To have even fit in here, she would've had to be the size of a six- or seven-year-old. A giddy sense of anticipation gripped her, as though something wonderful would happen at any minute.

I'm dreaming... seeing something Robin did.

A firm *thud*—the front door closing—came from downstairs. Two men spoke in harsh tones, though they didn't seem angry with each other. Their exact words made no sense, speech reduced to raw scraps of emotion and noise like barking mongrels.

Footsteps thundered up the stairs.

The head and shoulders of an unfamiliar, slightly chubby, older man in his sixties appeared, white shirt, black suspenders, wispy grey hair in a sad combover, as if three strands could hide a giant bald spot. He had a dour frown, the sort of man Mia expected would just as soon kick a sleeping cat out of his way than walk around it.

She really didn't like him.

As soon as he set a foot on the upstairs hallway, Mia jumped out of her hiding place, held her hands up like claws, and screamed. The man jumped back, starting to clutch at his chest, but too late realized a grip on the railing was more important. He fell over backward, crashing into a younger man behind him, and the two tumbled to the ground floor.

Mia giggled, then skipped down the hall to her bedroom, full of boring model boats on shelves. A folding table in the middle held several small shelves of tiny jars as well as an unfinished model boat, paintbrushes, and various fine tools. She didn't like any of it, and knocked one of the models to the floor on her way over to where her little bed stuck half out of another shelf of toy boats.

The room vanished to blackness. Darkness lingered for only a few seconds before it receded to forest. She hid in the shadow of a tree at the edge of the yard behind the house, peering around the trunk at the same older man trudging across the grass to a rider lawn mower. Mia grinned with anticipation and stared at the mower.

MIA'S EYES OPENED TO HER BEDROOM CEILING AND A WASH OF warm sunlight.

A small scrap of paper sat on the pillow where Adam's head should've been, and the quite noticeable weight of a child pressed into her from that side. Robin didn't show herself, but the heaviness settled against her chest made her think of Mrs. Vaughan's near suffocation— and her attack last night. Had Vic attacked her as well as Mrs. Vaughan? It might be possible that the child had been 'playing mean games' and didn't really try to harm the woman, but why would Robin try to kill *her*? That made no sense. Especially considering the girl cuddled up beside her. Maybe she'd only tried to seek comfort from Mrs. Vaughan as well? The weight of even a normal seven-year-old sitting on the chest of a woman in her fifties could feel like suffocation, especially when added to the freakiness of ghosts.

Of course, the old people had to have overreacted. Robin wouldn't hurt anyone.

"Morning, kiddo," said Mia in a sleepy half whisper.

"Hi," replied a faint whisper near her right ear.

Mia disregarded the feeling of being a mouse sleeping in the embrace of a cat and reached over with her left arm to grab the paper.

Hon, they sprang weekend office hours on me at the last minute. Twice a month on Saturdays, just until noon. We can hit the yard when I get back.

She groaned internally at the thought. True, she'd suggested they clean up the back yard before the weather became much colder. Whoever had been checking on the house while it remained unoccupied hadn't done a good job with the groundskeeping in back. Loose branches, leaves, grass up to her knees… it would probably take several weekends to push back the encroaching forest into any sense of civilization.

The ghostly child released her grip on Mia's arm and her weight lifted.

Mia got out of bed and made her way to the kitchen by way of the bathroom, still in the long T-shirt she'd slept in. Whenever she wore it —these days only as a night shirt—it reminded her of the six-day weekend caused by a blizzard when she'd been in college. Almost all the girls in the dorm—and Timothy—spent the whole time in pajamas since no one could go anywhere.

Once in the kitchen, she grabbed the box of pancake mix and read the instructions again. A cold draft hovered close behind her, though it lacked the otherworldly gloom she'd almost become accustomed to feeling here, perhaps due to the kitchen being bright. It felt strange that a ghost would be active during the day, especially on such a sunny, pleasant Saturday morning. She could almost pretend that a horrible tragedy hadn't happened in the house.

The sense of a small child hovering close beside her persisted the whole time she re-taught herself how to make pancakes. Excited energy in the air grew with each passing minute she cooked a reasonable portion for herself, figuring Robin had no ability to consume actual food and would enjoy them vicariously. She carried the plate to the table, snagged the syrup, and sat.

A chill brushed across the back of her neck in the shape of a small icy hand caressing her.

About a third of the pancakes—and twelve minutes—disappeared in an instant.

Mia jumped, startled. The flavor of maple syrup lurked in her mouth, a fork clutched in her fist the way a small child might hold one. A soft scrape accompanied the nearest chair on the right scooting an inch back from the table. Strong contentment radiated from it.

She... possessed me? The happiness settled in the chair beside her somewhat assuaged her indignation at the child taking her over without even asking. Mia fidgeted, unsure how to feel. The ease with which it happened unnerved her, but perhaps she had already agreed to let her do it. A promise for pancakes had been made, and really, a ghost didn't have any other way to experience food.

With a sigh, she decided to let it go, though couldn't quite avoid worrying what might happen if she upset Robin. As sorry as she felt for what happened to her, forty plus years as a spirit could very well have changed her from an innocent child into an angry, wrathful specter. As Adam would say, the id of a young child demanding instant gratification combined with the as-yet-unknown ability to cause havoc that the living had no way to stop made for a dangerous combination.

Mia resumed eating her breakfast, not that she remembered eating the first third. Evidently, Robin had become 'full' after a portion that would likely have been enough for a girl her size. Her anxiety waned with each mouthful, and the hope that a sugary treat might have offered some comfort to a child who'd endured the unspeakable.

She said it didn't hurt... does that mean she basically stayed awake the whole time? Did her ghost watch what he did? An unsettling thought hit her: Robin might have possessed her mother as easily as she'd jumped into Mia. *No. That doesn't feel right. That woman was destroyed emotionally... and Adam thinks ghosts gather strength the longer they exist. No wonder the first person to live here after them lasted the longest. The spirits hadn't gathered enough strength to be noticed then. Robin couldn't have affected her mother. She wouldn't have had the strength to do that so soon after her death.*

As eerie as the spirit could seem at times, Mia found herself inclined to think of her as an innocent in need of love and protection. Whatever she might've done to the prior occupants of this house, she probably had a good reason for it. If an old man spent days shouting at her, calling her names, and screaming about God, Mia would've thrown him down the stairs, too. A dark little smile formed on her lips, daydreaming about her father taking the same fall.

"Did you like your pancakes?" asked Mia glancing at the empty chair.

"Yes, thank you," replied a whispery, childish voice. "They're my favorite."

MIA PERCHED ON A DINING ROOM CHAIR, FEET TUCKED UNDER her, chin on her hand, studying the layout of a checkers game. Steam wafted from the coffee mug next to her and the syrupy-sweet scent of pancakes still hung in the air.

A red checker slid by itself into the next square.

"Hmm…" Mia eyed a few pieces she considered moving, but before she could decide on one, the doorbell rang. "Oh, drat. I'll be right back."

She got up, still in the shirt she'd slept in, and answered the door.

Wilhelmina stood on the porch, smiling at her.

"Oh, hi. Come on in… sorry if I'm not really dressed. Having a lazy morning."

"I don't mind if you don't." Wilhelmina entered, closing the door behind her. She removed her coat and draped it over the sofa arm. "How have things been?"

"Fine. We just had breakfast." Mia debated going upstairs to put on pants, but the shirt covered plenty, and Wilhelmina gave off something of a maternal vibe that put her at ease. She sat again at the table and resumed staring at the board. "Would you like some coffee or something?"

"If it's not too much trouble, coffee would be delightful." Wilhelmina entered the dining room and took a seat.

Mia approached the table and made a move. Seconds later, another red checker moved on its own.

Wilhelmina smiled knowingly. "The girl is here, isn't she?"

"Yes." Mia smiled. "She doesn't seem afraid of you."

"Good morning, Robin."

"Hi," whispered a small voice, though the woman didn't react to it.

"She says hi."

"Can you see her?"

Mia shook her head. "Not at the moment. Is it because it's daytime?"

"It might be. I'm hardly an expert on ghosts, but I believe that appearing to the living takes a significant amount of energy."

"You're a lot closer to being an expert than I am." Mia headed into the kitchen and poured a cup of coffee for her guest.

"Adam seems to know his stuff as well. From what I understand, the amount of effort it takes a spirit to show themselves to a medium such as yourself is significantly less than what it takes to appear to ordinary people. Even you can't simply *see* them unless they want to be seen."

Mia returned to the dining room with the coffee, the sugar dispenser, and a small carton of creamer.

"Thank you, dear."

"No problem." After returning the creamer to the fridge, Mia took her seat, pushed another red checker forward one square, and took a long sip from her mug. "Coffee is the elixir of the gods."

"I've looked over a few things, and I think there should be a way to address the darkness here. It is likely originating from a different spirit. Have you been to the basement or attic yet?"

"No." Mia shook her head, chuckled, and explained about how both places in her childhood home had terrified her. "Guess that left a mark."

"You shouldn't go down there," said a whispery voice from the empty chair.

Wilhelmina shifted her eyes in that direction.

"Did you hear her?" asked Mia.

"I heard something... a rasp or some such."

"Robin just told me not to go to the basement." She paused, watching a red checker jump over two of hers, which simultaneously slid off the board into the dead pile. "Is he down there, sweetie?"

"It's bad down there." Robin's voice came through clear, like an ordinary—albeit invisible—child sitting at the table.

Wilhelmina gasped, covering her mouth with one hand. "By the Goddess... I heard her. She sounds just like I remember."

"This house is infused with sadness." Mia gazed into her mug.

"That's putting things mildly," said Wilhelmina.

A moment of silence passed.

"She knows more than she's telling you," whispered Robin.

Mia glanced over at Wilhelmina. "What?"

"Hmm?"

"Are you leaving something out?"

Wilhelmina sent a sly smile at the empty chair before nodding at Mia. "Nothing I thought particularly relevant to the here and now."

"But...?" Mia swirled coffee around her mug.

"If you recall, the other day I mentioned my involvement with old traditions."

"She's a witch," whispered Robin. "She does magic."

Mia almost choked on a mouthful of coffee. "Magic?"

"Oh, don't seem so shocked, dear." Wilhelmina patted her on the hand. "Most people consider psychics to be nonsense."

"Willa did magic on Daddy," said Robin in a half-whisper. "Bad magic."

Mia stared at the empty chair. "Did you do something to Vic?"

"Oh, that." The older woman chuckled. "Perhaps. At the time it all happened, I was only thirteen, and I'd just recently begun dabbling in mysticism." She looked at the chair. "I'd been so horrified and angry at what he did to you that I tried to hex him."

"Did the magic make Mommy shoot him?" asked Robin.

Wilhelmina squinted, leaning forward like a much older person who'd lost her hearing.

"She wanted to know if your spell might've caused Evelyn to shoot him."

"Hmm." Wilhelmina sipped coffee, then leaned back in her seat. "Bear in mind that I had been quite young and inexperienced at the time. The energy of the spell I'd cast at him was far darker than anything I'd be inclined to touch nowadays, but as a teenager, I lacked the wisdom of age and lashed out with my emotions. By nature, the spell would have turned fate against him. Magic isn't like you see in the movies. No fireballs or meteors falling out of the air. If it worked, it would have caused a downturn of luck. Hit by a car, a terminal illness, a bystander shot by accident during a robbery... and so on. Though, considering he had already been arrested for murder, my spell—if it did anything at all—might have simply twisted the gears of fate so he got the death penalty."

"So it *could* have played some part in what Evelyn did?"

Wilhelmina mulled for a moment. "In truth, I don't think I performed the invocation correctly. These sorts of spells almost always have a degree of blowback on the person who cast them. Nothing noticeable happened to me, so it's likely I didn't do it right. A young girl like I was back then doesn't jump straight to advanced hexes and get them right on the first try. However, if we consider that I might've done something, I think it would have merely made it easier for Evelyn to do what she already desired to do."

"Like the police turning a blind eye until she'd shot him?"

"Exactly. You see, I had targeted the spell on Vic. It would not have affected someone else's mind or fate. I believe she resolved to kill him. Perhaps what I did helped her on that path, but I still don't think I had the power at the time to make a difference."

Mia nodded. "So do you think your magic can help here?"

"We're still not entirely sure what 'help' really is."

"Robin," asked Mia. "Is your daddy still in the house? Do you want us to try and make him go away?"

"I'm not allowed to talk about him... or bad stuff will happen," whispered Robin.

Mia reached past the checker board, trying to grasp a hand she couldn't touch, overcome with the need to hold the girl and tell her everything would be okay.

"What did she say?" asked Wilhelmina.

"Only that she can't talk about him. I think he *is* still here, maybe even listening to us." She looked back at the chair. "Robin, if there's a way for Wilhelmina to make him go away, would you want her to try?"

The girl faded into view, kneeling in the chair while staring at Mia with a pleading, frightened expression. Her grungy nightgown sorely needed a wash, a handprint in maple syrup on the chest that hadn't been there before. "I'm scared. If he goes away, I'll go away, too... and I don't wanna."

Wilhelmina didn't react at all to the child fading into view.

"Why would you have to go away? I don't want you to go away either." Mia did her best to hold the tiny, immaterial hand beside the checkers board. The longer she stared into the girl's sorrowful eyes, the more she wanted only to protect her from all that pain.

Robin looked past Mia. "The bad man is here."

The doorbell rang.

Mia glanced over her shoulder at a trace of khaki pants in the narrow strip of window beside the front door. "Ugh. That man again? This is getting out of hand."

"He's going to stand there ringing the bell for at least a half hour," said Wilhelmina. "You've got three choices: we deal with incessant doorbell, you send him on his way, or call Nate."

"Nate?" asked Mia.

"Nate Ross. He's Spring Falls' only cop. I think he's technically a sheriff, but he's all we got after the old man retired. Oh, wait, I think there's a new deputy now. A woman."

Mia slid from her chair and stood. She considered running upstairs for pants, but maybe having only a long T-shirt on would make Weston uncomfortable enough to leave—assuming she could avoid blushing. *I've worn shorter dresses in public.* "How did they handle the murder if the town only had one cop?"

"Nate wasn't even born then. Syracuse PD took it over. The former sheriff... Kline I think his name was, helped out but spent more time complaining that the 'city cops' ignored him."

Mia padded across the living room. A burst of late summer wind hit her as she opened the door, fluttering her hair back. Weston Parker waited on the porch, clutching a small book.

"Mrs. Gartner, sorry for disturbing you on a Saturday morning. I would be remiss if I didn't warn you that your soul is in peril the more you associate with evil. You know, tomorrow is Sunday, and we have services at nine."

She peered back at Robin watching her across the checkers board. That he called an innocent child 'evil' infuriated her. Mia scowled at him. "How can you call a little kid evil?"

"I was referring to your decision to allow a devil-worshipper into your house."

Wilhelmina laughed.

Weston leaned closer, lowering his voice. "I'm highly concerned for the sanctity of your soul considering what happened in this house. Nothing good will come of trafficking with those who have given their souls to the Devil."

"Don't waste your breath," said Wilhelmina, not bothering to get up. "I've been trying to convince him for years that I think his devil is a deliberate perversion of the pagan figures, Pan and Cernunnos, and don't worship it."

Mia paused before biting his head off. *He isn't my father.* "It's a little unnerving to think that you're either following her around or watching my house."

"I can't let this house take ano—" An old set of wind chimes leapt off their hook overhead and flew at Weston. "Gah!" He ducked, raising his arms to guard his face.

The chimes sailed through the spot where his head had been a second earlier, striking the ground at least thirty feet away in the grass with a disharmonic crash, breaking mostly apart from the force of impact. Mia gawked at the mess of corroded brass tubes.

Weston lowered his arms, his cheeks pale, mouth open. Lost for words, he kept glancing back and forth between her, the house, and where the chimes landed.

"I get that you mean well, but you're not helping." Mia took a step back into the house. "All that shouting you did with the Vaughans didn't change anything. If, for whatever reason, we decide we need your assistance, we will ask for it."

He closed his mouth, eyed the empty hook in the porch roof, and scurried off to his Jeep.

"I don't think he expected that." Mia eased the door closed. "I wonder if that's the first time he witnessed something he couldn't explain."

"I'm sure he's witnessed quite a bit." Wilhelmina set her mug down.

Mia walked back to the dining room. "Of course, but that look on his face. Everything before, he'd probably been able to rationalize away. Mr. Vaughan falling down the stairs for example. Anyone watching that couldn't say with perfect certainty that something unusual happened. Those wind chimes flew *sideways*, hard... like a tornado got them."

Robin jumped off the chair. Sniffling, she ran up to stand beside Mia, hiding behind her as if afraid of someone at the front door. The girl attempted to grab Mia's hand, but her fingers caught no purchase. Childish fright darkened to frustration.

"Shh. He's gone, now." Mia tried to pat her on the head.

"I don't like that man," said Robin in an ominous tone while glaring at the front of the house "He's mean."

"We won't let him hurt you." Mia smiled at her.

Robin again attempted to grab her in a hug, but her arms whiffed right through without contact. The child grew terrifyingly angry for a few seconds, blood seeping from her nose and mouth as she futilely attempted to cling—but she burst into tears and raced off up the stairs, sobbing. Seconds later, a door slammed overhead.

Wilhelmina jumped and looked at the ceiling. "What just happened?"

"She's upset... but not with us."

20

DOLLS

SATURDAY, SEPTEMBER 1, 2012

Old brass tubes clattered from Mia's effort to detangle the wind chimes.

Robin hadn't shown herself or responded to any attempt to console her. Not wanting to antagonize the child, Mia decided to enjoy the weather outside. She sat in a white wicker chair on the porch, a leftover from the previous owners. Wilhelmina occupied the chair to her right, still smiling from watching Weston nearly soil himself.

They discussed the pastor apparently either stalking them or spying on the house, and whether or not he might become more of a problem than a simple nuisance. According to Wilhelmina, he'd grown up in Spring Falls and had been around twenty at the time of the child's murder. From the sound of it, ever since he'd become pastor in 1974, he'd gotten into the habit of personally welcoming anyone new to the area and trying to bring them into his flock. She didn't think he had any truly sinister motivation beyond the simple belief that three types of people existed: God-fearing Christians, those who needed to become God-fearing Christians, and devil worshippers.

Wilhelmina shared a few stories about his reaction to the others in her 'coven' deciding against going to his church. He'd nearly come unglued when Lisa Donovan stopped attending and began associating with the 'witches.' At the time, she'd been seventeen or so, and Weston had managed to turn the girl's parents against her to the point they took her to a psychologist.

"Clearly, only someone with mental problems could *possibly* choose a path other than his," said Mia.

"Yes, basically, that's how he felt."

"Poor kid."

"She's not so much a kid anymore. Linda's about your age now."

Mia held up the wind chimes. Alas, her skills at restoring old and damaged paintings didn't translate well to this project. At least, not without tools and supplies she lacked. She did, however, manage to get them into a state where they'd work again, despite looking battered.

Adam pulled into the driveway and parked beside the Tahoe. He hurried up the walkpath to the porch, shaking his head.

"You look frustrated," said Mia.

"Just spent the past hour and a half working with a student. I'm half tempted to think he was messing with me since I can't imagine anyone being *that* dense. He couldn't have failed to understand the most basic of concepts if he *tried* to misinterpret everything on purpose."

"Ahh, then our mornings were similar," said Wilhelmina.

Adam quirked an eyebrow at her.

"Weston was here again." Mia sighed, then filled him in on the flying wind chimes while handing them over.

"Wow…" Adam examined the chimes. "Do you think Robin threw them?"

"Hard to say. It might have been Vic." Mia smoothed her hands down her jeans. "I definitely got the sense she is not fond of him, though. The man's fairly spry for being in his sixties. If he hadn't ducked, they would've smacked him straight in the face and probably knocked him out."

"That's impressive…" He stood on tiptoe to hang them again.

"She's upset I can't hold her."

"Aww." He put an arm around Mia. "I wish there was something we could do to make her feel better."

"Just being here should help with that." Wilhelmina tapped her foot.

"Have you had lunch yet?" Adam opened the front door. "Why don't we continue talking over sandwiches?"

They relocated to the kitchen, the women sitting at the table while Adam ferried an assortment of cold cuts, cheese, lettuce, and tomatoes from the fridge to the table. Everyone assembled sandwiches for themselves.

"Now that I think about it…" Adam slathered mustard on a slice of rye. "I remember reading something a while ago about a civilization—I want to say somewhere in Mexico or Central America—that maintained a practice of crafting special dolls to act as repositories for the souls of their departed ancestors. They believed the dolls allowed them to remain present."

"That does sound somewhat familiar." Wilhelmina dusted her turkey with an astonishing amount of black pepper. "You're thinking the girl might wish to inhabit such a doll as a means for physical contact? If I remember correctly, those vessels would've likely trapped the spirit."

"No, that would be cruel." Mia shook her head.

"Have you considered channeling her spirit?" Wilhelmina capped her sandwich with a second piece of bread and sliced it in half. "That might be worth looking into."

Mia smiled. "I think I already did that this morning…" She explained her pancake breakfast.

"Hmm. For that to address her apparent desire to be picked up, you'd either need to channel her while Adam held you, or she'd have to inhabit someone else that you embrace."

Maybe she wouldn't be jealous of a baby after all… Mia squirmed at the idea any future child she had might grow up having to deal with frequent possession by a spirit. Would Robin ask or just leap in as she had done for breakfast? Or might she dote over a baby like an older sibling? If she became jealous and the wind chimes hadn't been Vic's doing... enough force to hurl them so far away from the house could do serious harm to an infant.

Mia hated herself for worrying Robin could harm a baby. *What's wrong with me? She's still a child herself. A child who had a violent death... she wouldn't hurt another innocent.*

The words 'wind chimes' in Adam's voice pulled Mia back from her mental wanderings.

"... at Weston, who knows what might happen if she became really upset. You told me that several people who previously lived here suffered injuries."

"That's true." Wilhelmina dabbed mayo from her chin. "Though, we don't know for sure if the aggression came from her. It could be Vic."

"It can't be her," said Mia. "She's a frightened, lonely child. Robin doesn't want to hurt anyone."

Adam made thinking faces while chewing, then took a sip of water. "The people who lived here before us were probably normal."

"What's that supposed to mean?" asked Mia with a hint of a smile.

"That means they quite likely weren't psychic and didn't expect a ghost or ghosts to be here and, consequently, didn't react well when Robin tried to get their attention." Adam set his sandwich down. "Picture this: a lonely child finally has people around after years of rattling around an empty house. So, what's she going to do? Try to get their attention, play, make contact. The average person is going to freak out."

"Quite." Wilhelmina nodded. "George O'Ryan left the house in the middle of the night after only a month. The Vaughans... well, they went to war with her."

"And lost," said Mia, grinning.

Adam glanced at her, one eyebrow up.

"Did something happen with Mr. Vaughan and a lawn mower?" Mia took a bite of her sandwich.

Mouth full, Wilhelmina made a *mmm* noise along with a nod.

"What?" Adam glanced at her, then peered at Mia. "And why do you seem so happy at them being hurt?"

"They were cruel to her." Mia plucked a stray bit of tomato from her plate and tossed it in her mouth.

"Mr. Vaughan had an accident with his tractor mower. He somehow managed to put it in the creek behind the house. Rolled the thing over and got stuck there for a few hours until his wife found him."

"Ouch," said Adam. "Was he hurt?"

"Sprained or broken ankle I think... nothing too serious." Wilhelmina waved around in a blasé manner. "I didn't much speak with them. Weston had them convinced I worked for the devil, you know."

"All we've seen so far of Vic is a repeating latent image." Adam glanced at the small foyer by the back door with shelves and a coat rack. "Drops a giant toolbox in there, then bee-lines to the stairs. We think it's an imprint from the night of the murder. If Vic is merely a repeating image, then that could mean Robin is strong enough to harm the living."

"You saw the shadow figure." Mia gestured over her shoulder, not wanting to look at the basement door.

"Which we don't know is definitely Vic. It had no features. It could be anyone—or any*thing*."

"Hon, she's a kid. She wouldn't try to hurt people." Mia scowled at nothing in particular. The vindictive glee she'd felt in that dream while watching the man fall down the stairs and again while he approached the mower needled at her doubts. She refused to accept that. What choice did Robin have? The man had invited Weston over and they spent hours screaming horrible things at her. The girl couldn't leave, or even tell them to stop. Her only want had been not to be alone, and they treated her like something evil. All her brother Timothy wanted was to be treated like a human being, and her father had vilified him as a devil spawn. *Good for that old bastard he fell down the stairs.*

Adam picked up on her defensiveness, his expression shifting to concern. "Hon, are you okay?"

"Yeah. I'm just upset at the idea of a kid being murdered in her bedroom by her father. It's not fair. She didn't hurt those people... on purpose. She's only a child."

"Yes, a child who suffered a cruel, brutal death. Just saying, you should be careful. Even a month ago, you had no interest in children. Now, it almost feels like you consider her *your* kid." He looked at Wilhelmina. "Could Evelyn still be here? Is she affecting Mia?"

"I'm not sure. Your wife is the psychic. I merely cast spells, talk to old gods, and according to Weston, dance around fires at night while having carnal relations with Satan." Wilhelmina appeared to be fighting the urge to laugh.

Adam chuckled.

"I don't think it's Evelyn. I've picked up scraps of her, but they feel like more imprints. Basically like I'm getting small peeks into the past for seconds at a time."

"Hmm. I should probably look around the basement or the attic tonight for EVPs." Adam took a big bite of his sandwich.

"Not yet… we shouldn't mess with the basement." Mia bit her lip. "It could be bad."

"How so?" mumbled Adam around a mouthful.

"I don't know exactly."

Wilhelmina gestured at her. "The girl said *you* shouldn't go to the basement. It might not mean he can't."

"Is there something horrible down there? He didn't like keep her remains here or something?" Mia shuddered.

"No. He left her on the floor where he killed her for Evelyn to find. The authorities collected the poor girl's remains. No one ever suspected he had killed anyone else," said Wilhelmina.

"Based on what I know of the events of September 1970, I think it would be unlikely for Vic Kurtis to have killed anyone else. His motivation wasn't seeking pleasure from the act of murder, but to specifically hurt his wife by destroying the person she loved the most. It may have even been jealousy."

"Vic was jealous of Robin?" asked Mia.

"It's possible." Adam nodded. "Men like him can lash out at anyone or anything they think competes with them for their woman's affection or time. That might have been what ultimately gave him the ability to kill his own daughter as an attack on the wife. He believed Evelyn chose Robin instead of him and that enraged him."

Mia looked down. "Should have left that night."

"So why would Robin not want us in the basement?" Adam picked at his eyebrow.

"Maybe Vic is down there and for whatever reason doesn't know anyone's moved into the house yet since we haven't been down there." Mia shrugged.

"Joe and I went down there the day we arrived for a cursory inspection. Nothing stood out as unusual or even creepy. As basements go, it's pretty welcoming." Adam grinned. "Not like a finished basement, but normal as far as I could tell."

"I still don't want to go down there."

He nodded. "That is most likely your parents' house talking."

"No, it's Robin warning me."

Mia swept her toes back and forth across the floor. He had a point about her inexplicably strong desire to protect Robin. It didn't strike her as external, not like the girl's mother had influenced her. This whole situation made her feel as though she'd gone back home, putting herself between her parents and her little brother. Timothy hadn't asked to be gay any more than Robin asked to become a ghost. For the Vaughans to be cruel to her after everything she'd gone through went beyond unfair. Mia clenched her right fist in her lap, glaring at the half-sandwich in her other hand. If Robin—and not Vic—had been responsible for their attacks, she'd give her a back pat and say 'good girl.'

Granted, that would also mean a being with the temperament of a child had the power to hurt the living. It might not take much to sway such a volatile temper against anyone, even Mia... but she couldn't let that worry her. All kids had temper tantrums. The girl probably didn't understand what effect she could have when lashing out, and didn't mean serious harm.

Mia smiled to herself. Whatever it took, she'd protect that poor little girl.

21

CLOSER

SATURDAY, SEPTEMBER 1, 2012

Wilhelmina roamed the house performing a sage scrub.

Mia had initially worried about the cleansing ritual possibly having an effect on Robin, but upon assurances that the minor invocation would only reduce negative energies, she agreed to it. Neither Robin nor Vic made any noticeable objection, though the smoke detector in the upstairs hall didn't appreciate the burning sage. After making a full circuit of both floors, Wilhelmina went with Adam into the basement while Mia waited in the kitchen.

They both emerged a few minutes later, unscathed. Wilhelmina left soon after, bidding them contact her if anything else happened. Yardwork consumed the rest of the daylight hours, mostly collecting branches, removing weeds, and taming knee-high grass. Every so often, Mia looked back at the house, certain someone—most likely Robin—watched her.

Hours of work later, daylight weakened. Mia and Adam hauled bags of grass clippings around to the side of the house where they'd wait until Wednesday pickup. Rock-paper-scissors said Mia would cook dinner. Adam set up shop in the dining room and proceeded to grade tests or essays from his students.

A cold spot formed beside her while she chopped onions and garlic.

"Hi, sweetie," said Mia. "I'm glad you're okay. Wilhelmina's sage didn't bother you, did it?"

"No," replied a faint whisper. Small fingers clutched at the fabric of her shirt.

Mia sighed, relieved. "Good. I was worried."

She rambled along as if talking to a normal child all the while she cooked up a batch of chicken and mushrooms over pasta. Robin—or at least the cold spot—remained by her side. She figured the girl kept herself invisible out of fear. The child had yet to appear while Adam was anywhere nearby. Taking a chance, Mia changed the topic of her random conversation to him, telling the girl about when they first met. He'd been a senior doing volunteer work, delivering meals to elderly people living around the campus during her second year of university.

"I knew right away he was kind," whispered Mia. "More than simply bringing food to old people. Something about him… Now that I think about it, maybe it had been a psychic read."

A small giggle came from behind her.

That's better. She sounds like a normal little girl. Mia smiled. "I'm so glad we found this house, and you."

"You won't go away?" asked Robin, a smidge louder than a whisper.

"Nope. Those other people were silly."

"You want to stay with me?"

"Yes." Mia patted the top of the cold spot. "Of course."

She portioned out two plates and carried them to the dining room.

Adam shoved his paperwork aside, grinning. "Ooh. That smells wonderful."

"It's just chicken, mushrooms, and cream-of-mushroom soup over noodles. Nothing fancy."

"Being simple doesn't mean it can't be good." He ate a few forkfuls, overacting how much he enjoyed it.

"Those noises you're making make me want to check under the table for a mistress."

Adam laughed into coughing. "Seriously, though. It's good. So, I'm thinking of checking out the basement now that it's dark. See if I can get some EVPs."

Small fingers dug into Mia's side.

"That's probably not a great idea. Robin's not saying don't, but she's scared."

"Hmm. Perhaps he is down there and disturbing him could cause her problems. All right. I'll hold off."

Mia relaxed, not having realized she'd grown tense. Over the rest of dinner, they discussed what Wilhelmina or they could possibly do to help Robin. The child didn't appear distressed at haunting the place, only being alone. Thus far, nothing had happened to explain what chased the prior owners away... beyond them overreacting to a benign spirit. Then again, the bathmat flying out from under her and Adam being so scared he blacked out on his run from the kitchen to the front yard would probably have sent most ordinary people running for the hills. But Mia wouldn't give up on Robin so easily. It no doubt helped that being psychic allowed her to see and talk to the child relatively normally. Even innocent requests for help would be terrifying otherwise.

Still, something unsettled her. The first moment she'd ever laid eyes on the house, she got a bad feeling. It hadn't been so strong she wanted to run away and never look back, so she hadn't raised any objections to Adam's enthusiasm to buy the place. Of course, the price helped convince her to set aside that bit of worry, as did a sense of belonging here. The lingering question remained as to what caused her initial trepidation. It had to be Vic, or perhaps she had been sensitive to the dark emotional energy such a horrible crime could leave in a place. The walls had also likely soaked up fear and panic from the prior occupants who couldn't handle Robin trying to say hello.

Who better to move into a haunted house than a psychic and a wannabe paranormal researcher? She eyed Adam across the table, somewhat surprised he hadn't yet tried to ask Robin to demonstrate something he could catch on video. Either making footprints in more dust, moving objects, or EVPs. Perhaps after hearing her history, and seeing her active interactions with Mia, he didn't want to think of her as a test subject.

After dinner, Adam got up to load the dishwasher and planned to finish grading his papers. Mia, tired of feeling funky from all the yardwork, went upstairs. She collected a clean shirt and sweat shorts from the bedroom, then headed to the bathroom.

Soon, she lay in a tub of milky-purple water, basking in the fragrance of a lavender bath bomb. The warm water drew the soreness from her arms and relaxed the muscles in her legs. Whoever had let the yard get so out of control needed a swift slap upside the head. They'd kept the front and sides neat, but anything that couldn't be seen from the road had been left to sit.

Amazing we didn't find a nest of snakes or wasps.

She reclined in the awesomeness of the bath, teetering on the edge of sleep.

A sudden odd feeling made her open her eyes and look around. All the hairs on her arms stood up in response to the sinister vibe in the air. Mia tried to open her 'psychic eyes' to find the presence she felt certain stood in the room with her. The corner by the door had nothing but shadows, and the cabinet along the wall to her right appeared normal.

Mia tilted her head up and back, peering at the sink in the corner behind the tub. An instant after she looked, her hair dryer leapt into the air straight toward the bathwater. She shrieked, thrusting her arms up at the flying instrument of death, deflecting it off to the side.

The dryer hit the bathmat with a soft *thump* at the maximum extension of its cord, which dragged it back toward the sink. Heart racing, Mia leapt out of the tub and stood there dripping, staring in horror at the innocent device that nearly took her life.

"Vic, you motherf—" She clenched her fists, glaring around.

Tickling droplets ran down her body. Her gaze focused on the outlet at the end of the hair dryer's cord. It had a little red breaker button. In theory, it would've cut the circuit the instant a short happened.

But an eerie feeling told her it wouldn't have worked.

She lunged forward and unplugged the cord, then kicked the hair dryer into the corner by the toilet.

"Ow..." Mia stood on one foot and grabbed her toes. "Okay, that was dumb."

Taking on a malevolent spirit while soaking wet and naked didn't sound like the best idea in the world. She dried herself off, opting to wrap her hair in a towel rather than use the machine. After letting the tub drain, she crept to the door, afraid to shut off the light. Mia rested her head against the door and stood there a while listening to her heartbeat, still thrumming well beyond normal.

Maybe I was wrong. Is Evelyn still here and she's pissed at me? I've been worried that Robin would get jealous if I had a baby, but I never even thought her mother would... wait. If her mother still haunted this house, Robin wouldn't be lonely. She—they—might not even make contact. The ghosts at my parents' house kept to themselves. Robin tried to get our attention within hours.

She gripped the doorknob and turned, dreading what she might see in the hallway. Though nothing appeared wrong, she couldn't shake a sense of dread, even stronger than what she caught upon seeing the house the first time.

"Is this what scared everyone off?"

Mia stepped out of the steamy lavender-scented bathroom, toes squishing into the cool rug in the hall. Ill energy saturated the upstairs. *Someone's pissed.* She shuddered. If she'd fallen asleep, or not looked up at the exact moment she did, she'd likely be dead. If not Evelyn being possessive of another woman trying to 'steal' her daughter, it had to be Vic. But that, too, didn't line up with Adam's psychological assessment of the man.

He hadn't been angry with Robin specifically. In fact, the man barely viewed her as a person... simply an object to be taken away from his wife to hurt the woman. That the child had to die in the process most likely didn't register to him. His lack of real effort to avoid the police, simply going to one of his known hangouts and drinking until they came for him, said he'd given up. If he had no particular animosity toward the girl, why would he care if Mia tried to make her happy?

Ghosts change, said Adam in her memory. *They're no longer the people they'd been in life. There are things on the other side, energies, secrets, who knows... seeing that all affects a mind.*

True, Vic may have succumbed to his anger, becoming less of a human sentience and morphing into something akin to an elemental force of rage. In that case, it wouldn't matter as much that she tried to comfort the girl. Merely being in this house could be enough to incur his wrath.

She trembled, feeling much the same as she did whenever she'd been forced to go into the basement back home. When she'd been fourteen, her father figured out being down there scared her witless and thought sending her into the basement on an errand and locking the door behind her might scare her into 'reopening her heart to God.' Mia had purposefully blocked out much of her memory of that day, but did remember slamming herself into the door at the top of the stairs over and over, as panicky as if a pack of lions roamed loose in the darkness below waiting to devour her at any moment.

Her screaming had evidently become so extreme and incoherent that her mother demanded he open the door—one of three times she could ever recall the woman defying him. Mia had collapsed on the kitchen floor and cried like a three-year-old after they let her out of the basement. She had always been fearful of her father, but after that, she avoided him as much as possible... until she had to get in his face to keep him away from Timothy.

Mia peered into Robin's bedroom, but found no sign of her.

The dread in the upstairs hall didn't drive her to the point of trying to scratch down a wooden door with her fingernails. It had a darker quality that made the basement feel like horror movie fear: lots of screaming, but deep inside, she knew nothing could really hurt her. The mood surrounding her didn't make her want to shriek, cover her eyes, or crawl under something to hide... more as though something wanted her to die.

She cautiously approached the top of the stairs, eyeing the floor for any objects she might trip over—or that might rush into her path at the last possible moment. Nothing appeared dangerous, so she gripped the railing in both hands and made her way down to the living room.

"Adam?"

Only the echo of her voice replied.

She padded around the couch and peered into the empty dining room. Curious, she advanced down the hall to the kitchen, and stopped short at all four burners glowing bright, no pots on them.

"What on Earth?" She rushed over and shut them off, then stood there watching the ceramic cook top dim to plain black. "Who turned on the stove?"

Light from the back porch drew her to the window. Adam sat out on the small deck, still grading papers while enjoying fresh air. He didn't appear aware the stove had been on, nor likely the cause of it.

Did this place originally have a gas range? Does Vic still see that stove as gas... is he trying to kill us both?

"Robin? Are you here?" Mia shied away from the basement door, backing into the counter. "Hey, sweetie? Where are you?"

The girl appeared abruptly, halfway between Mia and the doorway to the living room, eyebrows knit in a flat line, a perturbed scowl on her little face.

"Gah!" Mia jumped, staring at her.

Robin walked closer, giving off a sinister aura that pushed Mia back step for step.

Oh, shit... is she *trying to kill me?*

"Honey? What's wrong? What did I do? Why are you mad at me?"

The child stopped walking. "You're not turning into a ghost!"

"W-what?"

Robin's anger faded. She looked down at her bare feet like a child who'd been told to go to bed early. "If you're a ghost, too, you could hold me... we could be closer."

Anger, heartbreak, and confusion collided, leaving Mia blank. "Umm... That's not a nice thing to do, Robin. What your father did to you is about the worst thing imaginable. He betrayed your trust.

Hurting people is *not* the right way to do anything. I expected better from you."

Robin ground her toe into the floor.

Good grief. Am I really scolding a ghost?

"Sweetie," said Mia in a softer, non-accusatory tone, "I understand why you did it, but I need to be able to trust that you won't do anything like that again."

Robin kept staring at the floor, lower lip thrust forward in a pouty expression.

"I'm happy to be here for you, and I'll do everything I can to make sure you're safe and not lonely… but if you keep trying to kill us, we'll have no choice but to leave."

"No!" Robin looked up, tears brimming at the corners of her frightened eyes. "Please don't go away." She clamped onto Mia in a hug that felt as though she leaned against a cold metal wall. "I promise I won't do anything bad."

The pervasive sense of dread hanging over the house dissipated. Mia looked up at the ceiling, more than a little unnerved that she no longer felt as though her life was in imminent danger as soon as the child changed her mind about making her a ghost, too. *I should get the hell out of here. This kid is… maybe not quite a child anymore. It's foolish to… no. She's just a kid. An adult couldn't handle being murdered, and I'm expecting a seven-year-old to take it in stride?* Despite the alarm bells ringing in her mind, Mia lowered herself to sit on the floor and wrapped her arms around the spectral figure. The pressure of the child's embrace shifted to her chest, making it difficult to breathe. Tiny fingers stabbed into her back like icicles.

Those people couldn't see and talk to her like I can. We can make this work.

Robin sniffled. "I'm sorry. Please don't be mad at me."

"Did you make that woman fall down the stairs?"

"She was gonna go away and abandon me. I wanted her to stay."

"As a ghost…"

Robin shrugged. "I didn't want to be alone. I'm sorry if that was mean."

"What about the woman who stopped breathing in her sleep?"

The child's face twisted into a scowl. "They were nasty. I didn't like them at all. I sat on her chest and squeezed her neck, but I didn't wanna make her a ghost."

Mia sighed. "Stopping someone from breathing will turn them into a ghost."

"No." Robin shook her head. "Not all the way. I only scared her so the mean people would go away. They didn't like me. Told me I had to leave because it wasn't my home. The man made Daddy angry."

"He's here?" Mia swallowed.

Robin bowed her head. "Yes. In the basement."

"Does he still hurt you?"

"Only if I go down there, but I don't go down there. He's a monster now."

"Sweetie, he was a monster before... anyone who could do what they did to you..."

"He was always mean to Mommy." The girl glowered off to the side, saturating the kitchen with paranormal dread.

Electromagnetic detectors in the dining room erupted in a cacophony of wailing beeps.

Mia yelped.

Robin looked back at her, once again a complete vision of innocence. The squealing electronics in the other room fell silent. "Daddy's a different kind of monster now. He's a puddle of black stuff that crawls around the basement, an' won't do anything 'cept sit there 'til he gets mad. Then he does *bad* things."

"What makes him mad?"

"Mommy." Robin bit her lip. "An' runnin outta beer. An' bein' on fire, an' the man next door makin' a fence too close." She shrugged. "I guess everything makes Daddy mad."

"Being on fire?" Mia blinked, and shot a worried look at the stove.

"No. Not that kind of fire. Like bein' on employed."

"Oh." Mia almost laughed. *She's so creepy she's adorable... and I think I'm going insane.* She raised her right hand, pinky extended.

"Pinky swear. No trying to make Adam or me into ghosts, and we won't leave you."

The girl smiled and reached out, stopping an inch short of touching pinkies. "What if Daddy makes you a ghost?"

"Robin..." said Mia in a scolding tone.

She went wide-eyed. "I don't want him to, but I can't stop him." She shivered. "He has the hammer, an' I'm scared of it."

"Oh you poor..." Mia choked up.

Robin curled pinkies with her, an odd gleam in her eye. "Pinky swear."

22

THE DARKEST MOMENT

SATURDAY, SEPTEMBER 1, 2012

A woman hovered over Mia, her smile exhausted and frightened.

She appeared to be in her later thirties, dressed in a blue-green uniform like a waitress from a 1960s diner, her strawberry blonde hair up in a dated style that matched. Hints of a bruise ringed her left eye, poorly concealed under a hasty layer of foundation.

Mia snuck a hand out from under the blanket and waved goodbye, then clung to a battered stuffed rabbit.

"Tomorrow, I promise," whispered the woman. "Grandpa couldn't get down here tonight, so we'll go visit them in the morning, okay?"

"Okay," chirped a child's voice from Mia's mouth.

No… I'm dreaming.

The woman shut the light off and backed out of the room, closing the door.

Mia struggled to get up, but her body wouldn't move. No matter how much she refused to be a spectator watching the events of the past, she had no control. Her eyes closed, her arms cuddling the plush rabbit tight. She knew Grandpa would've come whenever Mommy asked, even if he lived really far away. Most likely, Mommy had been too scared of Daddy to go away at night. He should have been home already, and would've caught them carrying things to the car. Mommy didn't like leaving her home alone, but she was a big girl now and could take care of herself for the little while it would take Daddy to get home from work.

I don't want to see this. Please, no. Please don't make me see this, shouted Mia's voice in her thoughts.

A heavy crash came from downstairs.

Mia's eyes opened. Fear propelled her tiny body out of bed. Every time Daddy stomped around hitting stuff in the house, she hid because Mommy told her to. She dashed across the room and climbed into her big toy chest.

In what felt like a mere second, the lid flew open. Daddy stood over her, but he didn't look angry—he looked scary. Mia cowered, trying to hide behind Princess Rabbit. Daddy's giant hand reached down and grabbed her by a fistful of her nightgown.

"I'm sorry, Daddy," screamed Mia in Robin's voice. "What did I do?"

With all the emotional expression of a corpse, he hauled her out of the toy chest and dragged her across the room, tossing her to the floor at the foot of the bed. Her head bounced off the wall and she slid down, flat on her back, staring up at him, sobbing, begging to know why he'd gotten mad at her.

A glint of moonlight flashed from the face of a small one-handed sledge.

She abandoned the stuffed rabbit, reaching both hands up toward his arm. "Daddy, don't. Please!"

No! screamed Mia in the back of her mind.

He grasped her wrists together in his left hand, pushing her arms down to her chest and pinning her to the floor with so much force she couldn't draw a breath in. Mia-slash-Robin kicked and squirmed, but he weighed too much for her to move.

The instant the hammer started to come down, Mia's absolute refusal to watch any more erupted as a mental scream that hurled her out of the awful nightmare. She sat up in bed, screaming. For a few seconds after her lungs emptied, she stared into the darkness of her bedroom. Adam lay beside her, stirring in reaction to her cry of terror. Her right arm had gone numb, as cold as if it had been in a fridge. The reality of what she'd witnessed crashed into her psyche and she lapsed into heavy sobs.

Adam sat up and blearily put an arm around her, patting her back while rocking her. "You're okay. Just a bad dream."

"Oh my God," whimpered Mia.

"Ack. Are you okay?"

She sniffled. "Not really."

"Must be bad if *you* invoked God."

"Stop." Mia sighed. "I grew up hearing it all the time. It's just something to say. After what I just saw, there's no way he's real. That was so horrible... She's so little. She couldn't get away, couldn't breathe." She broke down in tears again.

He squeezed her close, holding her until she calmed. "Do you want to talk about it?"

"How could any parent do something like that?"

"Your parents were awful to your brother."

She ran one hand up over her head until she clutched the back of her neck. "Not even approaching the same degree of awful. Mommy was going to take—umm, I mean Evelyn was going to take Robin out of there *the next day.* Holy crap that was horrible." She struggled to breathe past the weight of grief.

"Mommy?" asked Adam.

"Just had a nightmare from her eyes." Mia rubbed her thawing arm. "Pretty sure she curled up next to me after I fell asleep. Not sure if she tried to show me that on purpose or if I just picked it up from being near her, but I was watching the murder from *her* perspective."

"Ouch."

"I couldn't handle it. Snapped awake before the hammer came down."

"That's fairly typical for nightmares of death. Our brains have a defense mechanism. We're programmed for survival, to fight death as much as we can... even in dreams. The brain won't process it, so it kicks us out of any nightmare right before we'd see ourselves die."

"Yeah, well... it worked. That poor child..."

The bed shifted to Mia's left. A handprint sank into the mattress, then another, and a knee. Mia stared at the approaching indentations, stuck between an instinctual urge to flee an invisible child stalking toward her and her need to comfort the girl after such a dream.

A frigid spot in the shape of a small hand touched Mia's side, straight on the skin as though she didn't have a night shirt on. Her arms and legs grew leaden, nearly impossible to move. Her head lolled forward, as heavy as a bowling ball. The chill migrated inward, enshrouding her core, sweeping over her into a state of full-body numbness. Mia's arms moved without conscious command, tucking her hands beneath her chin in the posture of a frightened little girl.

Robin wants to be held...

Mia mentally relaxed, deciding not to resist the girl taking over her body.

"Hon? Are you..." Adam gestured at her childish posture.

"Not... regressing..." whispered Mia with no small degree of effort to control her lips. "Robin..."

"Oh, hello there." Adam resumed rocking Mia and rubbing her back.

Mia let the girl soak up the sense of loving contact, content to watch from somewhere inside her brain. She'd lost all sense of touch, and couldn't even control where her eyes pointed. An ephemeral sense of crying came from an indeterminate place, simultaneously internal and external. No sound reached the outside world; Mia pictured Robin clinging and wailing as if Vic had merely punched her in the head and she'd run to Adam for comfort.

A sense of confusion accompanied it, the girl not quite able to comprehend a man who didn't act mean to her. Unlike the way Vic had treated Evelyn, the men who had taken this house had been kind to the women with them. Robin had thought them nice at first, but they'd all been nasty to her, even if they didn't hit the women. Those men had called her bad names and screamed. Some had done bad things, like going away and leaving her all alone.

Minutes later, Mia swooned, dizzy. The sensation of pins and needles swept over her entire body. Feeling returned, and along with it, a tremendous chill. Barely able to move, she scooted under the covers.

"Are you Mia again?"

"Y-yeah. S-so cold."

Adam lay back down. "I guess she's decided to give me a chance."

"She's still nervous, but I think you'll be good as long as you don't freak out at having a ghost in the house." Mia attached herself to him like a koala bear clinging to a tree. "I'm not scared. This is purely in the interest of warmth. She sucked up all my body heat."

"Hon… when have I ever freaked out about ghosts? Except in the sense of being excited to find one."

"How's your toenail?"

"Missing. It's a giant scab at the moment. And touché. So one time."

"That asylum in New Jersey you went to with the group… what was it two years ago?"

"Oh. Well… there's a distinct difference between ghosts and shadow figures. That thing might've had the power to kill." He cleared his throat. "I maintain that anyone would have screamed in that situation."

The repeating image of glint flashing off the face of the hammer kept her from laughing, or even smiling. "I think we might have one of those in the basement."

"Vic?"

"Yeah… or what's left of him."

Adam hissed air in between his teeth. "Ooh. That's going to be fun… not. Any idea how dangerous he is? Odd we didn't notice any sign of him earlier when we smudged."

"Robin said he just kinda slithers around aimlessly, ignoring the world."

"Hmm. Sounds like his mental state after the killing. Just sitting there drinking, not caring about anything."

"We're not safe." Though Robin pinky-swore not to try to kill her or Adam, children could lash out in anger without thinking. More than ever, she'd become convinced that Robin *was* an actual child, but one who'd developed a dark streak. Perhaps the house also had a creature akin to a demon… and that demon ticked like a bomb.

"What are you thinking?"

"Vic." Finally free of the paralytic chill, she relaxed her death grip on Adam, though remained close. "The way she made it sound, anything might randomly set him off."

"Well, we have a plan then." Adam kissed her. "It's seeming more likely that they're separate entities, and the child isn't dangerous."

Mia bit her lip, but kept quiet.

"So, all we have to do is see if Wilhelmina can get rid of Vic."

"Hon?"

He looked over at her. "Yeah?"

"I think that'll probably piss him off."

"Yeah. Most likely. But if we don't, something out of our control will eventually do that."

Mia closed her eyes. "Maybe. It could be thirty years, or three days. Who knows?"

"Exactly the problem. I think we should deal with him on our terms."

"Robin seemed afraid that getting rid of him would make her go away, too."

He yawned. "We haven't seen any absolute proof that they're separate entities. I'm still not sold entirely on that girl being what she appears. Not until we see both her and the shadow entity in the same place at the same time. It's possible we're dealing with a combined entity with aspects of both her and him… like a Dissociative Identity situation."

Mia shook her head. "No. Doesn't feel right. But why did she tell me not to go down there?" *Is she afraid I'll not see Vic and discover that she's the source of the darkness? I can't believe that. She's too genuine as a child to be faking it.*

"Well," said Adam, "Either she knows you won't find Vic down there, or you will and she's afraid he'll hurt you."

"Why would she be afraid he'd hurt me? Then I'd just wind up as a ghost and I could be with her forever… and able to touch her." *She tried to kill me, but doesn't want Vic to? Kid logic.*

"Hmm. What if his presence is what's trapping her here, and she's not moving on to wherever it is that most people do after death because of him? Get rid of him, it's like pulling out the drain plug and she can go somewhere else… but doesn't want to?"

"That's an idea…"

"As far as protecting you goes, she might be afraid you wouldn't end up haunting the house and would go away like her mother did. Or, she's traumatized and is phobic of him."

"Can you blame her?" *She's not afraid I won't haunt the house… or she wouldn't have chucked the hair dryer at the tub. I should really tell Adam about that…* She sighed. *Tomorrow.*

"Not really."

"I can't stop seeing that damn hammer." Mia shuddered. "I'm probably going to freak out if I see Vic."

"So, stay out of the basement."

Mia smiled. "You don't have to tell me that twice."

A few minutes passed in silence.

"Night, hon," said Adam.

She exhaled. "Night, babe… if I can sleep."

A moment later, a slight weight settled into the bed between them.

"Night, sweetie," whispered Mia.

23

THE PINECONE

MONDAY, SEPTEMBER 3, 2012

The giant impressionist painting had so many tiny holes in it, Mia wondered if it had pulled duty as a BB gun target. Most of the holes measured about three millimeters across, though numerous pinholes and a few larger rips marred the canvas as well.

She'd finished cleaning it last week, so today, she started the process of patching all the holes. Scrubbing a surface the size of a refrigerator door with a Q-tip offered endless tedium, but no less so than cutting out tiny pieces of canvas to match each hole and gluing them in place on patch backing.

Mia got to work, but found herself unable to fully immerse in her usual trance that made the monotonous repetitiveness slip into a groove and the day race by. The nightmare remained fresh in her thoughts. The more she tried to push it out of her mind, the more it devoured her thoughts. Never had she felt as helpless as that moment where Vic crushed her into the floor, no way to escape the hammer about to smash her head.

Her father had sometimes held her down, but not like that… not crushing her arms into her chest so she couldn't breathe. Mia's father had bent her over the side of her bed, or the couch, or a table, and taken his belt to her bare backside often enough to leave deep mental scars.

As long as she lived, she'd never be able to look at him with any trace of familial affection. He had made himself an object of fear, and as such he would stay.

However, as much as she found him terrifying, he had nothing on Vic. Even at his worst, her father never intended to kill her or even inflict serious injury. That man merely had one way to deal with children who had conflicts of opinion with him. He wouldn't talk, or debate, or bargain. The leather belt would make his point for him. The last time he'd strapped her, she'd been around thirteen, maybe fourteen. She'd riled him up plenty often after that, but she'd become old enough to treat like an adult. Shouts, threats, and guilt had become his weapon of choice then. Fortunately for Mia, she lacked the fear that his promises of God punishing her would mean anything. Her parents had been quite austere and frugal, so they couldn't exactly deny her much in the way of toys, money for niceties like movies and fancy clothes, or going out. All of those things would have had to exist for them to be taken away as a punishment.

The worst thing she'd done in their eyes had been rejecting their religion and taking Timothy's side. Some of the girls she'd grown up with had experimented with drugs. One girl she didn't really know in her high school had robbed a place and went to juvenile prison. Two girls she'd known since first grade got pregnant before they turned eighteen, but as far as her parents were concerned, she'd been the antichrist for questioning God, more evil than any of those other kids. Getting knocked up or coming home high would've been fine—as long as she had faith.

Each time Mia settled into the task of patching a hole, muscle memory took over. She didn't need to think about the work anymore, so her mind ran off to the nightmare. Mia dropped the tweezers she used to position the tiny canvas patches and grabbed her hair, shaking her head like she could make the bad memory fall out of her ears. After a run to the coffee machine in the break room, she returned and tried to focus on her job.

It worked for a little while until a new distraction gnawed at her thoughts. She'd never had a strong urge to have a baby. Some of her high school and college friends already had kids before graduating. A few planned to spawn as soon as they reached a point of being comfortable in their careers. A handful wanted kids less than they wanted brain tumors. Mia considered herself in the middle group, no strong feelings either way. Though, she had been leaning toward the 'nah' camp. Even after meeting and falling in love with Adam, they'd both been otherwise occupied. Finding jobs, worrying about life in general... then the ridiculous commute, now the insecurity of his being new at the university and of course, having to deal with a house that had at least one—probably two, maybe even three—ghosts in it. Though she had yet to see concrete proof of Evelyn, she couldn't otherwise explain why she felt the woman's presence.

Therein lay the problem, or at least the conundrum presently interfering with her concentration on work. Despite her ambivalence toward kids, her increasing sense of protectiveness toward Robin perplexed her. Its strength made her question its veracity. Could Robin be influencing her mind, desperate for a protector? Mia didn't think that had happened. Or maybe she didn't *want* to think that. Did a childlike spirit hold her hostage or did she genuinely feel horrible for an innocent victim of such a ghastly crime?

And what on Earth ever possessed her to buy a child sized bed and dresser for an empty room? As best she could remember, she thought familiar things would make the girl feel better. She'd had a clear mental image of the way the room had been before, despite refusing to look at the body. Redoing the wallpaper—if she could even find that pattern—would be going too far. Besides, she feared what might lurk under the paint. Did the prior owners peel down the bloody wallpaper or simply paint over it? Could there be a massive bloodstain on the floor under that carpet?

Mia shuddered.

Her cell phone rang, startling a scream out of her. She fumbled it off the table and stared at an unfamiliar number on the screen. Something told her to answer it, so she did.

"Hello?"

"Mia?" asked Wilhelmina. "I hope this is the right number."

"Oh, hi. Yes. It's me."

Janet Newman peeked in the door. "Mia? Are you all right? I heard a scream."

"Sec," muttered Mia. She raised the phone toward Janet. "It rang and startled me. I'm okay. Thank you."

"Heh. You always did get deep in the zone." Janet smiled and walked off.

"What's up?" asked Mia.

"Adam gave me your number. I was wondering if you'd meet me at the Pinecone once you left work today. There are some things I'd like to discuss with you away from prying ears, and I don't mean your husband's. I suggested he join us as soon as he's able to."

Mia craved routine. A sudden change like going out for dinner on the spur of the moment unsettled her more than it should. Home had been like that, highly scheduled. She *still* kept her hair in the same plain long, straight style she'd always worn it in because her parents made such a big deal about girls having 'girl hair.' The mere suggestion of changing it, dyeing it, cutting it, or doing anything with it threw her mother into a fury like she'd suggested killing someone. Timothy got the same treatment, only they demanded he keep his hair short and neat.

Her mother made the same thing for dinner every Monday, same trip to the store for groceries every Sunday after church. When Mia stopped going to worship, they kept going to the store without her. To 'atone' for turning her back on God, they'd tasked her with carrying all the groceries into the house. *That*, she did without protest, figuring it a small price to pay in exchange for not having to wake up early and be dragged to a two-hour waste of time.

Considering recent events, she wondered if her aversion to sudden change might be related to psychic sensitivity. She rolled the thought of going to the diner around in her head, teasing with the idea of going, then teasing at the idea of declining. When she aligned herself with 'go,' she noticed a distinct sense of calm to her thoughts that stopped when she changed her mind.

"Okay. I'm out of here at 5:30. Never been there but I have a

Garmin."

"Oh, you really can't miss it. Spring Falls' downtown is *one* street. The Pinecone is the only diner."

Mia laughed. "Okay. See you there."

"Wonderful. Talk to you soon."

"Yep." Mia hung up, set the phone on the giant table, and resumed patching the old canvas.

The change of routine offered her something else to think about than the horrible nightmare or worrying if sweet, innocent Robin might be darker than she appeared. Smiling to herself and feeling more than a little like a rebel for deciding to go out for dinner without much forethought, she dove into her work and lost track of time.

THE PINECONE DINER INDEED TURNED OUT TO BE IMPOSSIBLE TO miss.

Split Oak Road branched away from State Route 69 and meandered mostly northward among the trees until it changed names to Main Street at the point it straightened out for a not-quite-two-mile L-shaped stretch in downtown Spring Falls. Past the downtown area, it once again shrank to a winding backwoods path and resumed the name Split Oak Road.

Mia glanced to her left at an old Gulf station with two pumps and a simple garage. A weather-worn sign bearing the word 'service' hung over the three rolling doors. The ghosts of where old lettering had been removed remained readable as 'O'Riordan's Garage.' Five cars sat in the front lot by the service bay, two clearly having been stationary for decades. The other three appeared more recent, suggesting a mechanic might still operate there. Only the middle door was open, exposing a shadowed room and the back end of a relatively new Toyota pickup.

The shadows beside the truck moved. A man in blue coveralls with shoulder-length scruffy black hair wiped his hands on a red-and-white cloth while stepping outside to check out the car driving by. Cold, dead eyes stared straight at Mia.

Vic.

She screamed and nearly drove up onto the sidewalk. By the time she regained control of the Tahoe, he'd vanished.

Mia slowed to a near standstill, clutching the wheel hard. No other cars were on the road nearby to honk at her, but two elderly men walking by on different sides of the street both shot her looks she read as them expecting calamity whenever a woman got behind the wheel of a car. If not for still shaking from the sight of Vic watching her, she might have flipped them off.

That's where he used to work. I just saw a vision of the past. He wasn't really looking at me. *The bastard didn't die at the garage. Why would he be there?*

She took a few seconds to clear her mind and resumed driving.

The diner took up most of the inner corner of the L, one building away from the only right turn in the town proper and the only traffic light. Anyone who didn't turn at the corner and went straight between the two stores there would find themselves on a one-lane dirt road that led off to who-knows-where. Mia thought it odd that such an intersection needed a traffic light. Maybe the town elders wanted one there purely so they could say the town *had* a traffic light. Could an area officially call itself a town without at least one?

A giant wooden pinecone hung from a pole by the sidewalk. The building appeared unchanged from when it had been built in the late fifties. Metallic silver siding covered the lower half of the exterior walls, the upper part aqua. On sunny days, the Pinecone Diner could be seen from outer space. An awning of faded green with numerous holes covered the door, the word 'Pinecone' stenciled in white letters at the front end.

Mia pulled into a parking lot that looked way too large for the size of the diner. It could probably hold one car each for the entire population of Spring Falls, including children. Her Tahoe raised the present population of vehicles in the lot to five.

She parked, got out, and peered across the street at the Sheriff's Office, flanked by a barber shop on one side and an ancient clothing store on the other with child-sized mannequins in the window, dressed straight out of the early eighties—or maybe late seventies. Gold lettering on the glass above a plastic boy in a goldenrod plaid shirt read 'Pfeffer's Boutique.'

The large front window of the sheriff's office looked in on a room with three or four desks and two people in khaki uniforms: a man with short, dark brown hair and a blonde woman about Mia's age. *Hmm. Guess the town has more than one cop now.* The man noticed her looking at them, and the woman turned toward her. She offered a pleasant wave and headed for the diner entrance.

This town is eerie. There's hardly anyone walking around.

Two flapping doors, also aqua, with giant round windows led to a long, narrow room with gaudy green-and-white tile floor. A row of aqua-colored stools lined up in front of a counter trimmed in mirror silver. Booth seating extended in both directions, perhaps twenty-four tables in total.

Wilhelmina waved to her from the fifth table left from the door. A bored-looking black-haired woman behind the counter glanced up from a book at Mia, but upon noticing Wilhelmina waving, went back to reading.

Guess I seat myself. She waved to the waitress despite the woman no longer looking at her, and walked down the aisle to the booth.

"I trust you didn't have any trouble finding the place." Wilhelmina wagged her eyebrows and took a sip of water.

Mia laughed and took the seat opposite her. "Nope. It kinda stands out." She sent Adam a text, letting him know she found the diner.

"You seem on edge, dear."

She waved dismissively. "I'm not usually the sort of person who does spontaneous things. And, this town is kinda creepy."

"How so?"

Mia glanced left out the window. "It feels like an abandoned movie set. One street set up with shops and stuff in the middle of the woods. Almost no one around. So different from Slingerlands, where we used to live."

"Oh, it's been like that for years. People here tend to either head to Syracuse for the 'downtown' experience or eat at home. Mostly, you get the older crowd here at the Pinecone Friday night and Saturday. Also rather popular for Sunday breakfast."

Mia's phone chirped.

"Can I get you anything to drink?" asked the waitress while walking up to the table.

"Unsweetened tea if you have it, or water," said Mia.

"Know what you want to eat?"

Mia held back the 'I haven't even looked at a menu yet' ready to fly from her lips. "Sorry, need a minute. First time here."

The woman nodded and walked off.

"Wow." Mia peered over her shoulder at the departing waitress. "I get the feeling we're inconveniencing her."

"Martha's not as rude as she comes off. It's just her personality. You've heard of 'resting bitch face?'" Wilhelmina smiled. "She's got 'resting bitch.'"

Mia laughed and picked up a menu, glancing at the phone before opening it. Adam estimated about a half hour before he'd be there and told her to go ahead and eat. He'd get a burger or something he could take with so they didn't have to wait for him to finish.

She sent back 'like we're going to be late for something.'

A wiry, fortyish man in a green flannel shirt, jeans, and blue ball cap, a week late for a shave, entered the diner. He nodded to the reading waitress and made his way down the aisle, seating himself two booths away with his back to them.

"I'm sure you're wondering what prompted me to suggest we meet here."

Mia skimmed over the menu, which proved rather limited. "Yeah, just a bit." *Hmm. Guess everyone who comes in here has it memorized already.*

"I'll assume you believe in ghosts at this point."

"Yeah."

"What are your thoughts on theology in general?"

Mia settled on a grilled chicken, bacon, and cheddar cheese sandwich, then closed the menu. "I told you about my parents already. My thoughts on religion aren't too nice. But, I suppose it's the political aspect of it that bugs me. Like, if there *is* something out there, that wouldn't bother me. I just hate it when people use unproven stories of a supreme being to justify being shitty to each other or hurting people. Obviously, the anti-LGBT morons are a close issue for me, but also like those whack jobs who have a sick child and refuse to take them to the hospital because they think their imaginary friend will magically zap the disease gone? That stuff pisses me off. Like, if they believe in this whole 'god plan' deal, why would they expect him to heal the disease he gave the poor kid in the first place?"

Wilhelmina patted the table. "Calm down, dear. I was asking about your feelings toward more esoteric concepts of theology."

"Oh, like magic? Wicca? Druidy... Thelema or whatever that was?"

"Well, every group has their *interesting* members, but yes, more or less what I mean. Would you be inclined to burn a witch, consider her insane, live and let live, or are you curious?"

Mia fixated on the older woman's bright blue eyes, certain she had a sense of where the conversation would go and why the question had come up. "I'm definitely not like my parents. No witch burning for this girl. But this isn't exactly new. You already told me you dabbled with hexes as a kid. A month ago, I would've said live and let live while thinking they might be a bit off their rockers... now"—she emptied her lungs into a sigh—"I guess I'd be curious. I used to think people who claimed psychic abilities were nuts."

"Hah." Wilhelmina covered her mouth to hold in laughter as the waitress approached.

"Make up your mind yet, hon?" asked Martha.

"Yes. Sorry. Can I have the grilled chicken, bacon, and cheddar sandwich, please?"

"Which number is that?" Martha scratched her head.

"Uhh..." Mia started to reach for the menu.

"B11," said Wilhelmina. "I'll have the S4."

Martha jotted on her pad, almost smiled, and hurried off. "You got it."

"Wow, you really do have the menu here memorized." Mia blinked.

"It has twenty-seven items. Twelve burgers, ten sandwiches, and five 'dinners.' Lloyd tried to add 'wrap sandwiches' about six years ago, but the locals accused him of hugging too many trees, so he got rid of them."

"What do wrap sandwiches have to do with trees?"

"Hell if I know." Wilhelmina shrugged. "So, you're curious?"

"I'm going to take a stab in the dark here and guess you're a witch or at least someone who practices some form of magic, and you want to make sure I'm not going to freak out before you tell me that you'd like to use magic at the house."

"Almost. I was thinking you might fit in with our group. And no, I'm not pulling a Weston and trying to recruit you. Any help I may be able to offer would require the assistance of my friends, and I thought you would enjoy the opportunity to extend your social circle. Perhaps meet with them in a few days."

"Oh. Okay." Mia shrugged with one shoulder. "That sounds nice."

Wilhelmina's eyebrows rose. "That was quick. Didn't you say you're a bit of an introvert?"

"Nah. I'm not an introvert... or really an extrovert. Kinda in the middle. It's not people that bother me, it's deviating from routine that puts me on edge. I can cope with a lot if I have advance notice."

"Grand. I'll run it by the others then and we'll pick a day."

"I'm getting the feeling you wanted to have this meeting before my husband showed up. Is your coven a 'ladies only' situation?" Mia took a sip of her iced tea.

"Not by decree. It *is* all women, but that happened merely by chance. He's more than welcome to come along, though it's been my experience that most men wouldn't choose to be stuck in a room with six women debating the proper amount of powdered bull penis needed for a luck spell."

Tea streamed out of Mia's nostrils, spraying all over the table. She half coughed, half choked for a moment before catching her breath. Martha walked by and dropped off a stack of paper napkins with a bit of an annoyed smirk.

Mia wiped tears from her eyes and fanned herself. "I wasn't ready for that."

"My dear, few people are ever prepared to hear the phrase 'powdered bull penis.'"

She giggled while mopping up the spatter. "That's really a thing?"

"It is, though difficult to obtain in this country."

"Wow. I suppose I shouldn't be so astounded that magic might be real considering everything I've witnessed over the past week."

"It's probably nothing like you're expecting. Almost everything we do could be explained away as coincidence."

Mia held up a dripping wad of napkin, wondering where to put it. "How do you know it isn't? Coincidence, I mean."

"To be perfectly frank, we don't. We strongly suspect the elements, the spirits, and the Goddess hear us and answer our requests, but short of a deep circle summoning—which I haven't done since 1988—there's little actual proof to be seen."

"Sounds a bit like prayer." Mia set the napkin on the edge of the table.

Wilhelmina nodded. "That is a valid comparison. Many similarities can be drawn between pagan spellcasting and certain religion's prayers. Much of the ritualism involved in modern religions has origins with earlier mystical traditions. Focused desire, a specific set of words, gestures, rites, even specific clothing or paraphernalia… voicing one's desire to the universe. Magic and prayer are different only in the semantics of their application."

"I don't think many priests or pastors use powdered bull penis," said Mia, not quite able to keep a straight face.

Wilhelmina chuckled. "Before you consider me hypocritical, bear in mind that I do not think the world is controlled by an all-powerful being with a plan for everything, and then ask him to change his mind because I personally disagree with how things are going. The entities we call upon during our rites are powerful, but not without limits or faults. That prayer exists as a concept is contradictory to an omnipotent being who has a plan. Somewhere, long ago, a message got mixed up."

Mia smiled. "Yeah, just a little."

Martha approached the table and set an enormous mound of bun, chicken, bacon, and dripping cheese in front of Mia, then a turkey club sandwich in front of Wilhelmina. "Can I get you girls anything else?"

"My husband will be here in about twenty minutes. He'll order something when he arrives."

"All right. I'll keep the check open then." Martha swiped the green slip back from the table and returned to her spot behind the counter—and book.

Mia watched her walk off, wondering if Evelyn had worked here, or if Martha knew her. The woman didn't look old enough, probably would've only been a toddler—if that—when Evelyn died. But, Spring Falls didn't have any other diners. Unless she commuted to Syracuse or worked in another, larger town nearby, Evelyn would've waited tables here.

"What's on your mind?" asked Wilhelmina between bites of turkey sandwich.

Mia looked around the room, but other than a mild sense of unease, didn't feel anything of significance. "Just trying to figure out if Evelyn worked here."

"No, she waited tables at a place in Fulton on the late shift, usually not getting out of there until one in the morning, provided she didn't get stuck longer than that. Not enough business here to make any real money."

"Vic worked at the Gulf station near the end of Main Street, didn't he?" Mia picked up half her giant sandwich, certain the other part would go home with her.

"That's right. Micky O'Riordan sold the place about, oh, twenty years ago. Died in 2008 if I remember right."

"On the way here, I just happened to look over at it and saw Vic standing in the garage. It had to be me sensing the past. Why would he haunt *that* place?"

Wilhelmina shook her head, making a strand of long pewter hair fall from her shoulder. "If he haunted anywhere, it would be Johnny's. The man spent more time there than at home."

"Wish he'd stayed there that night." Mia let her mind wander around what ifs while she ate a few bites of her sandwich and some fries. "How did he figure out she planned to leave him? And, if Evelyn worked in Fulton, she would've needed a car of her own. She told Robin they weren't leaving that night because the grandfather couldn't pick them up until tomorrow. But… if Evelyn had a car, they could've gone right then. Why did she leave that poor child alone in the house for him to find?"

"Well, you're a smart woman. I think you already know the answer to at least one of those." Wilhelmina nibbled on a pickle slice. "She chickened out. Grandpa was an excuse for little ears. *Why* she chickened out, I have no idea… but I'm sure she blamed herself for what happened."

"She did." Mia closed her eyes, fighting the urge to cry. "She absolutely did…"

"As to how Vic found out? That would be Suzanne Stroh. She worked at the same diner in Fulton. Overheard Evelyn on the phone with her parents, asking them if she and Robin could go there for a while since she wanted to leave Vic."

"Bitch," muttered Mia. "Jealous former girlfriend or something?"

"Not as far as anyone admitted. Back then, people were a lot more committed to propriety. Suzanne was part of a group of local busybodies who nosed around making sure everyone stayed right with the church, kept their lawns perfect, planted the right flowers, that sort of thing. Though, some people thought Vic might've been having an affair. *Who* he had an affair with changed depending on the person telling you about it. I can't say for sure if that's anything more than rumor."

"Ugh. So, a woman leaving her man would've been scandalous? Even though he beat the shit out of her?" Mia gawked.

"Somewhat. Suzanne and Vic were friends, though I doubt anything romantic happened between them. That woman wasn't the type of person to condone infidelity. I believe she thought marriage to be inviolate and any problem could be worked out if she'd only be willing to talk to him."

"Oh, like he was violent because Evelyn somehow failed to 'wife' properly?"

Wilhelmina frowned. "Something to that effect, yes."

"That bitch effectively killed Robin. She told Vic that Evelyn planned to leave him. I bet he probably expected she'd already be gone by the time he'd have gotten home from work, so he went straight to the bar to get drunk."

"Did you see something or are you guessing?"

"Mostly guessing, but it feels right." Mia wagged her quarter sandwich at Wilhelmina. "Somehow, he figured out that she *didn't* leave yet, maybe he called the place she worked. Possibly, he thinks he's going to try and change her mind, maybe 'knock some sense' into her… but somewhere between leaving the bar and arriving home, he just became furious with her for daring to think she could leave him. Decides to hurt her in the worst way possible."

"Sounds plausible."

"Men like that often view their wives as property," said Adam from the aisle beside the table.

Mia jumped.

"In my opinion, as soon as he heard she'd made the decision to leave, he'd likely have become enraged." Adam scooted into the booth beside Mia and gave her a brief kiss. "The man most likely went drinking as an outlet for his anger at *not* being able to get at Evelyn, believing she'd already left. When he learned she hadn't gone away yet and was still in his reach, he rushed home to… well, you know the rest."

"Hello, Adam." Wilhelmina nodded in greeting.

"Professor Marx." He smiled.

"Oh, pshaw." She smirked at him.

Mia handed him a menu. Martha, already on her way to the table, made a face at that, perhaps annoyed that a newbie needed time to decide. She continued past them to the booth where the lone man sat.

Adam glanced over the menu, but closed it after only ten seconds. "Interesting place. Where do they hide the time machine?"

Mia leaned on him. "I was wondering that, too."

Martha walked up to their table.

"B7 please," said Adam.

"Chicken parmesan sandwich." Wilhelmina toasted him with her water glass. "It's rather good here."

"Drink?" asked Martha.

"Water's fine, thanks." Adam smiled at her.

They proceeded to catch him up on the conversation he'd missed. Wilhelmina didn't mind staying while he ate, so to fill the time, Mia explained her dream of the murder.

"Do you think it's something I randomly picked up from the house or did Robin send it to me on purpose?"

Wilhelmina repetitively stroked her fingers down a strand of her hair while thinking. Eventually, a sly smile formed. "I'm not sure why you're asking me about psychic things. Now, if you have any questions about witchcraft, then we can talk."

Mia chuckled. She considered telling them about Robin trying to throw a hair dryer into the tub, but couldn't get it out. As much as Adam adored being this close to such a profound paranormal experience, if he thought she could be hurt, he'd drag her out of the house and she couldn't bear to abandon Robin. Besides, she'd reached an accord with the ghost and didn't think the child would try harming her again.

And... part of her feared what the girl might do to him if he tried to make her leave.

Lying had never been one of Mia's talents, so she didn't often try it. She couldn't recall ever having deliberately lied to Adam before with the exception of evading questions when trying to surprise him with a holiday gift. Playful lies she could slip through since no guilt came from it. That thought gave her the crutch she needed to keep a plastic smile for the rest of dinner, despite her lie of omission. Her motivation not to tell Adam about her near-electrocution came from her desire to protect him from what Robin might do.

Not being completely honest with Adam bothered her.

But...

That some part of her still feared the ghost might not be so innocent bothered her more.

BACK TO GOD

TUESDAY, SEPTEMBER 4, 2012

The constant murmuring of distant voices came from the window to Mia's left, coaxing her out of sleep.

She groaned and lifted her head to peer at the alarm clock on the chest-of-drawers, which read 6:51 a.m. *Grr.* Mia let her head fall back to the pillow. *Who stole nine precious minutes of sleep?* Rapid soft thumps went by her side of the bed from the door to the window, the unmistakable sound of a child running. A rustle came from the curtain, which fluttered to the side as though someone small ducked under it to get to the window.

The mood in the room shifted to intense anger.

Worried, Mia slipped out of bed and approached the window to peer out.

Some-teen number of people had gathered in a group on the grass a short distance from her porch. Weston Parker stood at the center holding a book, apparently leading them in prayer. The cold spot in front of her dissipated and the curtain fell draped against the windowsill.

Oh, please don't be about to do something bad...

Mia glared at Weston for a second or two before hastily changing out of her nightgown into a T-shirt and sweat pants. She grabbed her phone and ran downstairs, ignoring the hiss of water in the bathroom from Adam, who'd obviously gotten into the shower before the church brigade showed up.

Once downstairs, she rummaged around the kitchen until she found the tiny local phone book that had appeared on her porch a few days ago, and called the non-emergency number for the Spring Falls police department. Her alarm went off upstairs, the beeping annoying, but not so loud she couldn't ignore it while in the kitchen.

"Spring Falls Sheriff's office," said a man by way of answering. "This is Nate."

"Hi. My name is Mia Gartner. I'd like to report harassment, and maybe trespassing."

Noise came over the line that made her picture him holding an old-fashioned corded phone handset to the side of his head with his shoulder. "Mia... Gartner... Doesn't sound familiar. New in town?"

"Yes. We just moved in a couple weeks ago."

"Ahh. Welcome to Spring Falls. What's the address?"

"Six Minstrel Run."

Silence.

She waited about thirty seconds before asking, "Hello?"

"Yeah... still here. You said *Six* Minstrel Run?"

"That's correct."

"Mm-hmm. What is harassing you?"

Mia raked her free hand over her hair, sighing at the 'oh, here we go again' tone in his voice. "Not a what. A who. Weston Parker. He's standing outside on my lawn with a large group, chanting some biblical nonsense. I've asked him repeatedly to leave me alone, but he won't."

"Uhh huh," said Nate, drawing it out to fill time with sound while writing something down. "And what's got the good preacher stalking you?"

"I'm not entirely sure. Either my not being interested in going to his church or that he seems to think this house is haunted and my soul is in danger."

Nate chuckled. "That house does have a bit of a history. You said 'seems to think'… you don't believe your soul's in danger?"

Great. Do I lie to a cop or have him think I'm crazy? "I've heard the house has a dark history, but nothing has happened here yet that's made me concerned for my wellbeing. I do kind of object to being disturbed early in the morning by a bunch of living people on my front lawn."

Her alarm stopped going off.

She glanced up at the ceiling. *Thanks, Adam… or Robin.*

"Do you have reason to suspect the pastor or his people represent an imminent threat of harm to your person or property?"

She grumbled. "Not really. He's just annoying."

"Heh, yeah, ol' Weston can be a bit pushy, but he wouldn't hurt anyone."

Mia randomly pictured her father's 'church smile.' Everyone thought him so pleasant and moral. They never saw the tyrant capable of whipping his kids with a belt until she nearly fainted from pain or Timothy wet himself, nor would anyone have believed her if she told them such things. James Williams would never hurt a fly. That man couldn't possibly ever raise a hand to his children. Her father had claimed to be doing God's work, but she suspected he got a thrill from having a sense of power and authority over them.

Weston's got dark secrets, too, I bet. She narrowed her eyes, then felt guilty for assuming him sadistic merely for being religious. He probably was, but maybe—just maybe—she projected her father onto him.

"Can you please get them off my lawn, maybe ask him to leave me alone?"

"All right. I've known Weston a while. He's a little mixed up and that house of yours has some history with him. Do you feel comfortable asking him one more time to mind his own business? Let him know you spoke to me, and next time, it'll be me asking him to give you space. That should do the trick."

Mia didn't feel at all worried the older man would physically harm her. "Okay. I'll try one more time. Small town, right? Everyone knows everyone, and people who call the police over every little thing don't make friends."

"Heh. Yeah, little bit of that goes on out here, though most people don't have much problem with each other. If he gives you any trouble, call me right on back and I'll head out that way."

"All right. Thanks."

"Anytime."

She hung up.

"Hon?" called Adam from the top of the stairs. "Isn't it a bit early for carolers?"

"They're not singing." Mia stormed down the hall from the kitchen to the living room. "Just got off the phone with the cop. I'm going to try one more time to tell this man to leave us alone."

Adam, already dressed for work, hurried down the stairs. "Be careful."

She nodded to him, opened the door, and walked to the edge of the porch by the steps, arms folded. Sixteen people stood in two rows of eight behind Weston, all at least fifty or older, an even mix of women and men. Her gaze settled on a guy in the back row, third from the right... the same man who'd been sitting two tables away from them at the Pinecone Diner. She scowled at him, thinking it wouldn't be too tragic if he fell down a flight of stairs. The uncharacteristically violent idea vanished as fast as it formed.

Ack... where did that come from?

Weston approached, stopping at the base of the porch steps. "Mrs. Gartner."

The people on the lawn continued muttering prayers, asking the Lord to banish the evil from the house.

Adam moved up behind her.

"Mr. Gartner." Weston nodded in greeting.

"What's this?" Mia gestured at the group. "Normal people have to wake up early and go to work. I've asked you at least twice to leave me alone."

Weston clasped his bible in both hands against his chest. "It has come to my attention that you're at risk of becoming involved with that Marx woman and her collection of lost souls. I would be remiss in my duties if I allowed Satan to seduce you. It's quite evident to me that this house has already started to affect you and pull you away from God."

"I said it once already... if God wants to save me, he's free to do so. If his help is conditional, it's not coming from benevolence."

Weston moved up one step. "Those who suffer the delusions of Satan are not in a position to see the danger they're in. The Father of Lies deceives, he takes on the guise of innocence to lure the unwary to their deaths and eternal torment."

She opened her mouth, then closed it. "Before I say what had come to mind, I have a question for you."

He blinked, seeming surprised. "All right."

"You may have noticed I have been somewhat hostile to you from the moment you mentioned your being a pastor."

"I have."

She set her hands on her hips. "My parents are like you... God this, God that. They thought themselves so virtuous and pure, yet when they discovered that my younger brother is gay, their cruelty knew no bounds. If they wouldn't have been arrested for it, they'd have kicked him out of the house at thirteen. They constantly told him what an abomination he was, how he'd be better off dead, how he made God weep, how he wasn't really their son and they were ashamed to have brought him into the world... They wanted nothing to do with him and we haven't had any contact with them in years."

Weston cringed.

"Do you agree with them?"

"Not all who claim to follow the Word of God hear the True Word. They shouldn't have condemned him for who he is, and should have spent their time bringing him back to God."

"Back? Is this some conversion therapy bullshit?"

Weston shook his head. "No, I'm sorry you misunderstand. I believe God has a reason for everything he does, even creating people who feel physical attraction to others of the same sex. We are all His children. Who our mortal selves feel drawn to doesn't matter."

She blinked in absolute disbelief. "Wait, so you wouldn't have any problem with someone who's gay?"

"Not for that reason alone. We are all His children."

"Oh…" Mia fidgeted, biting her lip and feeling guilty for nearly ripping his head off verbally.

Weston reached out and grasped her hand. "I am afraid for your soul, Mia. Those people you are associating with traffic in foul energies and call on darkness. That woman you trust isn't what she seems. She had something to do with what happened here; I am sure of it."

"What?" asked Adam, emerging from the house behind her. "You think Wilhelmina was involved with Robin's death?"

"I do." Weston released Mia's hand and clasped his Bible again. "Even as a young girl, she'd been wont to spend her time alone in the forest talking to demons and other creatures. She eschewed God and sought the company of imps and goblins. Do you not think it suspicious that Wilhelmina Marx babysat the little girl, but Evelyn didn't call her to watch the child the night she was murdered? Why would the woman leave her seven-year-old child alone in the house and go to work thirty miles away in Fulton?"

"Because she expected Vic would come home at any minute. Maybe she tried to call Wilhelmina and… she was only thirteen at the time. She wouldn't have been able to stay up late, might've even been in bed already herself. You're criticizing Evelyn for leaving Robin alone, but think it's fine to drag a thirteen-year-old out of bed that late? I'm not even sure what time Evelyn left, but it was already dark out."

"You're assuming Evelyn *didn't* call her. I believe she did. What rational woman would leave a child that young alone? As soon as Wilhelmina Marx had the house to herself, she and her friends conducted a Satanic ritual that culminated with the sacrifice of a child she'd been entrusted to protect."

Mia gasped. "That's a lie."

"Vic discovered the body, and it broke him. They found him sitting on the bridge ready to jump because he'd been so grief stricken. The girls—Wilhelmina and her friend Pauline—used one of his tools to kill the child, so everyone naturally assumed he did it. Especially with the troubles he'd had with the wife."

"Stop!" yelled Mia. "You're wrong. I saw him kill her."

Weston shook his head. "Oh, child. You're already under the influence of the dark one. You couldn't possibly have witnessed it. The girl would be almost fifty years old now if she hadn't been killed."

"I'm psychic. I saw it in a dream... so vivid as though I lived it."

"You believe you're psychic?" Weston regarded her with a pitying expression.

"You believe in an imaginary sky wizard." Mia folded her arms. "I've received at least two pieces of verifiable information that I had no way to know otherwise. Do you have any proof your God is real? And I mean that as a sincere question."

"God is there if you know how to look for him," said Weston.

"That's not proof. That's brainwashing. You're wrong about Wilhelmina. I've seen *things*. I had to watch that son of a bitch hold that little girl down and... and..." She raised her arm as if holding a hammer. "I didn't want to see the rest... forced myself to wake up. You were all over this house when the Vaughans lived here. You had to have heard the damn toolbox smash into the floor every damn day at 1:03 in the morning." She pointed at him. "And I saw Mr. Vaughan reach the top of the stairs. The ghost jumped out at him and screamed. He fell over backward and knocked a younger man down the steps with him." She shook her pointing finger. "That was you like twenty years ago."

Most of the color in Weston's cheeks faded. He stared at her with an unreadable expression that could have been fear as easily as revulsion.

"There's no way I could have known that without being psychic, is there? The Vaughans moved far away from here, and may not even still be alive given their age. I'm sure you didn't tell anyone he knocked you down the stairs, or that he claimed to see a ghostly little girl jump out at him."

"I..."

"Look, Weston. We got off on the wrong foot. I'm sorry I assumed you were just like my parents. However, I need you to understand that there is nothing at all satanic about Wilhelmina. She doesn't even believe that Satan is a real entity. Just because *you* don't understand something and don't *want* to understand it doesn't make it the work of Satan."

He kept glaring.

"Before this escalates more... I'm not looking for any animosity here. But, you aren't helping the situation in the house. You spent months here with the Vaughans, tormenting an innocent child. And yes, she heard all the things you called her, all the horrible things you said she was. If your God is so benevolent, why did he allow a seven-year-old girl to have her head smashed open by her own father? Where was his protection then? Why is he letting her spirit linger here instead of... whatever happens after? Why does he need *you*, a mortal human being, to beg and pray for him to do something? Obviously, everything you tried to do twenty years ago didn't work. And honestly, the 'situation' in the house is fine. No one needs to do anything. We've come to an accord."

"An accord?" His hostility faded to confusion. "What are you talking about? With the Devil?"

"No. With the spirit. It's not the girl you need to worry about, it's Vic. And, no matter what you want to convince yourself of, Wilhelmina had nothing to do with her death. She was devastated."

"You need—" Weston gestured at the house. "There is—" He fidgeted at the Bible. "Sunday, you should—"

"Speaking from a psychological standpoint regarding Wilhelmina," said Adam, "for a girl of thirteen to be capable of murdering a younger child, she would have displayed various types of aberrant behaviors that would have been noticed by someone—parents, teachers, even other kids.... Children that young who kill don't have the capacity to process consequences and often make no effort to hide their crimes, or they lack the sophistication to conceal them well. Had she been both deviant enough to kill and intelligent enough to hide the crime like an adult, we're talking about the makings of a dangerous serial killer that's one in ten million. Has there been a string of unsolved murders in the area? Someone like that would not have stopped at Robin Kurtis unless they were caught and institutionalized."

Weston rubbed his chin, a note of doubt in his eyes. "No, not that I'm aware of. Perhaps then the Devil, or whatever dark force is in this house affected Vic and compelled him to kill."

"There are plenty of psychological reasons to explain what he did that don't require supernatural influence." Adam scratched at his eyebrow. "Men with histories of abusive behavior like that don't need a push from beyond to lash out when their dominance is threatened."

Mia fidgeted, anxious about making it to work on time. "I have no idea. It's possible some negative energy affected him. There definitely is something dark in this house, though I'm inclined to say it's Vic. Again, if I decide we need your help, we'll ask for it. Please stop harassing us. I'm about to be late for work. Please go home, have a nice cup of coffee, and relax. I spoke to Nate, and he thinks we can handle this like adults and he doesn't need to be involved."

Weston frowned, but retreated down the porch steps. "You're making a mistake. To beguile the unwary, Satan appears as one you will trust."

"It doesn't feel like I am being tricked. Really. I have to get ready for work. Thank you for your concern." She forced herself to smile, despite worrying about her earlier thought regarding the man who clearly told Weston about her meeting with Wilhelmina. She'd wanted him to fall down the stairs. Up until coming to this house, the worst thought she'd ever had about her father had been not wanting to see him. She'd never wished ill on him until coming here. Though, did an idle daydream about him going face-first down a flight of stairs count as 'wishing ill?' Also, she'd had a rather crazy reaction to Robin attempting to kill her... scolding her like a child who'd purposefully spilled milk out of spite. A sliver of doubt crept in that perhaps the pastor might have a point, but she trusted her intuition more.

"If things don't work out with the animism, we can talk." Adam offered a handshake. "Until then, please give my wife some space?"

Mia didn't wait for his answer, hurrying inside to change for work, grumbling the whole way upstairs to the bedroom. Because of him, she wouldn't have breakfast and worse, she'd have to wait until she got to the museum to have any coffee.

The energy in the house darkened as if in response to her annoyance.

25

BAD DEEDS

THURSDAY, SEPTEMBER 6, 2012

Weston's mind raced, trying to poke holes in the Gartner's argument.

The fools teased with powers they had no understanding or respect for. Clearly, the Devil had already gotten his claws into the woman. How else could she have known that Hal Vaughan had jumped back so forcefully at the top of the stairs he'd knocked them both into a fall, and that Hal later claimed to have seen a little girl leap out at him? The only other people who knew anything about his war with the Devil during those months in 2001 had long since left the area. And he doubted Hal or Ettie would've told anyone about it.

Doing battle with Satan in a house occupied by a scientist and someone so hostile to those doing God's work wouldn't be easy. On some level, he sympathized with the woman for having parents who misused The Word. He had a far dimmer view of them than even atheists—at least the atheists who only wanted proof and didn't actively mock the faithful. People who claimed to be Christians yet used their faith to divide and harm did more damage to God than those who refused to believe. In this woman's case, her parents' cruelty had pushed her away from Him and left the poor woman vulnerable.

Satan had affected young Mia Gartner, and Weston would save her —whether she wanted him to or not. A drunken man can't ask someone to help them walk home, but they still needed someone to walk them home. Her mind had been affected by the Devil too much already, his influence irresistible due to her lack of faith.

She kept demanding proof, *visible* proof, and God simply didn't work that way for whatever reason. Who was he to question the Creator, much less make demands of Him?

He'd been two years shy of fifty when Hal Vaughan swept him down the stairs. That had hurt quite a bit. Now, at sixty-two, a fall like that could have serious consequences. Perhaps he should let the poor fools suffer the fate they asked for and walk away, but he couldn't turn his back on people so clearly in need of God's help. Inviting them to services on Sunday had sent the wrong message. He'd wanted them to be surrounded by the energy of the Lord, but they—mostly her— assumed he merely desired their donations to the plate. A different approach was needed. As much as it worried him to attempt anything without the support of holy ground at his feet, he'd compromise and do everything here, tell them going to the church wasn't necessary. His flock had already done battle with the evil in that house and God wouldn't care if they prayed here, in a fancy building, or wherever.

He tried to pick his words carefully to formulate a suggestion, but before he could assemble a full sentence, Adam thrust out a hand.

"If things don't work out with the animism, we can talk. Until then, please give my wife some space?"

Mia abruptly dashed inside, and the instant she turned away, a palpable wave of evil radiated from the house.

The faithful behind him all stopped praying at the same time.

Weston's mind blanked. He feebly shook Adam's hand and backed up, gawking at the upstairs windows. *Something* seemed to be staring at him, but he couldn't pinpoint it.

"What do you want us to do now, pastor?" asked Violet, a sweet woman a few years older than him who, without fail, knitted afghans for everyone in the church each Christmas. She had to spend all year making them… every year.

Weston couldn't stop looking at the house, wary of danger. It seemed Mia had called Nate Ross to complain about him. Of course, out-of-towners would do something like that instead of actually talking like neighbors. City folk never understood how it was out here, how people ought to be to each other. Worse, what with Nate trying to 'modernize' and be all respectable as a law enforcement officer, he probably wouldn't be as receptive to him doing God's work as Ralph Kline had been. The former sheriff knew how to keep the peace in a small town. Nate, although he grew up here, spent some years away and brought back a notion of 'city police.' The man would likely take Mia's complaints of trespassing and harassment seriously, despite that she desperately needed Weston's help.

No sense provoking that conflict yet, at least not unless things got out of hand.

Adam pulled out his cell phone and hurried into the house while explaining to someone on the other end that he'd be a little late due to an 'issue at home.'

"Ehh… The house has got them both pretty deep." Weston turned to face the volunteers. "Thank you for coming out here to support these people. I'm sorry if it's frustrating. They don't appreciate what they're up against."

"I… *felt* the evil," said Walter, Violet's husband. "For a sec there, I'd swear the *house* was starin' at us."

"Yeah." Earl nodded.

Murmurs of agreement swept over the group.

Weston raised both hands in a placating gesture. "It's all right. I experienced the same thing the last time I fought the darkness here, and it did not prevail. The Vaughans escaped with their lives, even if we were unable to cleanse the building. My only concern is protecting these people. For now, we've done all we can do today. You folks ought to go on home, maybe offer a prayer or two for their souls."

The group muttered their assurances they'd definitely pray for the Gartners, and wandered off back to their cars, parked a short ways down Minstrel Run. Adam jogged outside again, having added a blazer, hopped in his car, and zoomed off.

Weston strolled down the driveway, but paused at the end, not quite ready to give up on two innocent souls yet. On sudden inspiration, he slipped into the trees beside the road. Crouched low, he watched the house for a few minutes.

Mia rushed outside, pausing long enough at the door to say, "Be good, sweetie. I'll come home as soon as I can." She closed the front door, twisted her key in the upper lock, and ran to her SUV.

"That old witch is going to take the poor woman's soul." Weston ducked while she backed out of the driveway onto the road. As soon as she drove off, he stood again, shaking his head. "There are foul, foul deeds afoot."

She could be going to meet the witch right now. Eyes wide with urgency, Weston climbed up onto Minstrel Run and fast walked to his Jeep. As he always did, he'd left the keys in the ignition. It prevented him from losing them, and if God thought someone else needed his truck more than he did, so be it.

He stared over the wheel at the retreating taillights of Mia's Chevrolet, and turned the key.

The starter whirred a few times then cut out. Weston backed off, waited two seconds, and tried again. No sound came from the engine.

"Blast... Dear God, why would the engine die now?"

Again, he turned the key.

"God had nothing to do with it," snapped a little girl—from the passenger seat.

Weston stared into the scowl of seven-year-old Robin Kurtis, her skin as pale as paper, her once light brown hair nearly black, nightgown stark white.

He screamed.

A sudden roar came from the engine. The Jeep lurched forward as though he'd stomped the gas pedal all the way down. Weston couldn't look away from the child glaring at him; the revving engine nearly drowned out his wail of panic. Branches clattered at the roof. Weston tore his gaze off the devil child and faced forward... at the tree ten feet in front of him.

He stomped on the brakes and crossed his arms in front of his face.

Wham!

STEAM HISSED OUT FROM THE JEEP'S GRILLE, GATHERING IN A cloud at the front end.

Robin stood in the middle of the street, smiling at the green truck.

The old man groaned from inside, knocked senseless by the crash.

He wanted to make Mia go away. Even Mommy went away and left her all alone with no one to protect her from Daddy. She said she'd be back, but she never came home. Robin wanted to wait for Mommy to come home, but she knew Mia wouldn't go away.

Mia would never go away.

The driver door opened. A delirious Weston Parker stumbled out of the Jeep, blood trickling down his face from a broken nose. He swooned to his knees, clinging to the door so he didn't fall completely over. Unfocused eyes swept over the road, oblivious to the child's presence.

Robin glanced away from him, down the length of Minstrel run at the sound of an approaching car. She grinned at Weston, who wheezed and fell seated, then skipped off toward home, gradually fading out of sight.

Seconds after she disappeared, the curtains behind the tall window to the left of the front door twitched.

NATE ROSS SHOOK HIS HEAD, SQUEEZING AND RELAXING HIS GRIP on the wheel.

He drove along Deer Path Road to the right turn where it met Minstrel Run, his thoughts circling around Old Sheriff Kline's stories about the house. Two possibilities waited for him at the house. Either nothing at all—or something horrible.

Ever since he'd gotten off the phone with the new woman living there, he couldn't shake the feeling he really ought to go out there and have a look for himself. Nothing about that house ever wound up being normal or routine. Every time Nate had come out here to check up on the empty house since taking over, he'd been restless for days, unable to sleep. He'd never seen anything, at least not with his eyes, but something had gotten into his head, distracting him with phantom worries.

Maybe he shouldn't have given into curiosity and checked out the old files, looked at those ghastly pictures of the little girl's body. It had been the sort of scene that could send a detective diving headfirst into a whiskey bottle or turned hardened cops into the worst sorts of clichés. He felt awful for the poor bastard who had to take those photos, and worse for the mother who had to find her daughter like that.

Sheriff Kline had been new in 1970, only a twenty-six-year-old deputy. Once when talking about that case, he'd said something cryptic to Nate like 'sometimes, a lady just needs a .38 special.' The man hadn't seemed too concerned that Mrs. Kurtis had smuggled a firearm into the courthouse and executed her husband in front of fifty witnesses, including two sheriff's deputies, two Syracuse cops, a bailiff, and a judge. It bothered him more that the woman had passed away while awaiting trial. Officially, they'd listed her cause of death as suicide despite she'd been found in bed, not a mark on her, no drugs in her system. Old Sheriff Kline said 'that poor woman just didn't wanna live no more.'

Nate rounded a bend to a roughly quarter-mile stretch of straight road that passed in front of the house. For a fleeting instant, he thought he saw the figure of a little girl in a nightgown skipping off the road into the trees. He slowed, staring into the woods while trying to figure out if he'd imagined it.

A flash of green drew his attention to a Jeep Cherokee about twenty feet deep in the woods on his left, crashed into a tree. Weston Parker sprawled on the ground beside it, blood all over his face. Nate cut the wheel hard, pulling a U-turn to that side of the street while switching on the emergency lights. He grabbed the radio mic.

"Clark, come back?"

"Copy, Nate," replied Allison. "What's up?"

"Need an ambulance out here by Six Minstrel Run. Send a tow rig as well."

"You got it. What should I tell them to expect?"

"One person injured. Weston Parker went off the road and hit a tree. Gonna go check on him."

"Copy, Nate."

He hopped out and ran over to Weston, taking a knee and looking him over. His nose appeared broken and he had a nasty cut over his eye. "Pastor, hang on. Don't try to get up. Medics are on the way."

The man wheezed, nodding.

Nate glanced over at the Jeep. Minor damage to the bumper, grille, and hood. *Couldn't have been going* that *fast... still set off the airbag.* He brushed the man's wispy grey hair away from his face and shone a penlight in his eyes. Dilation response appeared normal, if a touch slow. "What happened? Black out? Do you have any chest pain?"

"No pain." Weston coughed. He narrowed his eyes in suspicion, then shot a dark glower off to the left. "Nah. Wasn't a heart issue. Rabbit darted across the road. Tried to swerve."

"Right." Nate surveyed the woods between here and the house in the distance. "Little rabbit in a nightgown?"

Weston's eyes bulged, then relaxed with a guarded sense of agreement.

"Gotta watch out for them rabbits." Nate pulled a handkerchief out and dabbed the blood from the pastor's face. "They always jump out at ya when you least expect it."

26

THE POOL OF LIFE

THURSDAY, SEPTEMBER 6, 2012

The winding forest road led deep into the woods southeast of Spring Falls, past beautiful houses, small ponds, and a rocky cliff dappled with moss and trickling water. While pastoral, the dinky dirt trail consisted of little more than two ruts in the understory. Mia clutched the wheel, scowling at the useless Garmin, which showed her simply in the midst of a featureless green area.

Worse, whoever had made this road never imagined people would drive anything near the size of a Chevrolet Tahoe on it. Leaves scraped both sides and the roof for the past six minutes. Mia stopped where two trees flanked the road, so close she didn't think she *could* fit through.

Ugh. Why did Wilhelmina want to meet at her 'cabin in the woods,' not her house? She lives less than a mile from us. What's so special about this cabin?

She hopped out and walked around to fold the side mirrors in, then got back in. Jaw clenched, she eased the truck forward, a long, soft squeal leaking out her nose. The Tahoe fit with inches to spare on each side.

"Please don't let anyone come from the other direction... we'd both be stuck."

A few minutes of driving past the trees of doom, she reached a sharp bend in the trail to the right. She considered stopping and going home, but something told her to continue for Robin's sake. Setting her nerves aside, Mia sat high in the seat in an effort to see the ground better.

"This is too big, but the Nissan would never handle this road."

She glanced down at the glowing light on the four-wheel-drive switch. Driving a brand new truck she'd had for less than four months off-road didn't seem like a great idea. One wrong move and she'd be in a ditch, or wedged between trees, or scrape thousands of dollars' worth of body damage into the side. Adam wouldn't call this 'off-road.' He'd make some remark about there being nowhere near enough mud or rocks for it to count as true 'off-roading.'

As far as I'm concerned, any time there's dirt under the tires instead of pavement, I'm off the road.

After a few more close calls with trees, she found the end of the trail, a grassy clearing ringed with knee-high weeds. Five other cars— three Jeep Wranglers, a small pickup truck, and a little Kia—sat parked around the edges with their front ends toward the woods. She recognized the grey Jeep with all the beads and stuff hanging off the mirror from the diner's lot. *That's gotta be Wilhelmina's.*

The back end of the building stood a half-story taller than the near end, the roof a straight angled surface that probably dumped all the snow onto the rickety deck in front of the door. The woman had said 'cabin,' but the rectangular structure looked like an enormous version of a crazy bomb maker's shack. Lights glowing inside plus all the cars made it feel somewhat safer than a psycho's retreat.

A blonde woman in her mid-to-late twenties wearing a beige turtleneck and jeans emerged from the back door, squinting at her headlights.

Mia parked in an open spot near the deck by a pile of firewood. The scent of the forest and wood smoke flooded her senses when she got out. Though she'd only driven about eighteen minutes from home, it seemed like she'd gone *way* out into the sticks to go camping.

"Hi," called the woman. "You must be Mia. I'm Lisa."

Without the truck's headlights facing the deck, Mia couldn't see much of anything but the general shape of a person waving at her. She approached a wobbly set of stairs, little more than wooden planks, and made her way up, crunching on old fallen leaves. Lisa had no jacket or shoes on, but didn't seem the least bit chilly.

"Hello. Yep. That's me. Sorry I'm late. That road was... interesting."

"It's only scary the first few times." Lisa opened the door for her, grinning. "Even with that huge thing you drive."

"Still not really used to its size. I've only had it for a few months."

Mia entered a narrow hallway with an uneven floor covered in mismatched swaths of linoleum. A door to the right led to a plain room containing a twin bed that touched the walls on three sides and a battered dresser missing half its drawers. Another doorway on the left led to a room empty except for a few stray power cords lying on the worn brown carpet.

The end of the hall opened into a large space with a vaulted ceiling of exposed beams. To the left, it had the trappings of a living room: two recliners, sofa, tiny TV on a stand next to a fireplace, and a doorway into another bedroom two steps down from the floor level. The right quarter of the room had a fridge, counter, and sink beside the smallest bathroom Mia had ever seen.

Wilhelmina and three other women sat around a table that started in the kitchen and ended in the living room. Various odd items had been arranged in front of them including candles, knives, little jars of unidentifiable substances, bundles of herbs, bowls of feathers, twine, and so on. It looked more like she'd walked in on them doing an inventory of witchy supplies than she'd interrupted a ritual.

"Mia!" Wilhelmina stood from her chair at the living room end and hurried over into a hug. "We're so glad you could make it!"

"Easier to find than the Pinecone. I mean... you've basically got your own private road." She managed a weak smile and waved at the others.

She shifted to stand next to Mia, an arm around her back. "Let me introduce you. I see you've met Lisa Donovan."

Mia nodded.

Lisa waved at her again and plopped into a chair, likely where she'd been sitting before the Tahoe's headlights lit up the back hallway as evidenced by a cup of tea already there.

"This is Linda North." Wilhelmina gestured at a late-forties woman, her black hair liberally streaked with silver. "I've known her for years. Sometimes babysat for her, too."

Linda looked up as if to say hello, but froze, staring at Mia. "Oh, you're right. She does look... umm... in need of help."

The woman seated next to Linda appeared to be in her mid-thirties and wore her dark brown hair in a bob. She glanced at Linda with a note of confusion, but dismissed it, stood, and offered a hand. "Rebecca Todd. Nice to meet you."

"Hi." Mia shook hands.

"And finally, Cheryl Murphy." Wilhelmina gestured at a starkly pale woman with straight jet black hair. She had to be the second youngest in the room after Lisa and Mia, probably teasing at or just past her thirtieth.

"If you call me Murph, I will throw things at you." Cheryl grinned. "If you call me Cher, I will bite you."

"Okay..." Mia blinked at the odd greeting, but the woman had a humorous tone to the threat, so it didn't come off as anything more than a joke.

Wilhelmina ushered Mia to the seat at the kitchen end of the table. "Tea?"

"Sure."

Three of the women mostly smiled at her, waiting for Wilhelmina. Linda, however, kept looking at Mia the way one might study someone who closely resembled a minor celebrity, trying to figure out if they'd met the actual person.

Wilhelmina set a cup in front of her and poured it full from a large kettle, already containing brewed tea. She made the rounds refilling everyone's cups, then replaced the kettle on the stove.

Mia returned nervous smiles to the other four women, then sniffed at the steam rising from her cup. The tea smelled vaguely fruity, though she couldn't identify exactly what kind. She eyed the stuff all over the table, wondering exactly what she'd gotten into. A deer head mounted to the wall on the right roughly at the point where the giant space changed from kitchen to living room, felt as if it stared at her. It hung over another doorway that led to a room as long as the main one but only half as deep, packed with small beds. Except for the overwhelming aroma of herbs and incense coming from the table, the rest of the place mostly smelled like wet dog.

"Welcome to our little sanctuary," said Wilhelmina while settling back into her seat at the opposite end of the table.

"Thanks. Umm… This isn't exactly what I was picturing."

Cheryl laughed. "You were expecting what then? A hidden crypt under a graveyard? Skulls all over the place? Black cats? Or maybe a big bonfire with us dancing around naked?"

"It's too chilly for that now." Lisa sipped her tea. "But if the fire's big enough, I'm game."

"She's *always* game. I swear the girl's a dryad. Any excuse to fling off her clothes," muttered Cheryl with a big smile.

"I can't wait for it to warm up." Rebecca stretched.

Linda kept glancing over at Mia. Wilhelmina appeared to notice and nodded once.

Mia blinked, then blushed, having the distinct impression they really did dance naked around a fire.

The women smiled or laughed at her reaction.

"So you're a psychic, huh?" asked Lisa.

"Apparently." Mia explained some of the things she'd seen and picked up on at the house, including her dreams of Evelyn meeting a deputy in the courthouse who gave her a weapon.

"Ooh. I knew the police helped her." Linda snapped her fingers. "What did he look like?"

"Umm. Evelyn was staring down, I only saw his face for an instant when he cut in front of her. Young… Twenty-five to twenty-seven. Black hair."

"That could've been a few different people." Wilhelmina tapped a finger on her chin.

"Weren't you a kid then?" asked Mia.

"Six," said Linda. "I knew Robin, but we only played together a couple times."

Mia gave her a sorrowful look. "That's… ugh. Sorry. I meant how would Wilhelmina remember any of the cops from back then. She was like thirteen."

"I was. However, my mother brought me to the trial. The prosecutor was planning to question me about what I saw in the house while babysitting the girl."

"Oh." Mia blinked. "Wait… you were there when she shot Vic?"

"In the building, yes. I'd been attending the trial for a few days. The day of the shooting, a bailiff instructed my mother and me to sit outside the courtroom until we were called in." She shook her head. "I'm sure they all knew what was coming and didn't want me watching it at that age."

"So, what do you do, other than see psychic stuff?" asked Rebecca.

Mia rambled a bit about working for the museum restoring fine art. That led into chatting with the other women about their jobs. Linda didn't work in any official sense, as her husband—a lawyer in Syracuse—made plenty. She sold craft stuff online and also represented one-third of the Spring Falls Historical Society. Due to the town being so damn small, they tended to also preserve information of historical significance for the surrounding area as well.

Rebecca worked as a dental hygienist, lived with three cats, two daughters, and a husband and a half. Presently, married to the father of her younger daughter, she still had 'baby daddy one' around all the time, though nothing romantic existed between them anymore. The men got along quite well and even went fishing together.

Mia smiled outwardly but couldn't help but think that beyond strange.

Lisa waited tables at a TGI Fridays in Syracuse, being the least motivated of the group. She'd joined the coven at sixteen originally to piss off her parents (and Weston) but it clicked with her and she wound up resonating with the traditions. She mentioned Wilhelmina taught an elective class at the university about pagan spirituality, and Lisa sometimes helped her with it.

Cheryl had waited tables, played guitar in a band that never got anywhere, did a two-year stint as a cable internet tech before getting tired of going into people's houses and having her ass grabbed. She presently worked in Syracuse doing phone technical support.

As minutes stretched into an hour or so of banal conversation about cats, kids, husbands' annoying habits, and irritating co-workers, Mia's slight awkwardness at being around four complete strangers evaporated fast.

Her phone beeped.

Everyone paused to watch her read and respond to a text from Adam. He wanted to check in, make sure all was well. He'd stayed home to do some paranormal investigation of the attic and basement, since Mia wouldn't be there to get creeped out. She replied, telling him the girls were a fun group.

"Something important?" asked Wilhelmina.

"Just Adam letting me know he's still alive and wanting to know if I am."

"Relax, dear," said Cheryl. "We only sacrifice virgins."

Mia laughed, as did the others.

"Well, I told you about my kids," said Rebecca. "Let's hear about yours."

"I'm not sure I'd call her *my* kid, but yeah okay... I guess I've started feeling this odd need to protect her, especially from that Weston guy."

The women all groaned.

"Do you think she's more than she seems, maybe influencing me? Weston thinks so."

"That man is a pain in the ass." Linda frowned. "I wish he would just leave us alone."

"You're the psychic." Wilhelmina sipped from her third cup of tea. "What do you think?"

"It doesn't feel wrong to me but *would* it if I'm the one being affected?" Mia also drank from her tea, still unable to identify the specific fruit in it.

The women discussed that, seeming to come to the conclusion that she probably would have doubts if the protectiveness hadn't been genuine.

"Has anything happened to make you worry?" Lisa got up to grab the kettle. She yanked it off the stove into the air in a comically exaggerated manner, then sighed. "Damn. Empty."

Mia bit her lip. "Well… one thing freaked me out pretty bad, but we're okay now. I kinda yelled at her and she promised not to do it again."

"What happened?" Wilhelmina leaned in, curious.

"I was in the bathtub and my hair drier launched itself at the water."

Everyone froze, staring at her.

"The bathroom sink is right behind the end of the tub. I just happened to look up at it within a second of the thing jumping into the air. Managed to swat it aside. At first, I thought it might've been Vic. Then, I wondered if maybe Evelyn's ghost became jealous of me since Robin had gotten so clingy."

"Doubt that," said Linda.

"Hmm?" Mia looked at her. "Why?"

"Umm." Linda hastily sipped tea. "Only that no one's ever said anything about Evelyn haunting the place. What you've seen of her past was all in dreams. And dream visions usually come from…" She waved about as if trying to grab words from the air.

"Psychic imprints," said Wilhelmina.

Linda slouched, relieved.

"Evelyn released a massive amount of emotional energy into that house when she found Robin's body. It doesn't surprise me that you pick up scraps here and there." Wilhelmina gestured at Lisa as if to say 'go on, proceed with making more tea.'

Mia suspected the group—or at least those two women—left her out of something. She trusted Wilhelmina, but couldn't help but be annoyed. *I'm not one of their witches yet so maybe I don't have top secret clearance.* She swirled half a mouthful of tea around her cup, trying to come up with a polite way to sidestep the witchcraft thing if they tried to invite her to join. Not that she had anything against them, but despite having come to accept the truth of being a psychic, she couldn't quite believe that magic worked. Wilhelmina and her friends weren't that different from Weston. The names and rituals changed, but they all believed in stuff because someone else told them it existed. But at least witches didn't threaten people who refused to join them with an eternity of burning. And, Wilhelmina hadn't asked her to join at all, merely meet them on friendly terms.

"So, anyway… I was storming around the house yelling at Vic. Robin came out and admitted she'd tried to 'make me a ghost' so she could hug me."

"Aww," said Lisa, eyes wide. "That's murderously adorable."

"You need therapy, girl." Cheryl pointed a finger gun at her. "Those two words should not be used together."

"I basically scolded her like she was any ordinary kid who made a huge mess. Told her if she did anything like that again, I'd leave. Also promised that I'd stay no matter what if she behaved herself." Mia gestured at the air with both hands as if holding a giant beach ball. "From the moment that hair dryer tried to zap me, the whole house felt ominous, like it wanted me dead. As soon as she promised not to try and kill me, that dread went away. I can't tell if the energy in the actual house changed or if I somehow sensed the threat to my life, which stopped when she decided not to kill me."

"Interesting." Wilhelmina tapped a fingernail against her cup.

"She told me something else that kinda had me and Adam confused."

"Oh?" Wilhelmina raised an eyebrow.

The other women leaned in close to listen.

"Well, we'd been talking about your scrubbing the place, and that we didn't want to do anything to Robin. However, if we could get rid of Vic, we would. She became worried, said something like if Vic went away, she'd go away, too. Adam thinks that Robin might be trapped there because of him somehow. He also suggested we might not have a little girl *and* a shadow man in the basement, but one entity pretending to be a kid as a means to play with our heads. I don't believe that. She feels genuine to me. Adam's kinda stuck on the whole heaven/hell thing. He said a real child's spirit who's innocent wouldn't hang around as a ghost. They'd just move on right away."

The women nodded at varying speeds, except Wilhelmina who stared into nowhere, lost in thought.

"I've heard that too," said Rebecca. "Mostly in paranormal circles. They think every little kid haunt is a demon playing mind games. Some might be... but even kids can have unfinished business. Some might simply be confused, not realizing they're dead. Or maybe they're waiting for their parents to cross over so they can go together."

"I'm guessing you guys aren't too big on that whole Heaven or Hell thing. Where do you think spirits go when they, uhh, 'move on?' Where would Robin go if Vic is like a drain plug holding her there and we pull it?"

"The Pool of Life," said Linda, staring at her with an odd intensity. "We believe that all life energy in the Earth is constant. Everything that lives has a soul, and when it dies, that soul energy returns to a great swirling mass deep within the Earth, only to reemerge with new life elsewhere."

"Reincarnation." Wilhelmina smiled. "Have you ever heard of the first law of thermodynamics?"

"It sounds vaguely familiar, but college was a long time ago." Mia smiled.

"Bullshit," said Lisa. "I'm older than you and I'm twenty-seven."

Mia raised her tea cup in toast. "So am I."

"The only one here who can say college was a 'long time ago' is Willa, and she didn't go because they didn't let women go to college back then." Rebecca winked.

Wilhelmina picked her eye with her middle finger. "I'm not *that* old. And I most certainly *did* go to college. It is rather difficult to obtain work as a university professor with only a high school diploma after all."

Everyone laughed.

"Anyway," said Wilhelmina. "The first law of thermodynamics states that energy can neither be created nor destroyed. It's a scientific principle that also applies here. Souls can neither be created nor destroyed, only changed. Life proceeds to death, the energy of the soul retreats to Gaia, mingles with the Pool, then comes back eventually."

"When a new child is born, energy from the Pool of Life returns and provides a soul for the baby." Lisa approached and refilled Mia's mug with still-boiling tea.

"Speaking of that... We've been talking." Wilhelmina clasped her hands, eyeing the others.

Lisa moved one space to the right and refilled Cheryl's mug.

"We believe it may be possible to alter that process magically."

Mia nodded. "You've found a way to throw Vic out of the house?"

"Not exactly." Wilhelmina's lips stretched into a slow, but broad smile. "When a child is conceived, soul energy migrates to our world from the Pool of Life. However, we think it may be possible to take a shortcut—if there happens to already be a stray soul in the area who wishes to inhabit the baby."

Mia nearly dropped her tea.

"I think she understands where you're going with this." Linda fidgeted in her chair like a kid staring at presents on Christmas morning she hadn't yet been given permission to open. The look in her eye rather made Mia think the woman wanted her desperately to agree.

"So... you... you're saying if"—she swallowed—"I were to become pregnant, Robin could what? Just hop in? Come back to life?"

Wilhelmina raised a hand. "Not *exactly*. We're not talking about raising the dead. Everything that lives and dies reincarnates at some point. All we would be doing is skipping a few steps, namely Robin's soul going back to the Pool and churning around down there for who knows how long."

"People don't remember their past lives, do they?" asked Mia.

"Most of the time, no. Except for bits and pieces." Linda shook her head.

"It happens sometimes. Like this one kid spoke fluent Russian and had no reason to know it. Another little boy once told his parents exactly how he'd been murdered in a past life as a thirty-something-year-old."

"Remembering things with such clarity is super rare though." Lisa shrugged.

"But those reincarnations happened the 'normal' way? As if anything here is normal." Mia chuckled. "What possible effect would this have on her if it worked? Isn't it kinda important to go through the spin cycle between lives?"

They chuckled.

Wilhelmina grinned. "I can't say for sure, but I think she will remember her former life more clearly than most, and there's a good chance she will remain the same person mentally."

It sounded creepy as hell, but hearing that Robin would remain who she is paradoxically made Mia want to do it even more. She'd decided a while ago to do everything she could to comfort the girl... how better than to be able to hold her for real? The hair dryer incident only happened out of a child's desperate loneliness, not malice.

Mia choked up. *What's wrong with me? She tried to kill me and I'm getting misty-eyed at it being sad and cute.* "Umm... what if Adam's right and Robin isn't a child but something darker?"

"Then you usher in the harbinger of the End Times," said Lisa in a cheerful tone with a huge grin.

"Check the baby's head for three sixes," deadpanned Cheryl. "Oh, wait... Satan's a myth."

Wilhelmina let off a stern sigh. "I have good news and I have bad news."

"Ooo-kay." Mia leaned back, eyes wide.

"The good news is, I'm confident we can construct the ritual necessary to create a spirit bridge for her in such a manner as to prevent the trespass of negative energy. I am inclined to trust your instinct that she is who she appears to be, but if she isn't, whatever it is will not be able to invade your baby."

"What's the bad news?" whispered Mia.

"If the spirit *is* dark... you'll probably die from the resulting clash of energy." Wilhelmina cringed.

Rebecca smirked. "Don't scare her. There's only like a seventy-five percent chance she'll have a heart attack. We might be able to do like CPR or something."

"Umm." Mia gulped. "Just so I'm clear on this… you're suggesting that I let Adam knock me up and you can somehow allow Robin to become my baby?"

"Just her soul," said Linda.

"That's correct." Wilhelmina nodded once. "All souls come from the Pool. We aren't changing the workings of things, merely adjusting the selection process."

Mia stared into her tea. As crazy as it sounded, after watching the murder right out of Robin's eyes, she *had* to take the chance. That poor child didn't deserve her end. A do-over was most definitely in order. If only she could somehow ask Evelyn for permission, but that boat sailed long ago. Robin hadn't spoken of her at all, only to say she'd gone away. Maybe the woman's soul *had* gone back to the Pool of Life or Heaven if it existed. Though, a finite amount of soul energy that continued to recycle sounded more scientifically plausible than endless numbers of new souls streaming out of thin air and eventually winding up sorted into naughty or nice piles. Endless creation and endless storage didn't make comparative sense, at least in any scientific manner.

"Okay. Let's do it," said Mia.

Wilhelmina got up, walked around the table, and took her hand, her eyes brimming with concern like she comforted an old friend at the edge of death. "Are you sure? Are you certain a dark spirit hasn't influenced you?"

Mia stared at the tan skin of the hand gripping hers, wrinkled, cured from years of gardening and natural living. "I don't think I am. Not a hundred percent anyway, but I'm not sure I care. It feels right, and my gut's been on a roll lately."

"All right." Wilhelmina took a breath and stood tall, exuding confidence. A hint of a tear glistened at the corner of her eye. "The first step will be for you to approach Robin about the idea. It will only work if she is a willing participant. We will not force her."

"Okay. I can do that. So, umm, what's all involved with this? And please tell me it's not going to require any powdered bull penis."

Wilhelmina cackled with laughter. The others appeared confused.

"Isn't that for luck spells?" asked Lisa.

Mia laughed so hard she nearly fell out of her chair. "Oh, I needed that... Tension breaker."

"It will require a ritual." Wilhelmina, still chuckling, made her way back to her seat. "We will set up a circle in the balcony room, the one with the big bay windows. That's directly under your bedroom. The girl will stand in the circle and wait. The other part of the ritual involves painting sigils on your body to establish the other end of the gate. Then, you and Adam simply do what you would normally do."

Mia nodded.

"Naked time!" shouted Lisa. "Hey, would you mind if I went sky clad during the ritual, too?"

Mia raised an eyebrow. "What does that mean?"

"She's addicted to being naked," muttered Cheryl.

"Umm... that would be more than a little awkward." Mia bit her lip. "Is it required?"

Lisa fake pouted. "No. Just comfortable. Don't worry. It'll be plenty awkward enough lying there while we paint you up."

Mia blushed. "Can't be worse than the gynecologist. At least you're not going spelunking."

"Nope." Lisa grinned. "You only have to deal with about thirty minutes or so of trying to hold still while we tickle you with paintbrushes."

She shivered at the mere thought of that. "Okay. Let me talk to Robin and Adam about the idea."

Linda beamed. "I'm sure she'll be thrilled."

"Awesome." Lisa jumped up and headed over to the fridge. "Anyone want cake?"

27

A LITTLE UNCOMFORTABLE

THURSDAY, SEPTEMBER 6, 2012

Yellow flashing lights danced among the trees up ahead, farther down Minstrel Run.

Mia slowed, still overjoyed she'd gotten the Tahoe out of Wilhelmina's cabin without scraping a tree or losing a side mirror. Going there had required she drive in the opposite direction—a left turn out of the driveway—she usually took to go to work or downtown. About 200 feet from her home, a pair of guys stood beside a flatbed tow truck backed off the road into the woods. Amber bar lights on the truck's roof filled the nearby forest with an eerie glow.

"That's odd…"

She veered left a little before cutting the wheel right to pull into her driveway. After shutting off the engine, she opened the door to the high-pitched whine of an electric winch. Mia hopped out and squinted at a cluster of trees awash in the glow of floodlights. At the sight of a newish green Jeep Cherokee easing backward up onto the flatbed, she gasped.

Her usual amused reaction at bad things happening to overly religious people didn't extend to *actual* harm. Only inconveniences like spilled coffee or walking into sign posts. She still hadn't quite processed what Weston said about gay people—that he had no problem with them—and it made her feel guilty.

"Hey, hon," said Adam from the front door.

She raised an arm to point. "What happened over there?"

"Weston went off the road and hit a tree. That sheriff you called stopped by to take a statement from one of us about the harassment. Apparently, the old guy didn't leave right away with the rest of his people. Nate thinks he might've been in a 'highly agitated state' that elevated his blood pressure and caused a blackout. Says brake skids only started a few feet in front of the tree, probably when he regained consciousness. Fortunately, he didn't get up to much speed. Knocked him around a little, but he'll be okay."

Mia relaxed at hearing Weston hadn't been seriously injured. The pitch of the hydraulic noise changed. She glanced over at the tow truck's flatbed sliding upward and leveling off. Other than a mess of greenery sticking out of the grille and a crumpled hood, the Jeep didn't appear to be too damaged. "He was going to follow me."

"What? How do you know that?"

She paused, searching for the answer. "I don't know. As soon as I looked at his truck, I just got the idea in my head. I didn't even see him in my mirrors this morning. He couldn't have been that close. No idea why he would've wanted to follow me to work."

"C'mon inside. It's starting to get chilly at night."

"Okay." Mia trailed up the steps to the porch, staring at the workers loading the Jeep until she passed the doorjamb and couldn't see them anymore. "Bad games."

"What?" asked Adam.

Mia took her coat off. "Someone played a bad game on Weston. Hope he got the message."

"Wait, you're saying Robin did that?"

"I'm suspecting. She's quite protective of us, and I wasn't too happy with him this morning." She hung the coat in the closet and kicked her shoes off.

"You're not at all upset about it?" He lowered himself onto the couch.

Mia sat beside him. "I should be, but I'm not. He was trespassing and probably about to stalk me. Plus, he isn't hurt too bad."

"Never knew you to have such a vindictive streak."

She hugged his right arm, leaning her head on his shoulder. "It's not vindictive. He's threatening a child I feel a need to protect. Speaking of which…"

"Hmm?"

"Had a rather interesting—and bizarre—meeting with Wilhelmina and her friends. They're like witches or something, but it's not like Wicca. She's made up this blend of witchcraft and old druidy and some other stuff."

"I wouldn't say she's 'made it up,' as much as collected aspects of various old belief systems and mixed them. She researches that stuff for her work at the university."

"Remember how Robin said she was afraid of going away if we got rid of Vic, and then you asked why would an innocent spirit wind up trapped as a ghost?"

"Yeah." He squeezed her hand.

Mia explained what the women had told her of the Pool of Life and then went into a description of the ritual Wilhelmina mentioned. "So they think they found a way to let her skip ahead in line so to speak."

He stared at her with an unreadable expression that could've said 'you're crazy' as easily as 'I could really go for some buttered toast.'

"So, umm… how do you feel about that?"

"To be perfectly honest, part of me thinks it's outlandish. A larger part of me is intensely curious about the paranormal aspects."

"If we do this, you are *not* going to be recording us."

He laughed. "No, of course not. Well, at least not the fun part."

"*Adam*…" She poked him in the side. "I don't want anything to interfere with it. If you start setting up EM detectors and microphones and the video camera, it might be too distracting or get in the way."

"Wow… you really want to do this? And not even so much the magic part, you're suggesting we have a kid."

"I already have a—" She shot him a sheepish look. "Please don't think I'm nuts, but it feels like we already *do* have a kid."

"Luckily for you, I have both known you for years and also have a keen interest in the supernatural. I both believe you are psychic and there is a spirit in the house... so no, I don't think you're nuts. Perhaps attached somewhat quickly, but I think she appealed to the same part of you that defied your parents to protect Timothy."

Mia snuggled against him, overtaken by a sudden, inexplicable desperation to be able to hold Robin for real, to protect her from the cold, lonely existence she'd been condemned to for forty-two years. If Adam said no, she'd probably wind up in tears. "This is so crazy, but I want to do it so bad. It doesn't make sense how much I need to do this. I need to be with her."

"It's a big decision, not factoring in anything about the unusual parts. Having a baby at all is a project."

"Yeah, it'll completely ruin our party lifestyle," deadpanned Mia.

He chuckled. "Why do I get the feeling this is as much for you as it is for her?"

"No idea. I suppose she could be influencing me somehow, but I don't *think* so." She sighed at the ceiling. "This is going to sound bizarre coming from *me* of all people, but I feel like I came to this house for a reason."

"Yeah. That does sound quite unlike you to believe in fate or destiny. While it's going to be awkward getting romantic with other people around, if this is something you feel so strongly about, let's do it."

She looked up at him. "Really?"

He kissed her lightly on the lips, then nodded. "Yes, really." His serious expression shifted comic. "Please tell me we're not going to need to perform somewhere out in the woods while Wilhelmina and her friends chant and dance around us."

Mia's face burned with blush. "No. I'm the one who needs to deal with mostly total strangers drawing all over me. They won't be in the room with us when we get to do the fun part... though you'll have to be careful. If you smudge the markings, it could disturb the bridge."

"Aww. Pity. Of course we'll have plenty of time for 'fun sex' after that."

"There is." She leaned up and kissed him. "You're really okay with this?"

"It seems you're not the only one who is potentially nuts." He winked. "Besides, I'm too fascinated by the idea of the paranormal at work here to miss the opportunity."

Mia smiled while gazing at the blank TV screen.

They discussed the logistics of introducing a baby to the family and came to the conclusion that they could work it out financially.

"I think I get a couple months maternity leave. We're going to need the money, so I'm planning to go back to work as soon as I'm out of time."

"My parents will be thrilled. Hell, we have the space now. They might insist on staying with us for a couple months after you return to work to help out."

She sneered off to the side, thinking about her parents. Part of her felt guilty for not wanting to tell them about a baby at all, but after the way they treated Timothy—and her—she'd washed her hands of them. "That'll be nice. And there's always asking Wilhelmina to babysit."

"Hah." He kissed her cheek.

Mia sat up. "Before I get too excited, there's one more person I need to bounce this crazy idea off."

He looked confused for a moment before realization set in. "Oh... right."

"Yeah. We're not going to do this against her will. None of the girls said anything specific, but I got the feeling that would have... bad consequences."

"No doubt. I've read *Pet Sematary*."

Mia gasped. "Don't even joke about that." Sudden worry at the coven's warning of what could happen if Robin turned out to be a dark entity impersonating a little girl made her cling to Adam's arm as though it were the child she so desperately needed to help. If she told him she had a good chance of death should the spirit be malign, he'd certainly refuse to allow the ritual to proceed—at least, not without total proof of the spirit's innocence. That could take years to establish if at all, and she couldn't wait that long.

Robin needed her now.

"Are you okay?" asked Adam.

"Yeah. Just worried, freaked out, and excited all at the same time. I can't believe I'm honestly thinking a crazy 'magic' ritual might really do something. It's so far-fetched, yet at the same time, the way she explained everything kinda makes sense."

He brushed a hand repetitively over her hair. "Well, either way, we'll have a baby."

"Oh, wow... what if it's a boy and she's stuck inside?"

"Think that might explain people with gender dysphoria?" asked Adam. "Wrong soul for the body?"

"I have no idea and I really don't want to waste the hundreds of hours we could possibly spend debating why some people's insides don't match their outsides."

He chuckled.

"All right." Mia stood, shivering. "I shouldn't be this nervous. She's only a kid. Not like I have to give a presentation to the board of trustees."

"Let's go..."

Adam held her hand as she led the way upstairs to Robin's bedroom.

"Sweetie?" Mia knocked. "Are you here?" She waited a moment, listening to silence before nudging the door open more and peering in. "Robin? Can I talk to you? It's important."

The room appeared empty.

"Be right back," whispered Adam. He ran off down the hall.

"Please, honey... It's got nothing to do with what may or may not have happened to that annoying pastor."

"You're not mad at me?" asked a whisper from beyond the foot of the bed.

"No, not at all." Mia smiled, hope surging. She stepped into the bedroom. "I have something to ask you."

Robin faded into view, standing on the spot where her body had been found. She regarded Mia with a neutral expression that carried a hint of curiosity. When Adam returned to the doorway holding his video camera and a digital audio recorder, she shied away.

"It's okay, sweetie." Mia sank to kneel, sat back on her heels, and raised her arms.

The child tentatively approached, stopping inches from arms' reach.

"Do you see her?" whispered Adam. "There's a light ball floating right in front of you."

Mia nodded. "Yes. I see her like a normal person, only a little transparent."

Robin stuck out her tongue.

The urge to grab and hug the girl for the rest of time grew to the point Mia almost couldn't resist it. She gripped her knees to keep her hands busy and stared down at the girl's bare feet.

"Robin, I promised you I'd do everything I could to protect you. And one of the things I want to protect you from is being lonely, cold, and scared."

The girl tilted her head slightly to the side.

"I think I know why you don't want us to make the bad spirit go away. He's the reason you haven't gone back to the Pool of Life." *Assuming that it exists.*

Robin shook her head, staring at her. "I'm waiting for Mommy, but she went away. If you make bad Daddy go away, I'll have to go, too."

"You aren't the same spirit as him, are you?"

"No. Don't be silly."

Mia smiled. Of course, a malicious haunt wouldn't hesitate to lie, but she didn't feel deceit. "Do you remember Wilhelmina?"

"Yeah. She was sad when Daddy hit me."

"Do you understand that you're a spirit now?"

Robin nodded. "Yes. I couldn't walk through walls before."

"How would you feel about a way so you wouldn't have to be a spirit anymore?"

She stepped back. "I don't wanna go away."

"No." Mia reached for her. "You won't have to go away. I want to help you have the life that should never have been taken away from you." She rested her hands on her stomach. "Every baby has a soul. Wilhelmina told me that those souls all come from a place deep inside the Earth, where everything goes when they're done living. She's found a way to make a bridge so *you* can be the soul for our baby."

Robin's mouth opened, eyes widening.

"You wouldn't have to be a ghost anymore... and we could hold you for real."

The spirit's eyes brimmed with glimmering tears.

"I..." Mia looked down. "Can't promise it will work, but do you want to try?"

"Even after I played all those bad games, an' tried to make you a ghost, you still wanna do that for me?"

Mia scooted forward, wrapping her arms around a patch of cold air filled with the intangible shape of a small girl. "I do. Is that okay?"

Robin wiped her eyes and nodded, too emotional to speak. After a moment, she looked up into Mia's eyes. Her tears ceased, and a broad smile formed. "Mommy!"

"Whoa," whispered Adam. "I heard that."

28

THE CIRCLE

FRIDAY, SEPTEMBER 7, 2012

The day dragged at work.

Mia had trouble getting into the zone. Color-matching for the enormous painting frustrated her with the tedium. Her perfectionism collided with her impatience to be home. Normally, she adored this part of the process since it came closest to letting her feel like she made a living as an actual artist. The little portrait of Robin she'd painted *did* match the newspaper photo Adam found. It had been enough to prove to him that her gift was real, but any skeptic could dismiss it as she could easily have painted it after seeing an old picture.

She'd called Wilhelmina last night after Robin had calmed down, and they had agreed to give the ritual an attempt on Saturday night. When Mia asked if they should wait to sync it up with her cycle, the woman told her not to worry about that as she had ways to help the body along in that regard.

Janet, her boss, came in to ask after the project, since she'd been behind her usual schedule. Mia mentioned that she and Adam had decided to try for a baby and her excitement had her distracted. Janet erupted in a fit of congratulatory cheering, and seemed pleased to hear that Mia had no plans on quitting—only taking enough time off to deal with the delivery and settling in afterward.

She returned home with shaking hands, mostly out of anticipation. Despite the girl's assurance that she was, in fact, an innocent murder victim and not a demonic entity pretending to be a child to mess with the living, Mia couldn't help but feel a little dread that she could have only a day and a half left to live. However, in order for her to be afraid that a magical ritual gone awry could give her a heart attack, she'd have to believe that the magical ritual could actually do something. She'd seen nothing at all to give her the least bit of hope that it would work. If she were honest with herself, it sounded as ridiculous as her parents praying for things. They'd spent at least a half hour every night after learning Timothy was gay praying for 'God to make him normal.' For all she knew, they still did... Of course, that didn't necessarily prove no god existed or that prayer didn't work... only that perhaps God considered him already normal and didn't need to change anything. She still thought prayer a contradiction for people who believed in a god who already had a plan. If they trusted in His plan so much, why ask Him to change it?

Adam handed her a sachet of herbs when he walked in the door. "Wilhelmina gave this to me at work today... said you should brew it into a single cup of tea and drink it around nine or ten tonight. Also, sugar won't affect it if you want to add some."

She took the innocent little cloth bag. "This is her workaround for my cycle? She thinks tea is going to help ensure I get pregnant?"

"If the woman believes tickling you with paintbrushes for a little while and saying some words is going to let Robin slip into a baby, a fertility treatment via herbal tea seems downright sane."

Mia laughed. "Fair point."

"Hey, if this works, we're not going to have a haunted house for much longer. Do you think you could ask Robin to do me a little favor for scientific purposes?" He ducked into the fridge.

The girl appeared in the doorway between the kitchen and the little hall to the dining room.

Mia smiled at her. "You can ask her yourself, she's right here."

Adam leaned back from collecting supplies for dinner. "Hey, hon.

Remember the footprints in the pancake mix? How about you help me out with some evidence?"

Robin folded her arms. "I'm not a guinea pig."

"He's not experimenting *on* you," said Mia. "He's trying to show the world that death isn't the end."

"It's not the end, it's just lonely." Robin frowned. "Okay. I'll help."

ADAM COOKED A BATCH OF SHRIMP PASTA AS WELL AS GOT STARTED on a massive pot of soup, which he planned on serving as dinner for everyone tomorrow night. He maintained that soup always tasted better after it sat for a day.

While they ate, Robin hovered beside Mia, peppering her with questions she couldn't answer about what everything would feel like if the ritual worked, was she scared, and so on. When she asked what would happen if it didn't work, Mia cringed at a pang of heartbreak as strong as if she'd had her child taken away from her.

"Well, if it doesn't work, then Adam and I will have *two* kids. And… not working once doesn't mean we won't stop trying."

Robin smiled. "Okay."

At seeing no trace of envy on the girl's face, Mia relaxed. Her present worries consisted of: not being able to help Robin, dropping dead in the middle of the ritual, and having to deal with a jealous spirit child who might harm a defenseless baby. Upon realizing she dreaded Wilhelmina's plan not working more than dying in the attempt, she swished her fork around the shrimp pasta, questioning her sanity.

While Mia loaded the dishwasher, Adam ran to get his video camera. He returned to the kitchen with it, set it on the counter, and squatted in front of it, recording himself describing he was about to demonstrate interaction with a fully intelligent actual spirit. That done, he picked up the camera and narrated while dusting the floor with flour.

"Is she still here?"

Mia tried unsuccessfully to pat the girl on the head. "Yes. She's standing right next to me."

"Great. Sweetie, will you please walk over this flour like you did with the pancake mix?"

She gave a little huff of annoyance, but obliged. Adam focused the video camera on the white patch, not reacting at all to her approach until she reached the flour and left a trail of footprints across it.

"Okay, now to further prove the spirit is an actual intelligent being... Hon, would you please write your name?"

The girl squatted at the edge of the powder and traced 'Robin' with her finger in a childlike scrawl... then dotted the 'i' with a little heart.

Mia choked up at the cuteness, then remembered the tea sachet and got up to boil water.

Tomorrow night couldn't get there fast enough.

Saturday, September 8, 2012

MURMURING VOICES AND THE OCCASIONAL STIFLED SOB CAME from the crowd seated around her.

She gazed down at the shiny pastel blue purse in her lap. The judge had given her an odd look for sitting behind the defense table, as had her parents who remained behind the prosecutor. No one else seemed to care. When they'd brought Vic in, dressed in a prisoner's jumpsuit and handcuffs, he'd had a far-off stare in his eyes. Upon noticing her, his blank affect broke to a sneering grin.

He muttered, "Bye bye, Mommy" when he passed.

Mia had been so heartbroken so long, hearing that phrase only sent a single tear running down her cheek. Soon, nothing would matter.

His parents had thus far avoided her, almost implying they somehow blamed her for the situation their son faced. Never mind a child had been killed, the tragedy in their eyes was that their son might go to prison for the rest of his life—or be executed. Whatever they thought about her wouldn't matter either. They'd soon think even less about her.

Mia didn't care.

She sat there, head down, hands clasped atop her purse, not really listening to anything the lawyer, the prosecutor, or the judge said... until the word 'recess' broke through her mental fog with the *slam* of a gavel.

Again, the horrible image of her mangled daughter appeared in her mind.

She had no hesitation.

She had plenty of regret, but not for what she prepared to do.

Mia slipped her right hand into the purse and grasped the handle of the .38 revolver. People around her stood and shuffled away, but she remained. Two deputies approached Vic to pull him out of the chair, but paused, giving her the look.

I'm sorry, Robin.

She stood and pulled the gun out, raising her arm to point it at the back of Vic's head, not quite ten feet away.

"Gun!" shouted the judge, panic in his eyes.

Neither deputy moved. Vic twisted toward her, his dead-eyed expression challenging her to do it.

Bang!

Her first shot clipped Vic in the shoulder. He flinched, tugging at the handcuffs secured to a restraint belt around his waist.

She fired again and again, as emotionless inside as the look on his face. He almost seemed to welcome it. Her third and fifth bullets struck him in the face, blowing pieces out the back of his head. The sixth round caught him in the chest at the base of the neck.

Click.

The hammer fell on an empty chamber.

Indistinct screams came from behind her. People dove to the floor or ran for the exits. The judge froze like a deer in the headlights, his face a mask of abject shock. Screaming, the defense attorney curled up under the table like a terrified child. Vic emitted a gurgle and slumped over sideways, his face mashed into the floor, ass in the air.

Mia tossed the revolver at him and offered no resistance as the two deputies who had come to collect Vic grasped her arms. She held her head high as they walked her out of the courtroom, as gently as young men guiding an elderly mother. Mia appreciated their kindness, but didn't really care if their suggestion she had a good chance of pleading temporary insanity or simply being acquitted for justifiable homicide might hold true.

She had no interest in living long enough to find out.

———

MIA LURCHED UPRIGHT IN BED AND HUGGED HER KNEES TO HER chest.

The son of a bitch wanted to die. Not the least bit of fear in him. He even tried to take her revenge away from her.

She let off a long, hard sigh. That she wanted to shoot Vic all over again herself disturbed her less than the sight of his shot-open skull.

"Hey, kiddo," said Mia. "How about pancakes? Gonna be a while after today before you'll be able to enjoy them."

Robin faded into view beside the bed, grinning. "Pancakes!"

Smiling, Mia hopped out of bed.

———

SHE HEADED OUT TO THE BACKYARD WITH ADAM, CONTINUING the task of cleaning up the aftereffects of the house standing empty so long. While she had no tremendous love of outdoor work, it needed to be done and also gave her something to focus on instead of rattling around the house paying attention to the slow creep of time.

"Oh, I forgot to tell you." Adam dragged a large branch out of a tangle and took a hand saw to it. "The other day in the basement, I got a couple still images of a shadow figure."

Mia shuddered. "You should check that bar, Johnny's. If Vic is haunting anywhere, it would be that place."

"Hah, yeah. Attic was blank. Still haven't seen any sign of

Evelyn's ghost. You'd think she'd be haunting this place as well... to be with Robin."

"Yeah, you'd think." Mia stuffed mulch handful after handful into a giant lawn and garden bag. "If she died of a broken heart, maybe she gave up too much and simply let the forces of nature take her wherever. Maybe she didn't even think about ghosts or hauntings? If she killed herself on purpose, waking up as a ghost wouldn't have offered the escape from grief she'd been hoping for, so maybe she let herself 'go away' as Robin keeps saying, just to stop existing."

Adam tossed the last fragments of the branch in another bag. "Could be. What feels the most right to you?"

Mia stared at her white gloves. Except for the little rubber grip dots on the palms and fingers, they looked like they belonged to Mickey Mouse. Despite their silly appearance, they worked well to protect her hands. "I think she was so devastated she just let herself go. Vic's parents blamed her for their little boy getting in legal trouble."

"What? Where'd that come from?"

She resumed stuffing dead weeds and leaf bits into the bag. "Had another dream this morning. Wilhelmina thinks Evelyn imprinted a lot of energy in the house when she found Robin. Somehow, I'm picking up on it and dreaming scenes from her past. Saw her shoot him this time."

"Ack."

"He just sat there and let her. Honestly, I can't tell if he'd been so stunned she had a gun he couldn't move, or if he wanted her to kill him. The bastard taunted her on the way in, gloating about how he'd hurt her."

"Hmm. I doubt he had any reason to suspect she'd been armed, so it's unlikely he tried to goad her into attacking him."

Mia scooted to her left every couple handfuls, keeping in reach of the shrinking pile she gathered from. "He wanted to hurt her. But he didn't know he couldn't do any more damage. That man had already put her in a dark, dark place. Nothing he could've done after that would've made it worse. And who the hell let this yard deteriorate so badly?"

"The people we bought it from, the Weirs. They listed it in 2009 and dropped the price four times. I kinda feel bad for them in a way, but they didn't take *too* much of a beating on it since they'd gotten it cheap. Place sat empty for three years and I think Joe was keeping the front and sides clean himself."

"Joe?"

"The realtor."

"Oh, right." She shrugged. "Nice of him."

"Ehh, he wanted to sell the place. Bad enough it had a reputation, but if it looked like they filmed *The Jungle Book* here, he'd never get rid of it."

She laughed.

The rest of Saturday afternoon passed in a haze of grueling yardwork. If they hadn't been planning on adding to the family, she'd have suggested hiring a landscaper. Between saving money and wanting the work to occupy her mind, she abandoned that idea.

Once the light began to weaken, they headed inside. Mia took a nice, long bath to wash off the sweat and soil of nine hours' work. She gazed up at the ceiling while relaxing in warm water, sensing a change in the energy of the house. More than ever, it felt like home... even more so than the house she'd grown up in.

I need to call Timothy and see how he's doing in LA.

Considering the planned activity later that night, Mia put on one of her old college sleep shirts, a *Bugs Bunny* one in red that hung down to her knees. Adam took over the bathroom as soon as she left to go downstairs and turn the soup on.

Wilhelmina and Lisa arrived together a little after six, carrying four large cloth bags. Lisa still didn't have shoes on. Rebecca rang the doorbell at 6:14, and Cheryl pulled into the driveway a minute after. Mia waited by the door for her to get out, smiling as the woman jogged up the stone path to the porch.

"Hey," said Cheryl. "Wow, someone's ready."

Mia blushed at her super casual outfit. "Yeah. I guess I am."

Wilhelmina entered the area she'd referred to as the 'balcony,' the room with the bay windows to the left of the living room. They still hadn't done anything with it, resulting in a large, open space.

"It's so empty in here." Wilhelmina set her bags down gently.

"Yeah." Mia leaned on the archway between the rooms. "Our last place was a little apartment. This house is quite a bit bigger than we expected for our budget."

"Ghosts are the ultimate real estate scam," said Linda, giggling. "Or would be if it didn't take forty years to drop the price of a house."

Everyone chuckled.

Rebecca looked around. "Wow, so this is the infamous house on Minstrel Run, huh? Yeah, I feel it in the air. Something is here."

"You drank the tea, I presume?" asked Wilhelmina.

"Yeah. Not sure if it's related, but I've had some odd twinges in the plumbing all day."

"Good." Wilhelmina grinned. "That means I didn't accidentally whip up a batch of rat killer. It's one ingredient different."

Mia blinked.

"Hah!" The elder laughed and unpacked small wooden boxes, bags, and jars from the bags, setting each on the carpet. "The look on your face. I'm joking by the way."

"Thankfully."

Wilhelmina glanced up at her. "Rat killer is *two* ingredients different."

"Umm…"

"You're too easy, dear. Relax. The rat killer is *only* two ingredients, and neither one of them is involved in what I gave you."

"Maybe she could relax if you stopped teasing her with doom." Lisa playfully elbowed Wilhelmina in the side.

"I'd say the place looks totally different from what I remember," said Linda, turning in a circle, "but I was so little then and only visited once… and I think we spent most of the time out in the yard."

Mia scratched her left shin with her right foot, biting her lip in worry. Tonight could end with her suffering an excruciating death… or delighted beyond belief. That she still wanted to roll those dice worried her. *No… I trust her. She's an innocent.*

Adam came downstairs after his shower, wearing jeans with a T-shirt, no shoes. He got into an easy conversation with the women about parapsychology and witchcraft, which filled the time until they all relocated to the dining room to eat.

"This is the first official use of this table for a reasonably large gathering of friends." Mia raised her water glass in toast. "Here's hoping it's not the last."

The women raised their glasses—some with wine, some water, some tea.

Adam gave her a 'why would it be the last?' look, but didn't say anything.

They ate soup with some 'from-a-tube' rolls she'd baked. Over dinner, she mentioned the dream of shooting Vic, then Adam brought up Pastor Parker hitting the tree. Word had already reached the women about it. Most of Spring Falls blamed the dark energies here for the accident, at least anyone over thirty did. The younger residents tended toward a medical explanation. As far as anyone knew, he remained in the hospital.

After dinner, everyone gathered in the balcony room. Wilhelmina discussed her idea of the Pool of Life with Adam while she unrolled a plain white sheet over the carpet.

"What's with the sheet?" asked Mia.

"Would you prefer we draw on your rug?" asked Rebecca.

Mia shook her head.

"That's what the sheet's for." Rebecca grinned.

Wilhelmina peered up at the ceiling, moved the sheet a little to the left, then nodded in satisfaction. She opened a glass jar full of black liquid, dipped a large, round paintbrush in it, and traced a three-foot wide circle upon the sheet. A pungent berry smell filled the air. When she finished the circle, she switched to a smaller brush similar to the kind used to write Japanese kanji and added complex markings and symbols around the outside of the circle.

Cheryl and Linda set up five ceramic bowls around the sheet, each with incense that they didn't light yet. An arrangement of candles followed at varying distances from the circle. Evidently, precision placement mattered as well as color, as Wilhelmina kept asking them to make tiny adjustments, moving the candle holders an inch or two here and there.

Mia retreated to the living room and paced, too nervous and anxious to tolerate watching the laborious process. A few minutes later, Adam came up behind her and pulled her into an embrace.

"Are you okay?"

"Fine. Just on edge. I don't know why I feel like this."

"Like what?"

Mia leaned against him, staring down at her toes. "So impatient, worried... I want this too much. Whenever I start worrying about how deep Robin got under my skin so fast and how I just wanna do whatever I can for her, I see that face she made when I told her about this plan. A bad spirit wouldn't be able to simulate such an innocent reaction of joy, would it?"

"I'm not sure. Bear in mind that most of the people who have documented demonic entities pretending to be child spirits are affiliated with organized religion or at least strong believers. Maybe they only say that because it's less depressing to consider them fake than actual children. Or, maybe it's because evil spirits know most humans are going to want to pick up and hug that stray kitten on the side of the road. I sincerely doubt that any of them have seen full body apparitions or carried on actual conversations like you have. It's a lot easier to fake a child presence when all people have to go on is distant giggling or high-pitched voices."

"Yeah." Mia closed her eyes. "She's real."

A little after nine, Wilhelmina emerged from the balcony room. "All right. We're as prepared as we can be in there. I'm sure you're eager to continue?"

"Yes." Mia faced her and held up her hands. "I'm literally shaking with my need to do this."

"Try to keep your thoughts calm and open." Wilhelmina brushed Mia's hair off her face. "Now, we need to do two things. First, please go locate Robin and ask her to come down here and stand in the middle of the circle. It's important that she remain there no matter what she sees or hears. If she's not in that circle at the right moment, all of this is a waste of time."

Mia nodded. "Okay."

"Second, paint. That won't take too long. When that's done, we'll come back downstairs here to the circle. You stay in bed. I'll open the circle and start the ritual. Adam, you'll be somewhere down here where you can see me so I can give you a nod when it's time. Then, you go up to your wife and I'm sure you don't need me to explain what you two should do."

He laughed.

"Okay. Give me a moment."

"Rebecca, dear, will you put on some water for tea?" asked Wilhelmina.

"On it."

Mia ran up the stairs, cornered to the left, and jogged to Robin's room. The girl sat on the rug at the foot of the bed, arms wrapped around her legs, head down.

"Hey, sweetie."

"I'm scared," whispered Robin. "Daddy knows what you're doing. He doesn't like it."

Mia took a knee beside her. "Listen… That man isn't your father. He gave that up a long time ago when he hurt you. Even before that… no *father* would have been so cruel to your mother."

Robin tried to leap into a hug, but passed through, leaving Mia shivering. She collapsed on her knees behind Mia, sobbing.

"Hey, sweetie. It's okay." Mia brushed her hand down the vaporous girl's back. "I know you want a hug more than anything. If this works, you won't have to be lonely anymore."

She sniffled. "Okay."

"I need you to play a game tonight. Downstairs by the big window, there's a circle on the floor. Can you stand inside that circle and stay there? No matter what happens?"

Robin lowered her hands from her face, looking up at her with a note of suspicion. "You aren't trying to make me go away, are you?"

"Absolutely not." Mia wiped tears from her face, nearly overcome by emotion at the memory of Evelyn finding the body in here. "It's a bridge."

A loud *bang* went off downstairs along with two women screaming.

Mia jumped.

"Daddy's angry," said Robin. "He made a light blow up to scare them."

"Honey, listen to me. The thing they're doing tonight… if a bad spirit gets into that circle, I could die. Only you can be in that circle, or it's gonna hurt me."

"But you said you didn't wanna be a ghost." Robin ground her toe into the rug.

"I don't. I want you to be with me, here, alive, and warm. So I can hold you and keep you safe and let you have all the happy moments you should never have had stolen from you."

Robin sniffled, nodding. "You don't really want kids."

"It's not that I didn't want kids. I never gave it much thought before. But, after coming here, it's all so different. This feels right somehow. After seeing you… Wilhelmina telling me that something like this is even possible. I've never wanted to do anything so much in my life."

Robin smiled. "'Kay. I'll go to the circle. You promise it's not bad?"

"I promise. It might not work, but it definitely won't hurt you."

The girl faded away.

Mia glanced over at the bad spot. Something told her the boards under the rug still had blood soaked into them. She found Robin there so often it had to be akin to an anchor point or energy source. Perhaps if this worked, she'd have those boards replaced. Or maybe it wouldn't matter then, since she'd no longer be a spirit.

With a grunt, she stood and walked out into the hall. For no particular reason, she called for Adam, then rushed to the stairs to make sure Robin made it to the circle.

Icy sliminess grabbed at her ankle the instant she reached the top of the stairs. She stumbled over it and fell forward, thrusting her hands out, screaming. Adam blurred into view at the bottom of the stairs. She landed on her chest, tumbling for a disorienting instant before crashing into him and knocking him against the wall in the corner.

"Shit, Mia!" Adam sat up and checked on her.

"Ow." She clutched her chest, which bore the brunt of her impact on the stairs. "I'm okay. Damn that hurt."

"What happened?" Lisa ran over, wide-eyed.

The others in the coven filled in behind her.

"Something cold and icky tried to grab my ankle." She looked past Adam at the wall, then rubbed her shoulder where it hit his shin. "Vic."

"Good thing you called for him." Wilhelmina patted Adam on the arm. "If he hadn't been in the way…"

"Yeah. I know. Tonight's going to be interesting. We should get this over with before Vic does something even worse." Mia limped to her feet. "I'm good. Let's go."

"Is she in the circle?" asked Wilhelmina.

Mia looked around, spotting Robin standing in the corner of the dining room, her back pressed to the wall. "C'mon, sweetie. It's in here." She pointed toward the balcony.

Robin eyed the women warily, seeming afraid.

"Are you shy around people or is there something about them that frightens you?"

The girl whispered something too quiet to hear.

Mia walked over to her.

"I'm scared of people."

"They're not going to hurt you." Mia crouched to eye level. "Hey, you don't have to even let them see you, okay? All you have to do is stand in that circle. Why be scared of people who don't even know you're there? You're the best at hiding, right?"

Robin grinned. "Yeah."

Mia held out a hand.

The girl grasped it—somewhat. Faint pressure squeezed at Mia's fingers. She walked her into the balcony and over to the sheet. Robin gazed around at all the candles, symbols, incense bowls, and squiggly marks.

"It's like Halloween," whispered Robin, as if afraid the others might hear her.

"Yeah, a bit."

The girl paused at the edge of the sheet. She lingered a moment, then looked up with a teary expression. "Do you really wanna be my mommy?"

"Yes." Mia smiled. "I do."

Wilhelmina and the other women gathered around, observing curiously. None appeared able to see the girl, though Lisa and Rebecca whispered about feeling a presence nearby. Robin gazed into Mia's eyes a while more, then smiled despite crying. She stepped onto the sheet, which drew awestruck gasps from the coven, except for Wilhelmina.

"The sheet's moving," whispered Cheryl. "Look, there's little footprints in the circle..."

Robin looked down at her feet, then at Mia as if to ask if she stood in the right place.

Mia nodded. "Just stay there, okay? No matter what you see or feel, stay in the circle."

"Unless you feel something tugging you straight up." Wilhelmina winked. "Then you should go up."

"'Kay," said Robin.

Oh, I hope this works... "Be careful on the stairs." Mia brushed past Adam with a brief hug, and made her way up the stairs on all fours to avoid another fall.

Wilhelmina, Lisa, and Rebecca—who carried two small cups of steaming tea—followed her to the bedroom. Once inside, Mia gathered all her nerve and removed her shirt. Naked, she reclined on the bed and stared at the ceiling, trying not to blush too hard.

The women gathered around her, each with a small jar of berry ink and a paintbrush.

"Try not to squirm too much, dear," said Wilhelmina. "This will tickle a bit, but we're not trying to make it uncomfortable."

Mia focused on the ceiling, trying to keep herself as blasé as a trip to the gynecologist while she sat there with all her secrets open to the world—or at least the doctor and an assistant. Fortunately, the women had no interest in anything more than preparing her for the spell. Lisa and Rebecca spent the next half hour or so tracing sigils and marks on her body, most of which wound up on her abdomen as Wilhelmina arranged more candles and incense bowls around the bed. They made marks on her forehead, each wrist, and each ankle, which Lisa explained as the 'points of the star' that essentially turned her body into a pentacle.

"So I need to keep my arms out to the side like this?" asked Mia.

"Only until I've opened the circle. Once Adam walks in, it won't matter. Our circle downstairs will extend through the floor and also protect you." Wilhelmina looked over the markings. "Everything appears in order. Time to begin. Try to relax and let nature take its course."

"Easier said than done." Mia smiled, despite feeling completely mortified at laying spread eagle on her bed like some kind of pagan sacrifice. *Crap. Why did I think that? Sacrifice is not the sort of thing I need to have on my mind while doing something that can kill me.*

"One more thing." Wilhelmina gestured at the little teacups on the end table. "Before you start, you should both drink these."

"What is it?"

"Just some tea." She smiled. "Should help ease your nerves, and help the magic work. Please don't forget, it's important."

"All right."

The women left, shutting the door behind them.

Mia lifted her head, blinking in astonishment at the complexity of the circles, triangles, squiggles, and everything else painted on her stomach and upper thighs. She let her head drop back and sighed, doing her best impression of the *Vitruvian Man* pose, picturing her head, hands, and feet as the points of a pentagram star.

I hope she stays in the circle. Please don't let Vic step into that circle.

Less than a minute after the door closed, the drone of murmuring voices from outside teased at the window. Weston, or his people, praying.

Oh, shit. Not now!

Mia fought the urge to spring up and scream at them. *Hah! I should storm outside just like this and see how they react.* She kept herself as still as she could, holding the star position lest the slightest movement ruin the spell.

The front door creaked.

"I'd appreciate it if you went home and left us alone," said Adam, outside. "Your concern is noted, but it's late."

The voices kept praying.

"Didn't you hear him?" shouted Lisa. "You're trespassing. Freedom of religion doesn't mean everyone's got the 'freedom' to be *your* religion."

"I'd rather not have to take things that far," said Adam. "But at least move your meeting off my property to the street or will I need to call Nate to come out here and ask you all to disperse. Look, I appreciate your concern, but this is more than a little intrusive."

Mia sighed. "Oh, sure, hon. Argue with the religious wingnuts while I just lie here naked, waiting for you. Argh, the timing. Go away already. Why can't they just leave us alone?"

29

TWO CUPS OF TEA

SATURDAY, SEPTEMBER 8, 2012

Adam folded his arms, staring at Weston and his small group of worshipers.

Twelve of them gathered behind the pastor in front of the porch, all holding flashlights so they could read their Bibles. They continued reciting the same passage in unison, something about casting out demons, while the pastor dug in his heels, a defiant scowl on his face.

"Look, I respect your beliefs," said Adam. "But, you need to respect my wife's."

"This house corrupted every family to ever live here." Weston narrowed his eyes. "You're unable to see it because you are under the effect of the Tempter. I am trying to save your souls. The Devil has staked his claim here. This house belongs empty. Any who dwell within it risk their souls."

Adam shifted his jaw side to side. Mia *had* been acting a little odd as of late. He felt sure she experienced something that had scared her quite badly, but for whatever reason hadn't mentioned it. She'd been edgy and strange ever since that bath, and the basement certainly did have a strong dark energy. At no point in his life did he ever suspect he possessed anything close to psychic talent, and even he could feel malice down there. The sensation reminded him of going down the wrong alley at night while a giant man with bad intentions followed him.

Maybe the pastor had a point... but then again, a malicious entity wouldn't make flour footprints when asked or write its name in such a cutesy way.

"You must banish these minions of the dark one before they do permanent damage to your souls." Weston pointed at Lisa. "That child was innocent once, but look at her now."

Adam glanced to his right. The blue-eyed blonde woman standing beside him appeared angry enough to punch someone in the nose, but not at all demonic or evil. "I don't see horns or a spaded tail."

Her glower softened, but she fell short of laughing.

"If you wanted this house to stay empty, you should've bought it when it was on the market, empty for three years. Now, please, go home. I'm going to go inside, wait thirty seconds, and then bother the sheriff if I still hear voices outside. Got a feeling he won't be too happy at being disturbed at near ten on a Saturday night."

Lisa hurried into the house, heading for the balcony.

"You're throwing your soul away, Mr. Gartner," called Weston.

Adam paused at the door to smile back at him. "I'm not telling you to stop praying for me... just do it at the end of the driveway."

He went in and shut the door. Eighteen seconds later, the recitation outside stopped. Flashlights migrated down the driveway and collected in a group near the street. Whatever they resumed saying didn't quite reach the house loud enough to understand.

Good enough.

Wilhelmina held a small sword up over her head, though it didn't look sharp. She walked clockwise around the circle while speaking in an odd language he figured might be Gaelic. Two small indentations on the sheet shifted slightly, suggesting Robin remained there as Mia had asked, and turned in place to watch the older woman. Linda lit incense in bowls. Cheryl glided back and forth lighting the candles. After three orbits, Wilhelmina stopped at the point where she'd started. The other four women approached the sheet, each one standing at another star point.

"Linda North." Wilhelmina pointed her sword at the air above the woman's head. "I invite you to enter my circle of power. How do you enter?"

"With perfect love and trust," said Linda, raising her hands to the ceiling. "Praise be to the Mother Goddess."

One by one, she 'welcomed' the others. That done, she invited The Moon Goddess, The Horned One, Lady Morrigan, and the elemental spirits all to join their circle. Wilhelmina held the sword high for a moment, said a few lines in Gaelic, then set the blade on the rug by her feet, and they all joined hands.

Wilhelmina chanted:

"The spirits path so long entwined,

"For eons old the way did bind.

"A bridge to cross, the fallow dark,

"To mother's heart, the spirit hark.

"Lady Morrigan, hear our plea,

"So we beseech, so mote it be."

The others repeated the chant in unison. Nothing visible happened. Adam stifled a smile of amusement, mostly at himself for being disappointed the 'magic' lacked flashy special effects.

Deep anger radiated from the kitchen. Seconds later, a loud *slam* came from the basement door. A few of the women—and Adam —jumped.

Wilhelmina nodded to Adam.

He took a deep breath. *No pressure to perform right?*

Careful to watch for anything attempting to trip him, Adam went upstairs and crept down the hall to his bedroom. Mia lay stretched out on the bed, arms out to her sides, legs apart, her body covered with markings similar to what the women had written on the linen cloth downstairs.

He blinked at the sight of her.

Mia exhaled. "Are they done with the spell?"

"I think so. At least, she gave me 'the nod.'"

She relaxed from the uncomfortable—and highly vulnerable—pose, sat up, and plucked two half-sized cups from the table beside the bed.

"Are you sure this is what you want to do?" Adam shut the door behind him.

"Yes."

He removed his clothes, tossing them on the floor by the bed. "What's with the cups?"

"Tea. Wilhelmina said it's important."

Adam shrugged and downed the not-quite-hot tea like a shot. It scorched his throat with the bite of whiskey and a bizarre herbal taste like mint-berry cough syrup. Mia drank hers in three sips, cringing.

"Whoa. That's some... interesting tea." He coughed, patted his chest, and set the cup down.

Mia's eyes fluttered. "Yeah."

He sat beside her on the bed, taking in the beautiful sight of his wife's body. After about ten seconds, lightheadedness made him smile and forget entirely about having other people in the house.

Mia reached up with both hands, rubbing his chest. "I'm ready."

"You are so damn beautiful."

"C'mere, handsome." Mia tugged at him. "Careful not to smudge me."

30

HOPE

SATURDAY, SEPTEMBER 8, 2012

Mia lay back, sweaty, out of breath, staring wide-eyed at the ceiling.

Well, I didn't have a massive heart attack.

A rhythmic chant came from beneath the floor.

Since I'm not dead, that means Robin really is an innocent, or I'm a complete idiot for thinking 'magic' would do anything. Whatever had been in the tea hit her fairly hard. She grinned, snickered, then burst into full on laughter.

"I wasn't that bad, was I?" half-whispered Adam.

"No, you were amazing. I just thought it funny that I'd been so terrified of magic and believed it might've killed me."

"Killed you?" He sat up, propping himself on one elbow. "How so?"

"Yeah. If something dark got into that circle, it probably would've killed me."

He stared. "That would've been... bad."

"You're not upset?" She covered her mouth with one hand, almost in slow motion. "Oh, I didn't mean to tell you that. I didn't want to upset you."

"I am upset, but it's not coming out."

"We're high as hell, aren't we?"

Adam grinned. "I believe so."

She traced her fingers around his chest. "We just tried to make a baby."

"Yeah. No raincoat."

Mia giggled. "I feel so relaxed. Could lay here like this all night."

"We've got people downstairs still."

"Yeah. We do."

"We do." He flopped flat on his back.

"I think maybe we should do something besides just lie here. Wow… our ceiling is so damn white. So clean. Could eat off it. How would we get food to stick to the ceiling to eat from it?" Mia rubbed her face. "Oh, wow. I'm stoned."

"Have you ever been high before?"

"I told you already. Tried E once in college and dabbled with pot, but nothing serious."

"Oh. Yeah, that's right, you did mention that."

Mia hopped out of bed and made it halfway to the stairs before she realized she hadn't put any clothes on. She decided not to care, but only made it a few more steps before her embarrassment overpowered the effects of the tea.

"Hon? Forget something?" Adam leaned out the door, dangling her giant T-shirt from one hand. "You know, something tells me they wouldn't mind if we were super casual."

She scurried back to him. "Will you ask if it's okay if I wipe these marks off? I want to clean up."

"Sure."

Adam hurriedly dressed, then went down the hall to the stairs. "Wilhelmina? Is it okay if she cleans up or should the marks remain?" He listened for a moment. "Sounds like they're still doing something. Thanking various gods for helping them, closing the circle. Sec." He went downstairs. A minute later, he came back and nodded. "Got a thumbs up."

Mia hit the bathroom for a quick shower. By the time she stepped out of the tub, the hazy, relaxed effect of the tea had largely worn off, leaving her feeling sober but tired. She changed into a standard T-shirt and sweat pants, then went downstairs.

Adam sat in one of the recliners, Wilhelmina in the other with a pleased look on her face. Rebecca, Linda, and Cheryl occupied the couch, Lisa sprawled on the floor beside it like a teen.

Mia padded over and sat on her husband's lap.

"So, did it work?" asked Adam.

Wilhelmina pursed her lips. "It's difficult for me to say. I *can* tell you that nothing went wrong aside from Vic's attempts to distract us, but he couldn't breach the circle.

"I think it did." Lisa grinned. "I saw the little footprints fade away."

Mia opened her senses as much as she'd yet figured out how to do. "Maybe it did work… the house doesn't feel so infused with sadness as it did before."

"Or you're still glowing from a good boinking." Lisa laughed.

Adam cleared his throat.

Wilhelmina glanced off in a random direction, a hint of red in her cheeks.

"Robin?" called Mia. "Are you still here?"

She looked around at the silent living room, balcony room, and what little bit of dining room she could see past the arch from her present angle.

Wham!

Mia jumped, emitting a shriek of alarm—as did Lisa and Cheryl.

"What the hell was that?" asked Adam.

"Sounded like a cabinet door from the kitchen." Linda scratched at her eyebrow. "I think someone's pissed."

"Robin never slammed doors." Mia slipped off Adam's lap and cautiously advanced into the dining room, heading for the kitchen.

"I don't think Robin did that." Wilhelmina got up and followed her.

One of the cabinet doors above the sink hung open, though nothing appeared damaged.

"Is he going to be a problem?"

"Difficult to say. We did stir up quite a bit of spirit energy tonight.

It wouldn't surprise me if that attracted some other entities to check out what we were doing. However, they ought to disperse soon.

Mia nudged the cabinet closed. "All right. Here's hoping."

For the next hour or so, they sat around being social, chatting about everything other than spirits or magic... until the crash of a heavy toolbox slammed into the floor in the back of the house. The requisite thudding went by toward the stairs.

"Wow, it's late." Mia yawned.

"1:03 a.m.," said Adam without looking at any phone, watch, or clock.

"Whoa." Cheryl slipped her phone back in her pocket. "Good guess."

"Not a guess." He scratched at his chin. "Every damn night that same thing repeats at exactly 1:03."

"That one isn't an active ghost. Just a psychic impression." Mia pointed at the route the disturbance took from the kitchen to the stairs. "It's like a glitched video on repeat. No intelligence."

"A more forceful cleansing or banishing ritual might deal with it..." Wilhelmina tapped her fingertips together. "Unless of course, you enjoy a nightly reminder of that bastard."

"Getting rid of that noise would be great." Mia nodded. "Once we're sure you're not going to banish Robin, too."

Wilhelmina wagged her eyebrows. "Oh, I suspect you'll banish her... in about nine months."

Mia leaned against Adam, trying to prepare herself mentally to cope with the disappointment that at any minute, she'd see a crying little ghost emerge from a dark corner.

"And it is still one in the morning." Cheryl stood. "My bed is calling me, and I'm sure these two want some rest."

The coven got up to leave, all hugging Mia in turn, wishing her luck and good fortune with the baby. Lisa and Rebecca hugged Adam as well, the rest shaking hands with him.

"Thank you all so much," said Mia. "It's... I'm still not sure if I should believe that magic is going to work, but I can't thank you all enough for what you've done."

"You're welcome, dear." Wilhelmina patted her shoulder, then picked up the bags of ritual supplies.

The others filed out behind her. Mia stood in the doorway watching the women walk to their cars, Adam behind her. She slipped a hand up under her shirt, idly scratching at her stomach. It didn't seem likely that 'special tea' would hasten her cycle or magic would work, and hoping so much that it would made her feel a wee bit silly.

Car doors outside closed with soft *whumps*. One by one, engines started and the women drove off.

"Am I a hypocrite for hoping this could work after making fun of my parents for praying?"

Adam rested his chin on her shoulder and hugged her. "You know what the difference between prayer and magic is?"

"The supernatural beings the witches call on aren't supposed to be infallible or all-powerful?"

"I was going to say there's more supplies involved in magic."

Mia patted her belly and let her arm drop. Hope wouldn't hurt anyone... and it did stand out that she hadn't seen any trace of Robin since she'd gone upstairs. Maybe the spell *had* done something. For all she knew, perhaps merely suggesting to Robin that she *could* jump into a baby was all it took and the magic merely made everyone feel better. She sighed to herself, feeling as foolish as an adult who believed in Santa Claus to hope that anything they did tonight would work.

However...

The house *did* feel less sad... but also angry.

31

TIME

WEDNESDAY, JUNE 5, 2013

The fragrance of pancakes saturated the kitchen.

Mia patted her tremendously pregnant belly. Cravings for pancakes had gotten out of hand the past few days. She'd had them every morning that week. The baby kicked happily while Mia ate.

"I know you love pancakes, but if you keep making me eat them, you're going to be sending me to the gym once you bust out of jail, kiddo."

The ultrasound had confirmed she carried a girl. The tea allowing her to become pregnant at all out of her cycle had been enough of a shock to open the doors of hope, and that hope had reached dangerous levels of anticipation after she hadn't seen any sign of Robin anywhere in the house over the past nine months. Dangerous in the sense that if it *didn't* turn out to be Robin in her womb, she'd be crushed. That much, she *had* confided in Adam. If they determined that Robin had simply 'gone away' and they had an ordinary baby, he would be on guard to help her through the resulting depression.

While the girl had gone quiet, other supernatural events had picked up with increasing frequency.

She couldn't tell if the increased activity happened due to

Wilhelmina's banishing ritual or Robin's absence. If Vic had been a 'plug' of sorts keeping Robin from going down the drain to the Pool of Life, perhaps her absence agitated him. The toolbox crash had ceased as a result of the deep cleansing ritual Wilhelmina conducted in the little room between the kitchen and the back door, but now, doors opened and closed at random, lights turned on or off, the TV switched on and off, small objects moved around constantly. A few times, she'd been thrown out of bed. Lately, she'd taken to sleeping on an air mattress so a fall wouldn't harm the baby.

Thus far, the activity had been easy to overlook, mostly irritating things, the sort of occurrences that would probably send normal people screaming out the door after two weeks. But after having full conversations with a ghostly child and participating in a pagan ritual, Mia brushed the events off. She did worry somewhat at the feeling Vic, who'd mostly been dormant, might be teaching himself how to interact with the living so he could do something dangerous in the future.

Her gut said 'the day' would come soon. She'd been on maternity leave from the museum for the past month and spent the early part of it preparing the house for a baby with help from Wilhelmina and the others. Weston had shown up a handful of times over the past several months, ostensibly to 'check' on her. She had been pleasant with him, even inviting him in for coffee. He hadn't stayed long and hadn't again brought a group of people with him to pray on the lawn.

She'd been on the phone with Timothy roughly once a week after the pregnancy test came back positive. He still lived in LA, sharing a studio apartment with his boyfriend Shane. Timothy had gotten in the door as a sous chef at a fancy restaurant, but given the cost of living out there, he had about as much spare cash as a short order cook working at a diner. He couldn't afford to head east to visit, at least not anytime soon, nor did he want Mia and Adam to eat the cost of his travel expenses. He'd content himself with pictures and try to get out there as soon as he could afford to.

Mia stuffed a forkful of pancakes in her mouth. *Four days in a row. I should be sick to death of these by now.* A contraction hit. She gritted her teeth and stared at the clock. The doctor said if they happened closer than five minutes apart, she needed to get to the hospital.

She chewed slow, staring at the clock, waiting for another contraction to time it.

Bizarre lightheadedness came out of nowhere. The kitchen faded to white, then back to normal, only she watched herself from a distance, her point of view that of a faerie hovering near the ceiling. Other-Mia ate another mouthful of pancakes—and her water broke, gushing over the chair to the tile floor. She grabbed the cell phone on the table next to the plate and staggered to her feet, waving her arms for balance. A tendril of black emerged from the floor and snagged her left foot, causing her to slip in the puddle she'd created.

Other-Mia went over backward, her head striking the seat of the chair she'd just been sitting in. She landed flat, her head tilted at an abnormal angle... clearly dead from a broken neck.

Her point of view leapt back into her body, still seated at the table. She stared at the pancakes on her fork, then down at her dry lap.

"Back the hell off, Vic. You might be made from the very fabric of hate, but do not fuck with a pregnant woman wielding a fork!"

Mia eased herself off the chair and sat on the floor, then grabbed her phone from the table. She tapped Adam's contact.

He answered in two rings. "Hey. What's up?"

"It's time. My water's gonna break."

"Going to break?"

Another contraction hit—four minutes forty-two seconds after the first.

"Yeah. Real soon. And Vic's going to try and kill me." She explained her out of body experience.

"Damn. Okay. I'm on the way."

"Thanks." *Sploosh!* Mia cringed, trying not to freak out at a sensation similar to wetting herself and being unable to stop. "There it goes. Good thing I'm not wearing pants under this circus tent of a dress."

Adam's muffled voice informed his class he needed to cut the session short due to his wife having a baby. Cheering erupted in the background. "Sorry, hon, what?"

"It's definitely time. I need you here, now."

"On the way!"

Mia figured he'd already be driving like an idiot in a hurry. "See you when you get here. Don't drive on the phone."

"Okay." Sounds of him jogging down a corridor echoed in the background. "I won't be driving on the phone. I'll be driving on the road."

"Wiseass."

She hung up and looked around at the massive puddle she sat in. "Maybe sitting on the floor wasn't such a great idea. No way am I getting up on my own. Still… beats a broken neck."

Another contraction hit.

"Hang on, kiddo."

She pulled the chair around to her side, folded her arms on it, and lay her head down.

The power went out.

"Oh go to hell. It can stay off. I wouldn't go to the basement normally to flip the breaker, and I'm *definitely* not going down there like this."

A stronger contraction drew a gasp from her.

"Ugh. Hurry up, Adam."

She closed her eyes and mentally asked her daughter to wait another few minutes.

Mia blearily focused on a cluster of blinding overhead lights, her body still shaking from the worst pain she'd ever experienced.

"Hey, hon." Adam patted her shoulder.

She looked to her left at a man in teal scrubs and a face mask. "You're doing it wrong. I'm the husband. It's supposed to be *me* who faints when the kid pops out."

A weak chuckle escaped her lips. She felt like a bus had hit her, then backed up to run her over a second time. "Holy shit that hurt…"

"Congratulations, Mr. and Mrs. Gartner," said a woman. "You've got a healthy baby girl."

Mia looked up at the doctor. "Thank you."

One of the nurses eased a newborn infant wrapped in a blanket into her arms. The little one gazed around, her tiny mouth open in an expression of awe.

"Hey there, kiddo. Haven't seen you in a while," rasped Mia in a weak voice.

"Do you have a name picked out yet?" asked the nurse.

"Yes. Her name is Robin," said Mia.

The baby peered up at her, her beautiful brown eyes widening with a distinct sense of gratitude. She sputtered and spit as if trying to talk, but couldn't quite make it work. Robin glowered in obvious frustration, then went back to staring gratefully up at them.

"Whoa," whispered Adam.

Mia's eyes welled with tears of joy.

"Something wrong?" asked the doctor.

"No." Adam smiled. "I'm just umm, blown away by how perfect she is."

Tuesday, June 11, 2013

MIA SAT ON THE SOFA AT HOME, ROBIN IN HER LAP.

Linda, Rebecca, Cheryl, and Lisa hovered around her, *oohing* and *ahhing* over the baby.

"She's so beautiful," said Lisa. "You must be thrilled."

"I don't even have the words." Mia gave the baby a light squeeze. "It worked. It absolutely worked. This is Robin."

"Amazing." Linda tapped the girl on the nose. "You're sure already?"

"Beyond a doubt. She hates diapers. Tries to make a fuss so I carry her to a toilet, but her body isn't capable of holding anything yet."

Robin grunted and frowned.

"Oh wow, it's like she understood you." Cheryl whistled.

"She does." Mia grinned. "It's frustrating for her... I think she remembers a lot, but her body can't keep up with what she wants to do yet. Adam's fascinated at the disconnect between her being able to understand speech but not talk. He's not sure if it's a neuro-physical brain thing or something else."

"Totally cool." Lisa tried to play patty cake, but Robin gave her a look as if to say 'seriously?'

Wilhelmina came down the stairs. "The protection spell is done. That should keep anything dangerous out of her room for a good while. You girls ready to serve an eviction notice?"

"Long time overdue." Linda stood.

"Thank you, all." Mia leaned back in the sofa. "Sorry if I don't go down there with you, but I'm still kinda drained from the delivery."

Wilhelmina waved dismissively. "Think nothing of it. You shouldn't bring her down there for this anyway."

The women headed to the basement.

With any luck, the banishing spell would hurl Vic into the Pool of Life, or at least toss him out of the house. The last thing Mia needed would be to fall down the stairs while carrying a baby. If Vic had the strength to throw her out of bed, he could do much worse to an infant.

32

HAPPY BIRTHDAY

WEDNESDAY, JUNE 5, 2019

The cake came out perfect.

Mia hummed to herself while sticking six candles into pink icing. High-pitched cartoon character voices came from the living room, along with the chatter of children and conversation among adults.

Robin had invited four friends over for her birthday party, and each girl came with one or more parents. Wilhelmina and Lisa attended as well. Rebecca got stuck working late at the dentist's office, Cheryl was in Maine visiting family, and Linda—who'd turned fifty-four a month ago—had gone to Arizona on vacation.

Mia let out a happy sigh, checking the cake over one last time. She could barely believe that six years had passed already. The time had gone by in a blur of oddities. Robin learned to walk super early, potty trained herself, and as young as two had started speaking in full sentences with the vocabulary of a seven-year-old. As she grew, she gave off hints that she remembered quite a bit from her past life and the time she'd spent haunting the house. Much of the ghostly period had eroded, leaving her fuzzy on exactly how much time had passed. She recalled being lonely and scared in the dark, and that other people who she didn't get along with had been here, but described it more like it spanned mere weeks and not forty-two years.

And she'd been astoundingly clingy, even with Adam. Even after six years, sometimes she'd spontaneously cry whenever he did silly fun things with her or let her cuddle when they watched movies. Seeing the girl still overwhelmed with joy at having a *good* dad choked Mia up every single time.

Adam didn't think it necessary to rip up the floorboards in the girl's bedroom, nor did he want to peel the carpet back to even look for blood. Robin surprisingly didn't show any fear of her room, though at four, she had matter-of-factly stated once, "this is where he killed me" while pointing at the floor and then said, "toy chests are stupid hiding places."

As strange as it had been watching a toddler with the mind of a seven-year-old, the house being devoid of darkness bugged her more. Mia had become so accustomed to the persistent sense of gloom that its absence had been distracting at first... at least until a few months ago. She couldn't put a finger on where it came from, but had a growing sense that something bad drew near.

She whistled to herself, wondering where all the time went. Though, she took no small amount of happiness from knowing she'd offered Robin a far happier life than she'd had before. Smiling, Mia lit the candles, picked up the cake, and carried it to the dining room.

"Okay, everyone. Who wants cake?"

Cheering erupted from the kids. Robin, dolled up in a white-and-pink dress, zoomed in first, circling the table before crashing into a hug. The other kids scrambled in and climbed into chairs. Two dads and three mothers joined Adam, Wilhelmina, and Lisa standing around.

"Thank you for the cake, Mommy!"

Mia scooped her up. "You're welcome, sweetie."

Robin clung to her, grinning broadly. Sometimes, the girl's habit of constantly hugging, laying on, or otherwise wanting to be in physical contact with her or Adam worried her that she might need therapy. However, in light of what had happened, it made sense. Even if the child couldn't remember how long it had been, she *had* been desperate for human contact for forty-two years. And no therapist in the world would process *that* story without sending Mia to get fitted for a padded cell.

She still didn't quite believe in any sense of God (neither the one Weston followed or the ones Wilhelmina and the coven spoke to), but more than ever, she felt like something—perhaps fate—had definitely brought her to this house to be with her daughter.

She set Robin in the seat nearest the cake.

Everyone sang happy birthday in varying degrees of off key.

"Make a wish," said Mia.

Robin took a deep breath, concentrated for a moment, and blew out the candles.

Thud!

The floor shook as if someone had dropped a concrete block in the living room.

Most of the adults jumped. The children, except for Robin, all yelled in fear—she peered up at Mia with an 'uh oh' face. Wilhelmina's eyebrows knit in annoyance.

"What the heck was that?" asked Mrs. Bearce.

Her daughter Amy burst into tears.

"Oh…" Mia waved back and forth. "Just the house shifting in the wind."

"Sounded like someone dropped a giant frozen turkey in the kitchen," said Mrs. Wasley, Emma's mother.

Mr. Wasley wandered to the kitchen doorway and peered in. "I don't see anything."

Mia crept up behind him and looked around. Nothing looked broken or potentially responsible for such a loud bang… but a potent sense of malice hung thick in the air, strongest from the corner where the door led to the basement.

Oh… shit.

"Maybe there's an open window upstairs," said Adam. "Might've been something falling over. Be right back."

Mia backed out of the kitchen and locked stares with Wilhelmina, whose expression appeared to convey a sense of 'we'll deal with it after the party; don't freak out the little ones.' She hurried back to stand behind Robin.

The uneasy mood gradually faded as pieces of cake made the rounds. Soon, the children resumed having fun, and everyone seemed to forget the inexplicable noise, or at least pretend it hadn't happened. The parents' lingering wariness suggested the folklore of the house hadn't gone unheard even by the younger generation.

Mia couldn't stop worrying about it, and kept eyeing the kitchen. She lapsed into a state of hypervigilance, making sure no child— especially Robin—came within accident range of anything potentially deadly.

A few hours later, the other kids and their parents left. Mia collapsed on the couch, exhausted from worry. Adam sat on her left, Wilhelmina on the right. Despite two recliners being open, Lisa again flopped on the floor like a teen.

"Didn't you turn thirty-three last January?" asked Adam.

"Age is merely a number." Lisa stuck out her tongue.

Robin climbed onto the couch and curled up between Mia and Adam. "The house is scary again."

"I felt it, too." Mia looked over at Wilhelmina. "Do you think *he* came back?"

"It's possible."

Robin looked up. "Bad Daddy didn't go away. He's just been hiding in the basement."

33

PEER REVIEW

SATURDAY, JUNE 8, 2019

A dam leaned back in his chair, draining the last few gulps of his second coffee.

Although he loved his job at Syracuse University, every now and then, his needing to be there two Saturdays a month 'just in case' a student showed up for office hours annoyed him. He considered it a violation of the sanctity of the weekend. Granted, if a student specifically asked him to pop in for a meeting, he wouldn't mind at all —the sitting there doing nothing is what felt like a waste. The Saturday hours didn't always bother him, but with things at home taking a turn for the strange once more, he'd rather be there for Mia and Robin.

Having a kid had its frustrating moments, though by and large, he adored her. The idea to try for another one teased at his brain, but he hadn't yet suggested it to Mia. They'd had things easy so far. Despite her arriving as a newborn, they'd essentially adopted a seven-year-old. If they had another one with a soul sourced in the usual manner, it would be an entirely different experience. Robin didn't do any of the usual bad things a two- or three-year-old would do: no drawing on the wall, flour all over the kitchen, covering herself in peanut butter, random fits of crying at meaningless things... as soon as the girl developed motor coordination, they'd had a kid developmentally seven but physically younger.

Perhaps the weirdest event had been when Mia's brother and his husband showed up three years ago. Robin—who'd never seen him before—said, "Hi Timmy!" and ran to hug him.

Adam's parents had no idea about any of the unusual aspects of their granddaughter's life. They'd visited on and off several times over the years and the girl loved them. Her blurted comment about it being 'nice to have grandparents this time' when she'd been two caused some confusion. Adam had swept it aside in a 'kids say the strangest things' sort of way.

With no outstanding papers to grade, he spent an hour goofing off on the computer until his email chimed. He paused the fails compilation video he'd been shaking his head at and switched windows to the email system.

The first message contained another rejection from a scientific journal that didn't find his footprints-in-flour video (plus associated evidence of the prior haunting) compelling enough to withstand peer review. Of course, he couldn't recreate the events of the video since the ghost no longer haunted the place. Naturally, the scientists at the journal took that as an admission of fakery. It frustrated him, but he understood. An experiment that couldn't be repeated didn't prove much of anything.

Adam had started documenting Robin's peculiarities with a notion to do a research paper on reincarnation, but somewhere along the line, he'd changed his mind. It felt wrong to do that to her. His daughter didn't deserve to be trotted around as a curiosity.

Email number two came from Paul Reitman, his former teaching assistant who now worked in Albany as a clinical psychologist, both with a private practice and as a consultant for the police. He asked if he could consult with him regarding a patient he wanted another opinion on.

Adam replied with a 'sure, call me whenever.'

Grumbling, he deleted the rejection email, went back to the internet browser... and decided not to resume watching the fail video. He'd had enough fail for one day. He randomly searched the internet for reports of paranormal activity in the area, hoping to find a story about a site he could go investigate. Perhaps Mia would help out and they could find another spirit willing to disturb dust on command.

A few minutes into scrolling, he stopped short in confusion at a picture of Robin. *Who the hell is posting pictures of our kid?* It took him a few seconds to realize she wore a hideous shirt with brown, red, and blue horizontal stripes. He blinked, wiped his eyes, and blinked again.

Curiosity got the better of him and he clicked the link.

The website contained an article about the girl's 1970 murder with a slightly larger version of the same photo, showing her from the waist up. He picked up a picture frame with his daughter's portrait in it and held it side by side with his monitor. His stunned brain didn't process the text in the article much at all, rendering it as blurry lines. Robin Kurtis looked too much like Robin Gartner to be possible. The old newspaper photo lacked sharpness, but it had enough that he could tell the two girls weren't *exact* copies. Not identical twins, but way closer than even most siblings looked. Robin Gartner definitely had Mia's eyes, and an argument could be made she also had a bit of Adam's nose. Robin Kurtis also, oddly enough, had Mia's eyes, but a slightly different nose. About the only real difference he could discern between their faces amounted to his daughter having a somewhat smaller—and cuter if he did think so himself—nose.

"Holy shit," he muttered. "They say everyone's got a double somewhere, but whoa."

Forget simply not going public with the reincarnation research... as soon as I get home, I'm going to erase it all. He picked up a notepad and fanned himself while his mind jumped among random worries of the government whisking her away, to crazy internet stalkers, to plain old crazy people coming after her. He couldn't do anything about the old article, and complaining about it would make him seem like a crackpot or call even more attention to her. He'd stumbled across that picture on the twelfth page of results after searching for paranormal activity near his zip code. No one outside the state would be likely to ever see it.

After the freak-out passed, he skimmed the article. It didn't tell him anything he didn't already know about the case, merely a brief write up about a local girl found murdered, father arrested. The article ended with some links, one of which caught his eye.

Parents of murder suspect accuse police of facilitating his death.

He clicked over to that article, which contained a photo of Vic's parents.

It explained that his mother tried to sue the police for being involved in his murder. She blamed them for not doing anything to save his life and even accused them of providing the murder weapon since her son didn't have any firearms in the house. She also claimed that Evelyn had killed the girl and framed her boy, then murdered him at trial to keep the truth from coming out. The reporter had challenged the idea, asking if Evelyn had, in fact, successfully gotten away with framing Vic for the murder of the little girl, why would she shoot him in full view of a judge, police, and over fifty witnesses. The article quoted the woman's response as 'because she's crazy.'

Another link led to a related article about Evelyn being found dead in jail while awaiting her trial for shooting Vic. It started with a two-paragraph summary of basic facts: she'd been discovered unresponsive in the morning by a jail guard with no evidence of injury. An autopsy failed to provide a conclusive cause of death. The larger portion of the article contained brief interviews with local officials and townspeople who knew the Kurtis family. Some believed the family suffered a curse, others said she died of a broken heart over her daughter. A handful suspected suicide and claimed the police lied about there being no injuries or drugs involved. Most of the people expressed some degree of belief that the woman would've been acquitted, with one woman (Deborah B) calling it a tragedy she died since 'she would've walked.' The last interview—with Weston Parker—blamed the Devil. He used his three sentences basically as a warning that people should stay away from that house.

Adam rolled his eyes. "The woman is dead and all you can do is use her death to scare people?"

He glanced at the clock at the bottom of the screen and smiled.

"One more hour…"

34

SMALL TOWN

SATURDAY, JUNE 8, 2019

On a whim, Mia decided to stop at the Pinecone Diner for lunch on the way home.

She and Robin had gone to Syracuse to shop for some summer clothes. The girl loved dresses and hated shoes, hated socks too—except for frilly ruffled ones. Mia wondered if spending four decades stuck barefoot in a nightgown left a mark, or if being super girly had been some manner of defense mechanism to protect her from Vic. Today had been a compromise day: sandals, no socks. Mia didn't stress the shoes issue at home, but the kid needed something on her feet when going into the city.

Robin so far hadn't given her any trouble, never throwing tantrums or refusing to put shoes on when needed. About the most defiant she'd been over the past six years had been taking forever to finish broccoli whenever it wound up on the menu for dinner.

Adam suggested she behaved that way out of gratitude, which made Mia wonder how long it would last before the girl changed. Then again, some kids *were* that sweet. Not until she'd had the baby could Mia have ever imagined herself being so attached and devoted to a little person. Sure, she'd stood up for Timothy, but she wouldn't have wanted to stop living if anything happened to him. Maybe she qualified as an overprotective parent, but Robin didn't seem to mind.

Somewhere between leaving the city and arriving in Spring Falls, 'I'll make something at home' gave way to lazy convenience. The local diner didn't exactly break the bank. Like much of the small town around it, the owners still appeared to think time stopped twenty or so years ago.

The Tahoe made a funny squeaking noise when she cut the wheel to turn into the parking lot. *Oh, that's so stereotypical. Soon as it's paid off, stuff starts breaking. Darn thing is only six years old. It shouldn't be falling apart yet.*

"Ooh. We're going to a restaurant!" Robin cheered from her car seat.

Mia grinned at her via the center mirror. "Yep."

"Do they have pancakes?"

"It's lunchtime." Mia pulled into a space and cut the engine. "You want pancakes for lunch? You had them for breakfast earlier."

"I remember." She grinned. "Okay, I'll wait. Pancakes are Saturday morning."

Mia got out, unbuckled Robin from her car seat, and held her hand while crossing the parking lot to the diner entrance. A passing elderly couple smiled at them in greeting, but when they noticed Robin, froze with confused expressions.

"Hi!" chirped Robin, waving.

The old couple exchanged a glance and seemed to get over whatever had bewildered them. Both smiled at the girl, the woman patting her on the head. They again waved to Mia and hurried off.

That was weird... She watched them amble over to a large maroon Buick sedan, turning away as they somewhat clumsily allowed gravity to pull them down into the car.

Robin squinted at the diner. "It's too bright. Why is there shiny stuff on the wall?"

Mia laughed while leading her up to the door. "Because the people who own this place like it."

She went inside, stopping short as a young woman, possibly not even eighteen yet, in a coral orange waitress uniform almost collided with her in her haste to rush down the aisle among the booth seats.

"Sorry!" said the girl. "Be right back."

Mia stood there waiting for the time it took the teen to drop off a carafe on a table and hurry back.

"Hi." The girl grinned at Robin. "Hello there, sweetie."

"Hello." Robin waved.

"Umm, you can sit over here." The teen led them to the right, heading for a booth table almost at the end of the building.

Ten minutes after noon on Saturday, the Pinecone had a decent crowd of mostly older people. The lack of cars outside suggested many of them walked—or carpooled—as it didn't seem likely this little town had a senior bus. Only three booth seats and four of the nine stools at the counter remained open.

People in various stages of eating or waiting for their food looked up as they walked by, initially either smiling or offering neutral glances. Robin waved at everyone, and as soon as she did, they all wound up staring at her. The child either didn't notice or didn't care about the odd reaction she elicited. The young waitress stopped at the empty booth one space away from the corner.

"Thank you!" chirped Robin. She hopped up into the seat and scooted over to the window.

Mia slid in beside her, both on the same side of the table.

"Oh, you're adorable." The waitress made a silly face at Robin, who laughed. "Can I get you something to drink?"

"Milk please," chimed Robin.

"Iced tea for me," said Mia.

"Okay. Be right back."

The old people at nearby booths kept peering over at them and whispering. The effect crept along the tables over the next few minutes. By the time the waitress had returned with their drinks and taken their lunch order, everyone in the place except for the young waitresses and a busboy gave them strange looks.

Robin's happy demeanor faded to a sense of worry. She cuddled against Mia's side. "Why is everyone staring at us?" She lowered her voice to a whisper. "I can't see inside people's thoughts anymore."

"I'm not sure," said Mia, low. "This is only the second time I've been to this place and it wasn't this full last time. People in small towns sometimes don't trust outsiders. We don't stop here very often, so they don't know us."

"Oh. Are they mean?"

Mia looked over the room. Whenever she made eye contact with anyone, they shied away. "I don't think so. They seem more confused than angry."

"Good." Robin squeezed her arm and whispered, "I don't wanna die again."

Choked up, Mia could only hug her back.

"Sorry for making you sad."

"I'm not sad, sweetie. I'm beyond happy."

Robin narrowed her eyes. "Your face is sad."

"Thinking about that stuff makes me sad."

"It makes me sad, too. I'm happy I'm not lonely anymore."

Mia brushed her hand over the girl's hair. "I wish I could take all those bad memories away."

"It's okay. I kinda 'member stuff, but not lots from when I was squishy. Sometimes I dream about it. I know I died once and you saved me." Robin snuggled against Mia's side. "I love you, Mommy!"

"I love you too, sweetie." Mia hugged her back, struggling not to break down at the realization she completely *got* Evelyn—and grateful she'd chickened out of that psychic vision before looking directly at the girl's body. She understood the woman's mental state and why she'd done everything she'd done... from killing Vic to simply letting go of her hold on life.

"Don't cry," whispered Robin.

She took a few breaths to still her emotions.

The waitress returned with their food: chicken fingers and fries for Robin, a chicken salad sandwich for Mia.

"Thank you!" Robin grinned at the young woman, who smiled in return.

They chatted about the approaching summer. Robin wanted to go with her friends to the lake to swim. Mia cringed inwardly, worried at the thought. With all the 'accidents' that almost happened at the house, combining her precious daughter with a lake felt like taunting the forces of evil. Her mind tortured her with visions of drowning, or that fatal amoeba thing. A 'we'll see' placated the girl for the time being. It had been years since Mia put on a swimsuit, but she might agree to a lake trip if she went into the water alongside Robin.

"Something watched me sleep last night," said Robin out of the blue. "Can I sleep with you and Daddy tonight?"

Mia froze in mid bite. She lowered the sandwich away from her mouth and peered over at the girl, who continued nibbling on a fry. "Something was in your room? It's protected."

"A shadow on the wall. I don't wanna be alone."

Was Vic trying to get through the wall but couldn't?

Another young waiter walked by, smiled at them, and kept going.

Still, the elders all glanced at them, whispering.

It's only old people... Mia idly fussed at Robin's hair. The girl smiled at her despite a mouthful of chicken. *She looks so much like she did as a ghost. I bet they recognize her.* Despite her appetite fading, she forced herself to finish the sandwich. *The house* is *getting darker.* While rambling about the crazy old pastor, Adam mentioned he said something about the Devil selecting their house. With Robin no longer trapped there as a spirit, maybe they should move? It made little sense given everything that happened there, but Mia had developed a strong possessiveness toward the house and didn't want to lose it. They'd never be able to afford a place anywhere near that size at a normal price. Also, she had no guarantee Vic wouldn't simply follow them.

"Do you think we should go somewhere else to live?" asked Mia.

Robin looked up from her food. "If you want to. People here don't seem to like us."

"I meant the house... the bad stuff there."

The girl shrugged one shoulder. "I dunno. You and Daddy made it nice there, but the bad daddy didn't go away yet. It's okay if you wanna move. It's okay if you wanna hit him in his stupid face."

Mia chuckled.

"And I'm not scared of those people staring at us. They're old and gonna die soon."

"Umm…" Mia gawked. The tone of it carried ambivalence, not cruelty, so she didn't think the girl *wanted* them all to die, merely stated a blunt—if indelicate—fact. Then again, this child once threw a hair dryer at her bathtub and made Weston drive into a tree. Oddly enough, both of those actions had been motivated by affection. "It's not polite to say stuff like that."

"I'm sorry. But it's not polite to stare either."

"You're right." Mia kissed her atop the head.

"Bad Daddy got mad when you didn't listen to him. But you don't gotta be scared of him now."

"Okay. We'll make him go away. You don't need to be afraid either."

Robin picked up her last fry, but paused before biting the end off. "I'm scared 'cause I'm only six. You're not afraid of him anymore, Mommy."

Yeah, I am… just good at hiding it.

The waitress returned. "All set? Can I get you anything else?"

Robin patted her belly and puffed out her cheeks.

Mia looked over their plates of crumbs. "Thanks, I think we're done. Just the check please."

35

OUT OF THE ORDINARY

SATURDAY, JUNE 8, 2019

Nate Ross sat back in his chair, feet up on his desk, sipping his 'noon coffee' while observing Main Street.

So little happened in Spring Falls, he didn't mind the six-day work week. Getting paid to sit in his office, occasionally break up a fight at Johnny's Bar, or give a local a jump start made for the perfect life. So what if he put in ten-plus hour days? Most of it involved doing what he did at present… sitting there watching people. Not like he had a wife or kid waiting on him. He didn't much feel any great pull toward obtaining either one. Alone suited him fine. No one to feel guilty about not paying enough attention to or spending enough time with. No one to stay up late worrying about. He had plenty of people to worry about already by virtue of being sheriff—like Chris Wilmott, the youngest deputy. Good kid, couple months past his twenty-second birthday.

A new real estate development west of downtown, a whole mess of condos, threatened the quiet peace he'd grown accustomed to here. New people, most of whom wanted the benefits of a city job in Syracuse but the quiet life of the boondocks, flocked there. With more people came more taxes, and Mayor Charles finally saw fit to add a third deputy.

Across the street, a glint of sunlight flashed from the door of the Pinecone Diner.

Mia Gartner and her daughter emerged from the front door, holding hands. The woman exuded protectiveness toward the child, who hovered close to her but grinned and waved at everyone who looked her way.

Nate couldn't help but smile back at her contagious happiness. He followed them with his gaze until they stopped to talk to two of Wilhelmina's friends—Lisa and Rebecca—then glanced to his right at the corkboard on the wall by his desk... specifically at a newspaper clipping old Sheriff Kline had kept from the Spring Falls Gazette showing the face of the little girl who died when Nate had been one year old. She smiled at him every damn day from that clipping since he'd taken the job. The same little girl had just walked across the parking lot across the street.

She lived in the same house, hell, even had the same first name. The way she skipped along behind her mother reminded him of something he thought he'd seen about six years ago when Weston introduced his Jeep to a tree.

He took a long sip of coffee, savoring it for a moment before swallowing. Nate set the mug on its coaster and reached up to unpin the child's picture from the wall. It had been there so long the paper around the tiny hole where the pushpin covered appeared visibly whiter.

The grainy photograph of a child taken in 1969, a photo no doubt obtained from the house by a reporter, showed a smiling six-year-old in a hideous striped shirt. Though she appeared happy, those eyes held a permanent undercurrent of fear. He couldn't tell if he picked up on it due to knowing all about Vic or if his keen perception and law enforcement training would allow him to recognize the same look in any other child terrified of someone close to them. The girl who emerged from the diner moments ago didn't have that quality in her eyes. She looked genuinely happy.

Nate removed his feet from the desk and stood, carrying it across the office to a back hall, past the bathroom to the storage room. He thumbed in 4-1-8-2 using the silver buttons on the mechanical keypad in the doorknob and entered a small room containing six metal shelves stacked with file boxes. Near the back left corner, he found the box he'd spent hours with over the years. Sergeant Kline had a mild obsession with the case despite everyone involved having died. The evidence box should've been disposed of decades ago, but for whatever reason, there it remained.

He removed the lid and picked up a manila folder, opening it to tuck the picture in. A report from Kline sat at the top of the stack of papers inside. Nate skimmed over numerous entries detailing calls about domestic violence from Evelyn. Kline's notes didn't appear to take her too seriously, but back in the sixties, no one really made that big a deal about a husband slapping his woman around unless bones broke. And even then, in a little backwater town like Spring Falls where everyone knew everyone, they all assumed Vic wouldn't really hurt her. Even Sheriff Kline had remarked in his notes that Evelyn had been 'overly excitable' and didn't think much of her saying she feared for her life.

"Guess that's why you gave her the .38," muttered Nate. "Guilt's a bitch."

A few documents later, Nate turned a page to reveal the booking photo for Evelyn Kurtis. He brushed his fingers down the face of a woman with strawberry blonde hair and hazel eyes. Something about her seemed familiar, yet if he'd ever met her, he didn't remember it. He would have been a toddler at the time she died.

Her eyes held so much sadness, like she'd given up entirely on life and wouldn't have cared if the deputy taking the booking photo pulled out a gun and shot her. Nate found himself overtaken by curiosity, that cop-sense telling him something didn't quite add up. The shape of her jaw, but mostly her eyes spoke to him. He felt as if he knew her somehow.

Unsure why, he plucked that report from the file and carried it back to his desk. He stood there, gazing at the photograph, allowing his mind to wander in search of answers. When he pictured the eyes changing color, the familiarity deepened. Brown… and brown hair.

She looked an awful lot like Mia Gartner.

He glanced up from the photo, out the window at the three women still talking in the Pinecone's parking lot. The little girl weaved around them, giggling.

Evelyn Kurtis had been thirty-six at the time of her arrest. As far as he knew, Mia was a few years younger. Take away the fatalistic gloom in Evelyn's expression, tint the hair and eyes brown, and...

Wow... they could be sisters.

Robin clamped onto her mother, beaming a huge smile. She gave off so much joy that once again, Nate found himself unable to resist smiling at the sight of her. Mia had to have been born at least fifteen years after Evelyn's death.

Mia randomly looked over toward the sheriff's office. For a brief moment as she stared at him, worry invaded her features, making her expression match the woman in the photograph. Mia's hair had to be twice as long as Evelyn's but...

Maybe not sisters.

Nate raised a hand to wave in greeting.

Mia's forlorn stare vanished to a pleasant smile. She returned the wave, then parted company with the two women. Lisa and Rebecca went into the diner while Mia and the girl headed for the Tahoe.

Deputy Wilmott rushed out from the diner, carrying a small box. He walked in a straight line over the parking lot, across the street, and in the office door, then set the box on the little table by the copier before fishing out two huge sandwiches wrapped in silver foil.

"Hey, sheriff. Sorry it took so long. Place is packed." Wilmott handed over a hot turkey and cheddar sandwich with double bacon. "How are things going?"

The Gartner's Tahoe rolled out of the lot and drove off to the left.

"Nothing out of the ordinary." Nate picked up his mug, tossed back the last of the coffee, and muttered, "For this town."

Wilmott chuckled. "Yeah, you got that right."

36

DARKNESS BANISHED, DARKNESS RETURNED

SATURDAY, JUNE 8, 2019

R obin left her sandals on the floor by the front door and dashed over to the sofa.

Mia put the TV on cartoons, then debated what to do with herself for the rest of the day—other than laundry. Adam should be home soon, but she figured leaving Robin alone in the living room for brief periods wouldn't be too risky, especially with the mesmerizing effect of television.

She kicked off her flip-flops and headed upstairs to get the first load of laundry started. They'd turned one of the unused bedrooms into a guest room, which had become basically Adam's parents' room for whenever they visited. That still left two empty bedrooms. Mia suspected her husband had been toying with the idea of suggesting they try for another baby. She smiled, expecting Robin would adore being a big sister. If he didn't bring it up in another month or so, she'd drop a hint.

Her good mood at that thought lasted only until she entered Robin's room to collect the contents of the clothes hamper. The air plummeted in temperature the instant she went past the door. Mia stopped short, stunned at the sight of her breath appearing as puffs of fog. Nothing visible manifested in the bedroom, though she once again felt as though a malign entity watched her. The palpable sense of anger saturating everything reminded her of the way the house had felt when they'd first arrived.

Alas, whatever psychic ability Mia had only allowed her to detect a presence. Other than shouting at it to go away, she had no real ability to *make* it leave. Wilhelmina and the others could handle that part. It had been a while since they cast a protection spell on Robin's bedroom, perhaps those spells ran out of power eventually. Evidently, their effort to banish Vic hadn't fully succeeded. Or, whatever defense it had offered wore off and allowed him back. Maybe he'd only pretended to go away, building power or choosing to bide his time for no good reason.

Mia backed out of the room without grabbing the laundry and poked her head into the empty bedroom to the left. It didn't feel cold in there, nor radiate any unusual anger. The atrium to the right gave off a distinct air of creepiness, but also lacked the supernatural chill.

Is it the blood in the floorboards? That spot always attracted Robin's ghost. Damn. We should have had it cleaned up.

A shadowy figure as tall as a man drifted around the near right corner, directly behind the washer/dryer nook. Mia whirled toward it, but only a wispy black tendril remained, seeping into the wall. She rushed out of the doorway, glaring at the washer and dryer area, but the creature had vanished.

Everything Adam ever said about shadow figures was really bad. She took a tentative step closer, bracing herself for the jump scare. Robin had hidden between the machines—a space no living child could fit into—and leapt out at Mr. Vaughan. Inch by inch, she edged closer, expecting something to burst forth from the dark space at any second.

The doorbell rang.

Mia screamed, jumping back with both hands over her heart.

"Mommy?" called Robin from downstairs. "What's wrong?"

"N-nothing... just... bad energy." She kept staring at the spot between the washer and dryer as she hurried past it to the stairs.

Robin ran over to the bottom of the stairway and peered up at her. "I feel it, too."

Mia kept a death grip on the railing until she went down far enough that a fall couldn't cause serious injury. Robin waited for her to go by, then returned to the sofa to resume watching cartoons. Trembling gave way to contained anxiety by the time she opened the door.

The sight of Weston Parker standing on her porch knocked the words out of her brain. He had to be nearing seventy, though other than his hair having gone full white, he appeared reasonably fit, if a bit thin. He had a small kink in his nose where the airbag broke it years ago. The same green Jeep Cherokee, long since repaired, sat in the driveway right behind the Tahoe, like the horses of two old rival gunslingers having water together.

"Mia…"

She hadn't seen the man face to face since the day he'd crashed into the tree. He'd occasionally shown up at the street with some of his people to pray, but that petered out a few years ago. Seeing him here came as a bit of a shock. While he might be a pushy religious wingnut, she found herself not necessarily objecting to having another adult around at the moment after what she'd sensed upstairs. And, he didn't share her parents' opinions about people like her brother.

Her antagonistic urge faded. She took a step back. "Hello, Weston. Come in."

He nodded appreciatively and obliged.

"What did you mean when you said the Devil chose this house?" She glanced sideways at the stairs. "The place has been quiet for years, but I… just felt something upstairs. How much do you know about what really happened here?"

High-pitched cackling came from the TV along with a cartoonish explosion.

"The Devil attacked that poor family. Evelyn wanted to pray with us, but that man refused to let her."

Mia bristled, sensing deceit. Joining his church aside, she had a feeling the woman tried to seek help from Weston in regard to Vic beating her… and been blown off. She could just imagine a twenty-something Weston, a new pastor, telling her she had to honor her husband or some bogus nonsense like that. The same bullshit her father used to believe in. Women and girls belonged in the kitchen, quiet and obedient.

"They were like you," said Weston in a regretful tone. "Didn't hear The Word. The Devil got into him, made him break his vows. Got into her, too. Made her defy him."

"I'm sorry, Weston, but it's not 1960 anymore. A woman fleeing an abusive husband is not defying him. Women are people, not slaves."

"Vic had an... affair. The Devil changed him. Made him angry, drove him to Johnny's. Drinking made him angrier. Evelyn got wind that he'd known another woman, but she respected her duty as a wife and did the good Christian thing, forgiving him."

Bile rose in the back of Mia's throat. "She didn't forgive him. If an affair happened at all, she would've been too terrified to do anything. Evelyn wanted to leave him before he killed her."

Weston shifted his jaw back and forth. "Well, be that as it may, for whatever reason, she stayed, hoping he'd change back to the man he'd been when they first met. She confided in me that she feared him, but try as I might, I couldn't make the man hear The Word. One night, the daughter had enough of him hitting her mother and asked him to stop. He slapped her for it. I believe that's when Evelyn made the choice to leave him. The Devil loves nothing more than to ruin anything sanctified by God, like marriage."

If God loves marriage so much, he would've protected them. She bit her tongue.

Sirens and cartoony gunfire came from the TV along with a nasal voice repeating 'stop in the name of the law.'

"The Devil got into him too far to save, and he took his daughter's life." Weston looked down.

"And Evelyn shot him during his trial, then died of a broken heart while sitting in jail. No devil made her do that. Absolute grief did."

Weston snapped his head up, staring at her. "How did you know that?"

"It was in the papers. I might not have been alive when it happened, but I can read."

"Oh, well... yes, but... You need to take your family out of this house before the same thing happens to you."

"What's *he* doing here, Mommy?" Robin sidled up beside Mia and clung to her left arm while giving Weston a nasty look.

He blinked, raising a shaking hand to point at her. "W-who is that?"

"That's my daughter, Robin. But you know that already don't you?"

"H-how?" Weston backpedaled toward the door, his eyes glassy, cheeks pallid.

"Are you okay?" asked Mia with a feebly suppressed smile. "You look like you've seen a ghost."

Robin giggled.

Weston twitched, a tic in his left eye. A book leapt from a shelf beside the television and flew at Weston. He raised an arm fast enough to protect his face. The book bounced off with a dull thump and hit the floor.

"I didn't do that, Mommy," whispered Robin. "I can't do stuff like that anymore."

The old pastor pointed at the child. "It's too late for you, Mia. You've allowed the Devil into your heart."

"Your god did nothing to protect the life of an innocent. Don't you dare call my daughter 'the Devil.' She's a child. Have you considered the universe might not work the way you think it does? Ever hear of reincarnation?"

Weston stared into Mia's eyes for a long, quiet moment. "Yea though I walk through the valley of—" He froze, still as a statue, staring past Mia.

She twisted to follow his gaze.

A thick, vaporous shadow coalesced in the doorway between the kitchen and living room. Robin tucked close to her side, cowering from it.

The shadow rushed forward at Weston.

He screamed and bolted out the door. At the arch between living room and dining room, the shadow figure exploded into a burst of darkness that faded away. Mia shuddered as a wave of tangible malevolence shot past her, seemingly going right out the front door— though she couldn't see anything.

The Jeep's engine roared to life.

"Watch out for trees!" yelled Robin. She glanced over at the book on the rug, then up at Mia. "I don't think bad daddy likes him, either."

37

OUTSIDE THE CYCLE

SUNDAY, JUNE 9, 2019

Forks and knives scuffed at plates, the loudest sound in the dining room.

Mia, Adam, Robin, and Wilhelmina sat around the table working on eggs, hash browns, and sausage. The girl kept making silly faces at Wilhelmina, who returned them like a sixty-two-year-old going on seven.

"So, the feeling's back," said Mia.

"Hmm." Wilhelmina pushed hash browns into a pile on her plate. "I think he might have returned as well. Or maybe he never quite left."

"Did something go wrong with the banishing?" asked Adam.

"It's difficult to say. Spells aren't an exact science, so to speak. I can't really tell for sure if an entity is driven out or simply chooses to leave because it's tired of hearing us pester it."

Mia stabbed a bit of egg and smiled at Robin. "Your magic clearly *does* work."

"Uh, huh." The girl beamed. "I remember seeing a tunnel, an' it pulled me, tryin' to pick me up. I knew it went to Mommy, so I jumped. Saw a hole in the ceiling, but when I went through it, I was a baby an' this man was holding me." She flailed her arms. "That was *so* annoying. I couldn't do anything."

"Interesting…" Wilhelmina made a pensive face. "So, you went from being a spirit straight to birth as though it happened in an instant?"

"Yeah," said Robin.

"Hmm. Guess she slept for nine months." Adam chuckled.

"Oh, she was very much awake for at least the last three." Mia rubbed her stomach.

Robin shrugged. "I don't 'member that part."

"You're sure you're not reading a latent imprint?" Adam swiped another sausage from the serving tray.

"No. That shadow figure didn't feel like a 'recording.'"

Adam grinned. "Well, at least we agree with him about Weston."

Robin raspberried.

"It is certainly odd that he should show up here out of the blue like that." Wilhelmina furrowed her brow. "Vic, I can understand. Men like that can't stand to lose. He did what he did to hurt Evelyn, to punish her. I wonder if our changing things might have made him restless."

Mia smirked. "Wouldn't he be in hell?"

Wilhelmina laughed. "If only. I feel that when a soul returns to the Pool of Life, they become part of creation again. Like if you scoop some cookie dough out of the bowl, then stir it back in, no matter how hard you try to scoop it back out, you're not going to get the exact same lump. Some of the dough is going to be different. Every spirit from ants to humans goes around in an endless swirl, waiting to return and reincarnate. The ritual we did isn't required for someone to reincarnate, though it did basically allow Robin to remain the same lump of cookie dough."

"I'm not a lump." Robin stuck her tongue out through a grin.

"Souls do not need such a ritual to reincarnate." Wilhelmina smiled at Mia. "Though it is rare that they closely resemble the person they used to be. If something like that were to occur, it would surely speak to that soul's strong drive. Or perhaps they sensed an opportunity to set a horrible event right they believed they played a part in causing."

Adam shrugged, nodding. "The internet is full of stories of people who claim to have been reincarnated and remember pieces of their past lives. And there's that old wives' tale that everyone has a double somewhere." He fiddled with his phone for a moment, pulling up a post with a dozen historic photos that resembled modern celebrities. "Coincidence or reincarnation?"

"Regardless of why a particular soul managed to reincarnate so close to the person they once were"—Wilhelmina reached over and rested her hand on Mia's arm—"the fact remains that you have a shadow problem. Some, like Vic may have had the strength of willpower sufficient to keep themselves outside the cycle. I'm sure he seethed with hatred and anger. He would not rejoin the Pool until he let go of whatever desire kept him here."

"No devil?" asked Adam, grinning.

"I do not believe he fell victim to a negative spirit, though I'm also not saying such things are impossible." Wilhelmina loaded her fork with some eggs atop hash browns. "That man was enough of a demon unto himself. He didn't need outside help."

Robin ducked under the table and crawled into Mia's lap. "I waited for Mommy."

Mia hugged her and kissed her atop the head. "You sure did, sweetie."

"Any idea why Evelyn didn't wind up haunting the house?" Adam inhaled a giant forkful of eggs.

"Oh, sometimes spirits take quite a while to get where they're going. They don't always take the most efficient route." Wilhelmina kept her gaze on her plate, smiling to herself.

"So what can we do about him now?" asked Mia. "If he's upset about Robin... would he have cared if she went through the cycle?"

"I imagine not. She wouldn't have truly been Robin anymore. I doubt she would've had the drive to retain the person she once was as strongly. The energy that comprised her soul would've changed. Mixed with other energy, and so forth."

Adam drank a few sips of coffee. "What kind of thing would keep someone together like that?"

"Oh, I can think of a few reasons. Perhaps a soul lost to sorrow jumped too quickly into the Pool and realized they had someone precious waiting for them." Wilhelmina finished off the last of her potatoes. "But, I'm just an old woman. What do I know?"

Mia stared at her. *She's implying... Does she think I'm Evelyn reincarnated?* She held Robin tighter, resting her chin on the girl's head. If that were true, wouldn't she know? Wouldn't she remember things? She bit her lip. Those visions and dreams she'd had of finding Robin's body, the powder blue purse... could those have been *memories* instead of psychic readings? Something she often said about her job restoring art hit her square in the feels: she loved restoring life to things considered dead.

"Hon, you okay?" asked Adam.

"Mommy's got the sad. She's thinking about what happened to me."

Wilhelmina dabbed a napkin at her lip. "As for what to do about Vic..."

"Do you—" Mia took a deep breath to let her emotions settle. "Do you think there's any possible truth to what Weston said? Could there be some kind of curse or dark energy affecting this house? Like an ancient burial ground, or some awful event that happened on this land before the house was ever built?"

"I don't believe so." Wilhelmina shook her head. "I have already spent quite an amount of years researching that exact thing, trying to make sense of the tragedy. In my professional opinion, Vic Kurtis was just a psycho."

Adam held up a finger. "I concur."

Wilhelmina winked at him. "Take it from the psychologist."

MIA SAT ON THE SOFA, NOT REALLY WATCHING TELEVISION.

Wilhelmina and the others would be there in another hour or so to scrub the house and perform another banishing ritual. This time, Mia would get over her fear and accompany them to the basement. Whether or not she had been Evelyn in a past life, she had a daughter to protect and she couldn't let her childhood of being morbidly terrified of her parents' basement threaten Robin.

A sudden, intense pang of worry hit her.

Without a word, she jumped to her feet and ran upstairs. A slosh of water came from the bathtub.

"Hon?" asked Adam.

Mia sprinted down the hall.

"Hon?" yelled Adam again, from the stairway.

The bathroom door started to swing shut on its own, but she leaned into her stride, ramming shoulder-first into it before it could latch, slamming it open. Adam thundered up the stairs behind her. Mia crashed into the cabinet and shoved herself away, spinning to face the tub. Robin lay flat on her back underwater, thrashing, kicking, and grabbing at the air as though something held her down. Two rubber ducks and a plastic faerie bobbed around over her. Air bubbles leaked from her mouth.

"No!" screamed Mia.

She dove to her knees, grabbed Robin's hands, and pulled. The child seemed to weigh four hundred pounds. Adam burst in and stood there for not quite a full second taking in the scene, then grabbed Robin's left wrist in both hands. Mia shifted her grip to the right arm, and they pulled together, but couldn't dislodge the girl from the tub.

Robin's eyes rolled up in her head. Her legs stopped kicking.

Mia snarled, pulling harder.

"Easy... don't dislocate her arms," yelled Adam. "Get under her shoulders."

No! I'm not gonna lose her again!

Mia grunted, took a huge breath, and plunged her face into the water, breathing into Robin's mouth. The girl snapped awake and clamped on with both arms and legs, trapping Mia's face underwater. Her lungs mostly empty from giving the child air, Mia's head spun in a dizzy whorl. She braced her hands on the tub floor on either side of the girl's head and pushed. Robin's fingers scraped over her back, slipping away, unable to hold on against the force pinning her to the tub. Again, the child went limp.

Adam grabbed Mia around the chest.

She threaded her arms behind Robin's back, fighting the tremendous weight holding her down. It reminded her too much of the horrible dream when Vic pinned her to the floor. Mia screamed inside her head and pulled, beyond caring if she hurt herself.

Robin started to sit up, then broke free from the force.

Adam, Mia, and Robin flew backward. He landed sitting on the floor, Mia in his lap, Robin still wrapped around her like a koala bear. Both Mia and Robin gasped for air.

"Holy shit," muttered Adam.

Mia squeezed her daughter, clinging to the tiny body wracked with choking coughs. Adam held them both in silence for a while.

"Mommy?" wheezed Robin. "I changed my mind. I'm not a big girl yet. Please stay with me for baths."

I'm going to sit beside the tub until she's thirty. Mia nodded, rocking her. "I will."

"Son of a…" Adam exhaled hard. "Are you okay? Let me see her."

Mia shifted sideways, relaxing her grip.

A faint red handprint marked Robin's chest. Adam gently overlaid his hand on the mark, which extended a little bit on all sides.

"Vic," said Mia.

Adam nodded.

Robin sniffled. "Sorry for getting water all over."

"Oh, sweetie. That's not your fault." Mia kissed the top of her head. "C'mon, let's dry you off."

She toweled the girl off while Adam pulled the plug on the drain and retrieved a mop for the floor. A few minutes later, the doorbell rang. Robin zoomed out of the towel. Mia tried to grab her, but missed.

"Wilhelmina!" cheered Robin from down the hall.

"Get back here! You're naked!" shouted Mia.

"Oh, I don't think the witches will mind." Adam chuckled.

Mia scrambled to her feet and hurried down the hall with towel in hand. Robin had opened the door to let the coven inside, all of them laughing at her bouncing with excitement at seeing them. Lisa announced that since the little one went sky clad, she would, too.

Robin pointed emphatically at the stairs. "Bad daddy tried to drown me!"

Their mirth fell in an instant to silence.

Mia swooped in and picked Robin up, wrapping her in the towel.

"What happened?" asked Wilhelmina.

Robin pulled the towel open enough to show off the almost-faded handprint.

Mia explained.

Wilhelmina approached and cupped Robin's cheeks in both hands. "You're not going to go to sleep now, are you?"

Robin shook her head. "Nope. Too scared."

"Well, you might as well help us out with the banishing then." Wilhelmina patted her on the head.

"Are you trying to lure my daughter to devil-worship?" Mia managed a weak grin.

"She's already dressed for a bonfire ritual," said Lisa.

"I swear..." Rebecca rolled her eyes. "You're part wood nymph. Girl just can't wait to take her clothes off."

"It's good she'll be with us." Wilhelmina tapped a finger to Robin's nose. "We can directly involve her in the protection spell."

"Okay. But first... someone needs her nightgown." Mia looked down at herself. "And I need to change, too. I'm soaked."

THE GROUP WALKED FROM ROOM TO ROOM.

Robin dutifully held a smoking sage bundle, following Mia, who primarily kept quiet and watched. In each room, Wilhelmina led the others in a banishing ritual, during which she called upon The Goddess, The Horned God, Morrigan, and Brigit. They cleansed the upstairs after the first floor. When they reached Robin's bedroom, Wilhelmina hung three talismans of twigs and herbs, one by the door, one between the windows, and one on the wall above the bed.

Eventually, they returned to the ground floor and went down to the basement.

Mia steeled herself, but accompanied them despite her inherent fear.

The air smelled mostly of dryness and heating oil. Boxes stood against the walls in piles, all things abandoned by the house's prior occupants. Based on the thickness of dust, she suspected quite a few of them had belonged to the Kurtis family. Flaking white paint fell from the brick walls around a largely open space. An old workbench ran along the far wall, next to an alcove where an ancient washer and dryer still stood. They appeared as though they hadn't been used in half a century.

Mia shivered at the heavy presence lurking behind the furnace. A darker spot formed the vague hint of a humanoid outline in the gloom. If not for having the five coven members surrounding her, she had no doubt she'd have screamed and run back upstairs. The initial blast of fear faded, leaving her furious that he tried to kill Robin for the second time.

"Vic!" Mia stepped in front of her daughter and pointed at the shadow. "Go away! You're not welcome here. You have no power over me."

The shadow rushed at her. Physical force crashed into her with the presence of hands at her throat, lifting her off her feet and slamming her back against the wall, strangling her. Reality flashed away to a brief vision of Vic in his mechanic's uniform holding her—holding Evelyn—against the wall in the same manner.

"Who do you think you are, bitch!" he shouted, then slapped her hard.

Mia returned to the now, her cheek throbbing. Adam grabbed at the vaporous apparition, his hands passing through it without purchase. Unlike her vision, the shadow figure didn't scream at her or make any noise, merely stared into her soul with two pale white eye spots. She sensed Evelyn curling up on the floor, apologizing over and over again, begging him to stop. A snarl slipped from Mia's lips. "Get off me, you bastard!"

She punched the shadow figure in its vaporous head, but the

apparition flowed around her arm. Robin screamed. Hearing her child so terrified set Mia off like a bomb.

"You're a damn coward, Vic! I'm not scared of you. Go the hell back to whatever sad little hole you crawled out of."

The force pinning her against the wall dissipated. She slid down to her feet, still glaring at the hanging shadow. At her refusal to fear him, the malice inside him grew—but she sensed his ability to harm her waning. Mia took a defiant step toward him; the shadow receded.

Wilhelmina aimed a hand at him. "I call upon The Goddess to cast out all negative spirits. I call upon the Horned God to purge from this place all energies dark and malign." She raised her hands over her head, then swept them down. "We call upon the energies of creation, the protective forces of the universe. We establish this as sacred space free from all forces chaotic and malicious."

The others repeated the chant.

Wilhelmina recited an invocation of elements that largely skirted the edges of Mia's consciousness while the drifting shadow held all her attention. Despite its sinister appearance, she refused to give him the satisfaction of showing fear. He'd attempted to drown her daughter. Anger bloomed. She projected it outward at the shadow figure, telling herself mentally over and over that he had no power over her.

The shadow melted in place, sinking to the floor. She sensed it still watching her and glared at the spot until all sense of his presence receded from her awareness.

Robin waved the smoking sage bundle and yelled, "Go away!"

Mia jumped at the touch of a hand on her shoulder. She turned to find Adam beside her. Wilhelmina and the others roamed the basement, still muttering and spreading sage smoke around.

"You okay?"

"Yeah. Just had a staredown with the bastard. I think he's left the house... but I don't think we're done with him yet. This just got serious."

"Bad Daddy's angry," whispered Robin.

38

RULES

TUESDAY, JUNE 18, 2019

In spite of no longer sensing dread inside the house, Mia still tossed around the idea of moving.

She kept it to herself for several reasons. One, she no longer believed that Vic was exclusively bound to the house, and worried he would simply follow them if they went anywhere else. Secondly, this place had numerous protections in place from Wilhelmina and the others. Witch bottles, talismans, and an amulet or two stood guard in windows upstairs and down. Third, she didn't want to surrender to that bastard.

Fourth, and most compelling, she hadn't picked up on any supernatural doom in the week since the banishing. Robin no longer wanted to be alone for bath time, not that Mia would've permitted it anyway for at least another few years. She'd probably decide to be embarrassed about having Mom or Dad in the room with her while she bathed by eight or nine, and—provided Vic stayed gone—it shouldn't be a problem at that point.

Mia fixed a breakfast of oatmeal for herself and Adam, cereal for Robin. As had become routine, she'd drop the girl off at Wilhelmina's house—a bit less than two miles down Minstrel Run—then go to work. The extra stop (going in the opposite direction from Syracuse) necessitated her leaving earlier than she used to, so she wound up walking out the door only seconds after Adam.

"Rabbit!" yelled Robin.

She dashed off the front porch, chasing after a streak of white fur. Adam stopped by the Nissan, smiling at the child's gleeful but futile pursuit. Mia turned to pull the front door closed, and froze at a sudden pang of worry. She whirled back toward the yard and ran, calling for Robin to stop.

A dull *clunk* came from the Tahoe—and it rolled backward down the inclined driveway, picking up speed.

The girl tripped and fell flat on her chest with a yelp of startled pain, her head directly in the path of the SUV's back tire. Mia screamed. Without superhuman speed, she'd never cover the distance in time. Adam zoomed across the driveway, crashing into Robin with a slide. The Tahoe bounced over his foot, the right corner of the back bumper clipped the open door of the Nissan, and the truck rolled out onto Minstrel run, coming to a stop with a *whump* against a tree.

Adam rolled onto his back, clinging to Robin, who appeared unhurt but disoriented. He hissed in pain, but didn't make much noise, though his face had turned bright red.

Mia rushed over and grabbed them. "Adam... holy shit..."

"Yeah."

Mia held them both until she stopped shaking, her emotions a storm of fury and panic. "You've got serious 'dad reflexes.'"

"I'm sorry," whispered Robin.

"It's not your fault." Adam fussed at the grass next to him. "Damn gophers or whatever... she stepped in a hole."

Robin rubbed the side of her head where it hit the driveway. "No. I mean I'm sorry for being scared of you before when I was squishy."

He hugged her, then handed her off to Mia. "Already forgiven... before you were born." He winked.

"You're a good daddy." She smiled.

Mia cradled the girl, staring at the wayward Tahoe out in the street. "The parking brake didn't slip on its own."

"Hah!" Adam laughed.

She shifted her gaze to him, unimpressed. "What's funny about this?"

"Nothing."

"So... you're laughing at what?"

"Do you remember the first day we were here?"

"Kinda."

"When you pulled into the driveway, your left foot hurt." He pointed at his left foot. "I think it's broken. You probably sensed the truck would run me over."

Mia raked a hand through her hair. "I don't remember that, but I'll take your word for it."

"Looks like I'm going to be late for work today."

She eyed the Tahoe. *It's probably safe to drive. Damn Vic.* The rabbit reappeared in the brush at the far side of the yard, staring at them in an almost taunting manner. For the first time in her life, Mia glared at a cute, fuzzy thing with malice. Indifferent to her opinion of it, the rabbit sniffed the air and hopped into the brush.

"I guess I should be more careful until Bad Daddy doesn't wanna make me a ghost again." Robin brushed grass bits off her dress.

Dread built up in Mia's gut at the worry it might not be Vic this time. He hadn't shown any sign of being here for over a week. Sure, the bathtub had clearly been him... but this? Robin Kurtis had died at seven. What if The Universe caught on to them cheating the system and intended to make sure Robin Gartner also died by seven? Had they broken the rules?

No. I'm just being paranoid and worrying about everything. She would've eventually reincarnated anyway, and if the Universe would get pissy about us altering the rules, why did fate line up to send me to this house in the first place—assuming I really am Evelyn reincarnated? She almost scoffed at the thought of that, but it would help explain how rapidly she'd become attached to Robin's ghost... and the random dream memories of Evelyn's life. Perhaps they had come from within, unlocked by her return to this house or proximity to the ghost of the child she'd once failed so horribly. Never having been in a situation with a man like that, Mia couldn't fault the woman for making the decisions she'd made back then… but had she grabbed Robin and gone to her parents' place instead of work that night, tragedy *might* have been averted.

Of course, had she done that, Vic could have chased her there and murdered all of them…

Mia rocked her daughter side to side, half ready to spend the next few hours sitting there and holding her to keep her safe.

Adam on the phone with his boss brought her back to reality. "… yeah. Going to hit the emergency room. It hurts, but it's not *that* bad. I'll be in as soon as I can."

"You're driving like that?" Mia blinked at him.

"It's just my left foot. Don't need that one to drive." He waved her at the Tahoe. "You should probably get that thing out of the road before someone plows into it."

Mia let Robin stand, then got to her feet. "Okay. I can call out and drive you if you want."

"I'm good. Go on. No sense both of us being late. Might want to ask Wilhelmina about a charm for the truck."

"Wait here, sweetie." Mia gave Robin's shoulder a squeeze, then hurried down the driveway to where the Tahoe sat horizontally across the road.

The rear bumper had a small dent from the tree, in better shape than the Nissan's driver side door. She dug the keys out of her purse, hit the button to unlock the doors, and hopped in. The engine started without issue. After parking on the road at the base of the driveway, she got out to load Robin into the car seat.

Adam hopped on one leg over to the Sentra. "Ehh. About time to replace this one anyway. What do you think? Should we get another car or look at something bigger and bump the Tahoe to the 'second vehicle?'"

"We've only had it for six years." Mia secured the seatbelts around Robin.

"It's as old as me." She thrust her arms up, then patted the seat, talking to the truck. "It's okay. I know *you* didn't try to hurt me."

"I'm not saying we get rid of the Tahoe, just do we get a replacement 'second *car*' or something like a minivan."

"So you want another kid?" asked Mia.

Adam put on an innocent face. "The idea's been rattling around in my head."

Mia shut the back door after securing Robin in her car seat. "Are you sure you're okay to drive to the hospital?"

"Yeah." He waved. "Go. Don't be late."

Against her better judgement, Mia trotted around to the other side and got in. She tested the parking brake, which appeared to work normally. The second time she pressed down on it, she remembered the phantom pain in her foot from that day six-ish years ago. It had hit her the instant she decided to set the parking brake because of the driveway's incline.

Well, how about that…? I guess I really am psychic.

She started the engine and drove around in a U-turn toward Wilhelmina's.

39

MAD

TUESDAY, JUNE 18, 2019

The discussion they'd had over dinner played on a loop in Mia's mind.

It didn't seem worth it to fix the door on the Nissan when the car approached thirteen years old and already had several other issues. Adam wanted to maybe get a mini-SUV, something smaller than the Tahoe that could still handle the more extreme roads around here. A minivan would run into the same sort of issues as a car in bad weather on winding backwoods roads or dirt trails.

As frustrating as the idea of taking on the expense of a new car—or buying a lightly used one—was, she lacked the emotional bandwidth to get worked up over it after nearly losing Robin twice in about a week.

She reclined on the couch, not quite watching a Disney Channel movie about a frontier family. Robin, in one of Mia's T-shirts for a nightgown, sat between her and Adam, who had his left foot up on the ottoman. He'd suffered a simple fracture to the second metatarsal bone, resulting in a boot cast and crutch time. Mia marveled that he'd been able to drive himself to the hospital and went to work right after. Though, he did teach from his chair. He hadn't taken any of the painkillers they'd prescribed him until arriving home.

A soft knock came from the door.

Mia glanced over, half tempted to ignore it, but the flickering light from the TV made it obvious they were home. The part of her that hated being rude rose up and nudged her off the couch as Adam reached for the crutch.

"Sit still." She playfully swatted at him.

When she opened the front door to see Weston standing there, she damn near closed it in his face. Only an inkling of doubt stalled her hand. The coven's spells had proven mostly effective in shielding the house, but hadn't been able to permanently banish Vic. She didn't have much trust that Weston's brand of paranormal interference—prayer—would do much since it hadn't helped back when the Vaughans owned the place, but if it offered even a tiny chance of protecting Robin, she'd at least give him the chance to say something.

The man didn't look well, paler than usual, his hair disheveled, eyes wide. A faint essence of beer hovered around him as well, though it didn't come from his breath or from his clothing.

"What brings you here at such a late hour?" asked Mia.

"I've been praying for guidance. It's never been clearer to me than it is now. Those pagans are doing something unholy. You and your family must come to the church before it's too late. God will still protect you."

"Have you been sleeping? You… look a bit strung out."

Weston rubbed his forehead, eyes fluttering. "I've been pastor here for over forty years, and I am deeply concerned for the wellbeing of all God's children who live in my town. What's going on here is an affront to the Lord."

She gritted her teeth. Dad frequently called Timothy that, an 'affront to God.' "If you're here to try and do something about Vic's spirit, we can talk. Otherwise, you should go home and get some sleep."

"It's imperative that you and your family get out of this house as soon as possible. You're welcome to shelter at the church. Just follow Minstrel Run to Deer Path, take the left onto Brownbriar road."

"You can pray for us wherever we are."

"Holy ground!" shouted Weston. "You need to be on holy ground to shield yourselves from the influence of the Devil."

"For the love of…" muttered Adam.

"Pastor Parker," said Mia, "I think you maybe should consider talking to someone… like a therapist? You seem a bit obsessive."

"It's not too late." Weston's eyes flashed with a manic glint. He started to reach for her, but stopped himself. "Your souls hang in the balance."

Mia leaned back, not at all liking the energy he threw off. "Weston, you're unwell. You need to go home."

He stuck his foot in the door as she started to close it. "Listen to yourself. The Devil makes you reject the Lord. If you continue to do so, you'll be damned."

Robin walked up beside Mia, scowling at Weston.

"Back!" Weston flung his arm up.

Mia yelped and grabbed Robin, starting to drag her away from the gun she expected would be in his hand… but he had a crucifix.

"Back in the name of the Lord!" He wagged the crucifix at the girl. "This is not a real child! You have welcomed a demon into your home. Robin Kurtis is dead!"

Adam's groan of pain accompanied the rattle of an aluminum crutch.

"This is Robin *Gartner*. You're insane. Robin Kurtis was born in 1963. Don't you hear how delusional you sound, Weston? *I* wasn't even born when that poor girl died."

Weston emitted a raspy wheeze. The fragrance of stale beer grew stronger.

"Mr. Parker…" Adam limped up behind Mia. "As an actual psychologist, it's my opinion that you should seek help, and probably soon. You have an unhealthy obsession with this house."

Mia glared at Weston, who continued staring past his crucifix at the child. A new hostility simmered in the depths of his pale brown eyes that hadn't been there before. She had no doubt this man wanted to hurt Robin.

"You stay away from us, and stay away from my daughter." Mia pointed at him. "I have no idea what's gone wrong in your head, but you keep it away from here."

Robin darted over to the coffee table, grabbed Mia's cell phone, and ran it back over to her.

"I'm going to call the sheriff now, Weston."

He eyed the phone as if considering swatting it out of her hand, then shifted his gaze to Adam.

"Why are you so mean to us?" asked Robin. "We just want to be happy."

"You took their minds and their souls, demon." Weston waved the crucifix at her. "And they don't even know it. You're not real."

Robin edged behind Mia. "Mommy, I'm scared."

"See! The fiend fears the Lord!"

"That's it," muttered Mia. She swiped the phone open and called 911.

"Spring Falls sheriff," said a woman two rings later. "Deputy Clark."

Mia kept her eyes on Weston's. "Yes, this is Mia Gartner at Six Minstrel Run. Weston Parker's at the door threatening us. He seems to be out of his mind or something. I smell beer on him, but he's acting more like he's high… or paranoid."

"What's he doing now?" asked Deputy Clark.

"Just staring at us. He seems to think my six-year-old is some kind of demon and wants to destroy her."

Weston snarled and stormed off to his Jeep in the driveway. He yanked its door open, but turned to shout back at them, "The wages of sin are death!"

He got in and slammed the door.

"He's leaving," said Mia. "And totally nuts."

Robin clung to her side.

"All right. Wilmott's in the area. I'll have him stop by to check up on you folks."

"Thank you."

Weston cut the corner tight at the end of the driveway, going over a bit of lawn to the road.

"There's something definitely not right in that head." Adam grunted, shifting his weight. "I hate to say it, but I think he cracked."

"As soon as he got a good look at her the other day. I practically heard his mind shatter." Mia shut the door and rested her hand on Robin's shoulder. "All the old people in town seemed to recognize her."

"Little place like this, sure. The murder, the trial, the spectacle of it consumed their every waking moment for that whole year." Adam shuffled back to the sofa, fell seated, and let out a relieved sigh. "Most normal people would see her and file it away as a bizarre coincidence. The idea of reincarnation at all likely doesn't even enter their thought process."

"But Weston isn't exactly normal people." Mia returned to the couch and pulled Robin up to sit in her lap.

"Can I sleep with you guys tonight? I'm scared," asked Robin.

"Of course." Mia picked her up.

Adam reached over and ruffled her hair. "You're scared of that crazy old preacher?"

"A little. I'm scared 'cause I'm gonna turn seven next year, and *he's* mad at me."

"Weston?" asked Mia.

"No. The bad daddy. He wants to make me a ghost again."

Mia squeezed Robin and shot a desperate look at Adam. "If we have to move, we're gonna move. I won't let him kill her twice."

Adam put an arm around her shoulders. "Do you think it will help?"

Mia shivered with worry. "Not really. He didn't die here. There shouldn't be anything significant about this house to him. He should be haunting Johnny's since he spent so much time there or the courthouse since he died there."

"He should go away," whispered Robin. "I don't wanna be a ghost again."

"It'll be okay, sweetie." Mia clutched her daughter tight. *That's not gonna happen. Not until you're old and grey.* "I won't let him hurt you."

Even if it kills me to protect her, that bastard isn't going to touch her.

40

ASHES TO ASHES

SATURDAY, JUNE 22, 2019

The idea of moving out of the house resurfaced the next morning over breakfast.

"Not like out of town far, just out of this house. Maybe it *is* cursed," muttered Mia.

"Wilhelmina couldn't find anything to suggest this land is tainted, and she spent years looking." Adam stirred raspberry jam into his oatmeal. "I'm not convinced it will help, but if you feel strongly about it, okay."

"I'm kinda scared of my room, but I kinda like it, too. It feels like home. I don't 'member bein' made a ghost. Just that he did it."

Mia continued debating if they should move while finishing off her oatmeal, though didn't pick up on any feelings one way or the other, at least nothing stronger than the continuous background worry that had been nagging at her since yesterday. Deputy Wilmott had been friendly, even if he looked too young for the uniform. He claimed to be twenty-two but looked eighteen. She hadn't heard anything more from the sheriff's office about it yet. With any luck, they'd go see Weston, realize he'd gone crazy, and take him somewhere for evaluation.

Once Mia collected the empty dishes, Robin ran to the living room and flopped on the floor by the TV amid her collection of stuffed animals. Mia rinsed the bowls before putting them in the dishwasher as oatmeal turned into concrete if it dried out.

Adam relocated to the sofa with his laptop. Mia zipped around the house, still overwhelmed at having to clean a place that size. Even with Adam taking on his share, it *still* felt like an endless battle. For as long as it took his foot to recover, she'd focus only on the more critical cleaning. Robin pretended to paint her toenails with a miniature faerie wand and toy plastic bottle, half her attention on whatever cartoon show Adam had put on for her.

Mia's cell phone rang a little after eleven. Hoping to hear good news from the sheriff's office, she rushed to the dining room and grabbed it off the table. Upon seeing Janet Newman on the Caller ID, she cringed with hesitation, certain she'd picked up some kind of psychic warning. Whether it meant answering would be a bad idea, the call brought bad news, or something else, she couldn't tell.

She didn't see how ignoring a call from her boss could possibly end positively for her. Janet had been promoted to the number two spot overseeing the entire museum, and Mia took on the manager's position for the restoration department.

"Hey, Janet. What's up?"

"Oh, thank God you're there. There's been an... event at the museum. I just got a call from the fire department. The sprinkler system apparently went off, and I haven't been able to figure out exactly what's going on. They need a manager there, and you're the closest person with all the keys. I'm still in Albany. Is there any way you could head down to the museum and meet with the fire department? It sounds like there's no actual fire, but a malfunction set off the waterworks in the back areas."

Mia bit her lip, dreading the potential damage. Fortunately, she could bring paintings back from water. Fire, not so much. "Okay. I'll go right now."

"Thank you so much. I owe you one!"

"I'll call you as soon as I can with an update."

"Great. You're amazing."

Mia sighed and hung up.

"That didn't sound good," said Adam.

"No. The fire system went off at the museum. Probably dozens of artifacts getting a bath from the sprinklers. I'm the nearest manager, so I need to run over there with the keys."

Well, that explains the weird feeling. Bad news.

"Okay. I'll, umm… be here." He smiled.

Mia rushed upstairs to swap her sweat pants for jeans and sneakers—no sense dressing nice for an emergency call on a weekend —and hurried back downstairs. After a quick hug and kiss with Robin and Adam, she headed out to the Tahoe, hoping that Janet's tendency to expect the worst of things meant the damage wouldn't be all that bad.

ADAM WINCED, SHIFTING HIS LEG ON THE OTTOMAN INTO A slightly more comfortable position.

He looked up at the rev of the Tahoe's engine. *Easy, hon. Don't drive like a nut.*

Robin played with her plush animals and dolls, sprawled on the floor in front of the couch in a simple white dress with pink trim. She swished her bare feet back and forth, doing silly gibberish voices for the various dolls. He took a small break from grading the essays his students had submitted electronically to merely sit there watching his daughter be happy. Whenever Mia arrived home, assuming the chaos at the museum hadn't left her in a bad mental state, he'd bring up the idea of adding to the family again.

Thump.

Robin looked up at the ceiling.

"Think that was a fat squirrel falling off a branch?"

She giggled. "No, Daddy."

The house had been spiritually quiet for some time, long enough that a random noise with no apparent cause once again stood out as unusual. Nothing like the first few weeks they'd lived here. Somewhere along the line, he'd lost his 'kid-at-Christmas' excitement for paranormal events. At least, paranormal events going on where he lived.

Thud.

Robin jumped with a gasp.

That one came from the kitchen.

She crawled over to the coffee table, grabbed the remote, and muted the TV.

A long, slow *creak* broke the silence, then a wooden clatter.

That sounds like the back door's swinging in the wind. Dammit. Guess Vic is in a mood.

Footsteps passed by overhead, heavy, like a large, angry man.

Robin crawled under the coffee table.

Another *thud* came from the kitchen. The door creaked again.

Grumbling, Adam grabbed the crutch and wobbled upright.

"Don't go," whispered Robin. "I'm scared."

"Just need to close the back door. I'm not going anywhere." He hobbled across the dining room to the kitchen, and frowned at the back door wide open. "At least he's only being annoying."

After looking around at the floor to make sure no 'traps' waited for him, Adam limped over to close it.

Sudden motion came at him from the right. He pivoted, raising his arms to block whatever object Vic threw at his face—but realized too late that Weston had been hiding in the small foyer by the shelf of canned goods. The old pastor rammed a hunting knife into Adam's torso. His bones rattled from the blade deflecting off the bottom of his ribcage, but the pain of the wound itself didn't hit him right away.

Adam grabbed at the blur of flannel in front of him. Weston yanked the knife out and shoved him aside. His left leg gave out, dumping him to the ground on his chest, his fingers tearing the pocket off Weston's shirt on the way.

The man stepped over him and went into the kitchen, mumbling something about needing to slay demons on holy ground.

Adam dragged himself around with one arm to face the doorway, his left hand clamped over the wound. Gritting his teeth, he forced himself up on one knee and grabbed the doorjamb for support. He didn't think he'd survive a rematch with Weston in his present condition, but he didn't have to survive... he only had to keep him busy long enough for his daughter to run.

ROBIN STARED UP IN TERRIFIED AWE AT THE MEAN OLD PASTOR stalking across the dining room toward her, daddy's blood dripping off his knife.

Her father staggered into view in the kitchen, wheezing, "Run! Get to Willa's!"

She scrambled out from under the table and darted for the front door, screaming for help, but managed to pull it open only an inch or two before Weston mashed his hand into it above her head, slamming it. He tried to grab for her, but she shrieked, ducked, and raced up the stairs on all fours. She skidded to a stop at her bedroom door, afraid to go in there, not with an angry man chasing her—too much like how she became squishy last time. Her room made for a bad hiding place.

A fleshy *thud* came from the stairway. Daddy grunted. Weston growled. Several meaty *thumps* and the heavy *whump* of a body falling to the floor followed.

Robin managed not to scream. Eyes blurred with tears, she dashed down the hall to her parents' room and crawled under the bed. At the thud of footsteps in the hallway, she covered her mouth with both hands and tried to keep as quiet as possible.

The house hung in silence. She listened, but the mean pastor must be in her room, searching for her. Robin breathed through her nose, trembling. Minutes passed. She worried about Daddy. He'd been hurt real bad. If she waited too long, he might become a ghost. But if the mean old pastor found her...

She eyed the bedspread blocking her view of the room. If the bad man had gone into her bedroom, she might be able to sneak by and make it out of the house. An old man like him wouldn't be able to catch her.

Tears dripped off her face. Terrified, but also afraid of losing her good daddy, she crept toward the edge of the bed.

The bedspread whipped upward, revealing Weston's evil grin—and blackened eye. "Gotcha!"

Robin shrieked. She scrambled backward, but he grabbed her right ankle and hauled her out from under the bed. When she stomped at his face with her other foot, he grabbed that ankle as well, lifting her into the air upside down. Her dress fell over her face, blinding her.

She flailed and screamed. He swung her up and tossed her on the bed, then grabbed her in a bear hug, pinning her arms. Robin screeched and thrashed as he carried her downstairs, past Daddy—who lay face down on the living room floor, not moving—and into the kitchen. Upon reaching the small pantry room by the back door, he pinned her to the floor long enough to tie her hands behind her back with duct tape and bind her ankles together.

She squirmed and struggled, but couldn't snap the tape. "Let me go! You're mean! Please don't hurt me!"

"Your pleas fall on deaf ears, demon. You cannot fool me. I know what you really are."

"I'm not!" wailed Robin, wriggling.

He lifted her again, tossing her over his shoulder like a bag of dog food.

"Daddy!" screamed Robin. "Help!"

Weston carried her outside, across the deck, and over to the left side of their yard where he'd parked his Jeep Cherokee. He opened the back hatch and unceremoniously tossed her inside on her chest, then slammed it. Robin peered up at a wall of metal grating behind the rearmost seat that turned the back end of the truck into a cage. Similar bars covered both side windows. The space stank like wet dog and a few muddy paw prints marked the beige carpet. She twisted to look behind her. The inside face of the hatch didn't have any handles, buttons, or knobs to open it.

"Let me out!" screamed Robin.

She bent her legs back, picking uselessly at the tape between her ankles.

Weston got in and started the engine.

"Please leave us alone. I'm not a demon. Please don't make me a ghost!" She rolled over and got up on her knees, grabbing the cage behind her back and shaking it.

"That mesh will hold a pit bull," said Weston. "But keep on tryin'. You may have fooled that poor woman and gullible man, but my faith in the Lord is too strong."

She pulled at it for another few seconds before a turn flung her over sideways.

"Please let me go," wailed Robin. "I'm not bad!"

"I know exactly what you are," said Weston in a younger, deeper voice.

Robin froze, nearly peeing all over the floor from fright. He sounded exactly like Bad Daddy. Each time he steered around a slight bend in the road, she slid back and forth across the kennel area, bumping into small plastic doors over storage compartments on either side.

"The preacher and I are going to return you to where you belong."

"No!" Robin rolled onto her back and kicked at the grating again and again, scream-crying, "Mommy! Help!"

41

MOTHER'S INSTINCT

SATURDAY, JUNE 22, 2019

Mia drove west along County Route 69, heading for Interstate 81.

Out of nowhere, worry at what she'd find at the museum blanked entirely out of her head, leaving her wondering why she drove anywhere at that moment.

She blinked.

Robin.

An overwhelming need to check on her daughter fell on her like a sack of cinder blocks. She stomped on the brakes and swerved into the entry drive for the Parish Country Lodge, slammed the shifter into reverse, and backed out onto the road again, facing the other direction.

Mia floored it, accelerating well past the speed limit without giving a shit. A cop could chase her all the way back home for all she cared. She flew down Route 69, squeezing the steering wheel so hard she half expected it to break in her hands. Both cars she illegally passed honked at her. She yelled at her phone to call Adam and ringing filled the truck's speakers.

"Hi, this is Adam Gartner, well, no it isn't. It's my voicemail. Leave a message and I'll get back to you as soon as I can."

"Fuck!" screamed Mia.

"I'm sorry, I didn't catch that," said her iPhone. "Please repeat your command after the beep."

She slowed enough to avoid rolling the Tahoe into the weeds when she reached the turn for Split Oak Road. Between its small size and winding route, she could only get up to fifty before worrying too much about losing control. Killing herself in a car wreck would be no good to her daughter.

With each passing minute, her fear deepened to outright nausea. She again shouted at her phone to call Adam, and it again went to voicemail.

A few locals gave her nasty looks for speeding down Main Street, but she evidently didn't go fast enough to drag Nate out of his seat. Or maybe no one had been in the Sheriff's office at that moment. More likely, they knew exactly who buzzed Main Street at fifty-five and would be mailing her a ticket.

An agonizing four minutes later, she screeched the tires pulling into the driveway at the house. The sight of the front door ajar made her scream. She leapt out of the Tahoe, not bothering to kill the engine—or close the door—and hurried inside.

Adam lay on the floor, bleeding all over himself from a wound in his lower chest and several smaller cuts on his face. His lip had swollen up and blood leaked from his nose.

Mia dropped to her knees beside him and shouted at her phone to call 911.

"Oh, hi," wheezed Adam. "How was the museum?"

"Adam!" She clutched his arm. "What happened?"

The delirious quality to his expression cleared. "Weston... he's got Robin."

"I'm gonna kill him."

Adam grabbed his chest wound and grunted. "Hurry. Go. Get her. He's not gonna kill her until he's at the church. There's still time."

"Spring Falls 911, this is Deputy Clark," said the phone.

"Allison! Send an ambulance as fast as you can to Six Minstrel Run. My husband's been stabbed and my daughter's been kidnapped."

"Slow down, ma'am. You say your husband's been stabbed?"

"Go," wheezed Adam. "Move! I can make it 'til the ambulance gets here. The church…"

Mia set her phone on Adam's chest. "Yes. He's been stabbed. I gotta go right now or my daughter's gonna die."

"Ma'am?" asked Deputy Clark.

Mia ran outside, jumped in the Tahoe, and screeched the tires backing out of the driveway. The truck hit the road so hard she screamed, fearing it would bounce and roll over, but it only wobbled. Snarling, she glared at the road.

Deer Path to Brownbriar Road.

Snarling, she stomped on the gas pedal, too furious to cry.

42

WHERE YOU BELONG

SATURDAY, JUNE 22, 2019

Robin rolled around the dog cage in the back of the Jeep, helpless to stop herself.

The mean pastor didn't drive well at all. She curled up, trying to keep her face from bouncing off the storage compartments or the rear hatch. Screaming, she pulled and twisted at her hands even though it felt like the tape would rip her skin off.

Tight stickiness slipped down over her right hand. Robin strained, pulling as hard as she could with her arms in such an awkward position behind her. Twisting her hand side to side, she worked her hand loose a little bit at a time. A turn threw her to the right. She rolled like a log into the side compartments, knocking one of the plastic doors open.

At the end of the turn, the Jeep flung her onto her chest. She huffed, nearly out of breath. This man would make her a ghost again; giving up wasn't an option. Grunting, Robin tried to force her arms around her butt. The tape tore down over her fingers—and her right hand popped free.

The stinging made her cry, but when she pulled her hand around to look at it, the pain stopped. She hadn't ripped her skin off—it only felt like it. A wad of silver tape still clung to her left wrist, but she ignored it, grabbing at the tape tying her ankles together. It refused to tear no matter how hard she pulled at it.

Robin almost screamed in frustration but stopped herself, eyeing the open storage cubby. Maybe one of them had a knife she could use to cut herself free. Each had a little plastic door with a pushbutton to open it. The first door she checked contained a plastic shopping bag full of wooden talismans—the same ones Wilhelmina had put around the outside of the house.

He broke the spell!

The second one she opened contained a black plastic box and an orange gun that looked like it came from a cartoon. She considered the strange weapon for an instant, but kept looking. Before she did anything else, she had to get her legs untied. Among other tools, the fourth cubby had a retractable knife like the one from Bad Daddy's toolbox.

Holding her breath, Robin reached into the cubby and gingerly removed the knife, keeping low to the ground near the front of the cage, hiding behind the back of the rear seats so the mean pastor couldn't see her. She pressed the nub down and pushed about an inch of blade out the front end. Holding a blade that sharp near her feet in the back of a bouncing Jeep scared her, but not half as much as the man behind the wheel scared her. She twisted her feet as far apart as the tape allowed and raked the blade at the silvery binding. The utility knife sliced the duct tape open with such ease she whimpered, not wanting it anywhere near her skin. The instant the tape snapped open, she retracted the blade, then kicked her legs free.

Weston hit the brakes hard, flinging her against the cage wall. She caught herself with her hands and held on until the forces holding her stopped. The Jeep took a gradual right turn and the sound of tires chewing up dirt road filled the cabin.

Having no better ideas, Robin went for the cartoony orange gun. She grabbed the cage with her left hand, braced her right foot against the side wall, and rose up on one knee, sticking the fat barrel through one of the square openings in the bars, pointed at the back of his head.

"Stop and let me out or I'ma shoot you!"

He twisted to look back at her, wide-eyed.

The Jeep drifted to the right, leaving the dirt road. A bump bounced Robin upward. She involuntarily clenched her grip on the gun, which went off with a loud *bang* and a *fwoosh*. Bright orange light streaked past Weston's face, missing him by an inch. Still, he screamed. The blindingly intense orange ball bounced off the windshield and ricocheted into the passenger seat.

Stinky smoke flooded the front of the Jeep as the seat caught fire. Weston howled, coughing.

Robin tossed the gun aside and got down. The back door had no handles or any way to open from the inside. Overwhelmed and terrified, Robin resorted to the most logical thing she could think of doing: she screamed for her mother.

The Jeep bounced over rough ground, throwing her around the dog kennel like a tennis ball in a clothes dryer. She grabbed at the mesh, unable to see anything but smoke. Weston shouted a whole bunch of nasty words, the same ones Bad Daddy used all the time. He hammered the brakes, throwing Robin against the front wall of the cage, but the Jeep came to a sudden stop with a jarring impact and another loud *bang* from the front.

She coughed as smoke filled her prison, no longer screaming for her mother because it hurt too much to breathe. Fire glowed amid the haze, brightening as it crept down the passenger side toward her and spread up into the roof fabric.

A door creaked. A steady stream of grumbled bad words moved around to the back end.

Panic pushed her as close to the door as possible, the end of the Jeep as far as she could get away from the burning while locked inside. Weston opened the rear hatch, but grabbed her when she tried to jump out.

He hurriedly fished a roll of duct tape out of another cubby, then dragged her away from the burning truck. Robin screamed and fought, but lacked the strength to escape his grip. At a safe distance from the fire, he took a knee and draped her over it as if to spank her. The man appeared furious, eyes watery and bleary, breath wheezy, a bright red burn on his head above his right eyebrow, but he didn't say a word while forcing her arms together behind her back.

"Help!" shouted Robin as loud as she could make herself. "Mommy! Please help me, I'm being kidnapped!"

Weston clamped a hand over her mouth.

Lost to feral panic, Robin bit down on his middle finger with every intent to rip it off. He let out a yowl of pain and recoiled, cradling his hand to his chest. She twisted away from him, landing on all fours in grass that came up to her knees after she leapt to her feet. Weston swiped at her with his unbitten left hand. She ducked his attempt to grab her and ran.

A large building with a cross painted on the wall stood off to the right. The dirt-and-gravel parking lot had a few other cars in it—but anyone in it there might be as mean as the bad pastor. She kept going straight toward the woods. Dry grass whipped at her legs and snagged between her toes. Weston's coughing drew closer, coming up behind her.

She dashed out of the tall grass onto a swath of mowed lawn, which allowed her to run faster. At the other side, she plunged without hesitation into the woods. Thumping footsteps followed close along with the crunch of branches the taller man had to shove out of his way. She veered for a pair of trees too close together for a grown-up to fit, darting between them. Weaving back and forth around trees kept him far enough behind that he couldn't grab her, though she dared not look back. Instead, she aimed for every place she thought he'd be too big to follow.

An eternity later, she stumbled down a hill, waving her arms for balance. A belabored wheeze behind her sounded far enough away that she decided to risk looking. Weston emitted a groan, gasping for air between whispers about demonic little imps. Not being able to see him gave her hope and a second wind. She kept running for a little while more.

Thick undergrowth as tall as her chest covered a stretch of forest up ahead around a massive tree with a trunk as big around as a refrigerator. She ducked down and crawled in, tucking herself up against the bark under a canopy of broad leaves. If she could only stop breathing so hard and stay quiet, he might not find her.

Robin curled in a ball and wrapped her arms around her knees. She wanted to gnaw at the wad of duct tape still wrapped around her left wrist, but feared it would make too much noise.

"There's no point to running, demon," rasped Weston, distant, yet close enough to be scary. "You may think you know where you are because you've been wandering around here for forty years... but I've lived here just as long. You don't fool me! You aren't a real child. You're a demon pretending to be one. I know what you're doing to that poor woman and her husband! God will forgive you if you ask him to. Come with me to holy ground!"

She huddled down low. *Mommy! Hurry up! I'm here! Please help me!*

"There is no escaping the Will of God, fiend! You belong dead!"

Robin shivered at the sight of Weston stalking among the trees maybe a hundred feet away from where she hid. *Mommy, help! I know you're coming. I just know it. Please hurry!*

43

INTO THE WOODS

SATURDAY, JUNE 22, 2019

A great plume of black smoke rose up over the trees not far ahead on the right.

Mia growled at a big sign with a cross on it by a dirt trail leading away from Brownbriar Road that bore the words 'Spring Hills Christian Fellowship Church' beside a right-pointing arrow. She hit the brakes hard, skidding only a little as she steered the Tahoe onto the unpaved road.

The plume came from a fully-enflamed Jeep Cherokee crashed into one of a row of trees planted alongside the trail leading to the distant church building. Its back hatch appeared to be open, but she couldn't see inside for all the fire and smoke. Despite the frightfulness of the scene, she sensed Robin had gotten away from the fire.

Mia stopped far enough back to protect her truck from a potential explosion, and started running across the grassy field toward the big, white one-story building. Adam said he wanted to take Robin to holy ground before killing her. She swore under her breath for rushing off without grabbing any sort of weapon, but she didn't have time to do anything other than haul ass.

Weston's voice emanated from the forest to the left. He sounded too far away to understand, but the taunting tone came through clear.

The instant Mia looked in that direction, she *knew* Robin had gone that way. She changed course, barreling into the woods. Branches whipped at her face, roots threatened to take her feet out from under her, but she kept going, guided by the mocking voice.

"I know you're around here," called Weston. "Demons cannot conceal themselves from the eyes of the Lord. Repent and go willingly unto Him and you shall be forgiven."

Mia skidded to a stop, trying to catch her breath. Panic and urgency gave way to thinking. *He's lost her. Robin's hiding... He'll hear me coming if I just run in.* She resumed following the man's voice, moving with a focus on quiet rather than speed. If Robin screamed or he stopped trying to trick her into showing herself, she'd bolt.

"The Lord is thy Shepherd..."

She bristled at the rhetoric, but the man's babbling religiosity acted like a homing beacon. Soon, she caught sight of him up ahead, stalking among the trees with a roll of duct tape in one hand. A distant *kaboom* signaled the end of the Jeep. Hopefully, *that* would tell the sheriff's deputies exactly where they needed to be.

Weston flinched at the explosion, but didn't turn. He scanned the woods with wild, feverish eyes.

She hurried closer, circling left to stay behind him, and looked at her empty hands. *Oh, screw it. I don't need a weapon to take on a sixty-eight-year-old man.* Mia closed to within twenty feet, then burst forward in a sprint. He spun toward the rustle of her tearing up the underbrush. She ran straight into him, crossing her arms into a battering ram that she drove into his chest. Weston barked like a kicked goose and flew over backward. The duct tape sailed off into the weeds.

Enraged, Mia rushed in, kicking at his side. She landed two good shots on his ribs before spotting the hunting knife on his belt and squatting to grab for it. He caught her by the wrists and dragged her off balance before she could open the retaining strap. She fell forward, draped across him. Weston forced her arms behind her back and held her wrists together.

"You poor child," rasped Weston. "The demon's in your mind. "I'm trying to *help*—"

She hurled herself upward, mashing her head into his face. He lost his grip on her arms. She rammed her elbow back into his chest as fast and forcefully as she could a few times before he grabbed two fistfuls of her hair and tossed her aside.

Mia landed flat on her chest and screamed in pain tinged with fury. Wings of adrenaline carried her to her feet the same time Weston wobbled upright. He lunged in trying to grab her, caught off guard by her fist crashing into his jaw. He staggered away while Mia gasped and cradled her hand to her chest, surprised by how much it hurt to punch someone in the head.

Ow. Shit.

"As soon as I destroy the demon, your mind will be free. You'll see that—"

She shrieked and ran at him.

He caught her by the forearms, holding her at bay for a few seconds until she again surprised him by attempting to bite him on the shoulder. Weston flung her back and drew his knife.

"You're making things difficult. If you don't obey God's will, I'm going to have to knock you senseless until it's over."

"Why are so many religious people insane?" She rasped a few breaths. "My daughter is not a demon. A demon is someone who can murder an innocent child."

"That is no innocent child. What you did is against nature." Weston's voice shifted deeper. "She belongs dead."

Mia stared at him, stunned. "You... you're not the pastor anymore, are you?"

Weston laughed in the younger, lower voice. "Oh, city girl's a smart one. It's your husband's fault you got a mouth like that. You sit down and behave yourself. Me and the preacher have a demon to put back where it belongs."

"I can't tell where Weston ends and Vic starts, but I'm not going to allow either one of you anywhere near my daughter."

"Oh... you wanna be with that kid so bad huh? If it means that much to you, I can make it happen for you." He lunged, stabbing at her chest.

Mia leapt aside, darting around a tree for cover. The blade chipped a sliver of bark away with a dull *thump*. Weston strolled around the tree, wrinkly face twisting into a malevolent smile.

A wheezy elder voice muttering Bible passages leaked from his mouth at the same time the deeper voice spoke over him. "Preacher man cracked like an egg when he saw the kid, alive and breathing, same as he remembered her. Sending the 'demon brat' back to hell was all his idea. I'm only helping him out." Weston slashed at her again.

She caught his arm in both hands, holding the knife out to the side. Weston continued invoking scripture in an endless, incoherent half whisper. Goosebumps rose on her arms in response to the needling cadence of his raspy voice. Vic laughed. She grunted, struggling to hold his weapon back. The old man rambled in a loop about God and demons, eyes manic. Mia locked stares with him, certain that only she —or another psychic—could hear Vic's voice coming out of him, the same way she'd been able to speak with Robin before.

Sirens wailed from somewhere far behind her.

Unable to get his knife out from her grip, he punched her in the head with his left hand, knocking her staggering, then slashed, scoring a minor slice on her forearm. Mia yelped and scrambled away. He charged in, mashing a hand into her chest and shoving her over on her back.

"Bye bye, Mommy," said Weston, raising the knife.

"No!" shouted Robin, jumping out of the weeds.

Weston twisted to stare at her. "There you are…"

Mia reared back and drove both feet into his gut with a mule kick that launched the skinny old man into the air. He landed hard, barking out a heavy wheeze. She rolled forward, leaping on top of him and slugging him over and over in the head. Weston flailed his arms, babbling deliriously.

Robin ran around to stay behind Mia.

She hit Weston one more time and leapt off him into a run. Mia scooped Robin up and sprinted into the woods carrying her. Weston groaned. She ran a little ways looking around at the trees, but didn't seem to be going toward where she'd left the Tahoe. Every direction looked the same. Robin kept quiet, clinging, not even crying.

"Now you've pissed me off," grumbled Vic, over Weston's continued muttered scripture.

Mia stopped caring about going anywhere specific except away from him. She hiked Robin up a little higher and ran. Even carrying a six-year-old, she didn't have a problem staying ahead of him, but she also didn't appear to be leaving him behind. Hoping she had more endurance than the aged pastor, she pushed herself to keep going.

"Go faster, Mommy!" yelled Robin. "He's right behind us."

Trees and branches rushed by on both sides. Mia ducked her head, trying to spare her face from the endless low-hanging branches in her way. Twigs and leaves crunched behind her along with the grumbled curses and out-of-breath wheezes of a man too old to be running in the woods. Sirens grew louder off to the right, so she swerved that way.

Mia ran hard, ignoring the pain in her legs, ignoring the desire to simply drop where she stood and rest—right up until she found a ridge.

A clipped yelp flew from her throat as she skidded to a stop with inches between the tips of her sneakers and a steep downhill slope. She didn't have enough time to think 'oh shit' before the dirt beneath her gave out and she fell into a tumbling logroll, bouncing over rocks and jutting roots.

Robin's clear high-pitched scream followed her down the hill.

44

THE CABIN

Trees stretched up into Mia's vision, thrust like twisted spears into the clear blue sky.

It made no sense why trees would be sticking straight out in front of her like that. Or why the sky looked like a giant blue wall hanging. Or why her entire body felt numb.

A light patting jostled her cheek. "Mommy?"

Blurry whiteness crept into her awareness. She squinted, wondering what sort of ghost hovered next to her.

Small hands gripped her shirt by her neck, shaking her. "Mommy! Wake up. He's gonna get us."

Dozens of bruises throbbed in time with her pulse. The reality of her situation crashed into her all at once: Weston, the knife, falling… Robin. The blur sharpened into focus—her daughter, smudged with dirt and soot—kneeling next to her. The child trembled, wide-eyed in fear.

"The demons begged of Jesus," shouted Weston in a brittle voice, "Drive us out and send us unto the herd of pigs. I see you, demon, and shall drive you out!"

Shit! He sounded close.

Mia scrambled upright and took the girl's hand. She started to run, but hesitated upon noticing Robin's bare feet. The girl kept going, pulling at Mia's arm. The pain of crashing down a steep hill echoed in bruises all over Mia's body, but she fought past it. She considered picking Robin up so they could move faster, but her weary muscles could do only so much. Even with a much smaller stride, the child would've outpaced her if not for hanging off her arm.

Snapping and crunching echoed out of the forest behind her. No doubt, Weston had found a less painful way to the bottom of the hill, which afforded her enough time to recover from the daze. She couldn't remember most of the fall and worried she might've hit her head on a tree at the bottom.

Memory loss isn't a good sign. She clenched her jaw, determined to force her head clear.

"You cannot run from God, Mia," called Weston, sounding close but nowhere to be seen.

"Come on!" yelled Robin, pulling at her. "This way."

Mia grabbed at her pocket, but she'd left her phone in the truck. The thick woods surrounding her blocked the sky as well as the smoke plume from the burning Jeep. "Crap. Where are we?"

"Over here," whispered Robin, veering left. "There's a cabin where we can hide."

"How do you know that?"

"I see it."

Mia struggled to keep up with the child. She searched the woods ahead of them, not finding any trace of a cabin. Though, the direction Robin wanted to go *did* feel right.

Weston started to shout something about God but his voice shifted to a cry of alarm, then the thud of a body falling amid snapping vegetation. Mia grinned to herself at him falling over. She hoped it would give her the time to reach a safe spot—a locked cabin door should hold him off long enough for someone to find them or at least the cabin might have something she could use as a weapon.

The child pulled her along, heading for a steep hill of exposed dirt and rock roughly two stories tall. Without hesitation, Robin grabbed a stone and started climbing. Mia reluctantly let go of her hand and took hold of a jutting root. With seemingly practiced ease, the girl navigated the maze of roots, rocks, and weeds. Wherever she couldn't find purchase, she jabbed her toes into the dirt like a knife. Mia dragged herself up right behind her, flinching at a steady drizzle of soil falling on her face from above. A watermelon-sized stone near the top that Robin stood on for a moment gave out under Mia's sneaker, tumbling down the cliff face. All her weight hung on a cluster of roots, which tore out from the dirt after only a second of holding her.

Mia's scream started from fright but shifted to determination. A kick at the cliff shoved her sideways, swinging to the left. She caught hold of a thicker root and kicked her sneakers into the dirt, stopping her fall. There she paused a few seconds, waiting for the fear spike from almost falling to fade. Robin disappeared over the top, about six feet above her. Somewhere below, Weston's rambling about the fury of the Lord grew close.

With a grunt, Mia hauled herself up, grabbed another root, and tested a rock with her foot. It didn't budge when she kicked it, so she shifted her weight onto it and scrambled up to the ridge. Robin grabbed her shirt, 'helping' her up and over the top.

Flat on her chest, Mia gasped for breath.

"We're almost there." Robin tugged at her.

Mia pushed herself up to kneel. A ramshackle structure stood about thirty yards away, nestled in the woods beside a bizarre collection of copper tubing and large tanks. It made Wilhelmina's cabin look like the Waldorf, being one decent storm away from complete ruin. Whoever made this cabin hadn't used it—or the still—in decades.

So much for a locked door... maybe a weapon.

They sprinted across relatively flat ground to a dirt clearing. The air held a strong alcohol smell mixed with the pervasive stink of moldy wood and a chemical essence she didn't recognize. One doorway—without a door—peered in on a single-room space awash with graffiti. Five bare mattresses, all moldy and wet, lay around the floor among spent syringes, beer cans, disposable lighters, and bulbous glass pipes. She winced at the thought of going inside such a place, especially with Robin lacking shoes. A second building, somewhat more intact than this one, sat a short distance deeper in the trees behind the still. That one at least had a door.

Mia scooped Robin up, hurrying around the collection of rusty pipes and junk.

The door on the large shed refused to open, the knob either locked or rusted solid. Hazy windows coated in years of grime offered a partial view of a work table with a vice near a pegboard of old tools.

"Mommy," whispered Robin. "There's a hole on the side."

Mia looked where the child pointed. A couple boards on the left face of the shack had disintegrated. Termites—or some manner of little white insects—swarmed all over the wood fragments. "Umm..."

"The demon will not prevail," roared Weston from the base of the cliff.

She grimaced at the bugs, but her legs had enough of running for one day. Mia dropped to all fours. Robin stepped among the infested wood, unconcerned she walked barefoot over live bugs. The oddity of seeing such a girly-girl so blasé about the disgusting mess distracted Mia enough to crawl in behind her before thinking too much about it.

Once inside, Mia hastily looked around while Robin crawled under the workbench. A waist-tall wooden shelf holding a few paint cans stood against the wall not far from the hole. Mia jumped up and grabbed it, dragging the shelf left until it blocked off the hole. She backed up, clapping dust off her hands. The pegboard held mostly small wrenches, manual drills, and other old-timey tools she'd never seen before and had no names for. None of them looked worthwhile as any sort of weapon. Sections of pipe in various sizes leaned against the wall on the right in a pile with copper tubing.

"That'll work..."

Mia picked up a three-foot long piece of cobweb-covered pipe, clutched it like a baseball bat, and tucked herself under the workbench beside Robin. Her exhausted body trembled from fatigue, breaths rapid but short. Too much adrenaline flooded her system to even consider resting. *Just have to wait...* She eyed the small, dirty window beside the door. If Weston tried to get in that way, he'd be wide open for a pipe to the head. If he managed to shove the shelf out of the way and crawl in, he'd be even more vulnerable on his hands and knees. She doubted the door would open ever again... but even if it did, the old shed would force him to attack from straight in front of her.

It might not be much, but the place *did* provide some protection.

Don't see us. Just keep on running. The shallow slice on her forearm throbbed in time with her heartbeat.

"I'm scared, Mommy," whispered Robin, clinging to her arm. "Please don't let him make me a ghost again."

"I won't." She closed her eyes. *And if I mess this up, I promise we'll haunt the house together.*

Twigs crunched outside. Words like 'God,' 'demon,' and 'hell' drifted out of constant, incoherent rambling. Mia looked around at the junk, a sick feeling growing in the pit of her stomach. It didn't seem likely at all that anyone would find them way out here in time to help.

She swallowed the saliva in the back of her mouth and tightened her grip on the pipe.

45

IN THE NAME OF

SATURDAY, JUNE 22, 2019

The wind worried at the old shed's walls, rattling the ancient tools above the workbench.

Despite Mia's efforts to hold still, her muscles wouldn't stop quivering. Robin clung desperately to her arm, cutting off circulation to her hand. She trembled, her face wet with tears though she didn't make a sound. The stink of smoky burned plastic saturated her hair and dress. Mia risked looking away from the door for a few seconds to give her daughter a comforting smile, but wound up glaring at a tangle of duct tape still wrapped around the child's left wrist. She almost wanted Weston to find them so she could punish him for doing that to her daughter.

Minutes passed in silence.

They both jumped at a sudden flutter of flapping wings passing close overhead.

A swath of pale beige drifted by the window. Robin's grip on her arm tightened.

Mia stared at the door. As much as what he'd done to Robin infuriated her, she didn't want the girl to witness what would happen. Weston stalked by the window again, heading the other way.

That's it. Nothing in here. Keep walking.

Footsteps crunched around the shed behind her, passing so close she could've hit him with the pipe if not for the wall between them. He continued around the corner and lingered by the right side, near the hole she'd blocked off with the shelf... but resumed walking after a moment.

Mia exhaled.

The crunch of Weston moving among the weeds grew distant. Soon, only the clatter of tools and the rustle of wind reached her ears. She held still, certain Weston remained close enough to hear any noise they might make.

Robin looked up, her expression asking 'is he gone?' Mia relaxed her death grip on the pipe and reached across with her left hand to squeeze the girl's arm. She waited another moment before she entertained the idea that Weston might have missed them.

Sensing Mia relax a little, Robin stopped trembling.

The wall beside the shelf burst apart in a spray of splintering, rotted wood. Little white bugs rained over the floor, scurrying for cover. Weston ducked his head, stepping in the new doorway. Blue veins swelled beneath his eyes on either side of his face, his cheeks wrinkled and pale.

Robin screamed, let go of Mia's arm, and scooted back against the wall.

"There you are," said Weston, grinning. "Since you are both making things more difficult than they need to be, perhaps instead of bringing the demon to holy ground... I should bring the holy ground to the demon." He spread his arms to the sides, knife in one hand, crucifix in the other. "Lord, consecrate this ground with thy holy bles—"

Mia roared and crawled out from under the workbench. Weston kicked at her before she could stand, but she swatted his leg aside. The pipe hit him near the ankle, emitting a hollow, metallic *thump*. He howled, stumbling back into the wall, cracking the boards. A small shelf above him collapsed, dumping an old lantern and several small boxes to the ground.

She sprang up into a charge, swinging the pipe for his head. The old man dove out of the way with surprising agility then thrust the knife up at her chest. Mia shoved the pipe down, smacking the blade away. He slashed a second time before she could recover enough balance to counterattack. Again, she managed to get the pipe in the way.

Weston snarled and tried to duck around her to the workbench. She hefted the pipe over her head, chopping it down at him with every bit of strength she could salvage, grunting from the effort. Weston flung himself to her left, diving flat on the ground. Committed to a swing that hit nothing but air, Mia stumbled forward. Weston rolled on his side and sliced at her ankle, but she jumped aside and scrambled to put herself once again between him and Robin.

"This is for your own good, child," said Weston while clambering upright. "The demon has taken your mind, made you see things that aren't there. That isn't your daughter. It's a fiend"

"Bullshit!" shouted Mia. "You're insane!"

"That's right, preacher man," said Vic, though Weston's lips didn't match the voice. "You gotta save that woman. She needs to be alive to watch the demon go back to hell. Bye bye, Mommy."

"No!" roared Mia, stepping into another swing.

Weston mostly leaned out of the way, but she still caught him in the left arm, knocking him three steps to the side. He gasped in pain, losing his grip on the crucifix. She drew the pipe back, poised for another strike. Weston let out a crazed shout, lunging for her face. Mia rounded the pipe, trying to take his hand off.

Steel crashed into steel.

His wrist bent from the force of the hit, but he didn't lose his grip on the blade. Like a man possessed, he slashed at her again and again, invocations to God launching spittle from his mouth. She slashed and swatted while backing away, sword-fighting with a pipe until her butt hit the workbench and she had nowhere else to go. She had the advantage of reach—the only reason he hadn't drawn blood—but her ponderous weapon allowed no time to attack him between rapid slashes.

Weston leaned back for a thrust at her heart.

With a shout of rage, Mia dodged to the right while swinging in a flat arc. The knife missed her by a few inches and jabbed into the workbench. The pipe slipped under his arm, crashing into his ribs with a *thud* and a sharp *crunch*. Weston clamped his arm down, trapping her weapon. Mia set her heels and pulled at the pipe. His fist came out of nowhere and hit her in the cheek, the added weight of the knife in his grip knocked her momentarily senseless. She lost her hold on the pipe and collapsed over sideways. Her cheek on the floor, she stared vacantly at two fat termites a few inches in front of her eye.

"Mommy!" screamed Robin.

Weston stepped over Mia.

She grunted, wanting to push herself up, but her arm didn't obey. The termites crawled off over the dust, seeming in no hurry to be anywhere. Robin screamed in fright. Boxes and junk clattered from the girl's attempt to scoot deeper under the workbench.

No! Oh, shit what's wrong with me? Did he break my neck? Why can't I move?

"Mommy!" screamed Robin.

Mia's vision flashed white. The decaying shed became a courthouse. Mia raised a small, black .38 revolver at the back of Vic's head. A young deputy beside him merely watched.

Bang!

The courthouse vanished. At a tickle creeping over her left hand, Mia shifted her gaze to a termite climbing her thumb. Her fingers twitched. Despite the throbbing pain in her face, she drew strength out of the deepest recesses of her being. *You will not hurt my daughter!*

Half her body regained feeling; Mia struggled over onto her side.

Weston grabbed Robin by the ankle and dragged her out from under the workbench, the knife in his right hand raised over his head. The tiny child lay flat on her back, gazing up at him with the same look she must've had on her face that awful night almost fifty years ago.

Grunting, Mia forced her right arm and leg to move, pushing herself up to sit, refusing to surrender, refusing to allow the scene she couldn't bear to watch as a psychic vision happen in reality. She glanced around, but didn't see the pipe anywhere. A random urge drew her attention to the right—at an axe leaned against the wall, almost invisible under a thick coating of cobwebs and dust.

"Please don't kill me again!" screamed Robin.

Weston hesitated. "Close your eyes, girl."

"Do it!" roared Vic.

"If I close my eyes, you're gonna kill me."

Mia forced herself up to stand on shaky legs and grabbed the axe. An eruption of scurrying spiders raced up the wall at the disturbance, so many they resembled black smoke. The shed spun, wobbling side to side. She fixated on the small figure struggling to pull away from Weston's hold on her leg.

A deep chuckle emanated from Weston. "Keep them open then. The Lord has given me the strength to do what must be done."

"No, please!" yelled Robin, stomping her free foot at the hand around her ankle.

Mia raised the axe and staggered toward him as fast as she could make her stubborn legs move.

Robin closed her eyes, cringing away.

Weston shouted, "I condemn you to Hell in the name of—"

Mia smashed the axe blade flat against Weston's head, knocking him over sideways, out cold. "I condemn you to unconsciousness in the name of Craftsman."

"Mommy!" Robin leapt into a hug that almost took Mia off her feet.

She lowered the axe, bracing it against the ground to use as a cane. Her head still spun, the walls continuing to sway about... but not as much as a moment ago. "Crazy old bastard."

"Is he a ghost?" whispered Robin.

"No... at least not yet." She kicked the knife away, launching it under the workbench, and stood there for a few minutes until the dizziness faded. Unfortunately, a nasty headache took its place.

"Mia Gartner?" called a distant male voice.

She tossed the axe aside, picked Robin up, and carried her out the giant hole in the wall.

46

COMPLETELY TRUTHFUL

SATURDAY, JUNE 22, 2019

Clean air scrubbed the essence of moldy wood and dust from Mia's throat.

"Over here," called Mia, her voice more rasp than tone.

"Here!" shouted Robin, much louder than her.

She trudged a few paces away from the shed and stopped, her legs threatening to give out at any moment. She held—more like wore—Robin close to her chest.

Nate Ross and Deputy Wilmott emerged from the trees on the far side of the clearing, a bit of distance between them. Nate spotted her first, called "Chris" while pointing at her, and hurried over.

"He's in the shed," wheezed Mia. She swallowed saliva and found a bit more of a voice. "Weston… in the shed."

Deputy Wilmott went inside while Nate guided Mia to sit on a nearby fallen tree. He took a small knife from his belt and cut the duct tape from Robin's arm, then checked them both over. Mia flinched away from the penlight in her eyes.

"I know what this looks like," muttered Mia. "The whole town's aware we've been at odds with that man since we arrived… but he went crazy, wanted to drag my daughter to his church so he could kill her on holy ground. He stabbed…" She blinked. "Adam! Is he?"

"Your husband is doing all right the last I heard." Nate peeled Mia's left hand away from Robin to examine the knife slash on her forearm. "So, the town pastor randomly snaps and tries to wipe out a nice little family? I think you might not be giving me the whole story."

She looked up at him, too exhausted to care. "Okay... Weston thinks my house is cursed. He's been at war with that place for decades. He went nuts and tried to kill my daughter because she looks like Robin Kurtis. And I think he's possessed. Vic said killing her was Weston's idea and he only gave him the strength to do it, but I have no idea if he's lying. The man really did seem to snap when he saw her."

"He never liked me," said Robin.

Deputy Wilmott dragged an unconscious, handcuffed Weston out of the shed.

Nate half-smiled at Mia. "I'm still not sure you're being completely honest with me."

Mia sighed. "You think I wanted to kill Weston?"

"No." His smile became genuine. "That little girl doesn't simply *look* like Robin Kurtis." He winked. "Good to see you two back together."

Her jaw hung open.

Nate hooked his thumbs in his pockets. "Of course, I can't exactly put *that* in my report or I'll wind up in the padded cell right next to Weston. So, I imagine we're actually dealing with a senile priest who for reasons unknown decided to snap and attempt to abduct your daughter."

Robin stopped sniffling and lifted her face away from Mia's shoulder. "He didn't *try* to abduct me. He *did* abduct me."

"I mean..." Nate patted her on the head. "He wasn't successful. He attempted to kidnap you, but your mother stopped him. Anyway, right now, looks like you could use a doctor yourself. That's a nasty cut on your cheek."

Mia grabbed at the air. "Had a giant knife in his hand... punched me. I'm *still* a little dizzy. Knife's under the workbench."

"C'mon. Bit of a walk back to the truck." Nate helped her up and pulled her arm across his shoulder.

Robin squirmed until she slipped down to stand. "I can walk. Mommy's hurt."

Deputy Wilmott hoisted Weston over his shoulder.

Overcome with relief and exhaustion, Mia let Nate guide her along amid a blur of trees.

MIA FOUND HERSELF AWAKE IN A BED AT THE HOSPITAL, FLOATING on a mild high from painkillers.

Adam, as far as she knew, remained asleep in a different area of the hospital, but a nurse told her some time ago he'd made it through surgery okay. Her injuries had been less serious, requiring only disinfecting, stitches, and antibiotics. They wanted to keep her a day or two for observation since they suspected she'd suffered a mild-to-moderate concussion.

Wilhelmina had spent the rest of the daylight hours here with Robin and would watch her until they let Mia go home. The girl had *not* been happy to be separated from her, but her only protest had been quiet sobs.

Nate and a woman with short blonde hair, Deputy Allison Clark, walked in a little after nine that night.

"You in any shape to give a statement, Mrs. Gartner?" asked Nate.

"I'm a little high, but sure. Pain's stopped... or at least I can't feel it now."

"Great. We won't be long." Allison pulled up a chair and sat.

Mia grinned at Nate. "Which version do you want? The actual truth, or the truth normal people will accept?"

"People here in Spring Falls are quite familiar with that house of yours." He sat on the other visitor's chair. "Might surprise you what they'd believe, but it's not them we're concerned with. Why don't we get the 'reasonable' truth out of the way first, and if you still feel like talking afterward, you can give my deputy here nightmares."

Allison rolled her eyes.

"All right... From the day we moved to Spring Falls, Weston had been pestering us about joining his church. He thought the house had the Devil in it and our souls were in danger. When my husband met Wilhelmina Marx at the university and we became friends, Weston couldn't handle it. You know he thinks they're like actual witches? Who believes in that stuff?"

Nate smiled, as did Allison.

"So… anyway… I don't really know what made him lose his mind like that, but he thought my daughter was a demon." Mia blinked. "Oh, shit. I forgot to call Janet."

"Who's Janet?"

"My boss. The fire alarm went off where I work and I was supposed to go meet with the fire department."

"I'll call her when we're done here. Do you have her number?" Nate looked up from his notepad.

"Yeah, it's in my phone. I don't know it by heart."

Allison pointed. "The phone that's right next to you?"

Mia glanced at the little table beside the bed. Her phone and purse sat beside her. "Oh, where did that come from? Never mind. I'm high. They gave me the good stuff."

According to the phone, Janet had tried to call her nine times. After giving Nate the number, she proceeded to explain everything that happened after the inexplicable urge to turn around hit her. Due to the painkillers, she even admitted to speeding, though neither of them appeared to care.

"Nothing quite like a mother's intuition." Nate flipped his pad closed. "All right. Thank you for your time. Go on and get some rest."

"Thanks…" Mia closed her eyes and let the painkillers carry her off to sleep.

EPILOGUE

A LITTLE MAGIC

Saturday, August 10, 2019

The smell of pancakes filled the kitchen.

Robin bounced in her seat, a huge smile on her face at the plate Mia set in front of her. Adam eased himself into the chair at the end. He'd been home from the hospital for a few days, mostly recovered from a collapsed lung. Mia cooked his portion of pancakes, set them on the table, then made some for herself.

Janet had initially been upset, but Nate's call and explanation that Robin had been abducted with intent to kill and Mia had saved her life changed anger to overwhelming concern. Not that the woman had doubted the word of a sheriff, but when she visited Mia in the hospital and saw the bruises on her—and Robin—she had a mild freak out. Jerry Golden, the exhibits manager, had wound up dealing with the fire department. No one could explain what set the system off, but they'd gotten lucky. The computer reported a fire with sprinkler activation, but there hadn't been a fire *or* sprinklers going off, only a glitch in the electronics.

Robin had more or less set aside the kidnapping, returning to her happy and normal self after only a few days... or at least normal for her. She remained quite clingy, perhaps more so. Mia didn't mind. As soon as Adam felt up to it, they planned on giving her a sibling.

Wilhelmina arrived about an hour after breakfast to help Mia around the house and spend time with them. She'd taken on a bit of a grandmotherly role for Robin and almost a maternal one to Mia. They did some light housecleaning while Robin played with her stuffed animals and Adam worked on his laptop from a recliner in the living room, catching up with his classes' progress via the substitute who had been covering for him. Something around thirty students had stopped by to wish him well in the weeks after his injury.

Nate showed up a little past noon while everyone sat around the table with sandwiches for lunch. Mia invited him in and offered him a sandwich, though he declined food.

"Mr. Gartner. Hope you're feeling better." Nate shook hands, then nodded at Wilhelmina. "Miss Marx."

"Still sore, but I'm not having any problem breathing anymore." Adam rubbed his side.

Nate nodded. "I'm just stopping by to pass on some updates. Weston's lawyer got the judge to accept an insanity plea that will put him in a secure mental care facility. Considering he faced three counts of attempted murder in the first degree, he's unlikely to see the outside world again."

"Wow, he went for an insanity defense?" asked Adam.

"Not exactly." Nate chuckled. "Weston came unglued in front of the judge when his lawyer announced they would accept the plea and commitment. While trying to explain to the court that he wasn't insane, Weston insisted that the Devil lived in Spring Falls, the spirit of a dead man had possessed him, and Satan had brought a little girl back from the dead and she planned to kill everyone in the town."

Adam whistled. "Great way to try and convince a judge of being sane."

"Hah." Mia laughed. "That's ironic. A pastor trying to tell people that someone came back from the dead and no one believes him."

Everyone but Robin laughed. She scrunched her eyebrows in confusion.

"Anyway, I have a few things to take care of. Just thought you'd like to know you folks won't need to show up to testify... or worry about that man again."

"Thank you." Mia got up and walked him to the door.

"So," whispered Nate. "You planning on inviting anyone else back?"

She chuckled. "No, sir. Next one's going to follow the usual rules."

"Take care of yourself. Oh, you might get a bit of a break. I think ol' Vic is kinda attached to the pastor. Hearing a bunch of weird stories coming from the corrections officers."

"It would be nice if he stays away, but I'm not holding my breath it'll last long."

"Wish I could offer you more help on that front, but I only deal with the live ones." Nate tipped his hat.

"Thanks for everything."

"Happy it all worked out for you." He nodded in farewell, then walked off to his patrol vehicle.

Mia shut the door, sighed, and returned to the kitchen.

"You're going to ask about the house," said Wilhelmina.

"Yeah." Mia sank into her seat, frowning at her half sandwich. "It's crazy of me, but I like this house. But if we need to leave to keep Robin safe..."

Adam fidgeted at his water glass. "We'd lose a lot of money selling so soon. And with the reputation this place has? It will be years before anyone buys it at a price that won't be ruinous. *If* anyone does. Especially with the whole Weston-going-crazy story."

"That might make it famous." Wilhelmina wagged her eyebrows. "You'll be movie stars."

Mia cringed. "Pass."

"I'll be okay after I turn eight." Robin looked up from her plate, her expression part eerie, part way-too-adult. "We can be safe here if we're careful. Besides. He'll follow me anyway, and I like that Willa lives down the street."

"After you turn eight?" Mia blinked at her. "Why would..."

Robin flashed a creepy grin. "Once I turn eight, your souls are mine forever."

Adam and Mia stared at her. She didn't feel any strange paranormal dread in the air, but something in the girl's eyes unsettled her.

Wilhelmina fought the urge to laugh.

"Hah. Got you!" chirped Robin, once again the picture of pure innocence. She raspberried, then shook her head. "I died at seven. The curse stops when I'm older than that."

"Hmm." Wilhelmina rubbed her chin. "It is possible that once she's lived past the term of her first incarnation, his connection to her may break. Where did you get that from, child?"

Robin shrugged. "I dunno. It just made sense."

"Oh, dear." Wilhelmina glanced at Adam, shaking her head. "You're doomed, young man. You've got *two* psychic women in the house."

Adam brought his hands together with a clap. "Well, that settles it. We stay. This is home. We might as well enchant the place again."

Wilhelmina nodded. "Couldn't hurt."

Robin hopped off her chair and crawled into Mia's lap. "Can I help?"

"Sure," said Wilhelmina. "If your parents are all right with it."

Mia wrapped her arms around the little girl in her lap, hugging her close. "I don't see why not… maybe I should help, too."

"Every girl needs a little magic in her life." Wilhelmina winked. "Never hurts to learn how to work a spell or two."

fin

ACKNOWLEDGMENTS

Thank you for reading The Spirits of Six Minstrel Run!

I'd also like to thank Alexandria Thompson for the amazing cover and Lee Sheridan for her help editing this book.

ABOUT THE AUTHOR

Originally from South Amboy NJ, Matthew has been creating science fiction and fantasy worlds for most of his reasoning life. Since 1996, he has developed the "Divergent Fates" world, in which *Division Zero, Virtual Immortality, The Awakened Series, The Harmony Paradox, and the Daughter of Mars series* take place. Along with being an editor at Curiosity Quills press, he has worked in IT and technical support.

Matthew is an avid gamer, a recovered WoW addict, Gamemaster for two custom RPG systems, and a fan of anime, British humour, and intellectual science fiction that questions the nature of reality, life, and what happens after it.

He is also fond of cats.

Visit me online at:
Facebook: https://www.facebook.com/MatthewSCoxAuthor
Pinterest: https://www.pinterest.com/matthewcox10420/
Goodreads: https://www.goodreads.com/author/show/7712730.Matthew_S_Cox
Email: mcox2112@gmail.com

OTHER BOOKS BY MATTHEW S. COX

Divergent Fates Universe Novels

Division Zero series

- Division Zero
- Lex De Mortuis
- Thrall
- Guardian
- Harbinger

The Awakened series

- Prophet of the Badlands
- Archon's Queen
- Grey Ronin
- Daughter of Ash
- Zero Rogue
- Angel Descended

Daughter of Mars series

- The Hand of Raziel
- Araphel
- Ghost Black

Virtual Immortality series

- Virtual Immortality
- The Harmony Paradox

Divergent Fates Anthology

(Fiction Novels - Adult)

The Roadhouse Chronicles Series

- One More Run
- The Redeemed
- Dead Man's Number

Faded Skies series

- Heir Ascendant
- Ascendant Unrest
- Ascendant Revolution

Temporal Armistice Series

- Nascent Shadow
- The Shadow Collector
- The Gate to Oblivion

Vampire Innocent series

- A Nighttime of Forever
- A Beginner's Guide to Fangs
- The Artist of Ruin
- The Last Family Road Trip
- The Phantom Oracle

Standalones

- Wayfarer: AV494
- Axillon99
- Chiaroscuro: The Mouse and the Candle
- The Spirits of Six Minstrel Run

- The Far Side of Promise anthology
- Operation: Chimera (with Tony Healey)
- The Dysfunctional Conspiracy (with Christopher Veltmann)

Winter Solstice series (with J.R. Rain)

- Convergence
- Containment
- Catalyst

Alexis Silver series (with J.R. Rain)

- Silver Light
- Deep Silver
- Silver Quarrel

Samantha Moon Origins series (with J.R. Rain)

- New Moon Rising
- Moon Mourning

Vampire For Hire series (with J.R. Rain)

- Moon Master
- Dead Moon

Maddy Wimsey series (with J.R. Rain)

- The Devil's Eye
- The Drifting Gloom

Samantha Moon Case Files series (with J.R. Rain)

- Blood Moon

Immortal Operative series (with J.R. Rain)

- Broken Ice

Young Adult Novels

The Eldritch Heart Series

- The Eldritch Heart
- The Cursed Crown

Evergreen Series

- Evergreen
- The World That Remains

Standalones

- Caller 107
- The Summer the World Ended
- Nine Candles of Deepest Black
- The Forest Beyond the Earth
- Out of Sight
- Evergreen

Middle Grade Novels

Tales of Widowswood series

- Emma and the Banderwigh
- Emma and the Silk Thieves
- Emma and the Silverbell Faeries

- Emma and the Elixir of Madness
- Emma and the Weeping Spirit

Standalones

- Citadel: The Concordant Sequence
- The Cursed Codex
- The Menagerie of Jenkins Bailey
- Sophie's Light